"I'm not going to

"the woman whose bed you share whenever you happen
to pass through."

"Good. I'm glad you're not," Sloan said huskily. "It isn't
what I want."

Polly clutched her quilt tightly. "Then what are you doing
here in my bedroom?"

"Well, I won't say sleeping with you didn't occur to
me. And I won't pretend it doesn't have its appeal." He
raked a hand through tousled hair. "It has a hell of a lot of
appeal. But I want more."

Her gaze narrowed. "What sort of more?"

"How does marriage sound to you?"

* * *

"Anne McAllister writes some of the best cowboys under
the clear blue Western skies."
>   —Kathleen Eagle, bestselling author of
>   *The Last True Cowboy*

"A powerhouse storyteller, Anne McAllister crafts a warm
and tender love story."
>   —*Romantic Times Magazine*

Dear Reader,

When I was offered the chance to write a single title (and therefore longer!) book for my CODE OF THE WEST miniseries, I was delighted, as I've wanted to do something like that for quite a while. And as it happened, I'd just come up with the notion of a "cowboy auction" and was wondering what to do with it. Putting the two together turned out to be a perfect fit.

Polly McMaster, the mayor of Elmer, first appeared in *The Cowboy and the Kid* (Silhouette Desire, July 1996), and has popped up occasionally ever since. Sloan Gallagher was first mentioned in my Harlequin Presents novel, *Rhys's Redemption* (August 2000), and was, of course, Gus Holt's childhood buddy in *A Cowboy's Gift* (Silhouette Desire, November 2000). It was only after I got them together in *The Great Montana Cowboy Auction*, though, that I realized how much of a "past" they shared. One of the great joys of writing this series has been following the people in and out of each others' lives and coming to feel like they are part of my family and my community, too. Being able to revisit them in other books is like meeting old friends, and getting to know them fully in their own stories when they have had "walk-on" parts in earlier books is always great fun.

But sharing them with readers around the world is the most enjoyable part of all. Thank you so much for all the letters you've sent me about my books and the people in them. Thank you for welcoming them——and me——into your home and into your reading life for a while. And thank you very much for taking the time to share your views with me. It is always a pleasure to hear from you through the reader service address, my post office box or, most recently, via e-mail.

I hope you enjoy *The Great Montana Cowboy Auction*. I hope you like Polly and her family, and that you fall in love with Sloan, as I did. I also hope you'll join me again in a few months for Jace's story in *A Cowboy's Pursuit* (Silhouette Desire, June 2002), the next installment in the CODE OF THE WEST!

All the best,

Anne McAllister

ANNE McALLISTER

THE GREAT MONTANA COWBOY AUCTION

Published by Silhouette Books
America's Publisher of Contemporary Romance

SILHOUETTE BOOKS

THE GREAT MONTANA COWBOY AUCTION

Copyright © 2002 by Barbara Schenck

ISBN 0-373-48457-7

Visit Silhouette at www.eHarlequin.com

Printed in U.S.A.

**Also published by Silhouette Books
by Anne McAllister**

A Cowboy's Promise
(December 2001, Silhouette Desire, #1405)
A Cowboy's Gift
(November 2000, Silhouette Desire, #1329)
A Cowboy's Secret
(March 2000, Silhouette Desire, #1279)
Cowboy on the Run
(August 1999, World's Most Eligible Bachelors)
The Stardust Cowboy
(June 1999, Silhouette Desire, #1219)
The Cowboy Crashes a Wedding
(July 1998, Silhouette Desire, #1153)
The Cowboy Steals a Lady
(January 1998, Silhouette Desire, #1117)
A Cowboy's Tears
(November 1997, Silhouette Special Edition, (#1137)
Cowboy Pride
(November 1996, Silhouette Desire, #1034)
The Cowboy and the Kid
(July 1996, Silhouette Desire, #1009)
Cowboys Don't Stay
(December 1995, Silhouette Desire, #969)
Cowboys Don't Quit
(August 1995, Silhouette Desire, #944)
Cowboys Don't Cry
(February 1995, Silhouette Desire, #907)

Coming Soon:

A Cowboy's Pursuit
(June 2002, Silhouette Desire)
The Cowboy's Christmas Miracle
(December 2002, Silhouette Special Edition)

And don't miss Anne's Harlequin Presents title:

Nathan's Child
(Winter 2002)

For
all the men in my life

Peter, David, Patrick, James,
Tony, Eric and Griffin

and especially for
Bob and Jason,
thanks for being my help
at the end of the phone line!

Special thanks to
Nancy Ronek,
postmistress extraordinaire

Chapter 1

The last time Polly McMaster had missed a meeting of the Elmer, Montana, town council she had ended up mayor.

It had put the fear of missing meetings into her for two solid years. Some things, however, took precedence over leadership avoidance—and one of them was your nine-year-old son bleeding all over your kitchen floor.

"Look, Ma, I can spit through it," Jack said, taking a gulp of water and demonstrating how the inch-and-a-half gash in his chin, courtesy of his friend Randy Naylor's hockey stick, would work as an auxiliary mouth.

Polly, though not squeamish—who could be after four children and fourteen years of marriage to a rodeo bullfighter?—still wasn't overly fond of gross. "Here." She pressed a dish towel against Jack's chin, bundled him into the truck and deputized her mother, Joyce, to attend the council meeting in her stead.

"Keep my name out of things," she said. "I don't want to be commissioner of streets. I don't want to be town treasurer. And I especially don't want to wear funny hats or house any more livestock."

It was enough that she had to run the council meetings, oversee the snow removal and the Christmas pageant, and just last month had got stuck housing the baker's dozen out-of-work rabbits who had last been employed as the Elmer Christmas pageant's livestock on the hoof.

The only job she would do, Polly told her mother, was head the committee to raise funds for the library. The Elmer town library had seen better days. It had seen more books and more hours. Polly was among those who thought it needed to be improved. If she was going to be stuck with a committee, she wouldn't mind that.

"*If* no one else will do it," she told her mother on her way out the door.

Actually she had quite enough on her plate.

Besides being mayor, with all that entailed, she was the Elmer postmistress, a part-time college student and single mother of four. That meant, this year, helping Jack make a giant flour-and-water relief map of the Amazon jungle, being a chaperone at the school dances at Daisy's junior high, helping sixteen-year-old Lizzie, who was presently calling herself Artemis, rehearse her lines for the school play, and serving as a bad example for nineteen-year-old Sara who thought she could surely do a better job than Polly at living a well-ordered life.

Polly quite agreed.

Well-ordered was not a word she had ever used to describe her life.

Actually, she thought as she sat waiting for Jack to get stitches, and writing checks to pay her bills at the same time, she could be the poster girl for Ask A Busy Person If You Want Something Done. But when would she have time to pose?

Three hours, eleven stitches and seven bills later, she and Jack finally got home. Her mother was sitting in the living room with a pile of twine in her lap.

"So how did it go?" Polly unwrapped herself from the January snowstorm and shook snowflakes out of her unruly ginger-colored hair. She looked hopefully at her mother, who was sitting in her armchair by the fireplace doing her latest macramé project.

What Polly meant, of course, was *Am I home free?*

"Went very well," Joyce said with a satisfied smile. But she didn't quite meet her daughter's eyes and went straight back to the wall hanging she'd been macraméing for the past month.

Polly, who understood the subtleties of eye contact or lack thereof, reached back into the kitchen to hang her jacket on the hook by the door, then came back in to face her mother squarely. "How well?"

Joyce flicked a beaming smile in her direction. "Very well indeed." But then she looked at her mass of knots again.

"*Not* the streets committee?"

"Of course not. Artie said he'd do that. Come here," Joyce said to Jack. "Let me see." She admired his bandage. "Heavens, you'll look just like Harrison Ford."

Jack smiled widely. "Cool. Hey, Dais'," he bellowed up the stairs at his sister. "Grandma says I look like Harrison Ford."

"Not hardly," Daisy's disdainful voice floated down.

"Do, too!" Jack shouted back. "I'll get the *Raiders* video."

He started to sprint toward the kitchen where a door led into the small shop at the back of the house where his aunt Celie had her single-chair beauty salon and his oldest sister, Sara, rented out videos. It was called C&S Spa and Video and was among Elmer's most thriving businesses. It also provided Jack and his sisters with a never-ending supply of tapes to watch as long as they didn't mind them being at least six months old.

"Not," Polly said, using lightning-fast maternal reflexes to catch him by the neck of his sweatshirt as he bolted past, "on a school night. It's time for bed."

"But—"

Polly gave him her best I'm-the-mother-and-what-I-say-goes face. "Now."

Jack knew exactly how far he could push. He rolled his eyes, gave a long-suffering sigh, then shrugged, turned and pounded up the stairs instead.

"You'll see tomorrow," he yelled at Daisy. "Harrison McMaster, that's me!"

"He never talks when he can shout, does he?" Joyce wasn't complaining, only stating a fact. She'd raised three daughters and considered herself an expert on girls. But Jack, though the apple of her eye, was a mystery.

Even at nine, he was A Man.

"No, he doesn't." Polly felt the adrenaline begin to fade. She actually found Jack restful—loud voice, pounding feet, stitches and all. He might be a boy, but to Polly he was far less of a challenge than the girls. He was like his father had been—cheerful, mellow, easygoing, uncomplicated.

It still hurt sometimes, thinking about Lew. He had been gone almost six years, killed in a plane crash on his way back from Dodge City one stormy August evening. A day didn't go by that Polly didn't miss him. They'd been soul mates, best friends, lovers. They'd complemented each other.

"Together," Lew used to say with a grin, "we make one complete person."

Polly had discovered how very true that was after he was gone and she was left to do everything.

What would Lew do? she asked herself half a dozen times a week, especially dealing with Jack. And then she did it.

She knew he would have laughed when Jack had spat the water. So she had laughed, too. But inside she'd ached a little, wishing as she always did that he were here to be the father Jack needed.

But she wouldn't let herself think about Lew now. There would be time for that tonight when she was alone in bed. Now she focused once more on her mother.

Joyce was humming as she tied the knots. She hadn't looked up except to consult the directions and the picture in the Seventies era magazine she'd found the pattern in. It was supposed to be airy with a sort of fishnet quality to it.

Polly thought it looked like a hair shirt.

"So Artie's heading up the streets committee. Bless his heart." Artie Gilliam was ninety and he certainly didn't need to be worrying about Elmer's transportation future, but she was delighted he was. She would have to stop off at the hardware store in the morning and thank him. "So I got the library?"

Joyce stuck her tongue between her teeth and scowled at the

hair shirt. "Over, over, under, around. Loop. Loop," she muttered. "Carol Ferguson's doing that."

Carol wasn't even on the council, so she must have turned
up and volunteered. That was good. Unless...

"Don't say I've got to do the Christmas pageant again this
year!"

Polly flung herself across the legs of the overstuffed armchair by the fireplace and looked at her mother, dismayed. "I
thought we agreed Celie would volunteer for that. She's the
drama freak—I mean, the entertainment whiz—not me."

Celie knew more about actors than anyone alive. She sub-
scribed to every magazine, read every word, watched every
gossip show and saw every movie as soon as it was released,
even though she had to go clear to Bozeman to do it.

Well, not *every* movie. Just those starring hunky handsome
men—especially God's gift to women, Sloan Gallagher.

Sloan Gallagher and his colleagues were Celie's defense
against real men—the ones she met every day.

Ever since Matt Williams had jilted her ten years ago, Celie
had sworn off three-dimensional men. Silver-screen heroes,
with their two-hour staying power, were the only ones she
trusted. Her fantasy life was terrific.

Her real one was dull as dirt.

Polly rarely thought she knew better than anyone else how
they should live. She didn't care if Celie wanted to swoon
about Hollywood hunks for the rest of her life. She just figured
that, with all her dramatic expertise, Celie might as well put it
to work. She'd spent the last week telling Celie what a terrific
experience it would be if she ran the pageant.

Privately Polly thought, Let her see the nitty-gritty. Let her
get stuck with kids with measles and pregnant Marys and stage-
frightened ten-year-olds throwing up on her shoes. Let her talk
some bashful cowboy into being Joseph. Let her tell him to
bring his bathrobe to wear on stage, and be told with a grin
that not only didn't he own a bathrobe—he didn't wear paja-
mas, either!

Polly had been told exactly that.

She'd been chair of the Elmer Christmas pageant five out of

the past seven years. Only twice had she been lucky enough
to presume upon the ignorance of newcomers. But she'd just
taken advantage of the last newcomer when Charlie Seeks Elk,
Cait Blasingame's new husband, had run the pageant this past
year.

Now, unless some unsuspecting fool moved in or Celie volunteered, there was no one else but her—and Polly had run out
of ideas and patience with cowboys and ten-year-olds.

The only thing she hadn't run out of was bunnies—somebody's idea of "incorporating a touch of realism into the pageant" a couple of years back.

They were out in the shed behind the house right now. There
were thirteen of them at last count. By next Christmas, God
knew how many there would be.

Polly would deal with the bunnies. But she wanted Celie to
run the pageant.

"Celie let you volunteer her, didn't she?" Celie had evening
haircutting appointments so she couldn't go to the council
meeting herself.

"Mmm? Yes. Yes, she did."

"Wonderful!" Polly sighed and stretched her arms over her
head. The weight of perpetual responsibility began to lift. She
smiled and kicked her feet and wiggled her toes. "I'm off the
hook."

"Not quite."

Polly's feet stopped kicking. "What do you mean, not
quite?"

Joyce blinked over her half glasses. "Oh, nothing much."
She gave a little laugh. "There was just a bit of new business."

"What new business?"

"It's about Maddie."

"Maddie Fletcher? She's not ill, is she?"

Maddie was seventy-five if she was a day, and she still
worked as hard as two men trying to keep the family ranch
going. The Fletcher place, called the Arrow Bar, had been in
her late husband, Ward's, family for four generations. It wasn't
a large spread, but it was one of the nicest in the valley—and

since Ward's death two years ago Maddie had done her best to keep it up on her own.

"No. But it's almost as bad. Ward took out a loan to buy a new bull and fix up the buildings four, five years back. It wasn't any problem making the payments as long as he was alive, but…" She shrugged sadly.

Polly stared. "Don't say they're foreclosing!"

"Not yet. But they're expecting payment. It was one of those balloon things. Maddie got behind when Ward was sick and now she can't catch up. Worse, some Hollywood fellow is interested in buying it, and the bank thinks he's a better bet."

"They can't do that!"

"Actually, Will Jones is afraid they can."

Will, a retired rancher and an old neighbor of Maddie's, was well versed in the kinds of things banks could do. He'd dealt with them for more years than Polly had been alive. A few years back he'd left the running of the ranch to his son, Taggart, and moved to Bozeman, but it didn't stop him staying abreast of local business concerns. If Will thought the bank could do something awful, Polly was ready to believe him.

"Will came to the meeting?"

"He and Taggart. They think we, as a community, should help Maddie out."

"Well, of course we should. But…Maddie let them?" That didn't sound like the stubbornly self-reliant Maddie that Polly knew.

"Ha! You know Maddie. Proud as a post. She'd have gone under and never said a word. But Will ran into her at the bank right after she got the news and she looked so bad he thought she was ill."

"I'd be ill," Polly said flatly. She swung around and sat up straight. "So what are we going to do to help?"

Elmer and environs were home to a fair share of independent-minded folks who took care of themselves and went their own way—Maddie among them. But no one ever turned their back on a neighbor and they always took care of their own.

The Fletchers had always been good neighbors—the best.

They'd always lent a hand when anyone else was in need. They'd been right there taking care of the kids for Polly after Lew's accident.

They'd even had a hand in raising Lew himself. Ward and Maddie Fletcher had opened their home and their hearts to a passel of foster kids for over forty years. One of those kids had been Lew. He'd thought the sun rose and set on Maddie Fletcher. Madeleine was their Sara's middle name.

Joyce beamed at Polly over the top of the hair shirt. "I knew you'd feel that way. I told 'em you would."

The penny dropped.

"So I'm chair of the Save Maddie Fletcher's Ranch Committee?"

Well, fine. No problem. It was a job worth having. And Polly had run countless PTA fund-raisers. She'd helped the 4H raise money for the county fair, had baked several thousand cookies for several hundred bake sales, and had just this past month organized a snow shoveling contingent made up entirely of hyperactive nine year olds. She could raise money blindfolded with one hand tied behind her back—as soon as she figured out what would bring in the amount of money required.

"I don't think a bake sale is going to do it," she said, her mind whirling through possibilities as she stared into the fire. "It would take an awful lot of cookies and cakes to pay off even the interest on a bank loan."

"It would." Joyce nodded.

"And even if I got all the kids to shovel all the snow for the rest of the winter and donate all their proceeds, that wouldn't do the trick."

"You're right," Joyce said.

"Maybe a benefit dance?" Polly thought out loud.

"Not enough revenue," her mother said.

Polly blinked, surprised at Joyce's comment, even though her mother was certainly correct. "Er, right."

"We need something with broader consumer appeal," Joyce went on.

"Um, yeah." Polly stared at her mother. The hair shirt sat unnoticed in Joyce's lap now. There was a sparkle in her eyes.

It was the first sparkle Polly had seen in a long time.

Her mother had once been cheerful and content—a rancher's wife, doing all the things that needed to be done to keep the ranch running. But when Polly's father, Gil, had died of a heart attack two years ago, everything changed.

Joyce couldn't run the ranch by herself. So she'd sold it to Mace and Shane Nichols and their wives, and she had moved in with Polly. For a year she'd been a mere shadow of her former self as she'd grieved. She'd gone through the motions of living, but until last winter when she got a job four nights a week as the receptionist at the Livingston hospital, she'd hardly done more than stare out the window.

Finally, on her sixtieth birthday, four months ago, Joyce had woken up and realized she wasn't going to die—even if she wanted to. She was going to be stuck on this mortal coil for a while, and ever since she'd been determined to make up for lost time.

A week didn't go by that she didn't start a new project— like the hair shirt. The study of market economics was another.

"I want to know what a bull market is," she'd said over dinner three weeks ago. "And a bear. And cost-averaging strategy." She'd gone into Bozeman and bought an economics book. Now she used terms like *revenue* and *broader consumer appeal*.

It took some getting used to.

"Nothing we've done before will do," Joyce said now. "We need a large-scale effort and a lot of community participation. We need to take it beyond the local market."

"I'll give it some thought."

"I already have."

"*You?* I mean, er, wow. And you think your idea will, um…generate enough revenue?" She tried to sound economic.

"Oh, yes. Everyone else did, too." Joyce's eyes sparkled. "We're going to have an auction."

"An auction? You mean everybody contributes white elephants and stuff?"

It was a nice idea, but she didn't see how it was going to raise a pile of money, but then, she supposed her mother couldn't be expected to understand all economic issues in three short weeks.

"Not enough revenue." Joyce finished the knot she was tying and looked up quite pleased. "White elephants won't do it. And they won't get enough people involved. Besides, it wouldn't use up our surplus. You should always work from your surplus," she informed Polly gravely. "I read that in chapter four."

"Chapter four. Right," Polly said. "Of course. But I don't quite see. I mean, what have we got a surplus of...besides snow?"

Joyce tied one last knot, looked up and smiled beatifically. "Cowboys."

Well, yes. If there was one thing Elmer had a lot of, if there was one thing it was simply overloaded with—besides snow— it was cowboys.

They worked on the valley ranches, rode the fences, herded the cattle and came into Elmer to hoist a few beers and raise a little hell. They played pool in the Dew Drop, Elmer's tavern, they ate meat loaf at the Busy Bee Café, they hung around Loney's welding shop getting their trailer hitches welded and prowled the aisles of Gilliam's Hardware buying rolls of baling wire and cases of duct tape. And besides the local contingent there were always a couple of dozen passing through or going to bull- and bronc-riding school at Taggart Jones's place.

They were thick on the ground, all right.

But as far as Polly could see, that was the trouble.

"Who'd buy them?" Polly asked.

But before she'd got an answer, Jack and Daisy had begun scuffling upstairs and she'd had to go sort them out. And then Lizzie had wanted her to coach her on her lines for an upcoming audition, and by the time Polly got back downstairs, her mother had gone to bed.

Polly had gone to bed, too, and had spent a good part of the night thinking about Maddie, worrying about Maddie, and trying to figure out how this auction notion her mother was so proud of would work.

It was all well and good to say you should auction off your surplus, but if you had too many, who'd want them?

"Everybody," Joyce said cheerfully when Polly came downstairs in the morning and asked. Her mother was dishing up oatmeal for Daisy and Jack and humming as she did so. She still looked pleased.

"I wouldn't buy one," Lizzie said. But Lizzie had little use for cowboys. She wore black, read Harold Pinter and Edward Albee and wanted someday to star in an off-off-Broadway production because Broadway, she said when her mother asked her, was too commercial and didn't speak with the voice of real people.

Polly wasn't quite sure what she thought about that. "Liz...?"

"Artemis," her daughter corrected firmly. She pushed back her chair and glided to the sink with her empty dish.

Right. Artemis.

As Artemis, Polly noticed, her daughter didn't simply move anymore, she glided. When she wasn't gliding, she swept. She didn't talk, she proclaimed. And she didn't feel, she experienced—and then emoted.

Polly thought it was a lot of work being Artemis. She couldn't ever have done it. She didn't have that much energy.

"Did you feed the rabbits, Artemis?" Polly asked her.

"Not my turn," Lizzie said. "It's Jack's."

"It's always my turn," Jack complained.

"Maybe we could bid on a cowboy to feed the rabbits," Daisy suggested.

"What are we bidding on them for?" Polly wanted to know. "Mending fences and baling hay and working cattle? They do that, anyway."

"Yes, but this is extra," her mother explained. "They're donating time, and the money will go to Maddie."

"But that means the guys who are scraping by are going to be doing all the supporting."

"That's just part of it," Joyce said. "Virtually everyone in the valley can donate something cowboy related. Taggart and Noah are donating bull- and bronc-riding classes. And Brenna's donating one of her cowboy-hero paintings. Taggart said Tuck would donate a series of pen and ink sketches of last year's rodeo and he was sure Charlie Seeks Elk would provide some original cowboy photos. Artie said he'd donate some old cowboy postcards. There's a ton of cowboy-related items. People are still coming up with things.''

Polly began to see possibilities beyond, as her mother had said, the local market. They might get a few outsiders in for Brenna's painting. Brenna Jamison McCall's cowboy watercolors were well-known in art circles as far away as New York.

And Charlie Seeks Elk, currently one of Polly's favorite people because he had allowed himself to be talked into directing this past year's Christmas pageant, was something of a household name as far as photographers went.

''That might get us something,'' she agreed.

''Taggart said he was pretty sure Felicity could talk a few of the single guys on the rodeo circuit into being bachelor dates so the girls can bid on them.''

''That ought to get us a dollar or two,'' Lizzie said dryly.

''Lots of women love cowboys,'' Joyce said firmly. ''Your father was a cowboy.''

''I know, but—''

''And they will get the runoff from our big-ticket item.''

''What big ticket item?'' Polly asked.

Joyce was smiling smugly. ''We're auctioning off a famous cowboy.''

The only famous cowboys Polly could think of were Roy Rogers, Will Rogers, Gene Autry and Buffalo Bill. ''All the famous cowboys are dead.''

Joyce just smiled. ''Not Sloan Gallagher.''

Polly poured coffee all over her hand. She said something rude and unprintable, slapped the mug down on the counter, then hastily mopped up the spilled liquid. ''Don't be ridiculous. Sloan Gallagher's not coming here.''

''Sloan Gallagher's coming here?'' Her sister Celie appeared, her face going red, then white.

''Sloan Gallagher's coming here?'' Lizzie, for the first time, looked delighted.

Joyce rubbed her hands together. "Gus says he will."

Gus Holt was the foreman at Blasingame's ranch. His wife, Mary, had been the other newcomer Polly had roped into the Christmas pageant. Gus had helped out, too. Polly was very fond of both of them. But she couldn't imagine how Gus could promise them Sloan Gallagher.

"He and Sloan went to school together," Joyce explained. "They were best friends in elementary school and junior high. But then Sloan's mom died and his dad lost the ranch, and Sloan ended up down at Maddie's. You did know he lived at Maddie's?"

Polly finished mopping up the coffee, then turned around, her fingers locked around the mug. Oh, yes, she knew he had once lived at Maddie Fletcher's. She remembered him well.

"He was one of her foster kids," Celie said. "Like Lew. But that was years ago."

"Celie's right," Polly said. "It's been years. Why would he bother?"

"To save Maddie's ranch. Gus said he would."

"I don't care what Gus said," Polly said flatly. "He won't. Lizzie, time to get the bus."

"Of course he won't," Celie said.

Joyce shook her head at both her daughters. "How did I ever raise such doubters? You—" she fixed her gaze on Celie "—I should think you'd be over the moon at the notion. You could bid on him! Stop this mooning around and get the man of your dreams. I'd love to have Sloan Gallagher for a son-in-law." Joyce looked positively enraptured at the prospect.

Celie's face was bright red. "Don't be silly."

"Exactly," Polly said.

All these bright ideas were obviously going to her mother's head.

"Just because Sloan Gallagher was Maddie and Ward's foster child for a brief period of time doesn't mean he'd allow himself to be auctioned off," she told her mother. "Not everyone has fond memories of being a foster child. He might have hated it. Anyway, if he wants to help, he'll just send a check. Good grief, he could probably just pay the whole loan back for her if he wanted to." She tapped her daughter on the shoulder. "Lizzie, Artemis, whoever you are, get a move on. Now! The bus will be here."

Grumbling, Lizzie shoved back her chair and carried her dish to the sink. "*He* might be worth seeing," she said.

"Don't count on it," Polly replied.

Sloan Gallagher might once have been a tried-and-true, hell-bent-for-leather Montana cowboy, but he was currently one of the top five box office draws in America. Celie herself had read Polly that tidbit of information aloud from one of her many magazines not a week ago.

He was in demand constantly. The world's best directors clamored to work with him. His involvement with any project made it instantly bankable. So there wasn't a chance in the world he would waste his valuable time coming back here.

Of course even if he did he wouldn't remember her. The trouble was, she remembered him!

And it had nothing to do with Sloan Gallagher, America's heart throb. It had a lot more to do with Sloan Gallagher, the thin, wiry fourteen-year-old who had surprised her and Lew that day in the barn!

Polly shook her head, remembering. What a disaster! Every time she thought about it she felt equal parts mortification and amusement. She wondered what Celie would say if she knew Sloan Gallagher had seen her naked.

No one knew now except Polly—and Sloan Gallagher.

Fortunately, way too much had happened in his life for Sloan to recall one long-ago evening in Fletchers' barn. Polly was sure he'd seen far more memorable sights in the past twenty years.

Most of the rest of Elmer might have stayed here and stayed the same, but Sloan Gallagher hadn't.

He'd changed, grown up, moved on.

And despite what Gus said, Polly was sure he wouldn't come back.

Never in a million years.

Chapter 2

There were only three people in the world who had Sloan Gallagher's cell phone number—his agent, the director of his latest picture and Gus Holt.

His agent called every few days with projects, news and gossip. The director called when he needed something.

And Gus never called at all.

Well, almost never. Twice in six years. Last winter, like a bolt out of the blue, Gus had rung to tell Sloan that he and Mary McLean were getting married at last. He'd been laughing then, singing almost. "You're not going to believe this," he'd crowed.

And Sloan almost hadn't. *"Married? You?"*

After a dozen footloose, run-around years, the notion of Gus ending up back where he'd started—with the woman he'd started with—was one heck of a shock.

But nowhere near the shock he'd got last month when Gus called again.

"I'm a dad!" Gus's voice had broken, his words somewhere between a laugh and a sob. "Can you believe it? Poor little beggar. Imagine havin' me for an old man!"

Sloan had laughed, but he'd been awed, too—and just a little envious—though he'd been in bed with a starlet at the time.

"A dad? You've got a kid?" He'd echoed Gus's astonishment.

And the eagerness in his tone had sent the starlet scrambling away, as if parenthood was catching.

He'd assured her it wasn't. Sloan was always careful that way. He'd had sex with her—love had nothing to do with it— but all the while his mind had been on Gus and Mary and their brand-new baby boy, Daniel McLean, called Mac.

Sloan could remember that easily enough.

He could barely remember the starlet's name. He wondered if she remembered his.

Probably. That was why she'd slept with him—because of his name—because he was Sloan Gallagher, Hollywood star. He was a notch on her bedpost, a stepping stone on her quest for stardom.

After six years on Hollywood's short list, Sloan understood the way things worked. And he could hardly complain.

In the early days he'd been as eager as they were. Sex for the asking—women pressing their phone numbers into his hand, tucking them in his pockets, stuffing them down the waistband of his jeans—what was there to complain about?

There's too damn many women wanting to crawl into my bed!

Yeah, right. He'd win the sympathy vote with that one, hands down.

Gus would split a gut laughing.

Not that he'd ever find out at the rate they talked to each other these days. Gus was up to his ears in cattle and snow, working as a foreman on a ranch near Elmer, while Sloan was in Key West, land of sun and surf and sand, finishing up an action-adventure film that would be released in the summer. He wasn't even thinking about Gus tonight when his cell phone rang again.

"Don't answer it," murmured Tamara Lynd, one of the latest crop of up-and-coming actresses to try their wiles on him. She was curled around him in a hammock wearing little more than the skin she'd been born in, and she clearly had seduction on her mind.

But Sloan, who knew that Suzette, his agent, was trying to work out a meeting for him with the director on his next picture and Becca Hall, a possible costar, knew he had to. "Sorry," he said, reaching for the phone on the wicker table. "Duty calls."

"Oh, Sloan." Tamara smothered his mouth with one last kiss.

"Hey, Suz," he said, "What's up?"

"Sorry, man. I ain't your girl," an immediately familiar male voice said.

Sloan almost tipped out of the hammock. "Gus? What the—? Cripes, not another kid!"

"Mary'd see me dead first," Gus laughed. "Mac's not sleeping more than two hours at a time. We're walkin' the floor right now, him an' me."

"Mac's a goer," Sloan agreed.

"My respect for my parents goes up daily." Gus stifled a yawn and Sloan heard a baby's cry. "Shh, feller," Gus crooned in a tender, loving voice. It was so unlike his roughneck buddy that Sloan felt another jolt of surprise. "He's a peck of trouble," Gus said. "But I wouldn't trade him, tell you that. You oughta come visit. See the chip off the old block."

"Maybe this spring," Sloan said. "I should have some time. I got it written into my contract that no matter where I am, I get branding time off."

Tamara raised her eyebrows. He ignored her. No one understood why he insisted on going back to Montana every spring, least of all the women who were eager to get him into bed.

Even Gus thought he was a little crazy. "Why don't you come when you don't have to put in sixteen-hour days? Brandin's *work!*"

"Spoken like the true rodeo cowboy you are."

"Were," Gus corrected. "I'm a man of the land now. Or," he said wryly, "I will be when I find a piece I can afford."

Sloan could already afford it several times over. He had the land now. It had been the first thing he'd bought—the land that had been in his family for years and years. Five generations of Gallaghers had lived on the acreage Sloan's great-great-grandparents had homesteaded in the 1880s. It had always been a challenge, eking out a livelihood on it, but they'd managed until the depression. Then his grandfather had been forced to sell all but the house and a few hundred acres.

His dad had had to sell what was left the year Sloan's mother died, the year their lives—and their family—had fallen apart.

Getting the land back had been Sloan's first priority as soon as he had enough money. He couldn't get his family back. His father had died three years before. All the money in the world wouldn't bring the Gallaghers together again. But at least he had the ranch, and someday, he vowed, he'd have a family to live on it.

What he didn't have now was the time to enjoy it.

"You'll find yourself a piece," he promised Gus.

"I might," Gus said. "Actually, that's why I'm callin'."

When he'd first hit it big in Hollywood and had bought his own place, Sloan had made a point of telling Gus that when he decided to settle down, to give a shout and Sloan would help him out with a loan.

"Don't hold your breath," Gus had said. But that had been the old Gus, the footloose wanderer, not the man who'd come to his senses and married Mary McLean.

"You found a place?"

"No. But you remember Maddie Fletcher's place?"

Oh, yeah, Sloan remembered Fletchers' place.

"She's not sellin', is she?" Sloan was shocked that Maddie Fletcher might be selling out. He knew her husband Ward had died, but he couldn't imagine Maddie leaving the place except in a pine box. She'd married the ranch as much as she'd married Ward all those years ago. They'd loved it the way he and his old man had loved the Rafter Two T.

"Tryin' not to," Gus said. "She's got a problem."

Sloan rolled up and out of the hammock, leaving Tamara to stare at him. "What's goin' on?"

Gus told him.

"What d'you mean they're going to foreclose? How the hell can they do that?"

And Gus explained that, too—how Ward had taken out a loan, how he'd made only sensible improvements, how they'd been meeting the payments until he got sick—and now Maddie was in over her head.

"Shouldn't be happenin' to her," Gus said.

"No, it shouldn't."

There were no better people on earth than Maddie and Ward Fletcher. Even after Sloan had left their home, he'd thought of them often. Three years ago he'd got a couple weeks off in the summer and he'd flown into Bozeman, then rented a car to drive to the ranch. He'd been heading north when he'd come to the turnoff to Fletchers' ranch, and on the spur of the moment, he'd decided to stop.

He hadn't seen Maddie and Ward since he'd gone to live in Billings with his dad once the old man had stopped drinking and sorted himself out again. That had been eighteen years ago—but he'd never forgotten them.

They'd taken him in at the worst time in his life. He'd just turned fourteen, a miserable, angry kid whose world had been shattered—his mother had recently been killed, his father had turned into an emotional wreck, drinking himself into a stupor and into deeper and deeper debt. The family ranch—the past, present and future of Gallagher hopes, had had to be sold.

There had been nothing left of the life he'd known, when Sloan had been sent to live with Maddie and Ward. Sullen, angry and unresponsive, he had hated the world.

Slowly, with infinite patience, Maddie and Ward had helped change his mind. They'd given him the toehold he'd needed to hang on.

And even though he'd eventually gone back to live with his father, and then at eighteen had moved out on his own, he'd always remembered...and been grateful.

So that afternoon he'd stopped to see them. He'd seen Ward's new prize bull. They had talked bloodlines and birth weights and Ward had shown how pleased he was by the twinkle in his normally grave hazel eyes. When they'd finally left the corral to walk to the house, he'd clapped Sloan on the shoulder and said, "Glad you ain't forgot your roots."

Maddie had given him a bag of homemade cookies to take along. "You come back now," she'd said when he left. "Don't be a stranger."

"I won't," he'd promised. "You come see my place, too."

He'd meant to set a date and a time. He'd promised himself he'd have them up next time he was home. But his commitments kept him away most of the year. And the next thing he heard Ward had passed away.

Now he felt guilty as well as sad.

"I'll write a check," he promised Gus. "Just tell me how much and who to send it to."

"You know Maddie won't let you do that."

"Why the hell not?" Sloan demanded, pacing around the patio. "I can afford it."

"That's not the point."

"I thought the point was saving her ranch."

"Yeah. But it's not just you. It's all of us. Everybody around Elmer is helping out."

"Fine. Everybody else can pitch in and I'll write a check for the difference."

"We're having an auction," Gus said.

"So I'll buy something. What are you selling? Old fence posts and rusty barbed wire?"

"Cowboys."

Sloan stopped pacing. "What?"

"We're auctioning off cowboys," Gus repeated. "It was Joyce O'Meara's idea. Sort of takin' advantage of what's in our own backyard—besides barbed wire. We're auctioning off guys who'll work on a ranch for a certain amount of time. And Taggart Jones and Noah Tanner are auctioning off spots at bull- and bronc-riding school. Walt Blasingame's donating some trail rides. J.D. and I are offering some horse-training hours. There's other stuff. But the big draw, I guess, will be the bachelors."

"What bachelors?"

Gus laughed. "Oh, you know, they reckon we should have

one of those bachelor auctions where women bid on the guy they want to go out with. It's the weekend before Valentine's Day and Joyce said there's nothin' women love more than a cowboy—which is true, of course. All the local single fellas are up for that.''

"I'll bet they are." Sloan grinned.

"Thing is, we need to get attention, draw people in. Not very much good to have local women bidding on guys they see every day of the week. We need a bigger pool of bidders. So we need a big ticket item." Pause. "You."

"Me?" Sloan's laugh turned to a cough. "You're not serious."

"I am damn serious. This is Maddie's ranch we're talking about."

"Yeah, but an auction? A bachelor auction?" Sloan started pacing again. Tamara was watching every step he took, her eyes like saucers. Sloan snorted. "D'you know what a zoo that would be?"

His life was already a zoo.

He couldn't go out to eat without women popping up in the middle of his salad wanting his autograph and a peck on the cheek. He couldn't walk down a street without attracting a gaggle of gawking girls. He couldn't even go to the supermarket without causing a fan feeding frenzy. He had to have his damn groceries delivered. He didn't even want to think about what a hullabaloo being an auctionable bachelor would create.

"Of course it'd be a zoo," Gus said cheerfully. "That's the point. Get lots of people here. Raise lots of money for the ranch."

"I'll write a check!"

"You know what Maddie'd say to that."

Sloan knew. "Put your body where your money is," he said wearily—which was exactly what she and Ward had done for years and years.

They could have simply donated money to help starving orphans overseas. They could have simply "done their part" of taking care of needy kids by writing a check. But they hadn't thought that was enough.

"It's important," Maddie had told him the afternoon he'd stopped to visit them and had asked her why on earth she'd put herself through all the anguish she sometimes faced with ungrateful, unruly kids. "Kids matter. Ward and I needed to say so by what we did. My dad always said to put my body where my mouth was."

Sloan knew she felt that way about money, too.

In Gus's deliberate, calculated silence, Sloan grimaced. He flexed his shoulders and rolled his eyes ceilingward, trying to imagine what it would be like if he put his body where his checkbook was. It was a horrible thought. He had to find a way out.

"Before Valentine's Day, you said?"

"Yep. The Sunday before."

"Can't do it then," Sloan said, relieved. "I've got a film opening Valentine's weekend. There's always a ton of promo to do."

"So get on those late-night shows and tell 'em all about The Great Montana Cowboy Auction."

"The what?"

"That's what we're callin' it. Reckon it's maybe a little bit of an exaggeration, but Mary said we need a little hype. And of course it will be great if you're there." There was no one like Gus when it came to wheedling persuasion.

Sloan closed his eyes. "Aw, hell, Gus...you don't have any idea..."

No one did. They just knew his name would bring in lots of people—and lots of money. They had no idea what a headache it would be.

"How about if I just talk about it?" he said. "When I do those talk shows, I could mention it."

"Wouldn't do any good. Everybody'd go, uh-huh. In one ear and out the other. Except maybe we'd look like country bumpkins. No, thanks. If you're going to say no, just say it."

But Sloan couldn't say it.

A guy always paid his debts—and whether he liked it or not, whether he wanted to or not, he owed an enormous debt to both the Fletchers. "It'll be a mess," he warned Gus. "A god-awful mess."

"Never mind, then," Gus said. "Just forget it. I'll tell Polly you won't do it. She'll be thrilled."

"What?" Sloan's pacing came to an abrupt halt. "Wait! Polly who?"

"Polly McMaster. The mayor of Elmer. She's in charge. She didn't think you'd do it."

Polly McMaster? "Is that…Lew's wife?"

"Widow."

Sloan felt as if he'd been punched in the gut.

"What's the matter? Do you know her?" Gus demanded at his silence.

"I…remember her." Sloan felt vaguely breathless. "I knew Lew. I didn't know he'd…died."

"Oh, Christ! I'm sorry. I didn't realize."

"It's okay. I mean, we weren't close or anything. We were just both at Fletchers' at the same time. He was older than me, eighteen or so by the time I got there. He was workin' for Ward and bullfighting at rodeos on the weekends. What happened?"

"Plane went down. He and three other guys were comin' back from Dodge City maybe six years ago now."

He'd been in Mexico that summer. He supposed it wasn't odd that he hadn't heard, but it felt odd. It felt odd to think of Polly as a widow.

Actually it felt odd to think of Polly at all.

But now, as his thoughts drifted back, he could still see her in his mind's eye as clearly as he'd seen her that soft June evening there in Fletchers' barn.

She had been with Lew. Sloan had discovered them by accident when he'd snuck out behind the barn for a cigarette so Ward wouldn't catch him smoking.

The unexpected, soft sound of a female giggle had caught his attention. Quickly he'd stubbed out the cigarette, then crept up to press his eye against a knothole. At first he only heard voices, soft and intimate. But when he looked up he saw movement in the loft.

He should have turned and walked away.

He knew what was happening up there was private. But the evening light spilling through the open loft door caught a flash of golden skin, a tangle of gingery hair—Polly's hair.

And Sloan hadn't moved away at all.

He'd stood, mesmerized, in the thrall of the first real live naked woman he'd ever seen. All those airbrushed big-bosomed women he and his friends had ogled in the magazines they stole from their older brothers didn't hold a candle to her.

He pressed closer, tried to see more. He paid no attention to Lew, who was equally naked. His gaze was all for Polly.

She was glorious. The most beautiful thing he'd ever seen. Of course she didn't just stand there and let him gaze his fill. But he caught glimpses. He saw golden flesh and long loose wavy hair. He saw curve and line and light and shadow.

His mouth grew dry and his body grew hard and his breath caught in his lungs.

And then all of a sudden he heard Nicky, one of the little boys, pound around the corner of the barn and yell, "Hey, Sloan! Sloan! Whatcha doin'? Whatcha lookin' at?"

Abruptly he had stumbled backward and fallen, landing on his butt in the dirt. Inside he heard scuttering and thumping movements.

"What is it?" Nicky was demanding. "Whatcha lookin' at?"

"Nothin'," Sloan muttered, scrambling up, grimacing at the hard ache of his body, desperately hoping Nicky was too young to notice his very physical teenage boy reaction to the sight of naked female flesh. He grabbed the younger boy by the arm and pulled him away.

"You musta seen somethin'," Nicky protested. "You were lookin' in the knothole!"

Behind him he thought he heard Polly say, "Ohmigod, Lew!"

And Lew had replied with determined ferocity, "I'll take care of it."

Sloan hadn't stayed around to find out how. He'd grabbed

Nicky and hauled him off to the horse corral to watch Ward work with a couple of colts.

But it hadn't mattered. Lew had tracked him down later that evening. He'd hauled him back behind the very same barn and had had a few choice things to say as he'd pounded Sloan into the dirt.

Then, still holding him down and sitting on him, Lew grabbed Sloan's shirtfront and hauled him up so they were nose to nose. "You never saw a thing, did you?"

Sloan had swallowed and shaken his head. At least he would never tell. He wouldn't do anything to embarrass Polly. She was the most beautiful girl he'd ever seen.

"Never saw a thing," he'd choked out in the face of Lew's fists.

And what he said he hadn't seen, he remembered still.

And his body, which had been only mildly interested in Tamara Lynd's seduction, was definitely interested in the memory of Polly in the nude.

Now he swallowed, trying to get a little moisture in his suddenly dry mouth. "Polly's runnin' this show?"

"Yep."

"And she doesn't think I'll come?" Why? Sloan wondered. Because she thought he was too much a star to come back to Elmer and do a favor for a friend—or because she didn't want him to?

He wanted to know. He wanted to see her again.

Call it curiosity. Call it an itch that suddenly needed to be scratched. Call it the craziest thing he'd ever done.

But memories of Polly, young and lithe and golden in her nakedness, stirred him more than any starlet had in as long as he could remember.

"You're on," he said to Gus.

"A kelp body wrap?" Joyce turned her head and blinked over her shoulder at Celie as her daughter kneaded her back in the long rhythmic strokes that always loosened the knots created during her stint at the hospital in Livingston. "Er, no, dear, I don't believe I've thought about one."

As someone who, in sixty years of life on this planet, had never even seen the ocean, Joyce had never considered having her body swathed in seaweed.

"They say it's beneficial," Celie said. "I've been thinking about learning more about it."

"Sounds good." Joyce put her face back in the warm towel and gave herself over to Celie's ministrations. What did she know? After all, she'd originally been skeptical of Celie's interest in massage.

It sounded a little too risqué for a place like Elmer and she'd said so.

"For heaven's sake, Mother," Celie had protested. "I'm not going to massage naked men! I thought the women coming in for cuts and perms might like to try a little relaxation. That's all."

"Of course," Joyce had agreed. But she'd still held her breath when Celie had come back from Billings, bearing a piece of paper that said she was a certified massage therapist, and had added that to her list of "services" on her blackboard in the window.

She'd opened some eyes and raised some brows, all right.

A few of the guys who had come in to get their hair cut or to rent a video had looked at it and had said, "I wouldn't mind a massage," hopefully.

But Celie had merely looked down her nose at them and said, "Sorry, no."

"You're wasting a heck of an opportunity," Polly had told her cheerfully. "All those manly muscles."

And ever-practical Sara had said sensibly, "Not good business turning down half your potential clientele, you know."

But Celie had declined. She gave massages to local women. The men were out of luck.

It worried Joyce.

Celie wasn't getting any younger. She'd turned thirty the week before Thanksgiving. That wasn't really *old* yet, of course. When you'd just turned sixty, thirty sounded like kid stuff.

But for finding a lasting love, for starting a family, for doing the things that Celie had always wanted to do, time was getting shorter. So Joyce worried about her.

Of course Joyce worried about all three of her daughters. As she'd told her husband, Gil, years ago, it went with the job.

"I'm fine," Polly always said. "Don't worry about me."

And Polly had always been a fighter. Even after Lew had died, Polly had soldiered on. She'd said, "I have the kids. I'll be fine. It would be worse if I were alone."

And basically that was true. So Joyce stayed out of her way and kept her fingers crossed.

Mary Beth, the middle child, was a softer, gentler version of Polly, as if God had decided the second time around to add a little less pepper. Mary Beth and her husband, Steve, had moved to Cheyenne two years ago with their almost seven-year-old triplet daughters. Joyce worried about them as a matter of principle. When you were dealing with triplets, there was always reason to worry.

But mostly Joyce worried about Celie.

Celie was her baby. Quieter than her sisters, less outgoing, Celie had not been a tomboy like Polly or a self-sufficient sturdy middle child like Mary Beth. She'd never followed Gil around demanding to ride and rope and brand the way he did. She'd done those things well enough, but they'd never interested her. She'd always wanted to stay home and bake cookies and play with her dolls and read books.

From the time she was three, Celie had told her mother, "When I grow up I'm getting married and have babies like you."

And because Joyce had always been perfectly happy as a ranch wife and mother, she'd been pleased.

So Celie's whole life had been aimed at marriage. She'd had a hope chest, and she'd embroidered pillowcases and dish towels to put in it. She'd made a wedding ring quilt top before she'd graduated from high school. And when she'd started going steady with Matt Williams in her sophomore year of high school, she was sure she'd found the man of her dreams.

Matt was perfect. Handsome, tall, strong. A cowboy like her

father had been. Maybe, she'd confided to her mother, Matt would ranch with her dad.

Celie had had all their children named before she had a ring on her finger. And when she finally did get the ring, she'd been so busy planning the wedding she didn't care that Matt suddenly decided to do a little rodeoing before he settled down.

She didn't much like his traveling partners. Everyone knew Jace Tucker was a little on the wild side and Brent Vickers was a crazy kid. But once they were married, Matt wouldn't be around Jace or Brent anymore. He was just sowing his wild oats. Once they were married, Celie said, he'd settle down.

When the big day arrived, though, Matt didn't.

Instead, an hour before the wedding, Celie had got a call from Vegas—from Jace Tucker—telling her that Matt wasn't coming home, wasn't marrying her. He wasn't ready, Jace told her. He couldn't go through with it.

To say that Celie was devastated was putting it mildly. Any girl would have been. But being jilted, having her love spurned and her dearest hopes destroyed, had cut Celie's heart right out.

She had gone into a shell after that.

Of course there had been gossip. Of course people had talked, had speculated, had tittered and muttered.

Celie was still whispered about as ''the girl Matt Williams jilted.'' But only, Joyce was sure, because Celie had never got over it herself.

After a while other guys had turned up, had dropped in, had asked Celie out. To Joyce's knowledge Celie never went. She hadn't had a date in ten years.

Any interest Celie had had in the opposite sex, she'd turned to focusing on the men in books, on the screen and in magazines.

Men like Sloan Gallagher.

''Wonder if Sloan Gallagher really will come,'' Joyce said now and felt Celie's fingers tighten in the muscles of her back.

''Of course he won't,'' Celie said.

''You could bid on him,'' Joyce went on cheerfully, enduring another pinch of her back muscles as she determined how Celie actually felt about the idea.

"Ha-ha," Celie said, her fingers pummeling Joyce's muscles so hard her mother was sure she'd have bruises all down her spine.

"You should," Joyce insisted. "You know so much about him."

"Oh, Mother, don't be ridiculous. He won't do it," Celie said. "Polly's right."

Polly probably was right, Joyce thought. But there would be other eligible young men there. "Then you'll just have to bid on someone else."

Celie didn't reply to that.

That was the trouble with Celie. She never out and out said she wouldn't do what you wanted her to, so you couldn't argue with her about it. And you couldn't goad her into doing anything, either.

The "dare you" method of child raising that she'd used on Polly and Mary Beth had rarely worked on her youngest daughter.

"For Maddie's fund, of course," Joyce felt required to persist. "It's the charitable thing to do."

"Of course," Celie said, kneading rhythmically once more. "There will be lots of things to bid on."

Which was true—offers from cowboys and ranchers and families all over the area were pouring in—but agreeing to bid on *something* was as good as no agreement at all, Joyce thought wearily.

Celie didn't need a trail ride or a bull-riding scholarship. She didn't need her fences ridden or treatment for scours.

She needed a real live man in her life.

She needed to move on—to get a life!—once and for all.

What was a mother to do?

Chapter 3

He wouldn't come.

At least Celie hoped not.

Sloan Gallagher might once have lived at Fletchers' ranch, but she hadn't known him then. She only knew him in his films—and in her heart. And that was the only way she wanted to know him. He was just fine there.

Of course everyone else thought it was a great idea.

Alice Benn, one of Elmer's retired teachers, had stopped in the hardware store, where Celie worked mornings, to talk about it. She was delighted at the prospect. So was Cloris Stedman, another old teacher, and Carol Ferguson from the grocery store and Felicity Jones and Brenna McCall. Every woman who dropped in the hardware store that morning, married or not, thought it was a great idea.

"You should be delighted," they said over and over, because most everyone in town knew Celie was a "fan" of Sloan Gallagher's.

"Oh, yes," she'd murmured. But it wasn't true.

It would just complicate things. Celie liked her life as it was. It might be boring by some people's standards, but excitement wasn't everything. Ten years ago she'd had all the excitement she ever wanted. And after, she'd wanted to crawl into a hole and die. She knew people whispered and poked each other and murmured about "poor Celie O'Meara." She'd learned to tune them out.

She'd found solace in books and movies. She'd found reliable men in her dreams. And that was precisely where she wanted to keep Sloan Gallagher.

When she went to bed at night, she had him there. She could crush her pillow in her arms and feel cozy and warm and loved. That was what she wanted. And it was what her two-dimensional Sloan had given her.

Now when she went to bed, she didn't feel cozy and warm at all. She couldn't imagine murmuring to her pillow Sloan, telling him about her day, teasing him about the story she'd just read in the latest issue of a magazine or imagining what it would be like to do the things with him that she saw him do in films.

Tonight when she went to bed she thought about what it would be like to actually have Sloan Gallagher in her bed. The *real* Sloan Gallagher.

And instead of feeling that eager anticipation she always felt when she opened a magazine with Sloan's picture in it or watched a video of Sloan saving the day or charming a woman, or even better, sat in a darkened theater and relished his larger-than-life presence on the screen, then came home and imagined what it would be like to share her nights with Sloan, she had felt a cold clammy hand of panic grip her midsection.

She felt positively ill.

Of course it wouldn't happen. Polly had certainly been right about that.

Sloan would never come back to the place where, as far as Celie could figure, he must have been the unhappiest he'd ever been in his whole life.

Elmer was where he'd come after his mother had been killed in a car accident and something had happened to his father and the family ranch. The magazines never actually said what it was. All she knew was that Sloan, at age fourteen, had had his world turned upside down. She'd felt a rush of sympathy for the motherless boy, certain that he must have felt even more hurt and alone than she had felt after Matt had jilted her.

Reading of his early pain, she had identified with him. Learning that he'd lived in Elmer, aware that he knew some of the same people she did, Celie had felt an even closer kinship. She liked what she knew about him. She loved the characters he portrayed—men of honor even when they were battle-weary and in pain. She took those characters and what little she knew of Sloan, and she created the perfect man.

In her mind and in her dreams, Sloan was the embodiment of everything that Matt Williams hadn't been. Sloan had never hurt her. He'd never disappointed her. He'd never turned his back on her.

The last thing she wanted to do was meet the hero of her heart.

Either everyone in Elmer was suddenly writing more letters and buying more stamps and mailing more packages and checking two or three times a day for mail that was only delivered once before eight-thirty every morning—or they all wanted to see if Polly had heard from Sloan Gallagher.

Polly had assumed she'd be able to figure out the logistics of the auction during her slow times in the afternoons. But she didn't have any slow times the rest of that week.

A steady stream of stamp buyers and postal box checkers and people deciding that they might as well write their Christmas cards and mail them even if it was well into January appeared constantly. And, incidentally, every one of them asked if she'd heard from Sloan Gallagher.

Polly thought she ought to get cards printed. Instead she said, "Nope, haven't heard from him."

Gee whiz, what a shame.

"Guess he won't be able to make it. Can't say I'm surprised, busy man that he is. Hope *you* aren't too busy to help out. I sure could use a cowboy or two."

She shamed, cajoled and persuaded most of the town into

participating that way. Things were working out perfectly. She had plenty of volunteer cowboys—and no Sloan Gallagher.

No one else gave up hope.

"I'm sure he's just busy," Alice Benn said when Celie was washing her hair that week. "He'll call. You'll see."

"No," Celie said for what seemed like the thousandth time that week. "He won't. You're dreaming."

But Alice was stubborn. "I can hope, can't I?"

Other women said the same thing.

"Sloan Gallagher's coming," they insisted. "He won't let us down."

Celie resolutely ignored them. So did Polly, even though the topic of conversation at the hair salon and the post office remained the same.

"He won't come, will he?" Celie asked Polly every night.

And every night Polly said, "Of course not." And they smiled at each other and went to bed, relieved.

Then, on Thursday afternoon Polly marched into the salon when she got off work from the post office and announced, "Sloan Gallagher has arrived."

Celie gasped.

Everyone in the shop looked up—even Cloris Stedman whose gray hair Celie was highlighting and who suddenly had blue dye running down her face.

At their startled expressions, Polly grinned.

"Gotcha!" She waved the weekly shipment of new videos in front of their faces.

Celie dropped the hair dye and snatched the box out of her sister's hands. It was indicative of her agitated state of mind that she had forgotten that today was the day Sloan's latest film was being released on video.

Now with eager fingers she opened the parcel. She knew what was in it: two kung-fu action flicks and an Arnold S. movie for the guys, a couple of kiddie cartoons and the latest Disney, the new Tom Hanks film, and—yes, it was here!—*Whistle Up the Wind* starring Sloan Gallagher.

"See," Polly said. "Sloan Gallagher. I told you so." Giving

the box one dismissive glance, she went into the kitchen and didn't look back.

Celie, on the other hand, studied the box reverently. There were gorgeous photos of Sloan in roughneck-cowboy mode and tender-lover mode. It was all she could do to hand the box over to Cloris while she finished the older woman's hair. She kept sneaking glances at Sloan on the box, and Cloris's hair was perhaps a little more blue than gray when she left that afternoon.

Whistle Up the Wind went with her, as two months ago she and Alice had put in first dibs. Everyone else in the shop looked longingly after Cloris as she left with it.

"You should've ordered two," Kitzy Miller complained.

Celie didn't mention that she had. Now she picked up the pace, washing and cutting Carol Ferguson's hair as quickly as she could, then combing out Evelyn Setsma, and declining to give Kitzy Miller a massage tonight.

"Sorry, I have a commitment this evening," she said. She could hardly wait until she could close up shop, go eat dinner, then disappear into her room and spend two hours with Sloan.

Unfortunately, Jack pounced the minute she came into the kitchen. "Ma says you got Sloan Gallagher's new movie!"

"Cloris took it home."

"You always get two!" Jack was no fool. "So we can watch it after supper."

"It's a school night," Celie reminded him.

"Then let's hurry up an' eat!"

Celie gave in to the inevitable. After dinner she would watch it with Jack and her mother and whoever else happened to turn up in the living room. But later, after everyone else had gone to bed, she would take it to her room and watch it again. Alone.

Or rather, just the two of them—she and Sloan.

But until then it was a free-for-all, and chaos reigned supreme. Joyce was conjugating Spanish verbs out loud. Lizzie was reciting lines for the witches' part in MacBeth. Jack was pretending to be Sloan battling the bad guys. And above them all, Polly was reeling off a list of everyone who had volunteered for the auction.

"Otis Jamison is willing to do his old cowboy stories. Spence Atkins said he'd do the auction if anybody wanted to buy a deputy. And there were a couple of others. Maddie even came in and volunteered Logan Reese. He's her new hired hand."

Joyce's brows lifted. "She hired Logan Reese? *And* she volunteered him for the auction?"

"She said everyone had to do their part—and that meant her and Logan."

"Well, now…" Joyce shook her head. "Logan's going to be a bit of a challenge."

Celie couldn't imagine Logan coming back any more than she could imagine Sloan coming—for entirely different reasons. Sloan had gone off and become a tremendous success. Three years ago Logan had got thrown into prison.

"I don't believe for a minute he did it," Polly said stoutly.

"The jury did," Joyce reminded her.

"Even so. How many do we have?" Polly asked, brushing speculation aside. Joyce stopped speculating and pulled out her own notes. "Let's see. We're doing very well. We've got art and photos and trail rides and cookouts and fence mending and branding and doctoring and the bachelors."

She started to count the bachelors, at the same time giving Celie a significant look that said, *See, you can have your pick of one of these.*

Celie pretended she didn't notice.

The telephone rang.

To avoid her mother's gaze, Celie reached over and picked it up.

Lizzie stopped proclaiming and said, "If that's Louise, tell her I still need a witch's hat."

"If it's Frankie tell him I'll call him soon as we eat," said Jack.

"If that's Mabel, no, I can't work for her tonight," Joyce said.

"If it's Gus tell him his hot-shot superstar hero never called," Polly said loudly.

Celie waved a hand to shush them all. "Hello?"

There was a split second's pause. Then a rough-velvet voice said in her ear, "Tell Polly that Gus's hot-shot superstar hero would like to talk to her."

Chapter 4

"What's wrong?" Polly took one look at Celie, white-faced, trembling and thrusting the phone at her, and thought someone had died. *"What's wrong?"*

Celie opened her mouth, but still no sound came out. She looked halfway between stunned and panic-stricken.

"It's not Sara?" Polly's eyes were scanning the room as fast as her brain was moving. Only Sara was missing. Everyone else was accounted for.

Numbly Celie shook her head no.

"Well, for goodness' sake." Polly snatched the phone out of her sister's hand. "Who is this and what have you done to my sister?"

"Nothing," said an amused masculine voice. "Yet."

Oh, dear God.

Now Polly knew why Celie was white-faced and gibbering. And she had to admit she wasn't far behind—though not at all for the same reasons.

She squeezed suddenly damp fingers into a death grip on the receiver and said sternly, "Listen, here, mister, if you think you're going to get me to buy a vacuum cleaner by giving me a hard sell while I'm trying to eat my dinner, you've got another think coming.''

Celie gasped and dropped the spoon in the spaghetti sauce. Everyone else looked mystified.

Sloan Gallagher laughed. "You really don't want me to do it, do you?''

"I don't know what you're talking about,'' Polly stonewalled.

"Gus said you didn't,'' he went on, still amused. "I wonder why.''

Polly wished she was using the cordless phone so she could take Sloan Gallagher upstairs and deal with him there. Instead she was tethered to within ten feet of the kitchen wall while everyone in her immediate family eavesdropped.

Celie, still trembling, was shooting her desperate glances as she burned her fingers trying to fish the spoon out of the spaghetti sauce.

"What'sa matter with you?'' Jack was asking Celie.

Joyce frowned. "If it's vacuum cleaners, just hang up, dear,'' she said impatiently.

Wouldn't I love to? But Polly held up a hand to forestall her. "Sorry. Just a bit of quirkiness on my part, no doubt,'' she answered Sloan Gallagher's query. "Personal taste and all that.''

Polly was never snippy. At least not with anyone else. But Sloan Gallagher's lazy, teasing drawl seemed to bring out the awkward naked teenager in her. Deliberately she shut her eyes and started to count to ten.

She'd only got to four when he said, "Guess I'll just have to change your mind, won't I?''

"*No!* I mean, no.'' She made an effort to moderate her tone after the first squeak. She was an adult now. A mother of four. Mayor of Elmer, for heaven's sake!

"Who *is* that?'' Joyce mouthed.

Deliberately Polly shook her head and turned away. Time to stop acting like an idiot. She focused resolutely on the kitchen cupboard and did her best to sound like the sane, intelligent well-brought-up woman of thirty-seven mature years that most of the time she was.

"I'm sure how I feel is immaterial," she said, consummately professional at last. "Does this mean you'll be joining us?"

"It means Gus twisted my arm." She could hear the smile in his voice.

"You mustn't do it, then. Participation is entirely voluntary."

Although she was pretty sure Maddie herself had been doing a little arm-twisting this afternoon, before she'd turned up in the post office with Logan in tow. Still, that was irrelevant.

"So if you'd rather not…" she offered.

"I'm doing it," Sloan Gallagher said. "Gus said the Sunday before Valentine's Day?"

So much for graciously letting him off the hook.

"At one in the afternoon. First the auction, then a potluck supper for the volunteers. I'm sure everyone will be just delighted to see you." The understatement of the year. "Everyone is staying for that. So if it's not convenient…"

"It's fine. I'll manage. Where?"

Damn. "The Elmer town hall."

"Great. It's a date."

"Wait!" she yelped when she realized he was about to hang up.

"Yes, Polly?" His voice was a purr in her ear.

How could one skinny fourteen-year-old grow up to have that much sex appeal? It wasn't fair. "Er, um, what are we, uh…auctioning?"

"I thought you were auctioning me."

"Well, yes, but I mean…what?" *A night in the sack? A dinner at McDonald's?*

"What's everybody else auctioning?"

"Trail rides. Bull-riding school scholarships. A day's worth of riding fence. And dates, of course. Various kinds. Dinner. A movie."

"Well, I'd rather give you a day's worth of riding fence," he said, and he sounded as if he meant it. "But I suppose you want a date."

"Not me," Polly said quickly. "I mean, I won't be bidding."

"What a shame," Sloan said, his tone dry, "since I can tell how you'd just run up the price."

Polly felt her face warm. "Sorry," she muttered.

"Okay, let's do this," he said after a moment's consideration. "We'll offer a date for the following weekend. *Crossroads* opens that Saturday. My new film," he explained, as if she hadn't been seeing trailers for it on prime time television for the past month. "Whoever bids highest can be my date at the premiere."

"Are you serious?" Polly's jaw sagged.

"Why? Won't that work?" He sounded concerned that it might not. "The premiere's in Hollywood, but I'll spring for the airline ticket so that won't be a problem. Put her up in a nice place for the weekend. We'll do dinner first and party after. How's that sound?"

"Bidding will go through the roof."

"All the better for Maddie."

"It's not a vacuum cleaner salesman, dear...is it?" Joyce said, cottoning on at last.

"So are we all set, then?" Sloan asked.

"Er, actually, yes. Thank you. It really is very kind of you," Polly said, which was only the truth, little as she wanted to admit it.

"That's me. Kindness personified." He laughed. "You really didn't think I'd do it?"

Mortified, Polly muttered, "Gus has a big mouth."

"Always did. Why *didn't* you?"

"Because you're a busy man, and we're a very small place," she lied irritably. "You weren't with Maddie and Ward all that long."

"Two years is a long time at that age. And I remember it well," he added a second later in the soft whiskey drawl that made his bedroom scenes famous. It almost peeled the clothes right off you.

Polly willed herself not to react and definitely not to think about peeling clothes off. He wasn't talking about remembering *her*—and thank God for that.

"Well that's very nice," she said briskly. "I'm sure Maddie will be pleased. I know she'll be looking forward to seeing you."

"I'll look forward to seeing her," he said. Another pause, then once more that soft whiskey drawl tickled her ear. "I'm looking forward to seeing you again, too, Pol'."

Celie barely slept all night.

She held her pillow as if it were a stranger in her arms. She tried to recapture the easy quiet intimacy she usually escaped to when she made believe it was Sloan lying next to her. She tried to tell him about her day, to ask about his.

But she felt frozen in anticipation—and in fear.

Sloan was coming *here*. She had actually spoken to him this evening. Really spoken to him. Had heard his soft gruff voice speaking directly to her.

Talking about Polly!

Tell Polly that Gus's hot-shot superstar hero would like to talk to her. God, how embarrassing.

Why did Polly always have to smart off that way? And in front of Sloan Gallagher, for heaven's sake! Of course, to be fair, Polly had no way of knowing it was him on the phone. Chances had been a lot greater that it would have been a vacuum cleaner salesman.

But still…!

"She didn't mean it," Celie whispered to her pillow.

But somehow she couldn't fall into the fantasy she was usually able to conjure. There was no imagined murmur in return. There was only the echo in her mind of Sloan Gallagher's words on the phone, and Polly's announcement after she'd hung up.

Sloan was coming to Elmer.

He was going to be part of the auction. The highest bidder would get a weekend with him in Hollywood and she'd go as his date to his latest premiere.

It was the stuff of dreams.

But what did you do when they brushed so close to your real life that it was positively scary?

Celie thought about it most of the night. She tossed and turned and got up red-eyed and tired. She went to work at the hardware store still distracted, blinking and saying, "What?" to Artie Gilliam every time he spoke to her.

Celie worked at Gilliam's Hardware every morning. She opened the boxes, stocked the new merchandise and did the inventory, waited on customers and dusted the shelves. The locals knew if they wanted something in a hurry, to come during the morning when Celie was there. In the afternoons Artie worked alone. At ninety he still got around, but he was a little slower than he used to be, a little deafer and he couldn't lift quite as much. Still, he was damned if he was going to retire.

"Might as well put me in a pine box and nail the lid shut," he said nearly every day. "That'd be the next thing that'd happen if I closed my store."

Celie didn't doubt it. Artie had been a cowboy years ago, working on spreads in Oregon and Washington and Idaho before coming back to take over the store that had been in his family for three generations.

"Got my wandering done," he said. He'd married Maudie, a local girl and his high school sweetheart, and had settled down to town life. The two of them had been pillars of the community for over fifty years when Maudie died three years ago. Artie had even been mayor a few times and still worked hard to keep Elmer going. But they hadn't had any children, and since his only nephew had moved away years ago, no one knew what would become of the hardware store when Artie retired. It really didn't bear thinking about. Gilliam's was an institution and a necessity in Elmer. Everyone knew that when Artie retired, they'd all have to go clear to Livingston for a roll of baling wire or a half a pound of nails.

No one wanted that to happen. And no one wanted Artie nailed into a pine box. So they all encouraged him to keep coming to work. Tuck McCall came in once a week and helped hoist the heavy stuff around. The rest of the time Celie kept things going.

"If," Artie said now with just a hint of exasperation, "you can keep your mind on business, young lady."

"What?" Celie—in the midst of a stomach-churning fantasy of what it would be like to see Sloan Gallagher face-to-face, speak to him, smile at him, be smiled at in return—looked up from where she was absentmindedly stowing the new furnace filters on the bottom shelf. "Did you say something?"

"I did," Artie huffed. "I said we got us a customer." He jerked his head toward the counter where the cash register sat.

Jace Tucker was leaning against the counter, a weird sort of brace on his leg, a pair of crutches under his arms.

The smile Celie had automatically begun to form faded away.

She didn't smile at Jace Tucker. Ever.

As far as she was concerned Jace Tucker was the devil incarnate. Certainly he was handsome as sin with his thick unruly dark hair and vivid blue eyes, but Celie wanted nothing to do with him.

As far as she was concerned it was Jace's fault that Matt had jilted her.

Oh, he might not have tied Matt up and prevented him from getting to the wedding, but Celie knew Jace had exerted plenty of influence—wild influence, devil-may-care influence—exactly the sort of influence that makes life miserable for a guy thinking about settling down.

Jace and Matt had been traveling partners the year Celie and Matt had been going to get married. That meant they spent more time together in a few months racing around the west in Jace's rattly old pickup with the topper than most married couples spent together in five years. They rode together, talked together, drank together, caroused together. They made mischief together, no doubt about it.

Jace had grown up in the valley, too, on a ranch north of town. His sister, Jodie, still lived there with her husband and three kids. But Jace had taken off right after high school. He'd never been interested in settling down or in ranching. He'd been a hell-raiser from day one. Even Celie, who'd been three

years behind him in school, had heard about escapades Jace
Tucker had got up to.

To a "good girl" like Celie, he had always seemed terri-
fying.

She had not been happy when Matt had told her he wanted
to spend a little time going down the road with Jace Tucker.
If ever anyone in Elmer could have been named Least Likely
To Succeed, in Celie's view, it would have been Jace. In college. In business. In life.

But not in rodeo, Matt had been quick to point out.

In rodeo Jace had been one of the best.

He'd made it to the National Finals Rodeo in bronc riding
twice before he was twenty. He'd finished second in the world
the year Matt graduated from high school.

The only other two local boys who'd made good, Taggart
Jones and Shane Nichols, had both been bull riders. But Jace
rode broncs, same as Matt.

He'd become Matt's hero. Matt had patterned his rides on
Jace's. He'd chewed tobacco like Jace. He'd raised hell like
Jace. Not when he was around Celie, of course. Around Celie
he'd stayed pretty much a gentleman.

But on the road, things began to change. *Matt* began to
change.

He'd brought Jace home with him once and introduced them.
"My best friend and my best girl," he'd said, beaming at them
as if that would make them friends.

Celie had tried to smile and be polite. But Jace had only
watched her from beneath heavy-lidded eyes and barely said a
word.

"Charming, isn't he?" she'd said irritably to Matt later.

"You scare him." Matt had grinned.

"Oh, sure."

But if he hadn't talked to her, he apparently had said plenty
to Matt. From then on, every time they talked on the phone,
Celie heard, "Jace says…" and "Jace thinks…" and "Jace
knows…"

Jace said big weddings were stupid. Jace thought brides-
maids and ushers were a pain. Jace knew a lot more about what

went on in the real world than anybody…at least to hear Matt tell it.

And then one day he called and said that Jace didn't want to be his best man. Matt had been crushed. He'd thought it would be terrific to have his hero and best buddy stand up for him at the wedding. But Jace had declined.

Celie had been delighted.

She'd had a craw full of Jace Tucker by then. If he didn't want to be their best man, that was the best news she'd ever had.

"Lew can do it," she'd told Matt.

"Maybe," Matt had said over the static-ridden telephone connection. "I dunno. I'll talk to Jace."

She never found out what Jace had had to say, but the next thing Celie knew, Matt told her they might not make it home the week before the wedding. Later he called and said he might not make it in time for the rehearsal dinner. She should have realized then that something was seriously wrong. But she had been too caught up in the planning, too caught up in the moment.

"Try," she'd urged him. "How'll we know what to do on our wedding day if you're not here?"

"Oh, I reckon we'll figure it out," Matt had muttered, "when the time comes."

Only when the time came, Matt hadn't.

At first she'd just thought he'd got tied up in some emergency, that he was coming, that he'd just be late.

But then just before the wedding, the phone had rung. She'd felt a combined surge of panic and relief.

But that was before she'd heard the voice on the other end of the line.

"Call it off," he'd said. "Matt's not coming home."

After ten years Celie still felt like shooting the messenger.

Intellectually she knew it wasn't entirely Jace Tucker's fault, that Jace hadn't held a gun to his head, that Jace hadn't kidnapped him.

But he'd been there. He'd provided the inspiration, the role model. He had ruined her hopes, her dreams, her life.

She hated him for that.

But mostly she hated him because she was sure he thought she was a loser.

She'd lost her fiancé, hadn't she?

What kind of woman couldn't hang on to her man?

She was sure a lot of people in Elmer wondered the same thing. How could they not? She'd been jilted. Dumped. Left at the altar. Celie O'Meara had been branded as a girl not worth marrying. She was certain every guy in Elmer thought so.

And Jace Tucker headed the list.

Now she rang up his purchase without even looking at him, without asking about the leg she knew he'd broken last month at the NFR. Everyone in the valley knew, and plenty of them had talked about it. But Celie didn't care. She did her best not to make conversation or eye contact at all.

The trouble with not lifting her gaze above the counter was that she ended up staring in the general vicinity of his belt buckle. It was the gold one he'd won in Cheyenne a month after Matt had jilted her.

She looked away.

"How you been, Celie?"

She wished he wouldn't talk to her. It would be so much easier if he didn't. But in the dozen or so times she'd seen him in the past ten years, he'd always spoken to her—as if they were somehow old friends.

Ha.

She didn't want to have to be polite to him. And, broken leg or not, she didn't care how he'd been. She put the nails and screws in a bag, rang up the chit for the lumber, then dropped his change into his palm. "Fine, thank you."

"Still cuttin' hair?" Jace made no move to leave.

"Yes." She would have turned away and gone back to stacking the furnace filters, but Artie was watching and she knew he would get upset if she was rude to a customer. It didn't matter that he sometimes fell asleep waiting on them, but she couldn't be rude to them.

"Reckon maybe I could use a trim." Jace said. It was almost a question, as in, Did she think he needed a trim?

"Ask Jodie to do it."

"You think I'd let my kid sister near me with a pair of scissors?" Jace laughed and pulled off his hat. "What do you think?"

Direct confrontation. With Artie watching.

Celie had to look at him after all.

And yes, he was still damn handsome. No Sloan Gallagher, but there was a rugged appeal about Jace Tucker that—if you didn't know him—would make a woman stop and stare.

He wasn't as tall as Sloan. Or as classically good-looking. They were about the same age, and she knew both had seen their share of hard knocks. But she'd seen Sloan's face light with boyish mischief and soften with tender emotion.

She couldn't imagine Jace's doing that. His lean, rugged face and his oft-broken nose spoke of nothing but toughness and danger. If there was a gentle side to Jace Tucker, Celie had never seen it. She didn't believe it existed. He was hard and wild, and some women probably thought they could tame him.

The more fool they, Celie thought.

And why would anyone want to?

Looking at him now, she was surprised to see flecks of gray in his sideburns. Most of it, though, was still a thick dark brown, worn a little shaggier than most cowboys wore theirs. All the better for his bevy of buckle bunnies to run their fingers through, Celie thought sourly.

"It's fine," she said shortly, and turned away.

"You don't want to cut it?" He was smiling, teasing her almost.

Celie's fingers curled into fists.

I'm surprised you'd let me anywhere near you with a pair of scissors, she thought. But she just shook her head and said, "Excuse me, I have to get back to work."

She could feel his gaze still on her as she knelt down and went back to stowing the furnace filters under the counter. But she didn't turn around again, and finally she heard him limp away.

Celie breathed a sigh of relief.

Moments later Artie shuffled in from the warehouse. "Come give 'im a hand with that lumber."

Celie jerked up. "What?"

"Jace is buildin' a corral out on his sister's place. That was all that lumber you rung up. But he can't load it hisself, you know. Not on them crutches."

"He didn't say he needed help."

"Don't reckon he would. Do you?" Artie raised thin white eyebrows. "You bein' so warm and friendly like an' all."

Celie colored and pressed her lips together. "I was perfectly polite."

"Oh, yeah, you was. Mmm-hmm." Artie bobbed his head. "Regular Emily Pope, that's you."

"Post. Emily *Post*," Celie corrected irritably. But he just looked at her expectantly, and finally she yanked on her jacket and headed out the door.

Jace had his brother-in-law's pickup backed up to the doors of the warehouse part of the store. He'd pulled what he needed from Artie's stock, but he hadn't loaded it yet. When Celie emerged he was struggling to pick up the rails, his crutches abandoned against the side of the truck. He wasn't having much success.

Celie stalked over and grasped the rails he was holding. "Let me."

His gaze jerked up and he looked at her, startled, and for a moment she thought they might get into a tug-of-war. But after several seconds of seesawing during which they each hung on, finally Jace relinquished his hold and jammed his hands into the pockets of his jeans.

"Go for it," he muttered. He didn't sound all that grateful.

Celie didn't want his gratitude, anyway. "Open the tail gate. I'll slide them in."

He hobbled over and opened the tail gate, then stood back as Celie carried the lumber over and slid it into the back of the truck. It took her half a dozen trips to load it all while Jace stood watching her, scowling and looking uncomfortable.

Celie felt a perverse satisfaction doing something he couldn't do, even though, of course, had he been off crutches and not had one leg injured, he could have coped easily. She also felt annoyingly aware of his scrutiny, certain that, in his eyes she was a less-than-desirable woman.

To take her mind off it, she thought of Sloan. She made herself think about the way he'd been in the video last night. She focused on the love scenes, determinedly imagined herself in them. Imagined Sloan's mouth touching hers. Imagined his callused hands stroking her soft, heated skin. In her mind she'd touched him, too. She'd brushed her lips against the sunburned backs of his hands, had even nibbled a little. She'd run her hand up his arm, had caressed his—

"Ow!" Furious and embarrassed, Celie dropped the lumber and popped her fingers into her mouth, trying in vain to use her teeth to remove the splinter she'd just got from stroking a piece of wood.

Jace pushed away from the truck. "What happened? Let's see."

"Nothing! It's all right. I just—got a splinter."

"Let me see."

But she backed away, shaking her head. God, she was an idiot! "It's fine. It's all right." She examined her hand. She'd got out the biggest one. There were a couple of smaller ones still in there. She'd get them out later. Her hand stung, and she gave it a shake.

"I can get them out," Jace offered.

"No! It's okay. I just wasn't watching what I was doing." Turning away, she picked up the fallen wood and loaded it into the truck. Then she brushed past him and hurried back to get the last armful. Swinging it around as she hauled it out, she managed to make Jace take a quick step back. In fact she almost knocked him over.

He stumbled back and nearly fell. Thank heavens he didn't. She didn't want to have to give him a hand up—or feel guilty for knocking him down. She stowed the last of the lumber, then lifted the tailgate and slammed it shut. "There you go."

He nodded "Thanks." She turned to go back into the store when he said, "How 'bout a cup of coffee?"

The invitation stunned—and confused—her. Why was Jace

Tucker inviting her for a cup of coffee? Because he owed her for loading his lumber?

If it was payback time, he owed her for a damn sight more than that!

"No," she said coolly. "Thanks."

Jace looked at her speculatively. But Celie lifted her chin and looked away. He shrugged. "Another time then."

Sure, Celie thought. *Like never.*

This wasn't how Jace had planned to spend the winter.

He'd had close to a ten-thousand-dollar lead on the rest of the field when he'd gone to Vegas in early December to compete in the bronc riding at the National Finals Rodeo. He only had to hang on for ten rounds, stick on a few broncs and by God, come mid-December he'd finally be champion of the world.

This was his year.

All year long he'd been convinced of it. Everything had gone perfect since last January. He'd made money at Denver and Houston. He'd hit plenty of rodeos and had picked up steady money all spring.

He'd even won big during the Fourth of July rodeos, commonly called "the cowboys' Christmas," though they rarely had been for him. And even though he got stepped on in Dodge City in early August and had slowed down for a couple of weeks, he'd been going full bore again before Pendleton rolled around. All fall he'd hung in, finishing up with a third place at the Cow Palace and a good lead in the standings. He'd actually had time to rest up and shed his normal aches and pains. He'd gone to Vegas, believing that he was going to win.

And then the bottom had fallen out.

He'd been slammed into the chute gate by his first horse, cracking his knee so hard he'd seen stars. He'd got a reride for it. But in a field of fifteen of the best riders in the world, a 72 wasn't in the money. Not even close.

The next round he'd bucked off and landed on his bad knee. His lead was shrinking, but he was determined. He wasn't gonna give up. He'd always been a hardheaded son-of-a-gun.

But not hard enough. Sonny's Delight, his round-three draw, cracked his skull and broke his leg in two places.

So much for the world championship. There was no competing after that.

There was just surgery. And more surgery. There were screws and plates and pins. There was that big fat zero after his name in the Finals' winnings column. There was the misery of seeing his name fall from first in the standings to fifteenth.

Worst of all, there was the rest of his life.

"I'm not telling you that you can't ever go back to rodeoing," the doc had said to him just last week. "I'm just telling you that you're a damned fool if you do."

The doc politely didn't say, "But I reckon you're already that."

There wasn't much mischief Jace Tucker hadn't got into. For thirty-four years he hadn't led the most sensible life. But he'd always figured it was his life to screw up—or not—as long as he didn't hurt anybody else.

And he hadn't—so far as he knew—hurt anyone. He'd had a lot of fun. He'd made a lot of friends. And he wasn't the sort of guy to look back with regrets.

But at thirty-four he wasn't the fool he'd been at twenty-four.

It was a month after his wreck at the finals and he was still getting headaches from the concussion. His leg was taking its own sweet time healing up. The breaks had been nasty. His knee was already hamburger. He faced a long rehab. The doc told him he wouldn't be riding competitively until summer—if that.

He didn't talk to anybody about it. Didn't discuss the yeas or nays. It was his life, his decision. Only when he'd made it, had decided once and for all to quit rodeo, did he ask his sister and brother-in-law if they'd be interesting in letting him buy a share of the ranch.

He'd felt a little funny about asking since he'd never wanted any part of it before. He'd always been a headin'-into-the-sunset sort of guy.

But that was then. And even when he'd been heading toward the sunset, he'd always known where home was.

He'd never forgotten Elmer. He'd been a lot of places, but he'd never been to one he loved as much as he loved it here. If he had to hang up his spurs, he wanted to do it here.

Thank God Jodie and Ray said yes.

Of course it was to their benefit, too. Jace had saved a fair bit of his winnings over the years. Now and then he'd bought some cattle, and Ray had run them with theirs.

But Jace had just been dabbling then.

Now he was serious.

He was buying in, building this corral to do a little training, determined to keep his hand in with horses. He'd always been more interested in them than in cattle. And building the corral was one thing he could do—albeit slowly—while he healed.

He probably should have waited another week, though, to get the lumber. Then he could have handled it himself instead of making Celie O'Meara do it.

She hadn't looked real happy about it.

But then Celie O'Meara had never looked real happy with him. He reckoned it had something to do with that phone call he'd had to make when Matt Williams had chickened out of their wedding.

It had happened years ago. And she shouldn't have been ticked anyhow. The way Jace figured it, she ought to have thanked him!

He hadn't precisely talked Matt out of getting married. He'd just shown him that there were other things in life a guy his age might rather do.

Matt Williams, at twenty-one, had been no more ready to settle down than a prairie dog was to grow wings. He'd been starry-eyed and bushy-tailed—eager to cut a swath through all the women who tucked their phone numbers in his pocket and whispered sweet nothin's in his ear. Matt might have been engaged, but once he'd headed down the road, you'd never have known it.

The girls had come on to him, granted. But he hadn't often said no.

And as the date for the wedding got closer, Jace had seen him getting edgier and antsier.

"You sure about this?" Jace had asked when Matt kept putting off going home.

"Course I am," Matt had always said. But he'd grown more miserable even as he'd gone out and partied longer and harder than anyone.

Finally it was the night before the wedding, and he still hadn't gone. Instead of catching a flight to Bozeman, he'd headed down to one of the casinos, and as Jace watched, he'd switched from drinking beer to drinking the hard stuff.

"You better quit or you ain't gonna be in no shape to go home to your lady love," Jace had told him. "Come on, man. Let's get you sobered up."

But Matt had gone right on drinking. Eventually he'd taken off with two Vegas showgirls and Jace had spent the rest of the night looking for him. He'd found him with barely enough time to get him to the airport the next morning—only to have Matt stop, white-faced, in the middle of the parking lot.

"I ain't goin'. I ain't gettin' married. No how."

What was Jace supposed to do then?

Knock him cold and send him in a suitcase? Reason with him?

Reason, Jace knew damn well, had had nothing to do with what was going on in Matt's head. He'd seen it happen to Gus Holt a couple of years before. Gus, at least, had had the guts to call and tell Mary himself. And he hadn't waited till the very last minute, then balked.

But Matt had. And Jace had had to call Celie and give her the news.

It was the hardest thing he'd ever done—not least because, deep down in a dark, carefully unprobed corner of his heart, he was glad.

That was something Jace had never admitted to anybody—not even to himself.

But even as he'd hated calling Celie and telling her Matt wasn't coming home to marry her, some little tiny selfish part of him had celebrated the fact.

It meant she was free.

It meant he had a chance.

Not that he took it. Hell, she would've spat in his eye if he'd tried. And he hadn't been ready to settle down back then anyway. He wouldn't have been good for her—even though he'd hankered after her.

But now, ten years later...now he figured he was ready.

And Celie was still here. Still single.

And still acting like if she'd had horns she'd hook him and leave him for dead.

Chapter 5

"What do you mean you can't be there?" Suzette, Sloan's agent, demanded.

He held the phone away from his ear as her voice rose to the point of shrillness.

"You *have* to be there! My God, Sloan, this is Trevor MacCormack we're talking about! The hottest director in the business. That's like telling Steven Spielberg, Thanks, but you're sorry, you just can't make it this afternoon."

"I could make it this afternoon," Sloan said with more patience than he felt. "I just can't make it the first weekend in February."

"Of course you can. You'll be done in Key West next week. Then you've got one last location shot and—"

"Suzette." He cut across her argument. "No."

"But he's flying to New York all the way from Hong Kong. And he's arranged for Becca Reed to be there, too! My God, it's not enough you want to stand up one of the world's top directors, you want to stand up one of the best young actresses to hit Hollywood in years."

Sloan ground his teeth. Ordinarily he appreciated Suzette's

enthusiasm. She was a good agent—no, she was a great agent—and she'd done well by him for a long time. But Suzette's only concern was his career. For a long time that had been enough for Sloan, too, but just recently he'd found he was also interested in having a life.

"I didn't say I wouldn't meet them. I said I can't make it that weekend."

"But why? Why can't you make it? Are you getting married? Is your best friend planning on dying? I'm sorry, Sloan, but those are about the only reasons I can even remotely consider legitimate excuses."

"Then consider it illegitimate, but I'm not going to be there."

There was a huff of disbelief and annoyance on the other end of the line. "You've never been a big ego, Sloan. That's one of the things I've always liked about you. So what's the deal? This is your next film we're talking about. You're going to have to work with this man in a matter of weeks! What am I supposed to tell him?"

"Tell him I'm going to an auction."

"What do you mean you're going to an auction? An auction is more important than Trevor MacCormack? What are they auctioning off? The Mona Lisa?"

"Me."

"What!"

"It's for a friend," Sloan muttered, wishing he'd kept his big mouth shut. "Just a favor. No big deal."

"Big enough to put off Trevor MacCormack, obviously." Suzette was all ears now. "You're actually letting someone auction you off? A *bachelor* auction?" Suzette was laughing. "You? Mr. Privacy-Is-My-Middle-Name?"

"For one date," Sloan said through his teeth. "I'm not giving 'em my home phone number. It's not a big thing."

"The hell it's not. Where is it? When? Tell me." She was avid now. Hungry. A dog who has sniffed out a particularly delectable bone.

Sloan growled under his breath. "It's a fund-raiser for an old friend who's run into hard times."

"Do I know him? Her?"

"No! Leave it. You're not going to turn this into some publicity circus!"

"But if it's to raise money," Suzette said practically, "publicity is exactly what you need!"

Sloan groaned. Damn it.

"A little tasteful publicity never hurt anyone."

"Tasteful publicity? Isn't that like army intelligence?" They had a word for it, he knew, but he hadn't paid enough attention in English class to remember what it was.

"An oxymoron, you mean?" Suzette countered sweetly. "Like cowboy brain?"

Sloan laughed. "Exactly."

"Come on, Sloan. Give. Where is it?" Suzette never got off the scent. "What are you auctioning yourself off for?"

"You're not gonna leave this alone, are you?"

"No," she said firmly, "I'm not. I'm your agent. This is my job. They want you because you're famous, right? So let's give them a little publicity."

One of them, Sloan thought, didn't want him at all. But he didn't say so. Suzette would never believe there was a woman alive who was resistant to his charms.

"It's a friend in Montana," he said finally. "Just a local thing to raise money to help pay a ranch loan. Like I said, no big deal."

"And what do they get if they win you?"

"A date to the premiere of *Crossroads.*"

"Fantastic! Oh, it's perfect. Here's what we'll do—" The well-oiled Suzette Larrimer publicity machine was off and running.

"Look, Suze—"

"You'll do morning talk shows the week before. You can promote *Crossroads* and you can mention the auction at the same time. That will stimulate interest. Local boy does good deed. A little newspaper press and—"

"No!"

"Sloan," she said patiently. "They didn't ask you so they

can hide you under a bushel basket. They asked you so they can raise money for whatever cause it is.''

He knew that. But it wasn't only money. He'd offered a check and Gus had turned it down. Because, he said, the whole community needed to be involved.

Where had the community been when he'd needed them? Sloan wondered.

Then grudgingly he admitted that some of them had actually been there—or they would have been if he'd let them.

But he'd been angry in those days. He'd hated being in Elmer because of the mess his own life had become with his mother's death and his father's drinking. He'd resented everyone there who'd had what he didn't have—parents who were alive and still behaving like parents.

He'd been a jerk—not just to Ward and Maddie, who had understood his pain—but to a lot of people who hadn't.

It didn't matter, he supposed. But somehow he wanted to go back and prove that he was better than they remembered him.

And he wanted to see Polly.

He couldn't quite stop thinking about Polly.

He wanted her to see that he was better than she remembered, too. He wanted to see what she was like these days.

''What cause are we talking about?'' Suzette asked.

He didn't want to go into it. He didn't relish talking about those days. He'd never hidden his past, but he hadn't talked about it extensively either. If he did this, he knew it would be fair game.

''Remember when I told you that after my mother died I was in a foster home for a while? Well, my foster mother is in danger of losing her ranch.''

To give Suzette credit, she didn't leap on his explanation and tell him it was a marvelous opportunity. One of the things he liked best about her was that, on certain occasions, she could actually behave like a human being.

In fact she said, ''That's terrible. How awful for her. I'm so sorry.'' And then she said, ''But as a publicity opportunity for you, I couldn't have planned it better. Of course, we'll have to tell Trevor you can't make it, but he won't mind.''

"I thought he was going to have my guts for garters."

"He's not a fool, Sloan," she said impatiently. "He'll see that the publicity will help his film, too. This is a win-win-win situation. You get publicity for your friend's cause. You get publicity for yourself and *Crossroads*. And Trevor will be able to translate that into more exposure for his own film down the road. He'll love it!"

Personally, Sloan didn't expect Trevor to give a rat's ass. MacCormack had always been more interested in the quality of his films than the hype they got. That was one of the reasons Sloan wanted to work with him.

Sloan had got into acting because the opportunity fell into his lap. The camera loved him and he apparently had some God-given talent. That could have been enough to ensure that he had a reasonably successful career. But over the past six years he learned that he actually cared a great deal about the quality of the films he made. He wanted to work with good directors and good co-stars. He wanted to do a good job.

He supposed he even understood—to some degree—the importance of publicity, though it certainly wasn't his dearest love. He'd been naive enough when he'd started out to believe that if he just did his part in the film, that would be enough, that he could go home at the end of the day and forget about it.

Thirteen films had taught him that wasn't the case. He saw publicity now as a necessary evil. His buddy, Gavin McConnell, who liked that sort of thing no more than he did, gave interviews sparingly, but he did give them. And he'd explained the necessity of it in terms Sloan understood.

"If you don't talk to 'em, you got no control. They're gonna write about you anyhow. You might as well give them something of substance. And if you give 'em meat enough, they'll be so busy chewing on what you tell them, they'll have less time to write the stupid stuff."

That made sense. The auction was meat.

Phrased properly, the story of his role in The Great Montana Cowboy Auction would do everything Suzette said it would do. It would promote *Crossroads;* it would provide publicity for the auction and probably drive up the prices and thus the money raised; it would be good press for him; and it would ultimately please Trevor MacCormack.

It was a win-win-win-win situation.

No, Sloan thought, a grin spreading across his face.

There was one more win Suzette knew nothing about—it would drive Polly McMaster crazy.

Sloan wasn't exactly sure what made driving Polly McMaster crazy appealing. But the fact was, ever since Gus had brought her name up, he'd been remembering her, thinking about her.

For a long time after Lew had pounded him into the dirt, Sloan had been almost afraid to think about Polly at all, lest the older boy appear like some avenging cowboy and do it again.

God knew Lew would have, if he'd known the sorts of thoughts running wild through Sloan's adolescent brain!

Probably Lew had known—being human and male and still a teenager himself. Still he wouldn't have had time to dwell on it. He'd had lots more serious things to think about because Polly got pregnant.

Sloan remembered hearing they'd got married only a couple of months after the day he had seen Polly in the barn. At the time he'd been astonished that a guy as young as Lew would want to tie himself down. But as time passed and the reason became apparent—even to a fourteen-year-old—he'd understood.

The slender golden naked Polly of his fantasies had changed over the next few months. He hadn't had to see her naked again to see that things were different.

She began to wear loose floppy maternity tops. Her easy graceful walk became more like a duck's waddle. And her flat belly began to burgeon as she grew big with child. Sometimes when he saw her in town, Sloan couldn't help it, he just stared—unable to believe how much she'd changed.

Then, the last time he'd seen her, when he'd gone to pick up an order for Ward at old man Gilliam's hardware store, she'd looked like Polly again.

The old Polly was back—the slender, slightly curvy Polly, the Polly of his dreams—with maybe even more curve, more shape and fuller breasts.

He'd felt that primeval hungry masculine response surge through him.

And then the door had banged open and Lew had come in. "Here you go, kiddo," he'd said. "Here's your mommy." And he'd plopped a screaming baby into Polly's arms.

That Polly was one Sloan hadn't wanted to remember.

But now, perversely, like the phoenix rising from the ashes, thoughts of Polly were back. Hearing her name had awakened something inside him. It had set off a clamoring to see her again, had aroused a curiosity that he wanted assuaged.

He'd have been mildly curious even if she hadn't been widowed. She had been, after all, his first naked woman.

Sloan didn't fool around with married women. Never had. Never would.

But Polly was a widow.

And he was a single man who hadn't turned out too badly in the sex appeal department.

Would she be just the tiniest bit curious about him?

It had been a long time since Sloan Gallagher had thought he had anything to prove.

There were occasions when Polly, faced with an IRS tax form asking for her occupation, considered writing *juggler.*

Only the notion that the IRS might not have the same sense of humor as a thirty-seven-year-old woman with four kids, two dogs, a bionic cat and an indeterminate number of rabbits prevented her.

But if she thought she had juggled a fair number of demands and obligations before the auction to save Maddie's ranch, well—like Harry Hyena in the children's book she'd read aloud several thousand times—she was wrong.

The steady stream of curious townspeople and nearby ranch families—correction, make that towns*women* and ranchers' *daughters*—didn't slow as the news spread that Sloan Gallagher had agreed to be part of the auction.

On the contrary, as soon as anyone got word, instead of believing it, they all rushed right over to the post office to hear it from Polly's own lips. Things got busier than ever at the post office, and no one even bothered to use mailing letters or buying stamps as an excuse anymore. They only wanted to talk about Sloan Gallagher. And then they went right out and told two hundred of their nearest and dearest friends.

It was busier than December all week long.

Speculation was rife. Who would bid on him? How high would the price go? Was he really going to fly the winner to Hollywood?

Oh, my heavenly days! Hearts beat faster all over Elmer. It turned into a party, and Polly turned into the reluctant hostess.

"This is a post office," she reminded them.

"Right, right," they all said. "Wonder if he'll let the winner stay at his house."

The party rolled on.

Alice Benn made cookies and brought them over to share. "To get in the spirit," she said when she arrived bearing scrumptious chocolate chip cookies cut in the shape of hearts.

"He can have my heart," offered Kitzy Miller who had stopped in on her way to her job at the Mini-mart on the highway. She batted her sooty black eyelashes and smiled her best come-hither smile.

"Prob'ly ain't your heart he's after," chortled one of the cowboys from the Jones spread, then flushed at the glare Polly gave him. "Sorry," he muttered, and headed for the door, but not before he'd snagged a cookie off Alice's plate.

The furor would die down, Polly was sure.

But instead it grew. The small article on page six of Wednesday's edition of the *Livingston Enterprise* became a page-three half column on Thursday, and on Friday it was above the fold on page one complete with picture.

"We're going to have the whole damn valley here now," Polly muttered when the paper arrived that afternoon.

Alice rubbed her hands together gleefully. "Just what we want," she said. "Lots of bidders."

What they got were lots of volunteers. There was no shortage of women willing to help out. Every female for twenty miles called or dropped by to say she'd bring a hot dish to the potluck supper. Those who had husbands, brothers, sons or nephews volunteered them, too. No one was going to sit home when they could be a part of the auction that was bringing Sloan Gallagher to Elmer.

It was like a party every day at the post office. Polly began to look forward to the moment she could take down the flag, put out the mail to be picked up on the evening run and bolt the door behind her.

"It's insane," she said Friday afternoon when she huffed in the door. "Simply crazy! Thirty-seven women have stopped by this week to offer to help. Can you imagine?" She said to her mother.

Joyce didn't answer. She just turned and looked toward the Spa where someone shrieked, "She's here!" and a dozen women surged into the kitchen from the salon where Celie was cutting hair.

"Polly, I just came by to say I'd help—"

"Polly, I thought maybe that green bean casserole—"

"Polly, I can make mama's Dutch doughnuts!"

"Polly, just thought you might need someone to keep the cowboys in line during the auction—"

Polly took a step back toward the door—and bumped into Becky Jones and Susannah Tanner who went to school with Daisy and Lizzie.

"My dad said you might need a little help," Susannah said eagerly.

"We'd behave," Becky vowed. "We wouldn't get in the way, honest. Gus said he'd vouch for us."

Trapped between the oncoming women and the girls looking so earnestly at her, Polly gave up.

"Fine," she said to the girls. "You're hired. Make a list. Write down everyone's name, find out how they think they can help—realistically. I don't want a bunch of women willing to volunteer their services warming Sloan Gallagher's bed. Then tell them when we know what we need, we'll be in touch. And get them out of here."

"Right!" They beamed and headed off to do just that.

Wearily Polly sank down on one of the kitchen chairs.

Joyce set down her book on parachuting.

Polly stared—first at it, then at her mother. "You're not...?"

"Probably not," Joyce agreed mildly. "I'm not that keen on heights. You look tired."

"I'm exhausted," Polly admitted, which wasn't something she said very often. "What you just saw, I've had all day long. Everyone in the valley wants to volunteer. Who's going to bid if everyone is helping?"

"Oh, I think there will be a few bidders." There was something in her tone that made Polly look at her mother more closely.

Joyce smiled. "A reporter from the *Chronicle* called today."

So the Bozeman paper had got hold of the story.

"And another from the *Gazette* and—"

"The *Billings Gazette?*"

Joyce nodded. "—and the *Post.*"

Polly wrinkled her nose. "The *Clark Fork Post?*" That was a surprise.

"No. The *Denver Post.*"

"*What!*"

Joyce smiled. "News travels fast."

"The *Denver Post* is doing an article on Sloan Gallagher coming to our auction?"

"So they say. This might actually put Elmer on the map."

"And me in an early grave," Polly muttered. She leaped up again and started pacing the room.

"I think it will be fine. Better too many volunteers than too few. Besides it's just an auction. Calvin calls them every week."

"Calvin does livestock!"

Joyce shrugged. There was a twinkle in her eye. "And your point would be?"

Reluctantly Polly laughed. "It is turning into that, isn't it? The Great Montana Livestock Auction. Beefcake on the hoof."

"Well, I'm sure I'm going to enjoy it," Joyce said with

considerable relish. She fixed her gaze on her eldest daughter. "And you should, too."

If anyone else were doing the work—no, if anyone else was the beefcake on the hoof—she would be.

But not Sloan Gallagher!

If only he hadn't said it would be good to see her *again!* Polly had been feeling waves of mortification ever since.

"It's all a matter of attitude, dear," Joyce said complacently. "That's what my zen book says."

Her zen book.

Polly took a deep breath. "You're right. Of course you're right. We'll just take this cowboy by cowboy, volunteer by volunteer."

"And enjoy it."

"And enjoy it," Polly echoed, wishing she believed it.

"Here." Joyce held out a small piece of paper with a number scrawled on it.

"What's this?"

"Sloan Gallagher's cell phone number. He wants you to call him."

Chapter 6

She didn't call.

There was no way Polly was going to call Sloan Gallagher—not even to discuss morning talk shows, which was what Joyce said he wanted to talk to her about.

Morning talk shows!

As if she knew anything about them. As if she ever had time to watch them. She didn't, so she no opinion about them and, thus, no reason to call him back. Besides, she was busy.

And if she was lucky, in time she would forget.

But she hadn't yet. The number had been burning a hole in her pocket and her consciousness for twenty-four hours when, at supper Saturday night her mother asked, "What did Sloan Gallagher have to say?"

All conversation stopped.

All eyes turned to Polly, then, when she didn't reply, to her mother.

Joyce lifted her shoulders. "He called and left a message yesterday."

Polly shrugged. "I didn't call him back."

Celie gaped. "You didn't call him back?"

"I was busy," Polly said defensively, then took a bite of her mother's best stewed chicken so she wouldn't have to say anything else.

"He'll think you're rude!" Celie said.

"Disrespectful," said Daisy.

"Inconsiderate," said Lizzie.

"Ill-mannered," said Sara. "Or forgetful."

Jack looked up from shoveling mashed potatoes into his mouth. "Naw. He'll just think she's chicken."

"Chicken!" Polly was outraged.

"Well, he's a big star 'n' all. An' you're just a mom."

Just a mom.

And a chicken.

Jack was right. Wherever he was, Sloan Gallagher would be sitting there laughing at her right now because he believed she was chicken.

"I'm *not* chicken," she said firmly.

Dutifully her children nodded. But Polly saw them roll their eyes.

"Fine," she said, shoving away from the table. "I'll call him right now."

Teach by example, wasn't that what the parenting manuals all said?

Actually *hoist by her own petard* was the aphorism that sprang to mind as, glaring at the scrap of paper on the kitchen table, she punched in Sloan Gallagher's number.

It rang once, twice, three times. She breathed a sigh of relief. Of course he wouldn't be picking up his phone. She began composing a proper answering machine message to prove she'd called back.

"Hello?"

God, the man had velvet vocal chords.

Polly cleared her throat frantically. "Er, hello. It's Polly. Polly McMaster. From Elmer?" In case he couldn't remember. "My mother said you called."

That sounded all right. Calm. Adult. Professional. Well, all except the "my mother said you called" bit. That sounded like she was in junior high.

"Hey, Polly McMaster. From Elmer," Sloan Gallagher added, a teasing note in his voice.

Polly flushed. "I would have returned your call earlier," she said, "but I've been busy."

"I was betting you'd be chicken."

"What!"

He laughed. "Just kidding. So how're things in Montana?"

"Insane. We've created a monster. I have a list half a mile long of women who desperately want to volunteer to help out at the auction. Every female in the county, I think. And the newspapers have picked it up." She told him about the *Enterprise* article and about the *Chronicle* the next day and the *Gazette* and now the *Post*.

"The *Denver Post!* Can you imagine?"

"For my sins, yes," he said wearily.

And Polly supposed he could. His every move was probably noted and recorded by journalists whose job it was to trail him around.

The price of fame.

"I'd hate it," she said, feeling her first flicker of sympathy for Sloan Gallagher.

"It's not always fun. That's what I wanted to talk to you about. It's going to get worse. I'm doing two morning talk shows next week."

"About your film. I know that." Celie had already programmed the VCR.

"Not only about the film. The auction will come up, too."

"Not if you don't say anything." *Please, don't!*

"They already know."

"How can they?" Did everyone read the *Enterprise,* for goodness' sake?

He sighed. "My agent told them. She believes in publicity. It's her job," he said, cutting off any protest Polly might have made. "And it will be good for Maddie. More money to pay off the loan."

"Maddie will hate it. She won't want people pitying her."

"They won't. I'll see to it." He was emphatic. "And you'll have to do the same."

"Me? What are you talking about?"

"They're sending crews out to interview you."

"Don't be ridiculous!"

"I'm not. I'm just warning you."

"They can't interview me!"

"Why not?" She could hear the amusement in his voice.

But it wasn't funny to her. "Because...because—I don't do things like that!"

"Always a first time."

"No."

"It's painless. They'll love you."

"They'll think I'm an idiot. They'll think we're all idiots! A bunch of presumptuous hicks!" Imagining how the world would perceive their tiny town and its rough-edged, hardworking citizens made her cringe. She loved Elmer and she didn't want it turned into fodder for jokes by some smart-aleck, big-city folks.

"They won't do that. They'll be in awe."

"Oh, right."

"They will. They eat up stuff like this. They admire it."

Polly couldn't imagine. "Fine. You do it and leave me out of it."

"Can't. Once the word is out you can't stuff it back in. They wanted a local contact person, and Gus said that was you."

"Well then, *I'll* just tell them no." But as she said it, she knew it wasn't the brightest idea she'd ever had. Just because she didn't want to do it didn't mean the media would go away. They would just make a fool of her.

She sighed and faced the inevitable. It was just another meeting she hadn't attended and had been drafted to do all the work. So what else was new?

"When are they coming? What do I have to do?"

For the first time since Gil's death, Joyce was actually looking forward to getting up in the morning. Life, which had been pretty much shades of gray for the past two years, seemed to be taking on a little color at last.

The auction was the first real creative idea she'd had in ages, and the fact that it had been embraced by the community—and that Sloan Gallagher was coming back to Elmer because of it—gave Joyce a little tingle of satisfaction.

"Who'd have thought it?" she murmured aloud, talking to Gil as she always did when no one was around.

She'd talked to him less this week because she had rarely been alone. Everyone wanted to be involved. Everyone wanted to help.

"Everyone wants to get in the way," was how Polly put it.

But Joyce was grateful for the excitement—and intrigued by Sloan's return—even if it did seem a little like setting a wolf among the chickens.

"That's what you'd say," she told Gil as she mopped and dusted the Spa.

She wasn't crazy. She knew she wouldn't turn around and see him sitting there with his coffee mug balanced on his knee, that teasing little half smile on his face.

She knew she wouldn't hear his wry chuckle again. Not in this lifetime.

God knew she'd wished often enough. She dreamed. But she wasn't going to get Gil back—not the way she'd had him.

Still, as time went by she realized she hadn't really lost him, either. After nearly forty years together, he was such a part of her that even death couldn't completely come between them. She knew what he'd think, knew what he'd feel, knew what he'd say.

So sometimes when they were alone, she talked to him.

Now she talked to him about Sloan Gallagher.

"He's a looker. He's got charisma. Sex appeal. And you know I have an eye for a handsome man."

She could almost hear Gil chuckle knowingly at that.

"Celie is a nervous wreck," Joyce went on. "You know she thinks he's the perfect man."

Perfect man? She could almost hear Gil snort. *Ain't no such thing.*

Joyce smiled. How well she knew.

But a woman learned to put up with her man's little odd habits if she loved him. Lord knew she'd learned to put up with Gil's forgetting where he put his truck keys and never remembering to buy eggs when he went to the store for her.

Gil's mother had raised chickens and he'd been suspicious of any eggs he hadn't first met in a hen house. She remembered when they'd gone to Las Vegas on the one vacation they'd ever taken. The morning after they'd arrived, Gil had ordered eggs and bacon. He'd taken one bite and left the eggs. They tasted phony, he'd told her.

"Like everything else there," he'd said three days later on their way back to Elmer.

That was the only time they'd left home.

"Ah, Gil." Joyce leaned on the mop and smiled wistfully at the memory. Gil had loved his wife, his kids, his ranch, his home, his cattle. He couldn't understand why Lew had wanted to go from rodeo to rodeo or why Polly didn't mind going with him.

"Ain't no place on earth better'n right here," he'd often said.

And Joyce thought that was probably true. Still, she wouldn't have minded doing a little firsthand checking. That was why she'd bought that Spanish book and those tapes in Bozeman two months ago. Maybe she'd be brave enough to go to Mexico someday. Once upon a time traveling was something she'd wanted to do.

Beyond that one trip to Vegas, she and Gil never had.

There had been no time. No money. No inclination on Gil's part at least. You made choices, Gil said. And that was true.

Joyce didn't regret the ones they'd made. But now it was just her. She could travel now if she wanted to.

If she dared.

In her mind's eye she could see Gil again, looking at her with his little teasing smile, daring her. It was that smile that had got her to go out and get a job after his death. She hadn't worked outside the ranch since she'd got a job at Artie's store when she was seventeen.

At fifty-nine she'd been terrified at the thought of going out and looking for a job. But with the ranch sold, she'd had too much time on her hands and not enough money in the bank. She'd had to do something.

She'd thought about going back to Artie's. He'd even offered her a job if she wanted one. Artie had always looked out for her.

But Celie was working there. And Joyce knew she needed to do something on her own for once. But none of the other half dozen businesses in town needed her help.

Then Tess Tanner had mentioned that Ruby Truscott, the night receptionist at the hospital in Livingston, was retiring.

Joyce hadn't said anything about it that night. She hadn't wanted to make a big deal of it, just in case she didn't follow through.

Or, let's be honest, in case they didn't want her.

But she'd called and enquired. And a week later she had put on her best skirt and blouse, fixed her own hair, even though she knew Celie could have done it better, and had applied for the job as Ruby's replacement.

She'd been there now almost eighteen months.

It was the best thing she could have done. The job gave her focus. It gave her someplace to go and people who needed her. It had got her over the purposeless days following Gil's death.

But it wasn't enough. She was still lonely. She still felt hollow. She needed to fill that emptiness. She needed challenges.

That's what the macramé was.

And the finance class.

And the Spanish tapes.

If she got up the gumption, she might actually use her Spanish. She might get on an airplane and go somewhere far away. Somewhere foreign. Somewhere she never ever expected to be.

Mexico, maybe.

Or Argentina.

Or Spain.

Of course she never said that either. Like the hospital job she hadn't been sure she'd go after, traveling was a little scary. She didn't know if she'd ever get up the courage to do it. And she didn't want Polly pushing her to go on one hand, while Celie wrung her hands with worry on the other.

She had to do things in her own time.

"I'll do it," she said aloud now, "when I'm ready."

Behind her eyelids she could see Gil's grin widen just a little. He even winked.

"Ah, Gil."

She might cry if she kept on thinking about him. So she stuck one of the Spanish tapes in the player that Sara had lent her and began mopping with renewed vigor.

"¿Dónde está un buen restaurante?" The native speaker prompted.

"¿Dónde está...?" Joyce dutifully repeated.

She mopped her way through the part about it being two streets down and left at the corner. She learned how to say she didn't have reservations, how to order huevos rancheros and chiles rellenos.

"Now we'll pay the bill and go dancing," the tape promised.

"Dancing?" Joyce almost laughed.

"Dáme la cuenta por favor," said the native speaker.

"Dáme la cuenta por favor," Joyce repeated.

"Give me the bill, please," the tape translated. *"Vamos a bailar."*

And then the music started. Mariachi music. Accordions and violins, maracas and marimbas.

Joyce twirled the mop. *"Vamos a bailar."*

"Me gusta la música latina."

"Me gusta la música latina." Joyce parroted, dancing her way into the last corner.

"Yo quiero bailar un fandango—"

"Yo quiero—"

"Well now—"

Joyce whipped around.

Though she hadn't even heard the outside door open, Walt
Blasingame stood leaning against the doorjamb. Walt, who'd
been a friend of Gil's for years, pushed back his black felt
cowboy hat and scratched his head, perplexed—as if he'd never
seen a woman dancing with a mop before.

Joyce's face flamed. "I was just...studying Spanish."

"Spanish, is it?" Walt looked doubtful.

Joyce lifted her chin. "That's right." And even if he thought
she was crazy, she wasn't going to apologize. "I'm learning
Spanish," she said firmly. She shut the recorder off and turned
back to him. "Can I help you with something? Celie's at the
hardware store. She won't be cutting hair until this afternoon."

Walt took off his hat and rubbed a hand over his already
short, neat gray hair. "Don't need a haircut. Got me one in
Livingston last week. I just came into Loney's to get the ex-
haust manifold welded, and Caity asked me to stop and see if
you had Gallagher's new video."

"The official one is checked out," Joyce said. "And has a
waiting list a mile long. But Celie has one. I'm sure she
wouldn't mind if you borrowed it."

Celie and Cait, Walt's daughter, had been best friends since
they were old enough to toddle. The Blasingame ranch had run
between McCalls' and the place Gil's grandfather had homesteaded. Joyce and Walt's late wife, Margie, had been good
friends when the girls were in high school.

"Well, if you're sure Celie won't mind," Walt said. "But
we ain't borrowin'. We'll rent it. You got a business here."

"You will not rent it. You'll just borrow it and return it
whenever. We've all seen it. And," she added, "we'll be seeing the real thing before too long."

Walt grinned. "Yeah, ain't that somethin'?"

"Hard to imagine that boy growin' up to be a movie star,"
Joyce said.

"Hard to imagine him growing up, period," Walt countered
with a grin. "He was a hellion."

"And now he's Celie's dream man."

Walt's brows lifted. "No foolin'? Well, here's her chance."

"If she'll take it," Joyce said. "Celie's not one for risks. Not after…" Her voice drifted off. They both remembered the aborted wedding.

"Time she put that behind her," Walt said firmly. He paused for a second, doubtless remembering things he'd had to put behind him. He squared his shoulders. "A feller—and a gal—has gotta get on with life."

Joyce went into the living room and got the tape, came back and handed it to him.

Walt tucked it inside his jacket. "That's real nice of you. I reckon Cait and Charlie will watch it tonight and get it back to you tomorrow."

"No hurry."

It would do Celie good not to spend every evening watching the celluloid Sloan.

Walt zipped up his jacket, then opened the door and went down the steps. At the bottom he turned.

"How you doin' on that Spanish?"

Joyce blinked. "What?"

He shrugged. "I wondered if it's hard to learn a new language at our age?"

"Well, it's probably not as easy as for kids. You know Mace and Jenny Nichols's three learned English so fast I couldn't believe it. But it's not that hard. Why?"

"Just curious." Walt smiled. "Don't you go steppin' on that mop's toes now," he said. Then he winked and ambled off down the street.

Polly convinced herself that the television segment would be a five-minute wonder.

Or four. However long a segment of morning television lasted.

She never watched it herself, so how would she know?

Then she told herself that the whole business couldn't possibly be any more annoying than having a root canal or being audited by the IRS or dealing with one of the pompous postal bureaucrats who beleaguered her life at regular intervals.

She and Harry Hyena—wrong again.

The television crew didn't simply turn up five minutes before air time and stick a mike in front of her face—which was what had happened the only other time she'd been interviewed, when she won the goat-tying event at the Montana State High School Finals Rodeo in her junior year of high school.

Big-time network broadcasts, she soon learned, ran a different sort of ship.

The Friday before the Monday Sloan was scheduled to appear, a production staffer called Astrid rang to discuss "logistics."

"Logistics?" Polly, sorting the morning's mail and listening to Alice Benn read her the latest article on Sloan from yesterday's *Bozeman Chronicle,* didn't think in those sorts of terms. "What logistics?"

"The nearest lodgings for one thing. A place for the interview. The nearest airport and television station. I've had some trouble locating Elmore in my media facilities guide," Astrid said.

Elmore? Lodgings? Television station? Airport?

"It's El*mer.*"

"Right. El*mer.* Thank you. Odd name," Astrid muttered. "We also need a list of suggested sites associated with Sloan's boyhood and a list of potential interviewees. Ten or twelve should suffice. It's an auction, I understand, to save a ranch? So we'll want historical background on the ranch. And of course we'll speak with the rancher. The photographer will want to shoot some footage there. So if you could suggest some particularly picturesque spots, perhaps with a few cattle? He'll want to see where the auction is being held. And if you could hang a few of your decorations to set the mood—" she paused for breath for the first time "—and if you could have several other cowboys who will be auctioned off available all afternoon on Monday, that would be helpful. It's very simple, really. Nothing major."

The woman obviously had the lung capacity of a Navy

SEAL. Polly wondered if they had hired her specially because of it.

"Anything else?" Polly asked in her most sarcastic tone.

Astrid didn't hear sarcasm. "I'll need the information by three in order to see to the arrangements before five."

"Three? Today?"

But Astrid was already rattling off a telephone number. "Got that? Good. I'll be waiting for your call then. Bye-eeee."

Polly stood staring at the suddenly silent phone feeling as if she'd been run over by a very efficient truck.

"Trouble, dear?" Alice queried. "It's not one of the children, is it?"

"No," Polly said. "It's not. It's that flaming Sloan Gallagher."

Alice's grandmotherliness vanished in an instant. She did a credible imitation of a maiden going into a swoon. "That was Sloan Gallagher? On the phone?"

"No, that was some slick city chick called Astrid wanting me to organize the entire town for a spot on a morning talk show next week."

"Oh, my stars and stripes!" Alice looked positively delighted. "We're going to be on TV?"

Not if I can help it. Polly sighed. "Apparently."

She glanced at her watch. It was not quite eight-thirty. The flag was out, the scanner on and half the mail was in its boxes. She had the rest of the mail to sort and all her bookwork to do. She had forms to fill out, customers to deal with, training material to go over. And it was Friday so she had to inspect the car of Earl the rural carrier.

When he'd hung up from their last conversation, Sloan had said, "If you have any problems, give me a shout and I'll take care of them."

She wondered what he'd do if she called him and told him to get his butt out here right now and sort the mail.

And when he'd finished, he could decorate the town hall, find out the history of Fletchers' ranch, find lodging for a film crew, and, by the way, round up a dozen interviewees who had known him way back when, not to mention a few cowboys who would have work to do on Monday and couldn't be expected to stand around twiddling their thumbs.

She wouldn't call him, of course.

She hadn't juggled her kids, her job, her mayoral duties, her mother, her sister, her house, her dogs, her cat and God only knew how many Christmas rabbits only to admit defeat at the demands of some superefficient city chick.

She felt like Marshal Dillon on an old *Gunsmoke* rerun when the outlaw gang was about to invade the town.

"Alice," she said, "how would you like to be a deputy?"

Chapter 7

Sara glanced at her watch.

It was only a minute and a half since she'd glanced at it last. She knew exactly what time it was: three hours and twelve minutes past the time her mother was supposed to meet her and give her a ride home.

Three hours!

Sara glowered out the bookstore window as if doing so could conjure up her missing mother. But glower as she might, Polly didn't come.

This morning, before she'd caught her ride to Bozeman for class, Sara had stood right there in front of her mother in the kitchen and said, ''Gregg will give me a ride to Livingston on his way to Billings this afternoon. Could you bring me home after Jack's dentist appointment?''

And Polly, in the midst of scraping the charred bits off a piece of toast while she tried not to step on the tail of Sid the cat who was threading himself through her legs, had blinked nearsightedly because of course she didn't have her contacts in yet and said, ''Dentist? Jack?'' as if she'd completely forgotten, which she probably had. Then she'd turned and yelled up the stairs, "Jack, you have a dentist's appointment this afternoon! Thanks," she'd said cheerfully to Sara.

"You're welcome. So will you?" Sara had persisted. "If I meet you at the Page and Leaf?"

Polly was writing the appointment in ink on her hand. "What?"

"Give me a ride. This afternoon. If I wait at the Page and Leaf?" Sara spelled it all out slowly, knowing if she didn't, her mother would forget.

"What? Oh, yes. Sure. Of course I'll pick you up."

"The Page and Leaf," Sara had persisted, wishing her mother would write that down, too. "I'll wait there. I've got econ to read and notes to make for my paper, so I'll have plenty to do if you're late. But you will be there?"

"I'll be there," Polly promised through a mouthful of toast. "When have I ever forgotten you?"

Sara raised her brows.

"Well, besides the time Jack broke his arm." She'd left Sara sitting at Hastings in Bozeman, taken Jack to the hospital and had, after his arm was in a cast, driven all the way home before remembering to go back for Sara.

"The time at the library," Sara reminded her. "And when the washing machine broke and you went into Livingston to get the part."

Most of the time, though, her mother was the best mother in the world—with a few small qualifications.

Polly never used a day planner. She didn't check her calendar. And she hated making lists. She rarely knew what she was going to be doing ten minutes from now.

Sara knew what she was going to be doing for the next ten years.

"Waiting for my mother," she muttered now, glancing at her watch again. It was nearly nine. It was obvious that Polly had forgotten her. Actually it had been obvious by seven. No dentist worked that late, especially on a Friday night.

But Sara hadn't called home to remind her.

All the other times she had. This time she had poured herself another cup of herbal tea, determined to wait her mother out.

A little guilt never hurt anyone. And maybe then her mother would learn to write things down on paper!

At least that had been the idea six cups earlier.

The Page and Leaf, Livingston's current haven for sandal-wearing, granola-crunching, tree-hugging intellectuals, tolerated long-term customers. As long as you sipped while you read, you could spread out your things at one of the small round tables tucked against the front windows or scattered amongst the bookshelves and stay until the next millennium.

Probably they hadn't figured anyone would test that out. But as Sara was now past the three-and-a-half-hour mark, they must have been wondering.

It was what happened, Sara told herself, when you deviated from routine. Sara habitually stayed in Bozeman after class on Friday nights, cooking dinner for Gregg at his apartment and then either studying with him until late or, once a month, going with him to the movies.

They followed a strict schedule because if they didn't, they might do other things—things which might well get in the way of their goals. And while Gregg had said frequently he wouldn't mind at all if she would just sleep with him, Sara wasn't about to do that.

Her parents had had to get married because of her. She wasn't having any surprises like that in her own life!

She wasn't having any surprises at all. Not if she could help it.

But sadly she couldn't control everything—like her mother.

Now she tapped her pen on the tabletop, chewed on a fingernail and glared out into the snow-packed street. She couldn't see much, mostly just her own annoyed reflection silhouetted against the rest of the Page and Leaf's well-lit interior. Every now and then a couple would amble past, coming from Sage's, the restaurant down the block. And periodically she caught sight of a cowboy or two headed for The Barrel to spend their paychecks on buckle bunnies and beer.

Sara had never been in The Barrel.

Of course she wasn't twenty-one yet. She'd only turned nineteen last month. But other girls she knew tried to get into

The Barrel regularly to see what it was like, to flirt with the cowboys, to live dangerously.

Sara had no desire to do that.

Now she scowled out at the empty street and wondered once again where her mother had got to.

She'd moved to a table by the window an hour ago so while she worked she could watch for Polly's truck—and so her mother could see her patiently waiting when at last she drove up. But now, two econ chapters, one Spanish translation, six cups of herbal tea and three trips to the bathroom later, Sara was moving beyond impatience into worry.

Maybe her mother hadn't simply forgotten her.

Maybe something had happened. Maybe there had been an accident.

Sara found a phone. She called home, preparing a 'remember me? I'm your firstborn,' speech in case Polly answered.

She got the answering machine.

Now she was really worried. Someone was almost always home. Celie never went anywhere. Neither did Lizzie, except for play practice.

Maybe she should call the hospital. But if she did, she would get her grandmother who would be working in reception. She couldn't upset her grandmother when chances were there was nothing wrong. Sara bit down another fingernail.

She tried working ahead in Spanish, but they were just starting past subjunctive—contrary-to-fact statements—and her mind was far too contrary at the moment to deal with them. So she fetched another pot of hot water, more tea bags and went back to her table to stew.

By ten o'clock she had hypered herself into a frenzy. She couldn't work at all. So she gathered up her books, buttoned up her coat, pulled on her hat and mittens and shouldered her way out the door. She would find her own way home.

The street was basically deserted. There were a few cars and trucks parked near Sage's, the trendy restaurant next to the outfitter's shop. A block in the other direction there were a lot more trucks outside The Barrel.

Sara headed straight for Sage's.

"I don't want a table," she told the hostess when she went in. "I need to find my aunt," she said, which sounded better than "I'm just looking to see if I know anyone." "I need to give her a message."

The hostess hesitated.

Sara, who wasn't her mother's daughter in most respects, but who also knew how to get things done, thrust her backpack into the woman's arms. "Hold this," she commanded, and ducked past her into the dining room.

Of course she only had a moment before the hostess came to her senses, dumped the backpack and came striding furiously after her. But by then Sara had seen all she needed to. She didn't know any of the diners.

"Young lady!" The hostess's voice rang out and her nails bit into the sleeve of Sara's coat.

"Shh," Sara put a finger to her lips and glanced around at the startled customers. "We don't want to disturb the diners. I'm afraid she's not here." She peeled the woman's fingers off her sleeve and headed for the door, grabbing her backpack on the way out.

On the street again, with a north wind biting into her cheeks, she looked for signs of her mother's Jeep. But the only movement at all was two blocks down. Truck doors banged and she spotted a couple of cowboys heading into The Barrel.

The Barrel was a wilder, wickeder bar than Elmer's Dew Drop. It offered occasional honky-tonk entertainment to a cowboy clientele. It sponsored pool tournaments, free nachos on snowy days, something mysteriously called "progressive pitchers," and, if her friend Tina could be believed, monthly wet T-shirt contests at which a girl could win a considerable amount of cash—not to mention notoriety.

Sara might not have known anyone in Sage's, but she was virtually certain she'd find someone she knew at The Barrel.

Slinging her backpack over one shoulder, she headed down the street.

Friday night at The Barrel always got a little western.

Jace knew that. In fact, he'd been looking forward to it.

He'd had a bad week. A rotten week. A hellish week.

On Monday the doc had said he'd need extensive physical therapy on his leg—even if he never went back to rodeoing. On Tuesday the ground froze so hard that last week's slight thaw was only a memory and post-hole digging for the corral came to a complete halt. On Wednesday, Thursday and this morning, he'd gone down to Gilliam's to pick up stuff he'd forgotten—and Celie O'Meara had treated him like The Invisible Man each time.

He'd gone back to the ranch and taken out his frustrations hammering on the old corral—which meant he was now not only angry, gimpy and horny, he had two hammered nails and split knuckles, as well.

He couldn't do anything about the nails or the knuckles. He couldn't do anything about the limp or the frustration at being ignored.

But he didn't have to stay horny. No, sir!

He'd said thanks but no thanks to dinner with Jodie and Ray and the kids. He'd come down early to The Barrel, determined to find himself a woman.

A willing woman.

A smiling woman.

A warm armful of luscious, loving woman.

He'd been without one too damn long.

And there was sure no reason to stay celibate when the only woman he was interested in couldn't even bring herself to look his way.

He'd shot two games of pool, listened to a little rodeo gossip about who'd got hurt and who was having kids and who was getting married and who was running around with whose woman. Someone said Matt Williams had got married—for the second time. He wondered if Celie knew that. He didn't figure she'd want to, and he sure wasn't going to tell her.

And all the while he listened, he studied the women who came in.

Jace was old enough now to be a little choosy about who he would share a bed with. And he no longer needed the wet T-shirt contest to start his appraisal. Somewhere along the line he'd outgrown the notion that the size of a woman's breasts should be a major determining factor. Not that he didn't like a nice handful but—

What the hell?

Was that Sara McMaster over there?

Jace had been idly scanning the room, assessing various un- attached women, weighing whether it was worth getting up and wandering over to chat them up and buy them a beer—there was a redhead at a table near the door who'd smiled his way a time or two—when his gaze skidded to a halt at the sight of a slender young woman next to the jukebox being chatted up by a couple of cowboys.

In itself that wasn't unusual. That was what a lot of women came to The Barrel for—especially if they came by themselves. But those women all looked like they were having a good time.

Sara—because that was definitely who it was—looked mis- erable. And about as out of place as a bunny at a wolves' convention.

He was sure she wasn't old enough. So what the hell was she doing here?

Besides attracting attention. No doubt she was doing that. She looked more like her aunt than her mother, with Celie's glossy dark hair and wide, expressive eyes. Her cheeks were flushed, her eyes were huge—as if she'd just realized how hun- gry these wolves really were—and her short cap of hair was tousled. She looked alive, fresh, tasty—and scared. Her coat was zipped up to her chin, and she was hugging her backpack as if it were an iron shield.

She was talking to two cowboys, and there was a determined smile on her lips as she replied to whatever it was the cowboys were saying. Jace was fairly sure he knew what it was—cow- boys coming on to a gorgeous girl all sounded pretty much alike.

Just then the taller of the two cowboys chuckled and decided it was time to push his luck. He moved in close and slung an arm around Sara's shoulders, hauling her in.

Sara froze.

This particular cowboy apparently didn't read body language, or didn't want to. He leaned in and nuzzled her cheek.

Jace picked up his beer bottle, tossed some bills on the counter and began to sidle that way.

He was halfway across the room when Sara spotted him. Her face lit up. "Jace!"

"Oh, hell," Jace muttered under his breath. He'd intended to distract them, get them talking, move them away from her. He hadn't wanted to be set up as "the competition."

But at the eager look on Sara's face, the die was cast.

The cowboy with his arm around her looked around, saw Jace and scowled. His fingers seemed to tighten on Sara's shoulder. The other cowboy turned, too, and with Sara sandwiched between them, they both stood glaring his way.

Damn it to hell. He was too old for bar fights. Especially too old to be *losing* bar fights.

But with his leg, he couldn't imagine winning one tonight.

On the other hand, tempting as it was, he couldn't just turn and walk away. Trouble was, he had no idea how he was going to take her away from the moron who had his arm around her—without getting physical.

But just as he was wondering, the moron in question said to Sara, "S'pose you're gonna tell me *he's* your brother?"

Jace had never taken a drama course in his life, but even he couldn't miss a cue line like that one.

"As a matter of fact," he said with an easy grin at the moron, "I am."

Sara's eyes widened.

He fixed Sara with his best stern older brother look, one he'd never dared use on Jodie. "You're not half lookin' for trouble, kiddo, lettin' me catch you in here."

"I—"

"Save the explanations." He cut her off and clapped the moron on the arm in comradely fashion. "Thanks for keepin' her outa trouble. She's a hellion sometimes. Never know where she's gonna turn up. I figure it's a reaction to the old man."

"The old man?" The cowboy blinked.

"Didn't she tell you? He's a cop."

Whatever Sara had intended to say, she shut her mouth after Jace said that.

The cowboy's arm dropped from around her shoulders and he took a hasty step back. So did his buddy. "Sure. Right. No problem." They fell all over themselves backing away.

"Didn't want her to get in no trouble," the moron babbled. "We was just keepin' her comp'ny till you showed up."

"This ain't a place for a lady alone," added the other one.

Both of them bobbed their heads fervently.

Jace looped his own arm over Sara's shoulders and aimed her for the door. "You're sure as shootin' right about that." He gave her a little nudge, then glanced back, still smiling. "Much obliged, fellas," he said over his shoulder. "Reckon the old man will be grateful. Might even come looking to thank you."

"Oh, no, that's all right," they babbled. "You just go on home now. Don't give us another thought."

He didn't say a word.

He didn't let go of her until they reached his truck, his hand like a vice on her arm. Only when he had tucked her inside, got in himself, turned the key in the ignition and settled his hands on the steering wheel, did Jace look her way.

Sara held herself stiffly, waiting for him to yell.

She deserved it. She knew that. She'd been an idiot to risk going into The Barrel.

But after a long moment Jace only said quietly, "Home, I presume?"

It was such a relief that Sara almost cried.

Determinedly she didn't. She'd made fool enough of herself tonight. She wasn't going to compound it by falling apart now.

"Yes," she said. "Please," she added, because she owed Jace Tucker a great deal more than politeness.

He certainly hadn't had to come to her rescue. She hardly knew him.

She remembered him a bit from when she was little and her family used to travel with her dad to summer rodeos. She knew he rode broncs. She knew he was a hell-raiser. But at least he was a hell-raiser from Elmer.

That had mattered more tonight than anything else.

It didn't matter at all that her aunt Celie thought he was wild and had led her dear Matt astray.

Wild was relative, Sara thought now. And Jace's was the only face she'd recognized in the crowd.

She'd gone in claiming to be looking for her brother, hoping to find someone she knew and beg a ride home. Her worry about her mother, though, soon turned to worry about what she'd got herself into.

Several cowboys had offered her rides. But she didn't know any of them—and some of them, she was sure, had no intention of taking her anywhere other than to bed.

She might be foolish, but she wasn't a complete half-wit.

She'd tried to be polite. She'd done her best to keep them at arm's length and insist she was looking for her brother. But those last two hadn't wanted to take no for an answer. She'd been vastly relieved to spot Jace coming her way.

She'd been flabbergasted—and delighted—when, against all odds, he'd agreed that he was her brother. And his mention of their old man "the cop" had been inspired.

Now she slanted him a glance, wanting to compliment him on his inventiveness, but unsure what to say.

Jace was making a U-turn in the middle of the street and heading toward the interstate.

Once they had left The Barrel well behind, Sara drew a shaky breath. "Thank you." It was heartfelt.

Jace grinned faintly. "I'd say 'any time,' but truth is, kiddo, I'd really rather you didn't."

"I'd much rather I didn't, too," Sara said fervently. "I was just looking for a ride home."

"Not the best place to look."

"I went to Sage's first. I didn't know anyone there. I was waiting for my mother at the Page and Leaf. I've been waiting for hours. I don't know what happened to her." Sara's voice sounded high and reedy even to her own ears. Worry was making her shaky.

"Didn't you call?" Jace asked.

"Yes. Until I ran out of change. There was never anyone home. Not her. Not my sisters. Not even Aunt Celie!"

He shrugged. "It's Friday night. Lots of people go out on dates on Friday night."

"Not Aunt Celie."

Jace looked surprised. "Ever?"

"Not since—"

She'd started to say, *not since she got jilted,* but that seem somehow disloyal. True, but disloyal. Celie had been hurt badly. It wasn't her fault she was reluctant to try again.

"Not for a while," Sara said finally. She hesitated a second, then because she couldn't help herself, she blurted, "What do you think happened to my mom?"

She knew she sounded scared, but the truth was, she *was* scared.

When her father had died nearly six years ago it had been a day like any other—a day like this one, only in August—and suddenly their world had turned upside down.

Sara could remember it as well as if it had happened yesterday—the trooper who'd come to the door, the hushed voices in the living room, then her mother's stark white face.

It was her mother's face Sara remembered most of all. Polly had always been vibrant, sunny, smiling. But the trooper's words had knocked the life right out of her. Sara had understood then what they meant when they said someone "looked like death."

But it wasn't her mother who had died, it was her dad.

"What if…" she said now, her voice wavering.

"Don't," Jace said sharply, obviously reading her mind. "Don't think that sort of stuff."

"But—"

"Don't," he repeated, his voice still harsh. "What good does it do? You make yourself crazy. You don't help them." His voice was somewhere between ragged and edgy. He took a breath and softened his tone. "Don't worry. Not yet. Chances are it was just a mix-up. Don't ask for trouble."

"Okay." Sara tried not to. She tried to envision her mother

simply forgetting, running an errand, helping Alice or playing cards with Artie. She hugged her backpack as if it were a life preserver. "You're right," she whispered.

Please God, you're right.

It was a clear night so even with the snow cover things were fairly dark, not almost like daylight, the way they were when the clouds hung low. Jace drove fast but not recklessly, and before long they were turning off the highway toward the foothills where Sara could see the lights of Elmer.

She started to tell him where she lived, but he drove right to it. There were lights on in the house. It looked perfectly normal. Sara wasn't sure what she expected, but not that.

Jace pulled up in front and cut the engine. "Looks okay," he said, reading her mind again. "Shall I wait?"

"Would you? Please?"

"Sure."

Sara got out of the truck and gave him a bright smile, designed more to mask her worry from herself than to convince Jace.

Then she shut the door and, still hugging her backpack, walked around the side of the house to go in the door to the Spa.

The door was unlocked.

But the door was always unlocked. The last time anyone had locked a door in Elmer, they'd had to call the locksmith from Livingston to get it open again.

But unlocked or not, no one was there.

Of course it was late. Just past eleven. But Celie always told people they could pick up videos until midnight—on the honor system if she or one of the kids wasn't around. The honor system was obviously in force tonight.

"Celie?" Sara called. "Mom? *Anybody?*"

Good God, where were they all?

The panic she'd managed to keep reasonably well in check suddenly swamped her completely.

"*Mom!*" She dumped her backpack and began to run through the house. The McMasters and O'Mearas usually lived in a state of comfortable messiness. Nothing was any more out of place than it ever was. So no one had come in and kidnapped them all. Unless of course, they'd gone without a struggle.

Sara couldn't imagine her mother—or any of her siblings—going anywhere without a struggle.

"Mom!" Her voice reverberated in the silence.

It was time to worry her grandmother. She grabbed the phone and called the hospital.

With luck Joyce would still be there. With more luck she'd know where they were. With the best luck of all the rest of the family wasn't all at the hospital, too.

The receptionist who answered wasn't her grandmother but Mabel Kitchener who worked third shift.

"Mabel, this is Sara McMaster," Sara babbled breathlessly into the phone. "Is my grandmother still there?"

"Oh, Sara! How are you? Haven't seen you in ages. I was asking Thomas just the other day if he'd seen you lately." Thomas was Mabel's grandson. He was the apple of Mabel's eye, and she could go on for hours about Thomas's finest points if given the chance.

Sara wasn't going to talk about Thomas tonight.

"Tell him I said hello," Sara said. "Is my grandmother still there? It's important!"

"Oh, no, dear. She left early. She said she had to help your mother."

"Help my mother? Why? *What happened?*"

"For the auction, dear," Mabel explained cheerfully. "They're all there, decorating the town hall."

Chapter 8

Polly was sure Martha Stewart could have done a better job on the town hall.

Martha would have been more creative, more professional and, without a doubt, would have had more taste.

But not even Martha would have shown the enthusiasm for their work that Elmer's families displayed that night.

Alice had taken her deputization seriously. By the time Polly had closed the post office that afternoon, Alice had a group of school kids and their moms and little brothers and sisters already hard at work. Anyone who could be trusted with a pair of scissors was cutting out strings of cowboy figures, joined at the boot and the glove, or shiny red paper hearts. Those who who could be trusted with needles were attaching thread so the hearts could be hung to flutter from the ceiling.

When the grocery closed at six, Carol Ferguson brought in all the rolls of red and white crepe paper streamers she had on hand. She and several junior high school kids, including Daisy, were festooning the room. Jenny Nichols and a crew of boisterous fourth- and fifth-grade boys were making a huge banner to decorate the wall above the stage.

Maddie arrived with a stack of photos showing the ranch and all the children who had lived with her and Ward over the years. Alice had pounced on Charlie Seeks Elk coming out of the hardware store and requested that he scan and enlarge them.

He returned that evening with his mission accomplished. Since then he and Brenna and Jed and Tuck McCall were matting them.

Tess Tanner and Felicity Jones, with a little help from their daughters, Susannah and Becky, were adding hangers to the matted photos. And when Tess's husband, Noah, and Felicity's husband, Taggart, showed up, they took hammers and set to work providing nails to hang them on. Right behind the hanging brigade came Celie and Lizzie.

"The visual arts department," Lizzie said. They rearranged the photos for "a more dramatic effect."

On the other side of the room, Brenna had already hung the painting she was contributing, her nephew Tuck was hanging his rodeo sketches, Sam Bacon was putting up some prints he'd done of local scenes, and Charlie had put up a series of photos he'd taken at the roundup last fall.

All of them would be sold at the auction a week from Sunday afternoon—if they survived.

The ever-efficient Astrid had taken Polly's phone call at three, and her only comment had been, "You realize, of course, that it's five here already."

Actually Polly hadn't.

So I'm a bumpkin, she thought as she stood watching the room take shape around her. *So sue me. So don't ask me to run any auctions next year.*

But at the moment, all hassles aside, she was glad she was involved in this one. Despite the hassle, despite Sloan Gallagher, it was exhilarating. It had brought Elmer together, had given them all a sense of purpose, of commitment. It had made them appreciate one another.

Everyone was contributing.

Before she went to work, Joyce had brought over six dozen brownies. "I'll come home early if Mabel will come in. And I just ran into Loney and he said he'd be up after work to start the chili."

Loney Bates, who ran the welding shop was best-loved not for his talents with a torch but for his culinary accomplishments. He had won the Dew Drop's chili cook-off the past three years running, and the news that he would be cooking tonight brought more volunteers out of the woodwork.

When the chili was ready, Cloris appeared with tubs of salad, and Felicity Jones cut wedges of jalapeño cornbread. And long about seven Walt Blasingame and Otis Jamison showed up with two big racks of ribs. Someone brought a boom box and pretty soon Chris LeDoux was wondering, "Whatcha gonna do with a cowboy?"

Polly, watching half a dozen of them pitch in right now to help do Elmer proud, couldn't imagine you'd want to do anything with them at all—except hug them.

She got misty-eyed just watching. This was what small towns were all about—the care and concern of family, friends and neighbors. This was what those film crews Sloan Gallagher had threatened her with would see when they appeared.

"Bring 'em on," she murmured to herself, pausing as she punched a needle through one of the big glossy hearts. "We'll show you what Elmer is made of."

At a firm tap on her shoulder she turned around, beaming.

"Just exactly how long," Sara demanded, her face an alarming shade of red, "did you expect me to wait for you?"

Polly felt as if she'd been punched. "Oh, dear God. Sar', I'm so sorry. I—" But what could she say except the truth. "I forgot."

"Obviously." Sara's dark eyes were furious.

And Polly really couldn't blame her. "I'm so sorry, hon'. How did you—?"

But Sara just shook her head, clamped her mouth shut, spun on her heel and, pushing past Daisy, stalked out.

Staring after her, Polly felt the joy of the evening vanish.

Jack, halfway up the ladder, a threaded heart in his hand, asked, "What'sa matter with her?"

For just a second Polly didn't move. Then she gave herself a little shake and looked up at her son. "I forgot her. I was supposed to bring her home from Livingston this evening. After we got done with—" She paused, her mind spinning back and forward, touching on other things she'd forgotten in the push to get the town hall ready for the film crew invasion. "—after we got done with...your dentist appointment."

Jack's guileless blue eyes widened.

"You were supposed to go to the dentist this afternoon," Polly said. It wasn't a comment. It was an accusation.

Jack blinked rapidly, innocently. "Me?"

Polly might be forgetful, but she wasn't a complete pushover. "Why didn't you remind me?"

She had no trouble reading the answer in his wordless gaze. *As if.*

Damn. She thrust the cardboard heart she'd been threading into Daisy's hands. "Here. Tell Aunt Celie I've got to go, and she'll have to close things up. I've got to talk to Sara." Even as she spoke, she was stepping around Noah and Tess Tanner's little boys who were chasing Becky Jones's little brother, Will. "Sara!" she called desperately after her daughter.

But Sara was gone.

Polly ran after her out into the January night, wearing only her jeans and a thin cotton shirt. "Sara! Wait!"

But Sara was halfway down the street and she never looked back.

"You might as well let her go."

Polly spun around to see Jace Tucker standing by his truck.

"I have to talk to her! I forgot her tonight. I was supposed to pick her up and I left her in Livingston. I don't even know how she got home!" She turned to run after Sara.

"I brought her," Jace said.

Polly stopped. "You did?"

"She's okay. She was just worried."

Polly sagged and shut her eyes. "Yes."

Underneath Sara's anger she had seen fear and understood it. Her mother hadn't shown up. Six years ago, late one night, her father hadn't come home. Hours later a trooper had come instead. She knew the connection Sara would make.

That was why her forgetfulness was inexcusable.

"I need to talk to her."

Jace smiled a little ruefully. "Right now I don't think she wants to listen."

"Probably not. I've blown it. Bad."

"I doubt it. She was worried, but she'll get over it."

Polly wasn't sure about that. She'd forgotten Sara before, but never in circumstances that were as likely to make her daughter recall Lew's accident. "Her dad..."

"I know."

"She told you?" Sara had never talked about Lew's death. She'd only got very self-contained, very controlled, very silent.

"Not in so many words. But I...knew."

Yes, Jace would know. He'd been at the rodeo Lew had left that night. He'd have heard the news that Lew had never arrived home.

Polly tried to paste together a smile that would express her gratitude. "Thank you for bringing her. I suppose she tried to call."

"Said no one was home. When she got home and you weren't there, she tried to call your mother. That's when she heard about the town hall. Fixing it awful early, aren't you?"

"There's a film crew coming." She didn't give a damn about the film crew now. She was too concerned about Sara. "Where did she find you? Were you in the Page and Leaf?"

He smiled wryly and shook his head. "I was in The Barrel."

"Sara went to The Barrel? Oh, my God."

It wasn't that The Barrel was terrible. It was just not a place Sara would ever go. It was completely out of her element—a rough-and-tumble, loud-and-noisy cowboy bar. A weekend evening didn't pass without a bar fight or five. Lew had taken her there on a couple of the rare occasions when they'd left the kids and gone out. Polly had always enjoyed herself.

But Sara wasn't Polly.

Sara didn't like rough-and-tumble. She hated loud-and-noisy. She would have been as uncomfortable and out of place in The Barrel as Polly would have been at a time-management convention.

Not only that, she was exactly the sort of beautiful girl that a passel of drunken cowboys would think was God's gift to them. Polly felt a shudder run through her.

"She's all right," Jace said quickly. "Nothin' happened. When you didn't come, she came looking for a ride." He spread his hands as if to say it was as simple as that.

But Polly hadn't been a mother for nineteen years without developing some instincts that sent her maternal warning signals into overdrive. There were things he wasn't telling her, she was sure. But she didn't press. She would talk to Sara.

She had to talk to Sara.

"I need to find her. To explain."

Jace shrugged and tucked his hands into his pockets. "Yeah, well, good luck."

Behind them the door to the town hall opened.

"Polly! What are you— Oh!" Celie didn't finish her sentence. The minute her gaze moved from her sister to Jace Tucker, her words dried up and she hugged Polly's jacket against her chest.

"Celie." Jace touched his hat in greeting.

Celie gave a quick nod, but her gaze stayed on Polly. "Daisy said you had to leave. You forgot your jacket."

But even as she said it, she made no move to hand the jacket over. Instead Celie clutched it like a shield.

Polly nodded. "Jace will explain." She reached out and wrested her jacket from Celie's grasp.

Celie let it go abruptly. "No need." She began backing toward the door.

"Well, I need to thank him," Polly insisted. She turned to Jace. "I will later, I promise. Go in with Celie and she can get you something to eat. I think there's still chili left and maybe some ribs if you're hungry."

"Why would he be hungry?" Celie demanded. "It's almost midnight."

"Actually," Jace said. "I'm starving."

Polly smiled. "There you go, then." She gave his forearm a squeeze of gratitude. "Thanks, Jace."

Then she turned and hurried home, trying to think what she would say to Sara when she got there.

Just what she needed. Jace Tucker.

The end to a perfect evening, Celie thought sourly. She could feel him almost literally breathing down her neck as she went back into the noisy overheated town hall and he limped along behind her.

He wasn't using his crutches anymore. She'd seen him three times this week—rather, she'd *ignored* him three times this week—when he'd come into the hardware store. She'd like to ignore him again now, but it seemed he'd done Polly a favor and she'd been appointed to thank him for it.

Well, she'd try. But she wasn't going to make a big deal out of it. "I'm not sure there's any food left," she said over her shoulder. "We ate hours ago."

This was something of an exaggeration. People had been dipping into Loney's chili pot all night and, even so, there always seemed to be more. There were also probably still a few of her mother's brownies left and maybe a little bedraggled lettuce salad.

"Anything's fine," Jace said.

He was still right behind her, but he was gawking around, not looking at her. "Pretty impressive."

"Lots of people worked very hard." In case he thought it was tacky or something.

But he just nodded. "I can tell." He turned and his gaze lit on the huge banner over the stage that proclaimed in big red letters: ELMER LOVES SLOAN.

He burst out laughing.

Celie bristled. "I believe they plan on rephrasing that tomorrow."

Jace grinned broadly. "Probably a good idea. Won't do much for his image otherwise."

Celie ignored him. She had pointed that out herself, but she didn't think he needed to laugh quite so hard. She looked in the chili pot and, yes, there was some left, so she handed him a plate.

"Help yourself."

"I will." And there was such hunger in his tone that she looked at him, surprised. And was even more surprised to discover he wasn't looking at the chili pot, but at her.

Celie turned away abruptly, flustered. "Go sit down." She pointed to a chair. "I'll see what else is left."

She wanted to just leave him there and vanish, but if she did, no doubt Polly would hear about it. So she scraped up some salad and found a couple of ribs lurking at the bottom of one of the pans. There was still cornbread and brownies, too. She heaped everything on another plate, carried it back to where he sat and slapped it down on the table in front of him.

He grinned at her. "Hey, great. Thanks."

Celie grunted. He wasn't welcome so she wasn't going to say it.

Jace kicked out the chair across the table from him. "Sit down."

"No, I—"

"Ah, Celie." Mary Holt came bustling up, her baby, Mac, in her arms. "Good. I've got to help Felicity in the kitchen and I need someone to give Mac a bottle." She pressed the squirming baby and a bottle into Celie's arms. "Thanks. You're a peach." Mary beamed and hurried toward the kitchen.

Celie looked down at the tiny bundle of baby in her arms and felt a stab of longing. Of course she'd held babies before. She'd held all of Polly's and Mary Beth's. But that had been years ago. Jack was nine now and the triplets nearly seven. Then she'd thought she would still have her own babies someday. But now—

Mac fussed and started to cry.

"Sit down." Jace Tucker shoved the chair out again.

Not looking his way, Celie sat. She cradled the baby against her breasts and gave him the bottle. He glommed on eagerly, sucking as if his life depended on it. She smiled and touched the baby's cheek tenderly. Solemn blue eyes looked back. Around her the noise and bustle faded. She was only aware of the baby.

God, she wanted—

"You should have kids." Jace's voice startled her back to the present.

Celie stared at him, suddenly furious that he should read the longing in her—especially since he was a good part of the reason that she didn't have them.

"Thank you very much for that brilliant observation," she said acidly.

He looked startled at her animosity. "Huh?"

Celie gritted her teeth. "Nothing."

She wished he'd go away. But he had a plateful of food in front of him, and he seemed determined to eat every bit. She ignored him, focusing instead on the baby, smiling at him, willing him to look back at her, wishing she didn't still want so very much to have a husband and children of her own.

"So," Jace said after a few minutes, "how much you gonna bid?"

Since he was obviously talking to her, Celie forced herself to look his way. "Bid on what?" she said with supreme indifference.

"Our man Gallagher, of course." He grinned.

Celie felt her face flush. "Who says I'm going to bid anything on him?"

"Just figured you might, you bein' such a fan and all."

Her cheeks warmed even more. "Who told you that? Did Polly tell you that?"

"Nobody told me. I watched you droolin' over him in that magazine."

She'd had a magazine with an article about Sloan sitting on the counter at the hardware store this week. "I was not drooling!" Her voice was so sharp that Mac's face crumpled as if he were about to cry. "Shh, Macko," she whispered, shooting Jace a furious glance as she tried to soothe the baby. "Shh, now. It's all right."

"Right," Jace said, amused. "You weren't drooling. You were seriously obsessed, though."

"I'm a student of film," Celie said loftily. "And Sloan Gallagher is a good actor. I admire his skills."

Jace mopped up his chili with a piece of cornbread, popped it in his mouth, chewed and swallowed. "And I buy *Playboy* for the articles," he said solemnly.

"You are such a jerk."

Jace grinned. "So you don't think he's good-looking."

"Of course he's good-looking!"

"His nose is crooked."

"It was broken." Celie knew that from the articles she'd read.

"Damn right," Jace said with considerable satisfaction. "I broke it."

"You! *You* broke Sloan Gallagher's nose?"

"He was asking for it. Shootin' off his mouth about how much better things were where he came from. No big deal. He survived. Who knows? Maybe it's the nose that attracts them. Maybe he owes all those women in his life to me." Jace's grin widened.

"Oh, right!" Celie was furious. How typical of Jace Tucker to break someone's nose and be proud of it. She struggled to her feet, still holding Mac, still giving him his bottle, but absolutely unable to sit there and listen to Jace Tucker for one minute more. "He should have broken yours!"

"Oh, he did," Jace said wryly. "He pounded the crap out of me."

"More power to him," Celie said, and meant every word.

Sara's door was closed. As usual.

Most of the time Polly told herself that was normal—that any nineteen-year-old young woman who had to live in a house with her mother, her grandmother, her aunt and three siblings would want a bit of privacy.

If it meant more, if there was something seriously wrong, Polly hadn't let herself think about that. It would have meant confronting Sara, and Polly had never felt able to do that.

From the day she was born, Sara Madeleine McMaster had always seemed cleverer, smarter, more organized, more focused—*older!*—than her mother.

Of course, while Sara had been a baby, Polly had managed to convince herself that she knew best. But as her daughter had grown older and smarter and more organized, it had been harder and harder to convince herself of that.

Especially when Sara seemed to be having so much trouble believing it, too.

Tonight it was especially hard to believe.

But whether she believed it or not, Polly knew she couldn't turn a blind eye to the closed door any longer. But before she faced it, she sent a prayer winging heavenward.

"She's your kid, too," she told Lew.

In fact, Polly thought Sara had always been more Lew's than hers. Sara had adored her father. She'd followed him everywhere. She'd always listened to Lew.

"So give me some inspiration now," Polly beseeched him. "Help me figure out what to say."

She tapped on the door. There was no answer, but she didn't walk away. She knocked louder. Still nothing.

As if silence would deter her tonight. Nothing would deter her tonight.

"You're in the right, Sara," Polly said loudly to the closed door. "So why are you hiding in there?"

There was another considerable silence during which Polly wondered if she'd once more said the wrong thing. Finally the door opened.

"I'm not *hiding,*" Sara said sullenly.

"Good." Polly tried a smile, hoping Sara would return it. She didn't.

So Polly took a deep breath. "I'm very sorry about not

showing up. Sloan Gallagher called and said there was a film crew coming on Sunday. We needed to be prepared. To decorate the town hall. I got involved and I...forgot.''

Sara's expression didn't change. She didn't move. Eventually she shrugged. ''It doesn't matter,'' she said indifferently. ''I got a ride.''

''Jace told me. That was kind of him. He also told me you had to go to The Barrel to find someone—''

''I was fine!'' Sara said sharply.

''I'm sure you were. But it's no place for a young woman alone and—''

''You should have thought of that before you forgot to come!''

''I should have. It was my fault. I should be more organized.''

''You always say that!''

''Because it's true. I find it difficult. I try. I'm sorry I frightened you.''

''I wasn't frightened!''

But even now Polly could see the fear flashing in Sara's eyes. She longed to take her daughter into her arms and hold her. She longed to bury her face in Sara's thick cap of dark hair and breathe deeply of the scent that was so uniquely hers, to hold her close and remember all the years when they'd been close. Before...

Before Sara had begun to shut the door.

She could see the rejection on Sara's face. Her daughter had her arms crossed over her chest.

If she put her arms around Sara, Polly knew there would be no answering hug. Sara would resist.

But Polly was Polly. She couldn't not reach out. She wrapped her arms around Sara, anyway.

She felt Sara's body stiffen in resistance. The arms stayed locked across her chest, trapped between them as Polly hugged her. Sara was as tall as she was now. There was no burying her face against the top of Sara's head. But there was the soft brush of her short hair against Polly's nose and lips. There was that indefinable scent that was and always had been Sara.

And Polly could feel her daughter tremble even as Sara remained rigid in her arms. As if her daughter feared she might crack if she softened her stance, if she gave an inch, if she let go.

Let go. Please, let go.

But seconds ticked by and Sara held fast to her pose.

She stayed stiff and unyielding in Polly's arms, except for one eventual small squirm of irritation that told Polly she'd pushed as far as she dared.

"I'm sorry," she said against Sara's ear one last time. Then she stepped back, loosed her arms and let them fall to her sides. She looked at Sara, who wouldn't look at her.

"I love you, Sar'."

Sara flicked a doubtful gaze in her direction for just an instant. It didn't last long, but its disbelief cut Polly to the quick.

"Yeah," Sara said. The positive that meant a negative. Then she stepped back. She swallowed and started to close the door again. "G'night."

It was all the olive branch Polly knew she was going to get. A one-word offer to return things to the distant politeness that had existed between them before she'd forgotten her daughter.

Come on, Lew. What do I do? What do I say? How do I change things?

But the silence from on high was deafening.

There had to be a way to reconnect. But Polly knew, with a sinking feeling, that she wasn't going to find it tonight. Not when she'd already undermined the little confidence Sara seemed to have in her.

She smiled sadly. "Good night, dear."

Sara shut the door.

Sloan had spent all day making love with Lily Bascombe in a cave in some cliffs above a windswept sea.

Just he and Lily—and fifty or so other people with cameras, lights, sound equipment—and opinions.

Sloan did what he was told. Lily lay back and, he presumed, thought of Sam Keane, her husband.

Sloan thought of Polly.

In his adolescent fantasies, he'd often made love with Polly. In his fantasies Lew had conveniently disappeared, Polly was his, and the glory of her golden freckled skin, soft curves and hidden secrets was his to explore.

There wasn't any dialogue in the scene they were shooting, only sighs and moans and unintelligible whispered endearments.

Convenient because it gave him the chance to fantasize again. Of course there were millions of men in the world whose fantasy it was to make love to Lily Bascombe. They would give their eyeteeth to be where Sloan was now, to do what Sloan was pretending to do now.

Because, in fact, the woman he was making love to in his mind wasn't Lily, but Polly.

What was she like now?

He supposed she'd changed. Just as he wasn't a gangly pup with big feet and no coordination anymore, she probably wasn't the slender lissome beauty she'd been at seventeen. Of course he remembered her pregnant. But he doubted she looked like that, either.

Still, she'd had four kids, Gus had told him.

Four!

And the oldest would be in college now, older than Polly had been when he'd known her. It boggled his mind.

But even when he thought of her as a middle-aged mother, he found that he was eager to see her again. Partly because she didn't want to see him. She'd been tart, dismissive almost.

People had, in general, stopped being tart and dismissive to him several years ago.

But Polly treated him with about the same disdain she had shown for his gawky, fourteen-year-old former self. It was a novelty. It sparked his interest.

It whetted his appetite and made him want to call her again. He could ask if the interview people had contacted her. He wondered if she'd been tart and dismissive with them. He wondered, if they asked her, what she'd say about him. Surely not that he'd been spying on her and Lew in the barn!

At least he hoped not!

Once he got done making love with Lily Bascombe, he'd call and find out. He was looking forward to telling her he'd done an interview at lunchtime with Andrea Antonelli for *Incite*, one of the funkiest weekly entertainment mags. And he'd taken considerable pleasure in mentioning the auction in Elmer.

Andrea had been delighted—and fascinated. She'd wanted to come out and cover it—after all, she flew to the ends of the earth for a good interview, she often said. But she was scheduled to cover the Sundance Festival and then had to fly directly to Paris.

She had, however, offered to mention it to Schuyler Van Duersen, *Incite*'s owner-publisher. "I bet Sky would get a kick out of sending someone out to Elmer."

She and Sloan had shared a laugh at the very idea.

Incite was so unabashedly urban that every week it came with a list of the best spots to get mugged. Its reporters wore sandals with socks, and if they wrote the word *horse,* it was a given that they were writing about either heroin or basketball.

Sloan could just imagine what Polly would say if an *Incite* reporter turned up in Elmer. He spent the day looking forward to telling her.

But it was past two on Saturday morning when he finally called. He'd waited until then so there was less chance of having to deal with the kids or the sister or the grandmother.

He didn't want her distracted. He didn't stop to analyze why. He just knew he wanted her attention—all of it.

It was quieter and more intimate this way—just the two of them. And he could lie in bed while they talked—and pretend she was here with him.

He punched in the number on his cell phone and waited. Finally, on the third ring, she picked it up.

"Hello?" It was Polly, he was sure.

"Guess who's coming to Elmer?" He grinned and waited

for one of her quick, sassy replies, eager to tell her about *Incite*.

"I don't care," she said tonelessly.

There was a click. A silence. A dial tone.

She'd hung up!

The phone rang again a minute later.

Polly had known it would. Just as she knew who would be on the other end of the line.

She didn't want to answer it. She didn't want to talk to anyone, least of all to a single man with no cares or family responsibilities, a man who couldn't possibly understand the mess that was her life.

But if she didn't answer it, Sloan would think she was running away from him again and she didn't want that, either. She picked it up and said briskly, "Who's coming to Elmer?"

"What's wrong?" Sloan countered.

"Nothing's wrong! Who's coming?"

"You don't care who's coming," he said flatly.

Polly sighed. She tucked her feet under her and leaned back against the pillows on her bed. "No, I don't," she admitted. "But since I'll have to deal with them, anyway, you might as well tell me."

"Later. After you tell me what's wrong."

Why did he have to get nosey now? Irritably she shoved a hand through her hair.

"It has nothing to do with you. The world, you might be surprised to know, doesn't revolve around you."

As she said the words, Polly realized how rude they were. It wasn't his fault she'd screwed up. "I'm sorry," she said wearily. "It's my fault. I just…blew it this evening. I forgot my daughter."

"Forgot…?"

"Never mind." She shut her eyes. Weariness washed over her. The exhilaration of the evening had well and truly evaporated. She was left with nothing more than a sense of failure— and responsibility. "Who's coming? What do I have to do?"

"Just a reporter," Sloan said after a moment. "No big deal. It might not happen. Don't worry about it. Is your daughter okay?" He actually sounded concerned, as if he cared.

Polly huddled under her quilt. "Yes. She's...annoyed. Angry. At me. Which is understandable, considering." She paused, realizing she sounded whiny and sad. She made herself sit up straight. "It'll be okay," she said firmly. "We'll sort it out."

Somehow. Someday. She hoped.

"Anything I can do?"

"Adopt her?" Polly said, a glimmer of her usual wry humor surfacing.

Sloan sputtered.

She laughed faintly. "Is this what they call dead air?" she asked.

Sloan laughed, too. "Something like that."

"Don't worry," she assured him. "I wouldn't do that to you. We may have our moments, but I wouldn't give her up. She's mine, for better or worse."

"Good." He sounded relieved, though whether it was because she didn't mean it about adopting Sara or because she was sounding less pitiful, Polly didn't know.

She didn't want to sound pitiful. She didn't want him feeling sorry for her. It was bad enough that for a few minutes she'd felt sorry for herself. Deliberately she changed the subject.

"You should see the town hall," she told him. "We decorated tonight."

"Decorated?"

"Indeed. At the suggestion of Astrid the Efficient."

"Haven't met Astrid."

"Lucky you. Anyway, we've got hearts and cowboys everywhere. Also photos of the ranch and of the kids who lived with Maddie and Ward. Brenna McCall hung the painting she's going to be auctioning off. And Charlie Seeks Elk contributed a whole bunch of mounted photos. And right up front there's a banner that says ELMER LOVES SLOAN in big red letters."

"That'll be good for my image."

"I thought so," Polly said feeling marginally more cheerful. "There was some discussion about the wording, actually. We might change it."

"I'd be obliged," he said drily.

"I'll mention it to Jenny. She and the fourth- and fifth-grade boys did it. It's enormous. Takes up most of the wall above the stage."

"Sounds ominous."

"It just shows how much people appreciate what you're doing by coming back. It's very kind of you."

"I hope you think so in a week."

Polly did, too, but she wasn't saying so. "I'm sure it will be fine."

"I hope so." There was a pause and she expected he'd say goodbye. Instead he said, "Polly? If I can do anything to help, call me. I mean it."

And the oddest thing was he really sounded as if he did.

Chapter 9

After Friday night's disaster, Polly started making lists.

She had a list for each film crew as it arrived. She had a list for each of her children. She made a list of items to be auctioned, of volunteers willing to help out, of who was bringing what to the potluck after the auction, of what needed to be done every day before, and finally she made a list to keep track of the lists she was making.

She got a chalkboard from the hardware store and hung it in the kitchen. Everyone was assigned a column and instructed to note whether they were in or out—and if out, when they were returning—and with whom.

Sara, who had regained a little of her sense of humor by the following morning, stared at it and laughed.

"You actually think anyone is going to do that?"

"You will." Polly knew that much. "And I will."

Celie said irritably, "I'm here or at Artie's. I never go anywhere else!"

Polly thought there were a lot of other places Celie could go if she would just get out of her rut. But since starting an argument didn't seem like a good idea right now, she only said, "Then write down your schedule so we know."

"You only have to look." Celie grumbled. "If I'm not here, I'm there. See? Simple."

Polly saw. It was simple. It was the way she herself had run her life for the past thirty-seven years. But she'd also managed to forget Sara on Friday night, and she wasn't going to forget anything again. There was also such a thing as setting a good example.

"Humor me," she said to her sister and gave her a look she hoped Celie remembered from childhood, the one she used to use when she meant, *Do this or I will break your favorite doll in little tiny pieces.*

Celie said, "I'll just write down my schedule."

Polly smiled. It was nice to be remembered.

The kids wrote down their schedules, too. Artemis: play practice. Daisy: helping with horses at Joneses'. Jack: goofing off.

Polly wished she could goof off.

She'd assumed she would be able to point the film crews in the direction of Maddie's, show off the newly decorated town hall, give them a sound byte or two and get back to her life.

"Me and Harry Hyena," she muttered Sunday night.

They were like ants, she told her mother later about the film crews. "They're everywhere."

They were—at Maddie's ranch, in the town hall, on the main street. They poked their heads in every door that opened. They talked to anyone who moved. They shot cowboys playing pool in the Dew Drop and they borrowed a bunch of kids, stuck them in a classroom and filmed the local school. Worst of all, in Polly's estimation, they never left her alone. They asked about her life, her family, her job, and about Elmer. She couldn't imagine why they wanted to know.

"Background," they said.

She tried to be polite, cordial, small-town hospitable.

They asked her about Sloan.

"I didn't know him really," she said. "He's *much* younger than I am."

She longed to say, *Go away and bother someone else.*
Why were they so interested in her?

Sloan knew why.

There were some people the camera loved, some people who were so vibrant, so alive, whose charm and spontaneity was so contagious that you couldn't get enough of them. Some people said that about him.

But he knew it was true about Polly McMaster.

For almost twenty years he'd been carrying around a memory of a willowy golden girl. A stunning girl—especially in her nakedness—to his adolescent mind.

But the young Polly didn't hold a candle to the woman she'd become.

Polly McMaster, whose TV appearances on both morning segments had been spliced into footage of his own interviews last week, was a gorgeous animated woman with thick springy autumn-rust hair, a smattering of golden freckles and a dynamite smile.

Sloan, who had been curious enough to have the tapes flown in, had been anxiously awaiting them all day, and was still nervous when he shut himself in his room to watch them. It was nerve-racking to wonder how time had treated Polly McMaster. He'd prepared himself for disappointment.

He felt as if he'd been punched in the gut.

He couldn't take his eyes off her.

He watched the whole piece all the way through, then promptly ran it back and watched it again.

And again.

He must have watched each of them a dozen times. Or more.

Now and then he stopped it and just looked his fill. Time had treated Polly very well indeed.

"Who is this woman?" the voice-over asked as the camera zeroed in on her.

It was snowing in Elmer, and Polly was bundled up in a bright-purple down jacket, her glorious hair bouncing and tangling in the wind as she put out the flag in front of the post office, then went back in and began sorting the mail.

"And why does she hold the fate of Hollywood's most sought-after hero in her hands?" the voice continued.

It was titillating, of course. That was their job—to make Polly's task appealing. But they didn't need to work at it.

Polly sold herself.

The woman was golden. Bright. Funny. Charming and self-effacing at the same time as she showed the correspondent around tiny Elmer.

Sloan felt a hint of nostalgia as they did a quick tour of Main Street, of the welding shop, the hardware store and grocery. They showed the schools where Polly's kids went, where he had finished eighth grade. They showed one of her daughters acting in a play and her son feeding a hutch full of rabbits.

"Elmer," the voice over said, "the heart of America."

And the camera pulled back and showed the town tucked up against the foothills of the Bridgers, colored rose by the early-morning sun on the fields of winter snow. Then the camera moved in again. It cut from the grocery to the welding shop, from the school to the church, from Celie's spa to the tiny library to Gilliam's hardware store. It showed kids and cowboys, old people and young.

Then the clip cut to Polly telling the features correspondent, "It may not seem like much to outsiders, but we have everything we need right here."

The features correspondent who, Sloan happened to know, couldn't live without a deli and a dry cleaner in the next block, didn't argue.

She just smiled and chirped, "And next Sunday you're going to have America's heart throb, too."

That led into thirty seconds' footage on Maddie's ranch, on the foster children she and Ward had raised, with a panning view of a sea of young faces in photos—apparently the ones Polly had said were hung in the town hall.

And then the camera slowed and stopped on one scowling dark-haired adolescent.

"The man being auctioned off this Sunday," the correspondent said.

And then they cut to his own interview.

"Tell us about that," his interviewer had prompted.

And Sloan had done. He'd been personable, charming, said all the right things about Maddie, about the ranch, about Elmer. Then they'd asked him about Polly.

"I'm looking forward to seeing her again," he'd said with a grin.

He hadn't realized just how much.

The TV crews were supposed to come, film and leave.

They did.

But then the spots aired, and Polly realized that there would be one more day of excitement with some local buzz and commentary. With luck they would also get a few more bidders come Sunday.

But once that was past, she figured she could just get back to work and that things, however hectic they might become right before the auction, would still be more or less normal.

She and Harry Hyena. Oh-for-three.

Things didn't settle down after the shows aired. On the contrary, the world—discovering Elmer—went nuts.

The phone began to ring off the hook. Within minutes after the first spot had been aired, the show's booker was on the phone to Polly wanting more.

"I've told you everything I know about the auction," she protested.

But it wasn't just the auction he was interested in.

"The American people want to know more," he told her. "More about you, about your family, about what it's like growing up in this marvelous little Montana town. We want to do a full prime-time feature!"

"About *Elmer?*"

At first Polly thought it was Sloan Gallagher disguising his voice and putting one over on her.

It turned out she was oh-for-four.

She learned quickly that after the first spot, the network's phone lines had been jammed and their e-mail system overflowing.

"Well, of course," she said. "It's Sloan Gallagher. What do you expect?"

But it wasn't only Sloan. They wanted to know all about Maddie and the ranch, about what it was like to have foster kids, about how she, Polly, as a single mother coped with her children and her job and her mayoral duties and her multigenerational household. They all wanted to be just like her.

"You're America's heroine," he told her enthusiastically.

"Oh, good God," said Polly.

Life, instead of settling down, got worse.

By Tuesday afternoon Polly was getting calls from metropolitan dailies on both coasts, from entertainment magazines, from news weeklies and cable television shows. Reporters called constantly. Newspapers sent feature writers. Magazines sent stringers and freelancers and photographers.

They wanted all of Polly's life story. They wanted to know the history of Elmer in twenty-five words or less. They wanted to talk to Maddie, to Will Jones, to "real live cowboys," to Joyce who'd thought of the auction, to Sloan's boyhood friend, Gus Holt.

They prowled the town. They camped at the post office. They sat in their cars in the streets.

They started following her kids.

"America is fascinated with how normal they are," one of the news people told her. "How happy and well adjusted. They want to know your secret."

I forget when I'm supposed to pick them up. Polly could only guess what Sara would say if asked.

They followed Daisy to Jones's to ride horses. They watched Jack and Randy bash each other with hockey sticks. They went to play practice with Lizzie. They thought it was fascinating that she was calling herself Artemis. They did a small spot on children influenced by Greek mythology.

By Wednesday, Polly had decided that America needed to get a life.

At the very least it needed to get its collective nose out of hers.

"It's insane," she told Gus when he ducked into the post office to collect a package for Walt Blasingame.

Gus, who was looking just a little hunted himself, said, "I've had three reporters followin' me all week wantin' to 'get a taste of cowpunchin'' while they try to get me to talk about Sloan. Can't imagine how he puts up with it all the time."

Polly couldn't, either. But she didn't feel sorry for him. Sloan had chosen this. He got paid millions of dollars to show his face to the camera and be a public figure.

So where was he?

He'd done his three-minute interviews for the morning talk shows—and then he'd disappeared. She hadn't heard from him since Friday night.

She thought he'd ring Monday night. She fully expected a critique of her presence on television. But though the phone rang and rang and rang, and a lot of people wanted to do a postmortem, not one of those calls was from Sloan.

He didn't call Tuesday, either.

Not that she'd have noticed if he had. *People Weekly* called, and *Entertainment Weekly* and *Working Mother* and *Single Parent* and half a dozen other magazines she'd never heard of. They asked all kinds of questions about Elmer, about her life, about her children.

About her relationship with Sloan Gallagher.

"I'm going to be his murderer," she said to her mother, to Celie, to the rest of her immediate family.

To everyone else she said, "I am the mayor of Elmer and the head of the auction committee. No more. No less."

Wednesday brought more, not less.

There were twelve people standing in front of the post office when she arrived to sort the mail. Three of them were reporters. Five were groupies who had shown up early and wanted to know if they could bid on Sloan. Four were women who thought Polly sounded so sane and sensible on television that they simply wanted to talk to her.

"And tell me their problems! Because they think I have all the answers," she said desperately.

"Tell them to talk to us," Sara said dryly.

"No," Polly said. "Enough is enough."

Alice and Cloris had every room in their houses filled again. So did anyone else in Elmer who had a spare bed. The economy was booming, that was certain. Some came because of Sloan, some came out of curiosity, and some were there simply because they just wanted to be a part of this small-town extravaganza.

In 120 years there had never been a traffic jam in Elmer—unless you counted the time Wyatt Jackman got his team and brand-new buckboard stuck turning around on Main Street in 1904.

But there was a traffic jam on Wednesday morning.

When Polly called the sheriff's department, desperate, hoping she could get him to run some people in on loitering charges, he just laughed and sent his deputy Spence Adkins out to direct traffic.

The only way Polly could escape was to barricade herself in the back room of the post office at lunchtime, to take half an hour for herself in which she shut the service window, locked the doors and shut off the phone.

So she did.

And while she was eating her tuna sandwich and her apple, she prayed that something would slow it down, would stop the nonsense, would get everybody's feet back on the ground again.

"Anything," she said to the Almighty, who she doubted could hear her above the furor in Elmer these days. "Anything at all."

And then Artie Gilliam had a heart attack.

Celie knew it was all her fault.

If she'd been paying attention, she'd have noticed that Artie was looking pale. If she hadn't been trying to avoid those reporters who wanted to talk about Polly and Sloan—as if they were an item, for goodness' sake!—she would have seen that he needed to go home and rest.

Instead she'd been glad he was the one talking to the reporters and delighted she'd escaped to do the billing in the back room. Of course it wasn't only the reporters she'd been avoiding.

It was also Jace Tucker.

And if anyone shared the blame for Artie's heart attack, it was Jace.

He'd turned up bright and early to pick up the lumber that he'd ordered. And when he'd spotted her behind the counter, he'd grinned broadly and jerked his head toward the vast number of women who were already prowling the streets of Elmer.

"Looks like you're going to have a little competition bidding for your Mr. Gallagher," he'd said in that infuriating way of his.

"I'm not bidding on him," she'd said.

"Why not?" he'd asked, brows lifted, mouth twitching. "Chicken?"

Just thinking about it now, Celie still wanted to kill him.

But sadly, Jace Tucker was alive and well—and sitting just inches away from her—in the waiting room of the hospital in Livingston while the doctors worked on Artie.

"You don't have to stay," she said again. She'd been saying it for hours.

But Jace didn't budge. He'd been here the whole time. In fact, Jace was the one who'd brought Artie to the hospital.

It was Jace, actually, though she hated to admit it, who'd realized something was wrong and who had come to get her in the back room.

She'd railed at him when he'd burst in. "Get out! You don't belong back here."

He'd ignored that. "I think Artie's having a heart attack!"

At first she'd thought he was telling a bad joke. But when he grabbed her arm and hauled her out to where Artie was sitting, pale and clammy, at the register, she realized that this was no laughing matter. Artie looked up when he saw her rushing toward him, but he seemed to have trouble focusing on her.

"Don't feel so good," he said faintly, rubbing at his chest. "Reckon I'll maybe mosey on home, take me a little rest."

"No." Celie was reaching for the phone to call an ambulance.

But Jace took it out of her hand. "No time for that." He put it down again, then turned to Artie. "I think," he said calmly, "that maybe you oughta have a doc check you out. Get his coat," he told Celie.

"The ambulance—" she began.

"Will take longer to get here than I will to get there," Jace said flatly. "Get his coat. I'll bring the truck around."

He was gone before Celie could reply. But there had been nothing to say, anyway. This was one time she didn't argue. She got Artie's coat and bundled him into it. "We're just going to run you down to the doc," she said soothingly.

"Don't need no doc," Artie grumbled. "Just somethin' I ate."

"I'd feel better if we checked it out." She steered him out the door toward the truck, which Jace had idling next to the curb. He jumped out of the truck and helped Celie get Artie in it. She clambered in after.

"Here, now," Artie said, noticing the crowd of Sloan groupies and reporters who had gathered to gawk. "Who's gonna mind the store?"

Celie cast a glance around and saw her niece coming out of the grocery store. "Sara! Keep an eye on things!"

Before Sara could do more than look startled, Jace had shoved the truck in gear, jammed his foot on the gas, spun around in the middle of the street and headed toward Livingston.

That had been hours ago.

Since then she knew they'd called in a cardiologist from Bozeman. So it was a heart attack, though no one had come out and told her so.

Her own father had died in this same hospital two years ago. Memories of Gil's fatal heart attack came back to plague her now. She remembered pacing these same halls then, telling herself it would be all right, that her dad was only fifty-nine. He was strong, hadn't ever been sick a day in his life.

She remembered her mother's white face and desperate composure. "He'll be all right," Joyce had said over and over.

But an hour later they'd come out and said they were sorry, he was gone.

She wanted to call her mother, who had often called Artie, "the father she'd never had." But she couldn't. Not yet. She couldn't put her mother through this again. Not right away. After they had some real news, then she would do it.

Even if her mother hurried down, they wouldn't let her in to see him. And she would be here to work, anyway, in a couple of hours.

Celie walked over to stare out the window into the bleak winter landscape. The hospital seemed just as cold. She shivered and wrapped her arms across her chest.

The chair creaked behind her.

"I'm all right," she said before Jace could offer her his jacket. She was cold, but it was a cold that came from within and it wouldn't be helped by Jace's jacket.

Besides, she didn't want Jace's jacket. She didn't want him being nice to her.

He came over and stood beside her, close enough so she could feel the heat of his body. Fortunately not close enough to touch.

"You can go," she said without looking at him.

"No."

An hour later the doctor came out and wanted next of kin.

Celie's knees almost buckled. Strong masculine fingers gripped her upper arm, keeping her steady.

"He doesn't have any, does he?" Jace said.

"H-he has a nephew," Celie replied, mouth dry. "In Bismarck, I think."

Ted and his wife and boys had moved from Elmer a couple of years back.

"Is he—" She couldn't say the words.

"He's hanging in there. You brought him in?" the doctor asked. And when Jace said they had, and they were as close to blood relatives as he had in Elmer, the doctor talked to them.

"We want to keep a close watch on him for the first twenty-four hours," he said. "So he'll be in intensive care. Then if he's stable we'll move him to a regular room."

"Can I see him?" Celie asked.

"Can we?" Jace said. Celie glared at him.

"Five minutes," the doctor allowed. "Come this way."

"You don't have to come," she said under her breath as she hurried after the doctor.

"I don't have to do a lot of things," he said. "I want to see Artie, damn it. Stop thinking about yourself for once."

"I beg your pardon!"

"You heard me." He was striding along as fast as the doctor.

Celie tossed her head, lifted her chin and tried to brush past him, but he grabbed her arm just as they were going into the intensive care area and stopped her at the doorway.

"Let go."

"No. Not until you smile."

"What!"

"Otherwise Artie will think he's gone and croaked." He gripped her arm tighter. "Smile, damn it."

Celie bared her teeth at him.

"Perfect." Jace bared his own teeth at her.

The doctor looked back and did a double take at the sight of them. "Right in here," he said. "If you're, um, ready."

Artie hadn't died. But in that hospital bed with its rails and rollers and umpteen sophisticated machines all around him, he looked as if he'd come close. He was as white as the sheet that covered him. An IV ran into his hand, and a heart monitor was attached to his chest. Half a dozen other mysterious things were clicking and ticking and measuring and checking him. But other than the almost imperceptible rise and fall of his chest, Artie didn't move.

Celie had always thought of Artie Gilliam as wiry but strong. Not a big man but a powerful one even at the age of ninety. For the first time she realized how really frail he had become.

Her smile faded. She sucked in a sharp breath.

Jace's fingers dug into her elbow. "Smile."

Artie's eyes fluttered open. "Hunh," he said, his voice a gravelly parody of its normal self. "Will ya look at this?" One hand made a vague sweeping gesture toward all the modern medical paraphernalia that surrounded him.

"Pretty impressive," Jace said, his voice was firm and upbeat.

Celie nodded. She didn't speak because she didn't trust her voice, nor did she have a clue what to say that wouldn't upset Artie or bring Jace's wrath down on her.

Artie looked at her and frowned. "What're you doin' here?"

"I came with you."

"Who's mindin' the store?"

"Sara is."

Artie frowned. "She ain't no more'n a girl."

"She's nineteen," Celie said briskly. She didn't want to argue, for heaven's sake, but it was almost a relief to hear Artie's gruffness returning. "I'll mind the store," she promised. "Don't worry. Just get well and come home."

"Damned tootin'," Artie rasped. "Be there soon's I can." He scowled at all the paraphernalia hooking him to machines, then shifted his gaze to Jace. "Reckon you could do me a favor?"

"Anything," Celie vowed.

"Not you." Artie dismissed her. "Him." He fixed his gaze on Jace. "You mean what you said 'bout stickin' round?"

"Yeah."

Artie nodded. "Good. Ya can't start trainin' till spring though. So, reckon you could help me out?"

Jace blinked. "Help out? You mean—"

"Mind the store. Celie's a good girl, but she's got her own business goin'. 'Sides, she oughtn't t'be left on her own."

"What! Artie, I—" Celie protested, but Jace stepped on her toes.

"Sure," he said, nodding firmly. "Sure, I'll help out."

"Artie, I can—" Celie persisted.

"You got your own stuff t'do. And I know you can do most everything at my place, but I want a man around."

"That is so—"

"Want Jace," Artie said flatly and shut his eyes.

She thought he'd died. She stared, mouth agape, trying to

detect some faint rise and fall of his chest. He didn't even seem to be breathing.

Nor did she.

Then all at once his eyes opened once more. "You stay at my place," he directed Jace.

"Uh, sure."

"You can tell 'im what to do," he told Celie.

"I'd be happy to," Celie said with considerable bite.

Artie smiled faintly. "Figured you might."

"I'd like to talk to the old lady."

"You!" Polly's fingers clenched on the receiver at the sound of Sloan Gallagher's gruff voice in her ear late Wednesday night. Or maybe by now it was early Thursday morning. Time flew when you were having fun.

She'd got to bed just before midnight, exhausted, but she hadn't been able to sleep. Worries about Artie, about the auction, about what all the publicity was doing to her kids, were swirling around in her head.

And then the phone had rung just as she was starting to doze off, and that rough-velvet voice was in her ear asking for an old lady.

"What old lady?" she demanded.

"The one who's *much* older than me." He was laughing.

"Oh." She sighed and slumped back against the pillows and shut her eyes. "Well, it's true," she said. "I am. Old enough to be your mother."

"Math not being your strong suit, obviously." He chuckled again.

But Polly couldn't laugh right now. She couldn't even seem to talk. Her silence said enough.

"What happened?" he demanded. The concern was there in his voice again, just as it had been when he'd called last Friday. It was the sort of voice that made you want to gather up all your worries and woes and hand them to him because he made you think he could take care of them—take care of you.

He's an actor, Pol', she reminded herself.

"I saw the tapes," he told her. "They were great."

"Oh, yes," Polly said dryly. "We're the heart of America, don't you know?"

"What?"

"Where have you been?" she said testily. "On the north pole? Elmer is the flavor of the week. It's 'America's most wonderful little town.' Its citizens are 'the salt of the earth.' My kids are 'the best-adjusted children ever raised by a single parent' and I'm 'America's heroine.'"

"Ho, boy."

"A magazine from Puerto Rico sent a reporter who's charming my mother. Some stringer from a Texas monthly has invited Daisy to the cutting-horse trails in Fort Worth. Lizzie thinks she's got an in with a Broadway director, Jack is being offered a hundred dollars apiece—and more—for genuine Elmer Christmas pageant rabbits! And this morning...this morning Artie had a heart attack!"

"Artie? Artie Gilliam?"

She was surprised he remembered. "Yes."

"Because of all the hoopla?"

"Because he's ninety and has a bad heart," Polly said, because that was the truth. "But the hoopla hasn't helped," she added.

"How is he?"

"He's in intensive care. We don't know. We're worried. My sister works for him. My mother used to. He's like family. Like my grandpa. We're worried about him, and I'm worried about all this nonsense with the kids. It's just—" *Stop it, Pol'*. She took a deep breath. "I'm sorry. This isn't your problem."

"I caused it. I'll take care of it."

"What?"

"I'll take care of it, Polly," he said again. "Get some sleep. Don't worry. Trust me. I'll sort things out."

Chapter 10

Jace had never in his life seen himself as a storekeeper.

If anyone had told him he'd be opening the door of Gilliam's Hardware at 7:00 a.m. to get ready for customers at 9:00, he'd have stared in disbelief.

But that was what he'd done. He'd lain awake half the night marveling at the determination he felt to prove himself worthy of Artie's trust. But if his eagerness to get to work surprised him, it apparently poleaxed Celie.

"What are you doing here?" she demanded when she pushed open the door to the hardware store at 8:55.

Jace, who was sweeping the floor for the third time, said, "Getting ready to open up."

"How did you get in?" she asked suspiciously.

"Artie told me where he kept the key."

"I have a key!"

Jace shrugged indifferently. "He said you weren't supposed to open."

"But he should have known I would!" Celie protested. The color was high in her cheeks. She looked angry. She always looked angry when she was talking to him. Sometimes it was damned annoying.

"Oh, I reckon he thought you had a lot on your mind this week, getting ready for Gallagher," Jace said, moving away with the broom. "But then, he doesn't know you're too chicken to bid on him."

"Go to hell, Jace Tucker!"

He grinned. "Not just now, Miz O'Meara."

She glared at him. "You are so juvenile. I can't believe Artie trusted you to do this." She brushed past him and stalked into the back room. In thirty seconds flat she was back.

"Where's the change drawer?" she demanded.

Jace jerked his head toward the cash register. "Where do you think?"

Celie looked appalled. "Didn't Sara put it away last night?"

"Yeah. I put it back this morning."

"You took it out of the safe?" She opened the drawer and stared at the change. "Artie gave you the combination?"

"And I went to the bank and got change."

"But—"

"Did you think I'd steal everything and leave town?" Jace lifted an eyebrow.

"Obviously you haven't," she said gruffly. "Yet. Why don't I just go home then and leave you to it?" she said irritably, slamming the drawer shut. "Since you seem to have everything under control."

"Because it takes two. You know that," Jace said, refusing to let her annoyance get to him. "Somebody to mind the store and someone to deal with the warehouse."

"So fine. Which do you want?"

"I'll do the warehouse." But he stayed right where he was, even when Celie looked pointedly in that direction. "No reason to be out there now," he said easily. "Colder'n a son of a gun. I'll go when I have to. Meantime I'll just keep you company in here."

"And you'll do Artie's jobs?"

"Sure. Whatever."

Celie smiled. "Clean the bathroom."

* * *

It was odd, Joyce thought, how she could work in reception five days a week and cope perfectly well, and how the sights and sounds of ICU could set her heart to hammering.

But the second she set foot in the Intensive Care Unit, it was like Gil's death all over again. When she'd come in last night, she'd almost turned around at the door and left again.

There was no denying the feelings of loss, of helplessness, of pain that came with losing Gil. But there was no way around it, either.

So Joyce girded her heart against the pain and went in.

Last night Artie had been sleeping. She'd stood just inside the doorway and looked at him, aware suddenly of how much the old man had always meant to her. She'd known him, it seemed, all her life. Her schoolteacher mother had been a widow when she'd brought Joyce, her two-year-old daughter, to Elmer. She'd never remarried. ''I've never met anyone else who could take his place,'' she said simply.

So it had always been just she and Joyce.

And the Gilliams.

Artie and Maudie had befriended them from the first. Maudie had baked cookies with her and sewed doll clothes for her dolls. Artie had played catch with her and taught her to ride a horse. He'd let her come to the hardware store after school and had given her peppermints and let her count the change in his cash drawer.

When she was seventeen he'd given her her first real job. And he'd sized Gil up before she'd married him. Artie had, in fact, walked her down the aisle and he'd loved her children as if they had been his grandchildren.

In short, he was the father she'd never had.

And the thought that she might not have him much longer made her throat tighten and her heart ache.

She hadn't awakened him last night. She'd gone on to work and peeked in on him once more before she came home. Now he was asleep again. His normally ruddy cheeks were still pale and sunken, and his wiry frame looked insubstantial lying there in the hospital bed.

She would have crept away, as she had last night, but she'd

brought him a crossword book that Celie had found at the store.
"Give him this," Celie had said. "If he's well enough to do
it, it will keep him busy. Things will seem more normal because he does them all the time. And hopefully he won't fuss
so much about the store."

So Joyce carried it in, intending to leave it on the bedside
table. But as she reached the bed, his eyes fluttered open.

He stared at her, dazed. "Anna?" His voice was faint and
wondering.

Anna? Then Joyce realized he'd mistaken her for her mother.
She took his gnarled fingers in hers. "No, Artie. It's Joyce.
Anna's daughter."

His hand tightened around hers with a surprisingly strong
grip. His eyes closed again and he let out a shuddery sigh.
"Joyce."

"Celie sent you your crossword book," she said, putting it
on the table.

A faint smile touched a corner of his mouth. "She's a good
girl, that Celie."

"Yes."

"Needs a man."

"Oh, Artie!"

"Gettin' 'er one," he whispered.

"What?"

"Never mind." He closed his eyes again, but he still hung
on to her hand, his grip fierce.

Joyce watched the shallow rise and fall of his chest. Her
gaze went to the blip, blip of the heart monitor. It seemed
tenuous, thready. "How are you feeling?" she asked when he
opened his eyes again.

"Just peachy," Artie said with considerable disgust. "Can't
believe the ol' ticker did this now."

She smiled faintly. "I don't think the timing is a matter of
choice."

"No." Watery blue eyes met hers and he smiled, too, a little
wryly. "Timin's a funny thing." His gaze slid away and he
seemed to stare off into space, seeing something that she could
only guess at. Peoples' lives were mysteries, Joyce thought.

Even when you had known them for years, how much did you really know?

She shifted from one foot to the other. "Speaking of which," she said eventually, wiggling her fingers as she glanced at the watch on her wrist, "I have to be on the reception desk in two minutes."

"Ah. Right." Artie reluctantly let go of her hand. "Forgot you had to come in anyways." He sounded disgruntled, as if he'd just realized she hadn't only come to see him.

Joyce brushed a hand over his soft gray hair. "I'd have come to see you whether I was working or not, Artie. I stopped in last night, but you were sleeping. I didn't want to wake you."

Fierce blue eyes bored into hers. "You wake me," he insisted. "I ain't got all that much longer that you can let me waste time sleepin'."

"But—"

"Wake me. You hear? An' you come anytime."

"Only family is allowed anytime."

"You see any family?" Artie demanded, looking around.

What Joyce saw was loneliness. "I'll tell them to let me in, Artie." She bent and brushed a kiss across his forehead, then touched his sunken cheek for just a moment.

He smiled. The smile wobbled and his eyes filled. "G'wan," he muttered. "Time you got to work."

"Yes." Giving him one more smile, but determined to leave him his dignity, Joyce turned to go.

He called after her. "You'll be here tomorrow?"

"I'll be here."

It wasn't that Sara wanted to be interviewed.

It was just that everyone else seemed to be. In the past three days she'd seen Lizzie and Daisy and even Jack on daytime and nighttime television. People at MSU had asked about it.

"Was that your sister?" they said when they saw a segment with Daisy where she was—typically—blathering on about horses.

"Is that cute little kid your brother?" they wanted to know, when Jack turned up on three different shows talking about hockey and how to feed rabbits and what he liked best about living in Elmer.

Sara didn't mind that Daisy and Jack were becoming media darlings. But it seemed a little far-fetched that even grumpy, theatrical Lizzie—Sara refused to call her sister Artemis—was getting airtime. She'd not only got to talk at length to one of those daytime TV hosts, but a whole camera crew followed her to play rehearsal, and afterward she was starry-eyed as she told everyone that she might get to meet a Broadway producer.

"Like he'd give you a part," Sara muttered.

But Lizzie was flying high. "Why not?"

"Because things don't happen like that," Sara said scathingly.

But Lizzie had just tossed her short dark hair and stuck her nose in the air. "Tell that to Sloan Gallagher."

Sloan Gallagher, to Sara's way of thinking, had a lot to answer for. He was the reason her siblings were acting like brats. He was the reason her mother had forgotten her. He was the reason Aunt Celie was more distracted than usual. He was the reason it was taking Sara ten minutes to cross First Street.

With all this traffic, it might as well be New York City!

Irritable and distracted, Sara darted between cars.

There was a sudden screech.

Sara leaped back to avoid being run down and smacked into something solid, hard and warm. She knocked it right over and landed on top of it.

"Ooof!"

Hard arms went around her. Smiling green eyes and a hard, handsome face were inches from her own.

"You okay?" His voice was wonderful. It had a lilt to it. An accent. Not quite English. But not American either. Not quite.

"Sara!" Loney Bates came hurrying up, followed by Alice Benn. "You all right?"

"Yes. Yes, of course." She was fine. Just stunned. And startled. She'd never seen eyes quite like those of the man she'd flattened. "Are *you* all right?" she asked.

His grin was as gorgeous as his voice. "Sure an' I always did like the notion of the lady on top."

Face flaming, Sara scrambled up.

Loney caught her arm, brushing snow and gravel off her jacket. "You sure you're okay?"

"Are you all right, dear?" Alice seconded.

"Fine. I'm fine. I just—" *never know what to say when men say things like that!*

"Break anything?" Loney was asking the impudent stranger who was hauling himself to his feet now.

He was tall. Taller than Gregg. Taller than her dad had been. Over six feet. With thick unruly black hair that brushed his forehead, high cheekbones, a nose that had been broken at least once, and those beautiful grooved cheeks that you saw in *GQ* and almost nowhere else. At least one cheek was. The other, she saw now, was scraped and bleeding. There was a red mark that would likely become a bruise on one cheekbone, too. He must have caught the bumper of the car as he'd caught her going down.

"Nothing broken," the stranger said. He touched his face where the scrape was and winced a little. "Nothing serious."

"Damn tourists," Loney muttered. Then he caught himself. "S'pose you're one."

"A writer actually. For my sins." He grinned a little ruefully.

"Time? Newsweek? People? Field and Stream?" Loney said hopefully.

The stranger shook his head. "I'm doing a story for *Incite* magazine."

Sara's eyes widened. "*Incite* magazine? Isn't that a little...trendy to be interested in us?"

The stranger's expression was wry. "Apparently not."

There was a wealth of meaning in those two words, but Sara didn't know exactly what. She couldn't take her eyes off him. He was dabbing at the scrape on his cheek. She was going to be late. She was going to miss Gregg's call. She ought to be picking up her backpack and going home.

"You need to wash that scrape off. Maybe put a bandage on it," she said to the stranger.

"Got some in the shop," Loney said, jerking his head toward the welding shop.

"I can take him home with me," Sara said quickly.

Loney looked surprised. So did Alice. So did the stranger.

"You sure?" he said.

"Of course," Sara replied. "I plowed into you. You're my responsibility."

"Ah." He grinned. "Is this a reversal of one of those 'if I save your life I'm responsible for you forever' sorts of things?"

"I...I don't know," Sara said. She'd never done this sort of thing before. She had absolutely no idea.

But Loney was nodding. "Right. You jest go on with Sara then."

Alice looked as if she would like to give Sara a stern motherly warning. But Sara was oblivious to warnings.

"Come on," she said, picking up her backpack and leading the way.

"You're Sara," he said, falling into step beside her. "I'm Flynn."

The last thing Polly expected to find when she got home from work was Sara sitting at the kitchen table with a handsome stranger drinking coffee.

"Flynn Murray." He stood up, held out his hand.

She recognized his accent at once. "FBI," she said, shaking his hand.

Sara gaped at her, then at Flynn.

"Foreign born Irish," he translated for her. He was grinning. "An' right you are."

"A priest?" Polly said. What on earth was Sara doing with a priest?

He shook his head. "Writer."

"My God, are they sending them to Elmer from Ireland now?" Polly was horrified.

But Flynn Murray shook his head. "Just New York. I came

to live there with my uncle, who is a priest. But I'm a freelanc-
er. Doing this on spec for *Incite* magazine.''

Polly couldn't imagine what a counter-culture interview and
issues magazine could possibly want with an article on cowboys and Elmer. She said so.

Flynn Murray grinned. "Me, neither."

"Then why—"

"Sky Van Duersen, the publisher, he was wantin' me out of
town."

Her own life was complicated enough, thank you very much.
Polly didn't even want to know why New York City wasn't
big enough for Schuyler Van Duersen and one freelance Irish
writer.

She studied the chalkboard, then fixed her gaze on Sara. "It
says you're at the library."

"Couldn't go," Sara said. "I was late. I missed Gregg's
call."

"You were late?"

"From the traffic. Norby dropped me off by Loney's and I
was trying to cross the street. I ran into Flynn—literally—and
knocked him down. He cut his cheek." Sara nodded toward
the red scrape on the Irishman's face. "So I brought him home.
I had to clean it up for him, didn't I?" she added piously.

Polly looked at her daughter narrowly.

Sara had the grace to blush, then look away and fiddle with
the handle of her coffee mug.

Polly almost couldn't believe her eyes.

Sara? Blush?

Sara? Late?

She looked at Flynn Murray again. He'd sat back down. He
was looking at Sara, who deliberately wasn't looking at him.

"I see," Polly said, and wondered if she did or not.

Jace cleaned the bathroom. He unloaded the freight, stocked
the shelves, cut the lumber orders. Though he was still clearly
hobbled by his leg, he seemed to be everywhere, doing everything—including flirting with the customers!

Not the men, of course. He joked with them, laughed with

them, talked horses and cattle and ranching and trucks with them, and dealt with them far more easily than Celie did. Of course that was to be expected.

But he also charmed the women. Every time a woman came in, he teased her, winked at her, chatted with her.

Flirted!

And they ate it up, every one of them. Several local women came in to see how Artie was doing and to find out if Celie needed any help. And then they saw Jace there and they said, "Oh, well, you don't need us!"

But they didn't leave. No, sir!

They stood around and laughed and talked to Jace. They barely paid any attention to Celie at all. They only talked to Jace. When he teased them, they teased him right back. It was like a hen party with all of them fluttering around one preening rooster.

Celie should have gone home at noon the way she usually did and left him to it—to *them!* But she didn't see how she could, since he didn't know where everything was.

"I'll be all right," he told her. "If I need you, I'll whistle," he said with a wink.

Celie glared at him. "Artie wouldn't want me to leave you alone," she said, though frankly she didn't think Artie would have cared. He seemed convinced that Jace could handle things better than she could.

"Whatever you want," Jace said airily. "Feel free to hang around."

It was infuriating that, as the afternoon wore on, Celie felt as if she was doing exactly that. Jace didn't pay any attention to her. He left Celie to run the register, directing customers to her when they'd finally decided on their purchases, while he chatted with them and generally acted like he owned the place.

She never minded when Artie did that—because he did own the place. But Jace hadn't been here for years! Except for the tourists, she knew all these people better than he did!

But they didn't care! They were all delighted to talk to Jace. They asked him what he was up to now. They cheered his decision to hang around and ranch with Ray and do a little horse training. They told him to drop by for a meal or invited him to have a beer after work at the Dew Drop. They never invited Celie anywhere.

Not that she'd have gone if they had.

She was surprised to hear him telling so many of them that he was intending to stick around. And when she and Jace were finally by themselves in the store late that afternoon, Celie couldn't help asking, ''Are you really planning on training horses at Ray and Jodie's?''

Jace, who had boosted himself up on the counter to sit, dangled his legs and began rubbing his thigh where, she supposed, it hurt. ''I am, yeah,'' he said.

''And that's why you've been buying all the lumber? For corrals?''

''Yep. And a house.''

''You're building a house?''

He nodded. ''I'm settlin' down.''

''Oh, right,'' said Celie and laughed. But before she could ask what he knew about settling down, the door opened and several giggly young women came in.

''We're here for the auction,'' they announced. And it didn't matter that they were two days early. They just wanted to know all about Sloan Gallagher.

''Do you *know* Sloan Gallagher?'' they asked.

''Is it true he grew up in this little bitty town?''

''Did you go to school with Sloan?''

''Did you ever, you know, date him?'' They looked at her, eyes wide.

''Make out with him?'' They giggled. Nosey, ditzy, silly women. All they could talk about was how gorgeous and ''hunky'' and handsome he was.

Annoyed, Celie gave them short clipped answers, then said, ''I have to do some billing.'' She was not sorry for the excuse.

Naturally, they turned to Jace. They liked him better, anyway. He was clearly a cowboy, a bit of local color.

And Jace, naturally, made the most of it. He flirted with them. He joked and chatted with them and regaled them with Sloan Gallagher stories.

"Sure, I went to school with him. Sat behind him in algebra... He was a hardheaded kid. Chip on his shoulder. Figured I oughta knock it off for him."

The women were fascinated. Every group that came in hung on Jace's tales of his boyhood fist fight with Sloan. They ogled the scar on his jaw that he said Sloan had given him, and they gasped in amazement when he claimed at least five times to be responsible for the bump on Sloan's beautiful nose.

Celie sat with her back to them and worked on the bills and answered the phone whenever it rang. She tried not to listen. She might as well have tried not to breathe.

Finally, when Noah Tanner called with an urgent order, she turned and pushed a paper across the desk at Jace. "Noah needs this now."

"Right." But he kept right on talking to the groupies while they made fools of themselves, oohing and aahing and giggling and laughing and wanting to touch Jace's scar. One of them even offered to kiss it and make it better!

Celie stabbed the pen right through the page she was billing. She spun around.

"Do you mind?" she said, frost dripping. "This is a business! We have work to do. Those boxes in the back need to be broken down," she told Jace, "and Noah Tanner will be looking for that lumber."

"I'll get right to it," Jace promised. But even as he spoke he was edging closer to the woman who was puckering her lips.

"Right here, sweetheart," he said, pointing to a spot on his jaw. "Every once in a while I still get a twinge right here."

Celie stomped away. She was getting the lumber herself when he finally came out to join her.

"You call that settling down?" she demanded, yanking out boards and laying them on a rack.

He slanted her a glance. "I'm workin' on it."

She snorted. "Have someone in mind, do you?"

"Actually, yes."

That rocked her. Jace Tucker was serious? He was looking to settle down? And he had a woman in mind?

"Who's the lucky lady?" Celie asked with an edge of sarcasm.

Jace just looked at her. "That's my business."

Daisy thought she was going to Fort Worth to get a cutting horse.

Lizzie thought she was going to get a part in a Broadway play.

Jack thought he had an inside track on becoming a millionaire because he had discovered that there were a ridiculous number of people who would buy an honest-to-goodness, 100 percent guaranteed authentic, Elmer Christmas Pageant bunny for fifty dollars.

"*Fifty dollars?* You didn't!" Polly exclaimed when he waved a stack of bills in front of her face.

"You been sayin' we need to find homes for 'em." Jack gave her a broad grin and tucked his loot into his Colorado Rockies minilocker bank.

"I didn't say to sell them!"

"But you didn't say not to, either. And they promised to take good care of 'em."

What was she going to do?

Tomorrow it would start all over again. The streets would be crawling with reporters. Their *house* would have had its own resident reporter if she hadn't refused to let Sara invite Flynn Murray to stay with them.

"I don't mean to be rude," Polly had said to him, "but you must understand that we can't play favorites."

"Mom!" Sara objected.

But on that Polly had held firm. She needed a reporter-free zone somewhere. Her house was going to be it.

"Sure an' you're right about that," Flynn had said, grinning amiably. "I'll be seein' you tomorrow perhaps, Sara? Will you be havin' lunch with me?"

Sara didn't even check her day planner. She just said, "Yes."

I should lock them all up, Polly thought as she sat in front of the fireplace that night and waited for her mother to get home.

It was after midnight, it had been snowing for hours, and Joyce was late. She'd probably stopped to see Artie, and that was why she was late. Polly wouldn't let herself contemplate any other reason.

She was exhausted and she should just go on to bed. But she wouldn't sleep as long as her mother was out in this weather. She got up and made herself a cup of tea. She scratched Sid's furry head and ruffled the dogs' fur. They were her great comfort most evenings when she sat alone in the living room after the kids were in bed. Now she barely had time for them.

"Sorry, guys," she said and got a purr and a tail thump for her trouble. "Two more days and we'll be on our own again."

She heard the door open and moments later her mother came into the kitchen.

"Brutal out there. Wind coming right down out of the north. Took me almost an hour." Joyce said as she unwound herself from her scarf and shook the snow from her hat into the sink.

"Did you see Artie?" Polly felt guilty that she hadn't even been down to see him since he'd had the heart attack.

Her mother took off her jacket. "Yes. So far, so good. He grumbles a lot. Won't do what the nurses tell him. Stubborn cuss. Only one he'd ever listen to was Maudie."

"They were a pair, all right." Polly poured her mother a cup of tea, too, then padded back into the living room and sat in front of the fire. "You'd almost think he'd want to be with her. They were together a long time."

"Fifty-nine years." Joyce smiled a little wistfully. She took her cup and sat on the sofa. "At least he had a whole lifetime with her."

"Yes." She and Lew had barely had fourteen. They had been great years. They'd packed a lot into them, and Polly knew she would never trade those fourteen years for fifty with someone she loved less. But Lew had been gone six years now. She was only thirty-seven.

If she lived to be as old as Artie—or even her own mother—that was a long long time to live alone.

"We had good men," Joyce said at last. "A couple of the best. You can't ask for more." Their gazes met.

Polly reached out and patted her mother's hand. "I know."

Joyce's fingers bent around hers for just a moment, giving a gentle squeeze. Then she stood up. "I think I'll just take this cup of tea and go on up to bed. You should go on to sleep now, too."

"Yes," Polly said. But after Joyce disappeared up the stairs, she didn't move. The fire snapped and crackled. And Polly sat rocking, watching it. Life seemed almost normal right now. Calm. Sane.

"Two more days," Polly murmured. Two more days and it would be calm and sane again. The auction would be over. Sloan Gallagher would have come—and gone.

It was odd that he hadn't called last night or tonight.

Was that why she hadn't gone to bed when she was so exhausted? She'd told herself she was waiting for her mother to get home from work. But had she really been waiting for Sloan's phone call?

"Of course not," she assured herself. She set her teacup down and curled into the rocking chair.

Her eyes closed.

She slept.

A knock on the door woke her.

She jerked upright, cursing because she had a crick in her neck and the room was freezing because she'd let the fire burn down, and it was, what? *One-thirty in the morning?*

Who on earth would be banging on her door at one-thirty in the morning?

Some idiot in search of a story, no doubt! It was the last straw. Polly scrambled up, stalked to the door and jerked it open.

Sloan Gallagher stood smiling on her doorstep.

Chapter 11

"Good God!"

"Not even close." The famous Gallagher grin flashed briefly, and Polly's heart kicked over in her chest.

"What are you doing here?" she demanded.

"If you don't know that, sweetheart, you're not living on this planet." He glanced over his shoulder. "Can I come in? I don't think anyone has seen me yet."

Even as he said the words, Polly realized there was a good chance someone might. And if they did, a full-blown stampede might result. She reached out, grabbed him by the hand, hauled him in and slammed the door as if to shield him from a horde of invaders—and realized as she did so that she was the one who might well need shielding—from him!

Or from her reaction to him.

She knew all about animal magnetism. She'd experienced it in spades with Lew. But while she had acknowledged countless times, at Celie's insistence, that yes, Sloan Gallagher was handsome, that he had gorgeous eyes and a smile to die for, the acknowledgment had been purely academic. She personally had never felt its impact.

Until now.

Now, face-to-face with Sloan Gallagher, she felt serious oxygen depletion. She stood there with her mouth open and couldn't seem to get her breath.

He had an impact on space, too, she thought. He shrank rooms. The entry hall, normally quite large, now felt no bigger than a phone booth.

He seemed much more substantial than he did on the screen. It probably had something to do with his three dimensions. He might be twelve feet high on a screen, but there was so much *more* to him in the flesh. Snowflakes glistened on his tousled dark hair. And even in the dim light of the entry hall he looked tan and fit and gorgeous in his blue jeans and black down jacket.

He looked roguish and dangerous—like a movie star. Imagine that.

Polly had never thought of charisma as having a physical presence before. But she could actually feel it emanating from him. He was looking at her exactly the way she remembered him looking at the female lead in his films—right before he took her off to the bedroom and they scorched the sheets.

The surge of heat that shot through her unsuspecting body was so sudden, so unexpected and so intense that it could have been her first hot flash. Then she realized that it had been the exact opposite—not the death knell of her hormonal impulse, but the first rush of sexual awareness that she'd felt since Lew had died.

"Hell," she muttered. "Oh, bloody hell."

"What?" Sloan said.

"Nothing!" Of all the inappropriate reactions! she thought, disgusted. She was as bad as Celie. Worse! Agitated, she stepped around him and hurried into the living room where, she hoped, his effect on the dimensions of the room would not be so daunting.

Sloan started to follow her, then stopped and took off his boots.

Polly almost told him not to bother, that he wouldn't be staying long enough. But for all her sudden sexual awakening, she was still Polly. She was still practical. And in the clear light of the living room he not only looked roguish and dangerous and charismatic.

He looked tired.

He looked positively shot.

He yawned even as he worked his boots off. And as he straightened up and shed his jacket to uncover a chamois cloth shirt the very same blue color as his eyes, she thought he might topple right over.

And she would have to catch him.

Oh, yeah, right, she thought. Better she should let him fall on his attractively broken nose.

Trust Sloan Gallagher to look exhausted in a most world-weary, mind-shatteringly handsome way.

There was no doubt that he would bring in plenty of money for Maddie's auction. If everyone's reactions to Sloan in person were as strong as hers, Polly thought that by the end of the bidding Maddie might own the ranch free and clear!

"The auction is Sunday," she reminded him now, just in case he'd got his days mixed up.

"Someone mentioned that." He sounded amused as he padded into the room, still smiling, looking around, taking things in curiously.

"I just meant I was surprised to see you so early."

"I told you I was going to help."

He'd said something about "taking care of things," but she hadn't paid much attention. If she'd thought about it at all, she'd imagined him riding in on a white charger and slaying reporters right and left.

"This is help?"

"It was meant to be." He yawned again, so fiercely this time that his jaw cracked. "Sorry. God, I'm tired." He glanced at his watch, blinked, then shrugged and shook his head. "Whatever time it is, I know it's not almost seven." He squinted again at the watch face. "I wonder if that's morning or evening."

"Where were you? Where did you come from?"

She realized that in all the times she'd spoken to him on the phone she'd never known where he was. She'd never called him. He'd always called her. And somehow she'd always imagined him in his California bachelor pad, toes tickled by the waters of the Pacific, as they talked.

"Tierra del Fuego."

She stared. "You're kidding."

"I'm not, actually." He yawned again and kneaded the muscles at the back of his neck. "We had one last sequence to shoot. They wanted barren, windswept cliffs above the ocean. Uninhabited. Rugged. Lots of hours of daylight so they could shoot and shoot." He shrugged. "Tierra del Fuego."

"You came all the way from…?" Polly's voice died out. "Today?"

"Started yesterday sometime. Flew to Buenos Aires. Caught a plane to Newark. Snowing in Newark, too," he told her, through another yawn. "Waited seven hours for them to get a flight going this way. Flew to Salt Lake. Then to Butte."

"Butte? Bozeman would have been closer."

"There would have been press in Bozeman."

And he'd had the good sense to avoid it even when it meant going out of his way.

"But why did you drive all the way? Why didn't you stay…?"

"Someone would have noticed."

That was true, too. "But if you rented a car, someone must have seen…"

"I called Davy, my foreman, from Salt Lake. Told him to get a couple of the hands to take his truck to Butte and leave it." He tipped his head toward the door. "I picked it up. Drove here. Hell of a time going over the pass."

Polly could imagine.

"I parked up behind the Dew Drop."

By Alice Benn's. She hoped there were no insomniacs among the news crew that was staying with Alice. "But why? If you plan to be unnoticed, why come here early?"

"To get you. Thought we could go to my place."

She stared at him. "What? Who?"

"You. Me."

"You and me?" Polly thought he'd lost his mind.

"Your kids, too," he said helpfully. "You said they were bein' distracted. Reporters buggin' 'em. Figured they'd like the ranch. If they like horses and—"

"No," Polly interrupted him, refusing to even entertain the possibility. "Thank you, but no."

"It's just up by Sand Gap. Couple a hours. Well, maybe more in the snow. Thought if I got here tonight we could drive on up an' hide out there." He gave her a sleepy conspiratorial grin. "Give 'em the slip." There was a faint twinkle in his eye before the grin morphed into another jaw-splitting yawn. He swayed and blinked, struggling to keep his eyes open. The twinkle vanished. He sighed and rubbed a hand through his tousled hair. "It sounded like a good idea yesterday."

"It might have been," Polly said, giving him the benefit of the doubt, "if your flights had all connected."

"Yeah."

"And it wasn't snowing."

A shadow of the Gallagher grin flickered hazily. "That, too."

"And those nosey reporters wouldn't suddenly realize that all the McMasters were missing? They might wonder. They might come looking."

"They dunno where my place is," he insisted.

"Well, since we're not going, it doesn't matter."

"Mmm..." He continued to sway. His eyes closed.

She thought he was lucky he hadn't fallen asleep at the wheel driving all the way from Butte after that many hours flying halfway around the world. "You need to go to bed."

His eyes flicked open. The haziness became an almost slumbrous laziness as they suddenly seemed to focus directly on her. Dark brows lifted. "Now there's an idea," he drawled.

"By yourself," Polly said firmly. "And not here."

"Why not?"

"Because." It was enough of an answer for children. It didn't work on Sloan.

"Because why?" he persisted.

"Because there's no room."

He looked around the living room. His gaze lit on the sofa. Polly followed his gaze. "Absolutely not."

But, like a zombie, he started toward it. "Looks comfortable enough."

"You are *not* sleeping on my sofa!" She could just imagine Celie coming downstairs in the morning and finding Sloan Gallagher asleep on the couch. "No! Go to Gus's."

"Can't. Drove past Gus's already. Press."

"What?"

"There's a TV van parked out there," he enunciated slowly. "Right by the gate."

"Oh, for God's sake."

His mouth quirked. "Not God's sake," he corrected her dryly. "Ratings."

Polly racked her brain, trying to think of someplace in town where she could put him. There wasn't anywhere. Even Artie's place, now taken over by Jace, was full of Sloan groupies, according to Celie. There was only one real solution.

She sighed. "Come on." She turned toward the stairs.

"Taking me to see your etchings?" A grin quirked one corner of his mouth.

"I'm going to stick a sock in your mouth if you don't shut up," she hissed. "I've got a houseful of sleeping people. I don't need you waking them up."

"I'll be very quiet. Will you?"

"Hush." Polly, cheeks burning, gave him her back and marched up the stairs. Fortunately he followed silently. The last thing she wanted was anyone hearing a strange—or worse, familiar—male voice in the hallway to stumble out and discover her leading Sloan Gallagher into her bedroom.

Because, like it or not, it was the only place she could think to put him.

There were six bedrooms—her mother's, Celie's, Sara's, the one that Lizzie and Daisy shared, Jack's and, at the very end of the hall, her own. It wasn't large, and the minute they were both inside, her room shrank the way the entry hall had. Sloan looked around interestedly, his eyes lighting on the one big bed.

"I'm sleeping on the sofa," she said.

"Don't be stupid."

"I'm being sensible." She started to strip off the covers, to put clean sheets on the bed.

"Just leave 'em." He crossed the room and pulled the quilt out of her hands. He was so close she could feel the warmth of his breath on her cheek.

Abruptly Polly let go of the quilt. "Fine. I'll get you a clean towel. The bathroom is right next door. It's the only one on this floor and everyone uses it. It's not what you're used to, I'm sure."

"It's fine."

"Do you have a bag out in your truck?" she asked, and when he nodded, she said, "I'll get it. You stay here." Leaving him in her room, she hurried back downstairs, grabbed her jacket off the hook, stuffed her feet into her boots and let herself out into the snowy February night.

It had just gone two. Bad timing, as the Dew Drop was just closing.

Pulling up the hood of her jacket, Polly ducked her head and trudged up the hill, hoping that she wouldn't run into anyone she knew.

She was almost to Alice's when a voice hailed her. "Pol'? That you?"

Within seconds a pair of longer legs than hers caught up with her. It was Jace. "Hey. What're you doin' up?"

"I, er, had to get something at Alice's. No time before. I've been dealing with reporters and film crews and groupies all day. I've never seen so many groupies."

Jace grinned. "They're somethin', aren't they? Got a couple of 'em stayin' with me."

"I heard."

Celie had been appalled, but whether she was more disgusted by the women or by Jace's offering them a place to stay, Polly hadn't figured out.

They had reached the corner by Alice's, and Polly could see a white pickup parked out front. It was pretty battered and

GET 2 BOOKS FREE!

®

To get your 2 free books, affix this peel-off sticker to the reply card and mail it today!

MIRA® Books, The Brightest Stars in Fiction, presents

The Best of the Best™

Superb collector's editions of the very best novels by some of today's best-known authors!

★ **FREE BOOKS!** To introduce you to "The Best of the Best" we'll send you 2 books ABSOLUTELY FREE!

★ **FREE GIFT!** Get an exciting mystery gift FREE!

★ **BEST BOOKS!** "The Best of the Best" brings you the best books by some of today's most popular authors!

GET 2

HOW TO GET YOUR 2 FREE BOOKS AND FREE GIFT!

1. Peel off the MIRA sticker on the front cover. Place it in the space provided at right. This automatically entitles you to receive two free books and an exciting mystery gift.

2. Send back this card and you'll get 2 "The Best of the Best™" novels. These books have a combined cover price of $11.00 or more in the U.S. and $13.00 or more in Canada, but they are yours to keep absolutely FREE!

3. There's no catch. You're under no obligation to buy anything. We charge nothing – ZERO – for your first shipment. And you don't have to make any minimum number of purchases – not even one!

4. We call this line "The Best of the Best" because each month you'll receive the best books by some of today's hottest authors. These authors show up time and time again on all the major bestseller lists and their books sell out as soon as they hit the stores. You'll like the convenience of getting them delivered to your home at our special discount prices . . . and you'll love your *Heart to Heart* subscriber newsletter featuring author news, horoscopes, recipes, book reviews and much more!

5. We hope that after receiving your free books you'll want to remain a subscriber. But the choice is yours – to continue or cancel, anytime at all! So why not take us up on our invitation, with no risk of any kind. You'll be glad you did!

6. And remember...we'll send you a mystery gift ABSOLUTELY FREE just for giving "The Best of the Best" a try.

SPECIAL FREE GIFT!

We'll send you a fabulous surprise gift, absolutely FREE, simply for accepting our no-risk offer!

Visit us online at
www.mirabooks.com

BOOKS FREE!

Hurry!

Return this card promptly to GET 2 FREE BOOKS & A FREE GIFT!

The Best of the Best ™

▼ DETACH AND MAIL CARD TODAY! ▼

Affix
peel-off
MIRA
sticker here

YES! Please send me the 2 FREE "The Best of the Best" novels and FREE gift for which I qualify. I understand that I am under no obligation to purchase anything further, as explained on the opposite page.

(P-BB3-01)

385 MDL C6PQ   185 MDL C6PP

NAME   (PLEASE PRINT CLEARLY)

ADDRESS

APT.#   CITY

STATE/ PROV.   ZIP/POSTAL CODE

Offer limited to one per household and not valid to current subscribers of "The Best of the Best." All orders subject to approval. Books received may vary.
©1995 MIRA BOOKS

The Best of the Best™ — Here's How it Works:

Accepting your 2 free books and gift places you under no obligation to buy anything. You may keep the books and gift and return the shipping statement marked "cancel." If you do not cancel, about a month later we will send you 4 additional novels and bill you just $4.24 each in the U.S., or $4.74 each in Canada, plus 25¢ shipping & handling per book and applicable taxes if any.* That's the complete price and — compared to cover prices of $5.50 or more each in the U.S. and $6.50 or more each in Canada — it's quite a bargain! You may cancel at any time, but if you choose to continue, every month we'll send you 4 more books, which you may either purchase at the discount price or return to us and cancel your subscription.

*Terms and prices subject to change without notice. Sales tax applicable in N.Y. Canadian residents will be charged applicable provincial taxes and GST.

BUSINESS REPLY MAIL
FIRST-CLASS MAIL   PERMIT NO. 717   BUFFALO, NY

POSTAGE WILL BE PAID BY ADDRESSEE

THE BEST OF THE BEST
3010 WALDEN AVE
PO BOX 1867
BUFFALO NY 14240-9952

NO POSTAGE
NECESSARY
IF MAILED
IN THE
UNITED STATES

If offer card is missing write to: The Best of the Best, 3010 Walden Ave., P.O. Box 1867, Buffalo, NY 14240-1867 nondescript, a regular ranch truck with Montana plates, but not local ones. She was sure it was Sloan's.

But she couldn't figure out what she was going to say to explain why she was getting into it when Jace said, "Want me to move Gallagher's truck?"

"What!"

Jace dipped his head in the direction of the pickup. "I could put it in Artie's garage."

"How do you know—I mean, what makes you think that's Sloan Gallagher's truck?"

"I saw him get out of it. I was just headin' down to the Dew Drop when he was headin' down to your place."

There was clearly no way to deny it had been Sloan. "Did anyone else see him?"

"Don't think so." He grinned wryly. "Only damn fools or cowboys would be out on a night like this."

"And you are…?"

Jace's laugh was rueful. "Both? One of the girls stayin' at Artie's was gettin' drunk an' flirtin' with a couple of guys she'd have regretted in the morning," he explained. "So I kinda cut in an' took her home. I figured she'd just go to sleep and she'd be better off, y'know? But when we got there, she sorta thought we'd be doin' somethin' else and—" he grimaced and scuffed the toe of his boot in the snow "—I didn't figure that was such a good idea, so I left again."

Which explained, too, why he'd been heading to the Dew Drop thirty minutes or so before closing. Polly looked at him, impressed. It was hard to tell in the dim pink light of the low cloud cover and snowfall, but it almost seemed as if Jace Tucker was blushing.

"You rescued another damsel in distress?" After all, he'd rescued Sara just the week before.

"Cripes, don't go sayin' that." He scowled at her. "It's no big deal," he muttered. "Do you want me movin' Gallagher's truck or not."

"That would be great."

"How's he gonna get around?"

"He isn't."

"Where's he stayin'?"

"With us."

"Swell." Jace kicked at the snow packed against the curb.

Polly unlocked the truck and took out the black duffel bag on the front seat. Shouldering the bag, she shut the door and held out the keys. "If you wouldn't mind?"

"I didn't know he was staying with you," Jace said.

"Is it a problem?"

"Oh, hell, no. Why would it be a problem?" Jace snatched the keys out of her hand and jumped in the truck. He flicked on the engine, spun the tires in the snow and shot away.

What on earth, Polly wondered, was *that* all about?

Since he was fourteen years old, Sloan had fantasized about being in Polly's bedroom.

He'd imagined what it would be like—how he'd kiss her the way he'd seen Lew kiss her—only better, how he'd ease her clothes effortlessly off her with no adolescent fumbling, how he'd know precisely what to do to make her melt in his arms. And how he wouldn't disgrace himself by doing something stupid.

For years he'd thought the stupidest thing he could do would be to get so excited at actually being here that he would turn into the poster boy for Premature Ejaculations R Us.

He was wrong.

He shrugged off his jeans and his shirt, sat down on the bed to wait for her to come back with his duffel bag, and then he did something even stupider than he had ever imagined.

He fell asleep.

All the way back to the house Polly rehearsed. Cheerful smile. *Here's your duffel bag. I'll just get you a clean towel. Remember, there's only one bathroom upstairs, so be sure to lock the door or you might regret it. I'll see you in the morning. Good night.*

Or a variation thereof.

Actually she rehearsed six or seven variations as she slip-slid her way back down the hill, clutching his duffel bag against her chest. But even as she said the words, she couldn't believe it. It was the middle of the night, after all. Maybe she had just dreamed she'd led America's heart throb, Sloan Gallagher, up to her bed.

But when she got back, the first thing she saw were his boots by the door. So she practiced her lines one more time as she climbed the stairs.

Here's your duffel bag. I'll just get you a clean towel...

When she got to her bedroom door, she stopped and tapped. He didn't answer.

She tapped again, a little more forcefully. No response. She glanced around to see if he might be in the bathroom, but the door was ajar and the night-light was on. He wasn't in there. So, knocking one more time and getting no answer, she pushed the door open.

He was sprawled facedown, asleep on her bed.

She should have tiptoed out. But she couldn't do it. He had spied on her a long time ago. Turnabout was fair play, she told herself. Besides, she wasn't really spying, she was just looking—and after all he was in her room!

So she stepped quietly into the room and pulled the door shut behind her. He didn't stir. He was lying on top of the quilt, clad in a pair of boxer shorts and a white T-shirt. His head was pillowed on one arm, while the other was flung out across the bed. His dark hair was tousled and brushed his forehead. Over a day's worth of dark whiskers shaded his jaw and chin. Another man would look seedy and unkempt. Sloan Gallagher just looked sexy as hell.

Polly's fingers itched to touch his soft thick hair. They wanted to rub down the line of his jaw, smooth one way and sandpapery rough with stubble on the way up. Involuntarily she pursed her lips as if they, too, wanted to touch.

Suddenly aware of the direction of her inclinations, Polly pressed them together in a hard, thin line between her teeth. *Enough!*

It was more than enough. And she had no doubt that if he didn't bother to shave until after the auction, the women wouldn't mind a bit. They would love it.

They loved him.

Hadn't they already come from countless places near and far—just for the chance to see him? Surely all of them weren't intending to bid. Most, she was willing to bet, knew the price would skyrocket right out of their league in the first few seconds.

But they came, anyway.

She ought, Polly thought with a wry smile, to charge admission to the auction. And, for that matter, to her bedroom. For five dollars come and watch Sloan Gallagher sleep!

She could probably raise a few more hundreds or thousands of dollars for Maddie's mortgage payment just by doing that, she thought and stifled a laugh. The sound made him draw his brows down, and Polly froze, afraid of waking him. But then he sighed, fisted his fingers around a handful of quilt and slept on. Polly stepped back warily, still afraid he might wake, not wanting him to find her staring down at him.

Here's your duffel bag. I've brought you a clean towel.... Somehow she couldn't make it sound convincing.

She started to leave, but couldn't—not without covering him up. It was hardwired into her, apparently. Over the years she had covered up too many sleeping children—not to mention drunken cowboys—to let anybody lie uncovered in the middle of winter—even if he had been named the sexiest man in Hollywood three years running.

Sloan sighed again and smiled slightly when the warmth of the quilt settled over him.

"C'mere," he murmured, still smiling, eyes closed.

I'll bet you say that to all the girls, Polly thought, for just an instant more tempted than she would have thought possible.

Then sanity prevailed, and she grabbed her robe and nightgown and hurried out the door.

When the alarm clock buzzed in her ear, Celie was more than half tempted to switch it off, pull the pillow over her head and go back to a very lovely dream—a Sloan Gallagher dream—the first she remembered having since she'd learned he was actually coming to Elmer for the auction. She'd been kissing him. Better still, he'd been kissing her. They'd been standing right there in the middle of Gilliam's Hardware Store with their arms around each other—and when Celie had opened her eyes long enough to look past Sloan's ear, she'd seen Jace Tucker staring at them in openmouthed astonishment.

That had made the dream all that much better!

She did not want to get up and go to the hardware store and deal with Jace Tucker on her own again this morning. She didn't want to watch him flirt with all the groupies. The man had no discrimination. No taste!

But if she didn't get up, she would have to see his knowing smirk later. He would believe she didn't come in because she was avoiding him. Doubtless he would drop by to find out what had happened to her. And he would probably even bring a couple of those floozies with him.

She couldn't believe he was letting them stay in Artie's house!

But Artie had thought it was a good idea. "Hell, why not let 'em stay," he'd said when she'd called him to complain. "Good for the town. They stay there, they spend money there. Eat at the Bee, drink at the Dew Drop. Maybe even get their hair done," he suggested.

"I don't think so," Celie said. She would dye their hair puce if they came in. "Well, I hope you have a house standing to come back to," she'd said sharply.

Of course she regretted her words the minute she'd hung up.

Artie was ill. He needed calm and rest and cheerful thoughts. He didn't need her growling at him and giving him reasons to worry. So she'd called back and told him she was sure everything would be fine, that she'd just been working hard and was a little out of sorts.

"You shouldn't oughta work so hard," Artie had said. "You let Jace handle things. He'll take care of you."

Over my dead body, Celie thought. If anything was capable of getting her out of bed and moving this morning, leaving behind a perfectly wonderful Sloan Gallagher dream, it was the notion that if she didn't turn up, Jace would start thinking he was now supposed to "take care of her."

The bathroom door was shut and the shower was running. Polly must be getting an early start. Celie sighed and headed downstairs to start the coffee and use the bathroom down there. When Polly was finished, she'd take her own shower.

She put on the coffee and stood staring out at the snow-covered town and the stirring of people—strangers, mostly—already moving on the normally deserted streets of Elmer. They were people who had come from all over because of Sloan. People who had come to see him, to ogle him, to bid on him.

People who were doing something—unlike Celie who had spent her life dreaming.

"And what's wrong with that?" she asked herself.

Dreams were good. Graduation speakers always talked about dreams, didn't they? They told you not to lose your ability to dream, to hope, to plan.

For what?

Celie poured herself a cup of coffee and stood staring out the window and thought about her dreams and her plans. She had dreams, but somehow the plans had vanished years ago. She had dreams, but she didn't have hope anymore. She had lots of fantasies of her perfect man—a man like Sloan—but that was all she had.

Even that damned Jace Tucker had more than she did! He had a woman he wanted. A real woman.

Sloan Gallagher's real, she reminded herself. And he'd be here tomorrow. The embodiment of her dreams was coming to Elmer. For a brief period—in real life—he would be available.

And then he would be gone.

And Celie would be left behind, knowing that she'd had a chance—one brief opportunity to make her fantasy into reality—and that she hadn't taken it.

"What am I going to do?" she murmured, wrapping her fingers around the mug, breathing in the steamy-hot coffee smell.

Sid the cat nudged at her ankles, demanding breakfast. She reached down and scratched him behind the ears. Then she opened a tin of food and gave him some. Sid purred his appreciation. Celie watched him eat and wished that life were as simple for her as it was for him. Sid didn't care about anything but his next meal.

Maybe she should just take life meal by meal. She smiled. "Ah, Sid. You inspiration, you."

Sid, apparently thinking a treat might be in the offing, butted her softly with his head.

"Not now," she told him. "Tonight."

"Mrowww," Sid complained.

But Celie, glancing at the wall clock, knew she didn't have time to listen to his complaints. She had to get a quick shower, get dressed and get over to Artie's where she could do battle with Jace Tucker for another day.

Battle by battle, she told herself as, clutching her coffee mug, she climbed the stairs. Groupie by groupie. She would just take the day as it came.

The bathroom door was still closed. "Come on, Pol'," she said. "You've hogged the bathroom long enough."

In a one-and-a-half-bath household you didn't take more time than necessary, and if you really wanted privacy you hooked the latch at the top of the door. Otherwise you simply got used to being burst in upon. It was Polly's own fault, Celie thought, for taking so long.

She pushed the door open—and stared into the mirror image of Sloan Gallagher's shocked, half-shaved face.

For a split second neither moved, their eyes locked in mutual astonishment. Then Celie's hand jerked, the coffee flew everywhere.

Sloan leaped to avoid it.

And that was when she noticed that he wasn't even wearing a towel!

Chapter 12

Dying didn't seem to be an option.

Too bad, Celie thought, as it was definitely the best solution.

Hyperventilation didn't have much to recommend it, either. It made her dizzy and light-headed and caused her to do things that a sane Cecilia Margaret O'Meara would never in a million years do—like grab a towel, kneel down and begin patting Sloan Gallagher's naked coffee-splattered body, gabbling all the while, "I'm sorry! I'm so sorry! I didn't mean—"

"I'm sure you didn't," he replied in that whiskey-rough voice that nearly sent her toppling right over. He had reached for a towel, too, and was slinging it around his waist and tucking it in even as he spoke.

A very good thing, too, Celie thought, because by kneeling to mop up the coffee, she had managed to put herself basically on eye level with, er, it…er…*him.*

She could only stare—until the terry cloth towel intervened and her gaze was shielded from Sloan Gallagher's very, um, impressive masculinity. Even then her heart was going like a piston in her chest, and the sudden surge of hormonal activity she was experiencing seemed to have robbed her of sensible thought all together.

"Are you all right?" He sounded concerned, but at the same time almost amused. As if he often had women throwing themselves at his feet.

Which, she thought, mortified, he probably did.

"Of...of course." That the words came out hoarsely mortified her further. Celie took a couple of desperate swipes with the towel at the little puddles of coffee, then giving up, she tried to struggle to her feet and tripped over her robe.

A hand came down to grasp her arm, and effortlessly, it seemed, hauled her upright.

Her knees felt like pudding. She clutched the towel rack to stop them quivering and tried to get a grip. But one look showed her that now she was right on eye level with the pulse that beat at the base of his throat.

Desperately she cleared hers. "S-sorry," she muttered, averting her gaze fast, before she did something totally unseemly, like lean forward and press her lips to the spot or start licking the coffee droplets off his chest. She shut her eyes as a shudder overcame her.

"You sure you're okay? You're shaking."

"I'm f-f-f-f-ine. *Fine!*" God, she had to stop this! "Are...are you?"

"I'm okay," he said easily, rubbing a hand towel over his chest, drying his shoulders, drying himself off. "I should've locked the door."

"I shouldn't have barged in. I thought you were Polly." She was talking to the wall now, unable to even look at him.

"I'm not Polly," he said gravely, but still with a hint of amusement in his tone. "I'm Sloan Gallagher." As if she didn't know!

But then Celie realized that he had introduced himself because he expected her to do likewise. She wondered if she dared use an assumed name. Probably not. She took a desperate, steadying breath. She pasted on what she hoped was a polite smile but which was probably a rictus of horror.

"I'm Celie O'Meara. Polly's sister." She dared to flick one

quick glance his way in the vain hope that she would see recognition in his face—that somehow he would betray an awareness that at last he'd met his one true love.

"Hey, nice to meet you, Celie," he said and held out his hand.

She took it and waited for electricity to arc between them. Nothing happened. His hand was large and warm and strong—and damp.

There was no electricity. Only coffee.

"Look," Celie said desperately, dragging her hand out of his grasp. "I'll just get out of here and let you have another shower to wash the coffee off. I'm really sorry. I...I need to talk to Polly."

She bent and snatched the mug off the floor, then backed hastily out of the room and banged the door shut after her.

Polly had fallen asleep on the sofa wondering how she was going to tell her family that Sloan Gallagher was sleeping in her bed.

A thousand scenarios had passed through her mind. None of them had worked. She'd tossed and turned, fretted and worried. What would Celie do? What would Joyce think? What about the kids? She didn't like any of the answers she came up with. Finally, somewhere near four in the morning, she fell into an exhausted sleep.

By the time she woke up, she didn't have to figure out how to tell them.

Everyone knew.

"Hi," Jack said cheerfully when she staggered into the kitchen feeling like death and, she was sure, resembling it, as well. "Want some pancakes?"

Polly shook her head, shutting her eyes against the sight of Jack's cheery face. "No. Just coffee. Give me coffee." A mug miraculously touched her hand. She grasped it gratefully, brought it up to her lips and breathed deeply. "Ahhhh. Thanks."

"You're welcome." The voice was gruff, masculine, entirely out of place and way too familiar at the same time.

Polly's eyes snapped open as Sloan's hand wrapped hers, steadying the mug before she dropped it.

He smiled a little wryly. "Been there, done that."

"What?"

"Your sister already dropped hers this morning."

So he'd met Celie already. Polly groaned. "Oh, dear."

"Your mother dropped her toast. One of your daughters dropped her day planner."

Guess which, Polly thought.

"Another one dropped her backpack."

"Lizzie," Jack chipped in.

"I thought she said her name was Artemis." Sloan shrugged as if he'd misunderstood, then grinned. "The youngest one didn't drop anything—other than her jaw."

"Neither did I," Jack said. He held out his plate to Sloan. "Can I have some more pancakes?"

"May I," Polly corrected automatically.

"Sure," Sloan said. "Pull up a chair and sit down."

"No, I mean—" Dazed, Polly just stared at him. Where was her family—besides Jack? And why was Sloan Gallagher cooking breakfast in her kitchen? She had way too many questions. She glanced at the clock and saw that it was almost nine.

"Yikes!" She had to meet Calvin, the auctioneer, at nine-thirty to go over the final list of cowboys and other items.

"Sit," Sloan said from where he was supervising another griddleful of pancakes. "These are almost ready."

Polly shook her head. "No. I've got—I'll just go get dressed." She turned and bolted up the stairs.

The view that met her in the bathroom mirror wasn't encouraging. Ginger hair stood out like a haystack all over her head. Her eyes were bloodshot from lack of sleep. And she had "couch face" from pressing her face into the upholstered pillows. She had no time to wash her hair, so she took a quick shower, then pulled on a pair of jeans and a hunter-green sweater. Quickly she braided her hair into one long plait—the only way, under the circumstances, to show it who was boss—and dabbed on a bit of lipstick in hopes of convincing people she hadn't died during the night.

Finally she stared at herself in the mirror for signs of improvement.

They weren't as great as she had hoped.

But she'd done all she could for herself. Now she had to figure out what to do with Sloan. Not about how to make him presentable. God knew there was no improving on that.

But how was she going to keep him under wraps for twenty-four hours? How was she going to get her family to keep its collective mouth shut about their house guest that long?

For all she knew they had already spread the news far and wide.

It turned out she didn't have to figure anything out.

Sloan had a plan of his own.

"You're just going to march out there and take them all on?" Polly was agog when he blithely announced that he would come with her when she went to meet Calvin. "Do you have any idea what it's like?" she demanded.

"As a matter of fact, I do," he said, amused, putting a plate of pancakes in front of her.

She flushed. Of course he did. He put up with it every day of his life. Which meant that he knew how to handle it far better than she did.

"Fine," she said. "Do what you want to do." She finished up the pancakes, then rinsed off the plate, put it in the dishwasher and went to get her jacket. Sloan grabbed his and stood waiting for her by the door.

"You behave," she warned Jack. "Don't do anything I wouldn't do."

"That's no fun," Jack grumbled.

"I bet it could be," Sloan murmured just loud enough for Polly to hear him as he put on his own coat.

Polly stepped back hard on his foot.

"Ouch!"

She turned and gave him a guileless smile. "Oh, I'm sorry. Did I hurt you?"

His own smile was wry as they stepped out onto the porch. "Not as much as Lew did when he pounded me into the dirt."

"You deserved it."

"No doubt," Sloan said unrepentantly. "But if you think I'm going to apologize, you're out of your mind. That day was the highlight of my life."

Polly wanted to sink through the steps. Every time she recalled that day—at least the part Sloan had played in it—she wanted to crawl under a rock.

"Not mine," she said firmly. "And I wish you'd quit talking about it."

"Afraid I might mention it at the wrong time?"

As far as Polly was concerned *any* time was the wrong time. But all she managed to say was, "Yes," before someone in the street called out, "Look! It's Sloan!"

"There's Sloan Gallagher!"

"It's Sloan!" shrieked a lurking groupie.

The stampede was on.

The last thing Joyce needed that Saturday morning was to drive to Livingston to visit Artie.

She'd taken the day off when they'd picked the date of the auction, sure that Polly would need her help—and that had been before Sloan Gallagher had signed on and Elmer had become the hub of the Western Cultural World.

But Artie had wanted her to come. When she'd tried to leave last night about eleven-thirty, he hadn't wanted to let go of her hand. "You only just got here," he complained.

"I know," she'd said. "But it's snowing, and it's a long drive."

Reluctantly he'd released her, rubbing her fingers between his old rough, gnarled ones before finally relinquishing his hold completely. "You be careful. Drive slow."

Joyce had smiled. "Couldn't possibly do anything else. It's coming down hard."

"Mebbe you oughta stay here." Artie had brightened at the notion.

"I can't. I've got to help Polly tomorrow."

Artie sighed. "Wisht I weren't missin' it. Don't reckon they'll let me out by Sunday."

"No." Joyce had been around the hospital long enough to know how patients with serious heart attacks were handled.

"You get plenty of rest, and I'll give you the whole story on Monday."

"What about tomorrow?"

And so, whether she was helping Polly or not, she had to drive down to see Artie. If she didn't, he would have no one. Everyone else was completely preoccupied with the auction. And since Maudie had died, no one was closer to Artie than her.

"I'll come early," she had told him, so she could get home in time to help. But in fact she didn't feel as badly about abandoning Polly as she had last night—not since she'd turned around in the kitchen this morning and thrown her toast up in the air at the sight of Sloan Gallagher.

That was the first thing she told Artie when she arrived. "Sloan Gallagher's here."

"In the hospital?"

"At our house. In the kitchen." Joyce laughed now as she remembered how he'd managed to catch both pieces of toast in midair and had gravely handed them back to her before he'd said, "Hi. I'm Sloan Gallagher. And you're Polly's mother. I've seen you on television."

She'd told him she'd seen him there, too. "And in movies," she'd said. "We've seen all your movies." But as she'd said it, she hadn't felt as if she were kissing up to him. For America's sexiest heart throb, he seemed surprisingly easy to talk to. She'd asked if he wanted toast or if she could fix him pancakes, and he'd said he would kill for some pancakes, but that he'd be happy to make them himself.

She'd thought he was joking, but when she'd got out the ingredients, he'd stepped in and taken over.

"So he cooked breakfast," she told Artie, grinning, still marveling about it.

"I'll bet Celie liked that." Artie grinned, too.

Joyce frowned. "Celie didn't eat."

"Prob'ly not," Artie said. "Reckon all she did was sit an' stare."

"She didn't do that, either. She came down while he was mixing up the pancakes, and he told her he'd be happy to make her a plateful, but she just shook her head and scooted out the door. Said she had work to do.''

Artie sighed. "Damn fool girl."

"Maybe not," Joyce said. "Maybe she's realized she needs to think about a man she can have, not dream her life away about the one she wants but doesn't dare go after."

Artie was silent for a long moment. He was looking at her, but she didn't think he was really seeing her. Then he seemed to come back from wherever he had been and he reached out and he patted her hand. "That's what I thought, too."

Friday night Sara wrote "Flynn Murray" in her day planner under "appointments" for Saturday lunch.

"I don't see how you could have made a mistake like that," Gregg complained when he called to see what time she was going to meet him at the biology lab. "You know we work in the lab every Saturday afternoon."

"I guess I didn't write it down because of the auction," Sara said. It was true enough. She *hadn't* written it down. "I guess I thought my mother would need my help."

"Your mother has to stop depending on you so much," Gregg said. "Your whole family has to stop taking advantage of you. You don't have time to do errands for them or baby-sit that store just because some old man had a heart attack. You have work to do."

"I know," Sara said.

"If you want to get a place in a good med school you have to have good grades."

"I know."

"And to get a good grade in biology, you need to spend a lot of hours in the lab."

"I know."

"In the long run it's far more important than talking to some reporter. What can a reporter do for your future? Nothing. You have to do it all yourself."

"I know."

"Well then..."

She knew what Gregg expected. He expected her to say

she'd call off her lunch date with Flynn and that she'd meet him at the lab to work. It was what she *should* do.

But somehow, just this once, she couldn't do it. "But I told him I would. And I don't know how to reach him to call it off."

There was a disapproving silence on the other end of the line. And when she didn't offer to try to find out how to contact Flynn Murray, she heard a long-suffering sigh. "You know your grades aren't as good as mine," Gregg said. "It's going to be harder for you to get accepted."

She only had two Bs. "I think I'll be all right."

"Complacency is the enemy of accomplishment," Gregg reminded her.

"I'm not becoming complacent," she said, feeling just a little snappish now. "I'm having one lunch with one man from out of town."

"Suit yourself," Gregg said. "But if you're going to waste your time like this very often, don't expect me to bail you out."

"I wouldn't think of it," Sara said frostily. "Goodbye."

"I'll call you at five," Gregg said. "It's our night to go to the movies." She and Gregg went to a movie the first Saturday of every month. She even had it written in her day planner.

"Suit yourself," she said recklessly. "But I might not be here."

Jace was dead on his feet.

No big surprise. He was beginning to regret he'd ever said those groupies could stay with him at Artie's. They might have come to bid on Sloan, but while they were waiting, they'd apparently decided he was fair game.

He'd gone to the Dew Drop early last evening because their innuendo and calculated touches had done more than suggest that either or both of his house guests wouldn't mind going to bed with him. Singly. Or together.

Jace wasn't a prude. But that sort of thing had never interested him—and lately sex with anyone but Celie interested him less than ever.

So he'd gone to the Dew Drop. And Serena, the redhead,

had come with him. She hadn't stayed with him. She'd drunk far too much and made a play for everything in pants. Colly Bishop had been about to take her up on one of her more suggestive comments when Jace, feeling responsible, had stepped in.

"Time to go," he'd said, taking her by the arm.

Colly had looked disconcerted, but not ready to fight over her, thank God.

"Come on, sweetheart," Jace had said, hauling her out the door and down the street, which turned out to be a mistake because when he got her home, she thought he wanted her to go to bed with him!

It didn't seem tactful to say he didn't. So he got her to her room and told her to wait. Then he'd ducked out, crossed his fingers and hoped she'd fall asleep. She did, but no sooner had she, than Kelsey, the blonde groupie, came to his room. That was when he'd beat a retreat to the Dew Drop until closing.

He'd spotted Sloan Gallagher heading toward Celie's and had downed three whiskeys imagining Celie's reaction to having her heart throb right there in her living room. The last one had still been burning in his gut when the bar closed and he'd run into Polly. His offer to move Gallagher's car was a sly way of getting Polly to tell him, "No thanks," that Gallagher had only dropped by to let her know he was in town.

Jace, like Polly—and the press—had expected him to stay with Gus and Mary. Finding out he was staying at Celie's hadn't done a damn thing for his temper.

Going home and hitting the sack only to toss and turn, thinking about Sloan and Celie was bad enough. Kelsey, the blonde, "sleepwalking" her way into his bed, was the last straw.

He'd pulled on his clothes, yanked on his boots and stomped over to the hardware store where he'd spent what was left of the night in the back room on a damned uncomfortable old sofa.

He gave up at 5:00 a.m., made himself a pot of strong black coffee and sat nursing a god-awful headache and cursing Celie O'Meara.

It was all her fault.

If it weren't for her he wouldn't care who he slept with. If she didn't spring to mind every time he had a sexual thought, he'd be a whole lot happier. He thought of a hundred nasty things to say to her when she came to work, scathing things about her and her dearly beloved Sloan Gallagher. He was on his second hundred when he opened the store and waited for her to turn up.

She was always early, looking annoyed and smug when he turned up.

Today she didn't even come.

Sloan was as good as his word.

He'd said he'd "take care of it," by which he'd meant all the reporters poking their noses into hers and her kids' lives, and he did. The minute they spotted him, they forgot she and the kids existed. The only person who mattered was Sloan.

They surrounded him even before he got to the street, asking questions and demanding attention. The groupies swarmed, too, giggling and shrieking, pressing to get close to him, all talking at once, grabbing at his jacket, reaching out to touch him.

Polly was shoved aside, and all she could think was *Thank God.*

She was surprised he even noticed, but all of a sudden he stopped shaking hands and smiling and began scanning the crowd anxiously. Only when he spotted her, did a rueful smile flicker across his face. He lifted his shoulders, as if to say, *This is the way it is.*

Polly understood.

She took advantage of it, smiling and waggling her fingers to say goodbye, good luck and all that. Then she headed toward the town hall and Calvin, and left Sloan to deal with his fame.

She and Calvin went over the list. She made notes for him about each item—or cowboy. He listened and grinned and shook his head.

"Ain't never sold no fellers on the hoof before," he said. "Pretty amazin'."

"This whole thing has been pretty amazing," Polly agreed.

"This all then?" Calvin looked over the list one last time.

"I think so. They're a pretty good group."

"Most," Calvin agreed. "Except Logan Reese."

Maddie's hired hand. "Maddie bullied him into it," Polly said. "I think she thought it would help him get reestablished in the community."

Calvin snorted. "Don't even know why he come back. Ain't gonna be no bidders for the likes of him."

Polly was afraid of that, too. Logan had come back to the valley only two months ago after having served time in Deer Lodge for setting fire to Mill Chamberlain's horse barn.

"He's paid his debt," she said. "Besides he told Maddie he came back to prove his innocence."

"Tell that to the jury," Calvin said gruffly. The jury that had convicted him. They'd heard testimony about motive and proximity, both of which existed. Most damning of all, they'd seen the cigarette lighter found at the scene, a lighter that Logan's best friend, Deputy Spence Adkins had testified belonged to Logan and had been his father's before him.

"Don't bring it up," Polly said. "Don't bring any of it up. He's a cowboy up for auction, that's all. He's a hard worker, you know that. He always has been." Logan had worked for her dad for a couple of years.

"Mebbe so. But won't none of 'em have 'im," Calvin said flatly.

"Maybe one of the groupies will buy him," Polly suggested a little desperately.

Calvin folded his arms across his chest. "And good luck to 'er."

And to Logan, Polly thought. She, personally, believed Maddie was being overly optimistic, pushing Logan into this, hoping to get someone to take a chance on him.

"Well, let's hope," she said now.

He left and Polly stayed where she was. She took one last look at the list, then folded it and put it away. Then she sighed and stretched and basked in the silence.

There was no one else in the town hall. Just her. It was wonderful. She got up and went to the window. There seemed to be a horde of people moving toward the Busy Bee. That must be where Sloan was.

Poor Sloan.

Jack didn't take his mother seriously when she said, "Don't do anything I wouldn't do."

There were way too many things you wouldn't do if you were a mom. All the fun, stupid, really messy things a guy could think of he'd just have to forget if he was going to do only what his mom did.

What kind of life was that?

Besides his mom was really pretty good as far as moms went. Some of his friends' moms were a lot worse. It was hard on her, he figured, because his dad was dead and she had to do the dad stuff, too. She wasn't bad at that, either. At least, he didn't think she was.

Jack didn't remember his dad real well. Except, riding on his shoulders and being taller than everybody else. Jack remembered that. And he remembered his dad's laugh. And he remembered wrestling on the floor with him.

Moms didn't wrestle.

And even when they tried not to, they worried.

Jack didn't want her to worry. But he wasn't going to stop being a boy, either. So he had worked out his own rules for getting along. Basically he tried to avoid the things that would get him killed. He tried not to mention the ones that would make his mom nuts. And he did the other stuff because how was a guy supposed to learn if he didn't try things out.

What Jack was learning this afternoon was that it wasn't as easy to wrangle bunnies as it was cattle.

Maybe stampeding cattle were tricky to control. He wouldn't know about that. But the times he'd gone with his grandpa to drive the herd to the summer range, it had been easy as pie. Herding rabbits wasn't.

Rabbits didn't like being herded. They didn't want to be in a group. They bolted and darted and ran all over the yard, which meant Jack was bolting and darting and running all over the yard, too. He'd given up trying to herd them, now he was just trying to catch them and put them back in their cages.

"Hi, there."

A woman's voice made him jerk around. She was tall and blonde and almost as pretty as his teacher, Ms. Stanton, who was just about the prettiest person Jack had ever seen.

"Hi," he said, out of breath and gasping. Then a black rabbit darted past and he flung himself after it.

"You must be Jack."

He grabbed the rabbit around the middle and hauled it against his chest, then stood up. "Yeah."

She beamed. "I thought so. Sloan mentioned you."

"Sloan? Gallagher?"

"Yes. We're very close. Is he here?" The lady looked past him toward the house.

"Nope. He left with my mom. But then he got mobbed and I don't know where he is. You could walk around and look for the mob," he suggested.

"I don't think so," she said, still smiling at him. "I don't like crowds. Is he staying with you?"

"Yeah."

She studied the house again. "It looks nice and big. You must have lots of room."

"Not so much," Jack put the black rabbit back in its cage and started going after the others. "There's lot of us."

"But if you have room for Sloan..."

"He slept in my mom's bed."

The blonde lady pressed her lips together. "I see." She wasn't smiling now.

"Could you maybe try and catch one?" Jack suggested as three rabbits hopped in her direction. He had two cornered, but then he tried to grab one and both of them got away.

"Damn! Er, sorry." Jack flushed. Swearing in front of company was something his mother wouldn't do, and she'd have his head if she knew he'd done it. But if she wasn't going to help, he wished she'd just leave. He had to get these rabbits back in their cages. He dived for another one and, thank heaven, caught it. But as he stood up a shadow fell across him.

Oh, no.

But it wasn't his mom, thank goodness.

"M-mmm... Hi, Jace!" he beamed, relieved at the sight of Jace Tucker standing by the fence. "Wanta help me catch these rabbits?"

Jace didn't look as if he wanted to do anything of the sort. "Not now. I need to talk to your aunt."

"She's cuttin' hair," Jack said. "Can'tcha help me catch just a couple? My mom's gonna be home soon. Please. Aunt Celie's busy anyhow, fixin' Ina Grace Leibold's hair. You don't wanta interrupt that." No one wanted to interrupt Ina Grace.

Jace hesitated, then sighed. "Fine. Let's catch your rabbits."

"I'll help," said the blonde woman. She gave Jace lots more of a smile than she'd given Jack.

Jace blinked, then stared. "You're—" He stopped.

"Tamara Lynd. Pleased to meet you, Jace." She held out her hand.

And that was when Jack figured out who she was. He'd seen her in a movie. She'd been Sloan's girl. They'd kissed right at the end. And then she'd pushed him into a swimming pool.

"Jace," Jack said impatiently because Jace had shaken hands with Tamara Lynd and he hadn't let go. "You gonna help me catch these rabbits or not?"

"Uh, yeah. Sure." But Jace was still staring at the actress. "You come for the auction, Ms., um, Lynd?"

"Tamara, please." She gave one of those tinkly bell kind of laughs. "And yes, I guess I did. Sloan talked a lot about it when we were together in Key West. We're very close."

"Jace!" Jack implored.

"Right. Right." Jace still looked a little dazed. Jack was disgusted. Tamara Lynd wasn't *that* beautiful.

"I'll herd 'em toward you, an' you catch 'em," Jack directed. He started moving, shooing rabbits out of hiding places in the snow and beneath the steps and under the woodpile. "Here comes!"

He counted on Jace's instincts to get him moving and he

wasn't disappointed. As he flushed two of the rabbits out, they skittered toward Jace. He dived for one.

So did Tamara Lynd.

They landed together in a heap in the snow, Tamara shrieking and Jace laughing. "Got one!" Jace said, clasping a rabbit.

Tamara Lynd kissed him.

The shrieking in the yard distracted Celie.

Not that she hadn't been basically distracted all day. She'd tried to behave normally, to act as if nothing had happened, as if her whole fantasy life hadn't passed before her eyes as she'd stared at naked bits of Sloan Gallagher this very morning!

But she had. And what was worse, she'd acted like an idiot after.

The woman she knew she was inside—or outside or *somewhere* in her being, the one who was kind and loving and tender and sane—vanished and had been replaced by a blithering idiot who tossed coffee mugs.

She had wanted to run as far and fast as she could. So she had. She'd run to the Spa. The day's worth of appointments, of hair to wash and cut and perm and style, had been her salvation. She could do that without even thinking. And she had. Even though every woman who came in wanted to talk about Sloan Gallagher.

She thanked God she hadn't had to work at Artie's today. She couldn't have faced Jace Tucker's knowing gaze and smart mouth.

Her panic had mortified her, made her aware of how silly she had been. He was only a man—a *naked* man, yes, a *gorgeous* man, certainly—but a man like any other.

She'd idealized him beyond all good sense. And she had humiliated herself by her reactions.

It was time to get a grip. It was time to face the facts.

She'd had the day to do it.

She hoped she would develop some semblance of sanity by the time Polly and Sloan—*Sloan,* she made herself say it again in her head casually, matter-of-factly—came back this evening.

By then, she assured herself, she would act like an adult.

She would smile, she would be polite. She would meet his gaze and not drop things and blush.

Yet when she heard the shrieks, her resolve wobbled and her fingers trembled.

"Careful there!" Ina Grace Leibold snapped. Ina Grace didn't have a lot of hair, and what she had she expected Celie to take exceptionally good care of.

"Yes, yes." But Celie had to put the scissors down for just a minute. She had to close her eyes and draw a deep breath and tell herself that she could do this.

The shrieks continued. Celie heard laughter.

"Is that Sloan Gallagher coming?" Ina Grace asked. She preened in a futile attempt to look gorgeous.

"It must be," Celie said, trembling a little. "I'll just look." She wiped her palms on the sides of her jeans and went to look out the window. She saw Jack chasing rabbits, whooping and shrieking as he went. And she saw two people, a man and a woman, rolling and laughing in the snow.

Sloan? And who else?

Celie stared intently as they staggered up, both still laughing. And Celie saw that it wasn't Sloan at all, but Jace Tucker who stood there holding a rabbit and grinning like a fool.

And then the woman—*My God, was that Tamara Lynd?*—leaned forward and kissed him!

Chapter 13

It was the coolest sleepover Jack had ever had.

Sloan Gallagher was in his bottom bunk!

"You still awake?" Jack whispered loud enough for Sloan to hear if he was, but not loud enough to bring in his mother telling him to quiet down and go to sleep. Jack didn't want to sleep. At all.

"Still awake," Sloan confirmed.

Jack rolled over and hung his head down so he could peer through the darkness at the man in the bunk below. "I never seen so many people as followed you around today. Is it like that all the time?"

"Not always. But sometimes it get a little hairy."

"Lotsa girls."

"Yep."

"Too many girls." In Jack's opinion. He knew that someday he was supposed to think that having girls paw at you was a good deal, but he couldn't quite imagine it. As far as he could see they tattled on you when you were doing things that weren't any of their business anyway. And if they weren't tattling they were bossing or just getting in the way.

"More than I need, that's for sure."

"You could get rid of 'em."

"Oh, yeah? How?"

"Easy. Get married."

"Think that would work?" Sloan sounded intrigued by the possibility.

"Oh, yeah," Jack said, hauling himself back up onto the bed and flopping down on his back. "There were lotsa girls who liked Gus. But when he got married they went away. Gus says it's lots more restful."

Sloan laughed. "Hard to imagine Gus enjoying restful."

"He's not so bad. He still likes to do dumb stuff," Jack said. "Like ridin' broncs for fun. An' him an' me go four-wheelin' sometimes. Girls don't do that so they don't bother you."

"But if I got married, I'd have one girl around all the time."

"Yeah, but she'd be an okay girl."

"You think there are some?"

"Sure. My mom's an okay girl. So's Mary. An' Mrs. Nichols at my school. She's my friend Mark's mom. I don't know about that Tammy person," Jack added doubtfully.

"What Tammy person?"

"I forget. Tammy Somethin'. She said she knew you. She's an actress. She pushed you in a swimming pool."

"Tamara Lynd?"

"Yeah. Her. Not so sure about her."

The bed creaked as if Sloan had sat up. "She's here?"

Jack leaned down again. "Yep. She came by this afternoon lookin' for you."

Sloan didn't say anything to that.

Jack had thought he might say, "Oh, good!" and he'd hoped he might say, "Oh, hell." But he didn't say a word.

"Is she, like, your girlfriend?" Jack asked after the silence continued.

"No." It was flat and firm. There wasn't much question about how Sloan felt about that.

Jack was relieved. "I think she'd like to be."

"Not likely."

"She's gonna bid on you."

The grunt became a groan.

"She said she was gonna win you."

"I bloody well hope not," Sloan muttered.

"Who do you want to win you?"

Sloan didn't answer right away. "I don't know who's bidding, do I?" he said at last.

"Guess not. Guess you'll just have to wait and see. That would be terrible. I'd die if Mandy Kramer bid on me! Yuck!"

"Who's Mandy Kramer?" Sloan asked with a smile.

"A girl in my class. She sits behind me and she pokes me with her pencil when I put my elbow on her desk, and she kicks my chair when I tip back. She made me tip over once an' the teacher yelled at me!" Jack still felt indignant at the injustice every time he thought about it. He sat up and settled back against his pillows with his arms crossed over his chest.

"That happens sometimes." Sloan said.

"Did you ever get in trouble in school?"

"Oh, yeah."

"Lots?" Jack didn't get in trouble lots, but he had been known to talk maybe a little too much. And sometimes he forgot not to punch his friend Randy when they were standing in line.

"Now and then," Sloan said easily. "All guys do."

"That's what I tell my mom."

"Does she believe you?"

"I think so. She says my dad used to sometimes. She says he was a cut-up." Jack smiled when he thought about things she said his dad had done. "She tells me some stuff, an' Sara tells me things he told her. I don't...I don't remember him much."

"I do."

Jack sat up straight. Then he flipped around and hung down again so he could stare at Sloan in the darkness. "You knew my dad?"

"I lived at Maddie's with him the first year I was there."

"Whoa. Really? Did you like him? Was he cool? Was he a cut-up?"

"He was funny," Sloan said. "Sometimes. He was a good guy. And, yeah, I liked him. He always had a good word for everybody."

"He didn't, like, ever get in fights?" It was kind of hard to live up to that, Jack thought.

Sloan smiled. "Oh, he fought now and then. He pounded me once."

Jack hung so far over the side he almost fell on his head. "Really? How come?"

"I did something to upset your mother."

"Did you spit?" Jack knew that upset his mother.

"No. I can't tell you what I did. I gave your dad my word that I wouldn't."

"Oh." Jack would have liked to know—especially because, if Sloan still couldn't talk about it, it must've been way worse than spitting. But he understood. A part of him was glad. It meant Sloan could be trusted. After all, he'd made a promise all those years ago and was still keeping it—even though the guy he'd made it to wasn't even around anymore.

That was pretty good. The sort of thing you'd expect from a guy who grew up to be a hero.

Sloan had come back to prove he was a hero.

Well, maybe not a hero, because he was that only in Hollywood terms, but when Gus had called about the auction, Sloan had agreed not just because he genuinely wanted to help Maddie, and not simply because Polly O'Meara was in charge, but because he'd wanted to show the town of Elmer that, in spite of anyone's doubts, he'd done just fine.

What he discovered this morning was that the doubts had never been theirs. They'd been his own.

He'd been a displaced teenager, full of hurt and anger, aching to go home to a family and a life that wasn't there anymore. He'd spurned their overtures of friendship. He'd fought at the drop of a hat. He'd come with a chip on his shoulder. And though Ward and Maddie had succeeded in breaking through his armor and drawing him into the warmth of their love, he hadn't stayed long enough to make friends with many people in the town.

So he'd remembered them feeling about him the way he felt about them.

It didn't take long to realize he'd been wrong.

People remembered him. But they didn't remember him as especially surly or angry or tough. They remembered a dark-haired boy who had just experienced the death of his mother, who was enduring the emotional breakdown of his father, a boy who had seen his family ranch sold at auction, the herd sold, the furnishings carted away. They remembered a boy who was resilient, who was strong, who, as Will Jones had said this morning in an interview they did together, "had been dealt a bad hand and played it as best he could."

The look he'd given Sloan then wasn't one of pity, but of respect and admiration.

Other townspeople and ranchers had done the same. They'd come and shaken his hand and told him they were glad to see him back.

One interviewer implied that they were glad to see him because he'd become a Hollywood star, and for what he could now do for them.

Otis Jamison, the grizzled old rancher he'd been interviewing, had just stared at him.

Otis never hesitated speaking his mind and had once rightly chewed Sloan's ass for leaving a gate open. Later that summer, though, when Ward had sent him to help out at Jamisons', Otis had trusted him to drive a small herd of cattle up to the summer range.

It had been a vote of confidence at a time when Sloan had needed one.

This afternoon Otis had stared unblinking at the interviewer for what seemed like several years, though it was probably not even half a minute. And then he'd shrugged arthritic shoulders and shaken his head.

"My ol' ma always said, you'll find whatever it is you're lookin' for. You want to look for the worst in people, I reckon you'll find it.'' Then he'd turned to Sloan, shaken his hand and clapped him on the arm. "Glad you're home, boy."

Sloan was, too.

He lay now, with his arms folded behind his head, staring up at the bunk where Jack had finally run down and fallen asleep, and was very glad indeed.

And there was a laugh for you, he thought wryly.

He'd come to impress Polly. He'd been hankering to go to bed with Polly.

That, if the truth were known, was the main reason he'd come. When a guy had carried a fantasy with him as long as he had—even after bedding a fair number of the world's most beautiful women—he became a little obsessed with the one that "got away."

Not that he'd ever had her in the first place.

He'd only *wanted* her.

He still did. More than ever.

And yet he was happy just to be here—in Jack's room, in Jack's spare bunk, knowing that Polly was sleeping alone in the bed he'd slept in last night just across the hall.

Of course he'd have been happier to be there with her. But he'd realized first thing this morning that his fantasy and the reality of Polly's life couldn't possibly mix.

She had family everywhere. They obviously even felt comfortable barging unannounced into the bathroom if they thought it was Polly in there.

He expected they'd feel equally at home wandering into her bedroom at any time of the day or night. So, while he would still have enjoyed making love to Polly, he knew it wasn't going to happen here.

But even though his initial hopes had been thwarted, he still found himself enjoying life at the McMasters'. He liked being a part of the swirl of activity, of being one of the gang.

He'd liked making pancakes for her kids this morning. He'd gladly braved the reporters and photographers and groupies, not because he enjoyed all the hoopla, but because it meant he was on the team, that he was giving support, helping Polly get the break she so obviously needed. And he'd liked coming back to her place late that afternoon, shutting the world out and just being accepted as one of the family.

Sloan was used to being welcomed places. Everyone was always glad to see him, to invite him in. It went with being a household name. But it was rare that he—or anyone else—forgot he was a household name while he was there.

Somehow, though, this afternoon, once they'd shut the door on the groupies and the reporters and all the hoopla from the auction, he had simply fit in.

It was Polly who had made it happen. She had treated him with an offhand casualness that allowed him to relax. She wasn't in awe of him. In fact, she treated him more like a pesky younger brother than anything else.

But at least it made her kids and her mother treat him with less reverence and starstruck awe than most people did. Before he knew it, Joyce put him to work, and he sat in the kitchen peeling potatoes and carrots with Daisy, while Polly made a salad and Jack set the table.

When the daughter who was calling herself Artemis—and whom everyone else was calling Lizzie—came in, she'd been a little tongue-tied with him, slanting him awed glances until her mother said, "Lizzie, close your mouth." Then she'd turned to Sloan. "Would you like to be really helpful?"

"Sure."

"Great. Lizzie, get your script and let Sloan go over your lines with you," she'd said to her slack-jawed daughter, and to Sloan she'd said, "You'll do a lot better job than I could."

And so he'd ended up peeling potatoes and listening to Lizzie say her lines in *You Can't Take It With You.*

At first Lizzie had been stiff and awkward, but when he'd challenged her, reading the other parts opposite her, she'd started to get into it, to relax and do a good job.

That was what they were doing when the oldest daughter, Sara, appeared, bringing with her a dark-haired guy she introduced as Flynn.

Everyone had seemed surprised to see him. And Polly had said firmly, "No reporters. I told you that."

"Flynn's not a reporter. He's a friend," Sara had protested.

But Polly had stepped between Flynn and Sloan like a mother hen defending her chick. "*Are* you a friend?" she'd asked Flynn sternly.

He'd grinned. "Oh, yeah."

Polly hadn't looked as if she believed him. She'd looked from him to Sara and back again. Then she'd stepped forward, got right in Flynn's face and said, "If I read one word about whatever happens here this evening, you will regret it for the rest of your life."

Sloan thought Flynn might laugh. He was clearly bigger and stronger than Polly McMaster. But he didn't laugh. In fact his grin faded and he nodded quite solemnly.

"You won't read a word," he vowed.

"You won't breathe a word," she informed him, eye-to-eye.

"I won't," he agreed. Sloan thought Flynn might have to slit a wrist and give her blood to prove it as Polly still stared at him, long and hard. Sloan had never had anyone protect his interests so fiercely. He was amazed. Finally Polly seemed satisfied with what she saw in Flynn's face.

"All right, then," she said. "Jack, set another place."

They had laughed and talked all evening. While the streets of Elmer grew more congested and the time for The Great Montana Cowboy Auction drew nearer and nearer, while poor beleaguered Spence Adkins and a couple of other deputies kept things under control, inside the McMaster house, Polly, her mother, all her kids, her sister, Flynn and Sloan relaxed and enjoyed themselves.

Only the sister, Celie, seemed to feel awkward with him. Several times Sloan tried to smile at her, to tease her a little, hoping she would relax and forget what had happened in the bathroom this morning. But no matter what he said or did, she couldn't seem to look him in the eye. And finally he gave up.

Even so, it turned out to be a great evening. Not the sort he'd originally dreamed of—that had been a marathon of lovemaking with the Polly of his dreams.

But he'd enjoyed this enormously. And when, at the end of it, Polly had told him he could have her bed again, that she would bunk in with Jack, he'd said no, he'd sleep in Jack's room.

And he wasn't even regretting it.

Much.

Lust had never been a part of Sara's vocabulary.

Sex appeal had always been theoretical—an intriguing, but totally elusive abstract construct.

She'd never had trouble keeping her hands off Gregg. She'd never missed a plot point in the monthly movie because she was more interested in what Gregg's hands were doing to her. Because, in fact, Gregg's hands weren't ever doing anything to her—except meeting hers accidentally in the popcorn tub.

She had a timetable with Gregg. They had goals and plans for their engagement and marriage and their future together, and somehow urgency and intimacy had little to do with any of it.

They were in control. In perfect control. Like the sane, sensible people they knew themselves to be. Like everyone, Sara had told her mother flatly one day not long ago, should strive to be.

But that had been yesterday.

Now Sara wanted Flynn.

Sara had never *wanted* another person in her life. She very rarely *wanted* anything. She *planned* for things, thought out her goals and focused on them. Everything with Sara had always been long range.

Not now. Not Flynn.

They'd spent twelve hours together, in town and out driving around so she could show him the area, so she could ostensibly give him background for his article on Sloan Gallagher and the auction. They'd parked to look at the scenery from a place where Sara had told Flynn they could get a good view. But they'd done a little bit more than look at the valley.

In fact, if Flynn hadn't had the presence of mind to stop, to get out of the truck and stand, shoulders heaving, body taut, in knee-deep snow until he cooled down, they would have done more than a little.

Lying in bed now, Sara crushed her pillow against her breasts and wondered at her lack of control. More, though, she wondered how she was going to survive *not* going to bed with him.

She wanted him fiercely, desperately, urgently. Nothing she felt for Gregg could begin to compare to it. The urge to touch Flynn Murray, to run her hands over his body, to learn the secrets of his nakedness was stronger than anything she'd ever felt in her life.

She was hot, aching, just lying here thinking about him.

He'd left tonight about ten when Polly had politely shown him the door. "It's been lovely having you," she'd said in her most determined-mother, it's-time-for-you-to-leave-now tone. "I'm sure you'll want to get an early night so you'll be ready for tomorrow."

Sara had been mortified. "Mother!"

But Flynn had grinned. "Absolutely."

"I could walk a ways with you," Sara had offered.

But Polly, no fool, had said, "I would be obliged, Sara, if you would help me change some bedding."

"I'll see you tomorrow," Flynn had promised.

That was hours from now. *Hours!* Sara ached with the need of him.

She was tired of being alone in her bed.

Jace was alone in his bed.

And thank God for that, he thought. Though he could take a little credit, if he did say so himself. It had been one of his better ideas, inviting Tamara to stay at Artie's.

Serena and Kelsey could hardly believe it when he'd come back this evening with Tamara Lynd in tow. They'd been so excited to talk to her, to listen to her, that they'd followed her all over the house. They'd ignored Jace. Since that had been the general idea, he'd breathed a sigh of relief and left them to it.

He'd driven down to Livingston to see Artie—a better idea than sitting home listening to a trio of tittering women chatter about Sloan Gallagher, while the one woman he was interested in was having dinner—and God knew what else with—with the man himself.

Of course he knew, in that one small sane part of his brain, that Celie would never have *anything else* with Sloan Gallagher. She had a crush on Sloan Gallagher. That was all.

But it hadn't helped to walk into Artie's hospital room and have the old man say, "What? Just you? Where's Celie? Out with Sloan Gallagher?" He'd cackled a bit, then coughed so much Jace had thought he might drop dead right then. He started to get the nurse, but Artie waved him back.

Reluctantly Jace had stayed where he was.

"Just kiddin'," Artie wheezed when the coughing had finally subsided

"Yeah? Well, Gallagher's at her house. He stayed there last night."

"That's what Joyce said," Artie nodded. "Joyce thinks he's the right stuff."

Jace jammed his hands in his pockets and prowled the room. "He's not right for Celie."

Artie watched him, interested. "Got someone better in mind, have you?"

Jace glared out the window at the cars parked in the road. "I'm just sayin' Gallagher's not for her. That's all." He was damned if he was going to go setting himself up as a laughingstock—the guy who couldn't get Celie O'Meara to even look at him.

Artie nodded. "Could be you're right, too."

"I am right," Jace muttered. He pulled his hands out of his pockets and cracked his knuckles.

"You gonna be in the auction?"

"What? As an item? No way. I'll clean up the town hall after it's over," Jace said.

"Celie might bid on you."

Jace had glared at him. "Oh, yeah. Right."

Artie had looked as if he'd be up for discussing the matter, but, thank God, a nurse had come just then.

"Time for your medications now," she'd told him. Then she'd turned to Jace, "It's getting past his bedtime."

"Is not," Artie protested. "You'd think I was some young whippersnapper the way they boss me around," he'd grumbled.

"It is gettin' sort of late," Jace said, and he didn't want Artie probing the Celie issue anymore anyway. "Don't want you overdoing things."

"Like I could," Artie muttered. Then he looked up at Jace. "It'll be all right."

"Sure," Jace had agreed, though he wasn't at all sure what Artie had been talking about.

What would be all right? His health? The hardware store? Jace being hung up on Celie?

There were a whole lot of guys who would laugh at him now, Jace thought grimly.

Here he was, barricaded in Artie's bedroom, a delectable sexy female in every other room of the house, while he prayed that the chair he'd shoved under the doorknob stayed put and that tonight he got a little bit of sleep.

Celie lay there, clutching her pillow Sloan to her breasts, her normally fertile mind a barren plain of disorientation and panic.

She'd eaten dinner at the same table with Sloan Gallagher tonight. He'd gone out of his way to be friendly, to try to put her at her ease, to tease her gently so she would stop being so stiff and awkward around him. He was every bit as kind as she'd imagined he would be. He'd been easy to be with, not at all snobbish. He'd joked with Jack and had been patient with Lizzie. He'd talked horses to Daisy and told Joyce about places he'd traveled.

He was, in reality, everything she'd ever wanted in a man.

What was she going to do?

Sloan Gallagher had slept in her bed.

Polly felt a little like one of the three bears every time she thought about it. The notion made her smile, but mostly she yawned. And then she smiled again, because who'd have thought that tonight he'd be sleeping in a bunk bed in Jack's room?

Sloan Gallagher! In a bottom bunk!

There were lots of other places he could have gone. She knew that Gus and Mary would be happy to have him. And since the press now knew he was here and had, in fact, dogged his steps all day, there was no more need to worry about them knowing where he was. But he'd said no, he wanted to stay here.

And because he had been such a good sport all day—doing interview after interview, taking time for everyone who wanted to renew his acquaintance, and generally making her life much much easier and allowing her to do all the last-minute stuff that needed to be done—Polly had agreed. Another night on a too-short couch wouldn't kill her.

But Sloan had said, "I'll take the couch."

"It's too short," she had protested. "You'll never be able to sleep on it. You stay in my room. I'll bunk in Jack's. He has an extra bed."

"Then I'll take that." And no amount of arguing had deterred him. Sloan Gallagher had taken his gear and moved in with Jack.

Jack, of course, had been over the moon. He'd bounced his way to bed. And even after he got there, he kept right on bouncing. "Wait'll I tell Randy! Wait'll everybody hears!"

"You need to ask Mr. Gallagher if you can tell them," Polly had said. "And don't bounce, Jack! You'll drive him crazy!"

"He can call me Sloan." Sloan had said, coming into Jack's room from the shower, his hair damp. "And he can tell his buddies, but he's not allowed to tell the press. My credibility would be shot." He grinned wryly. "He can even bounce, but only until I get in bed. Then it's got to stop." He gave Jack a severe look, just like the one he gave the bad guys before he either mowed them down or hustled them off to jail.

Jack grinned. And bounced some more.

Sloan winked at the boy as he scrubbed at his own damp hair with a towel. He was shirtless and barefoot, but wearing jeans that Polly was sure he'd dragged on in order not to offend anyone, which she appreciated, even as she noted that the button at the top was undone. Her eyes had gone directly to it with the unerring instincts of a homing pigeon.

Realizing it, she deliberately—and quickly—had looked away.

"Good night," she'd said hastily, dropping a kiss on Jack's nose, then backing toward the door.

"Hey," Sloan had protested. "Don't I get one?"

"No!" Her voice had come out at barely more than a squeak. She was almost as bad as Celie!

Actually she was worse than Celie. She was a widow. A mature woman. The mother of four. She wasn't a giddy girl with a hope chest full of fantasies. She hadn't had a fantasy since she was eighteen and had dreamed of Lew.

But last night Sloan Gallagher had slept in her bed.

And tonight she couldn't stop her brain from wondering what it would be like if he was here tonight...with her.

Chapter 14

It was worse than the Christmas pageant, Polly thought, standing there amid a dozen milling muttering cowboys, all of whom were questioning their sanity and how long the line was for the bathroom.

"You just went to the bathroom," Polly told first one and then another twitchy-footed cowhand. "You don't need to go again. Honestly," she told them all, "you're worse than a bunch of third-graders."

"Yeah," one of them muttered darkly. "In third grade Miz Stedman told me I didn't have to go, either. I'm still livin' that down."

"Better let him go to the front of the line," another one cracked.

"Auction off the weak bladders first," another suggested from the back of the line. "Save the real men for last."

Bunnies, Polly decided, were easier to deal with. They were smaller. They stayed in cages. And they didn't have a cowboy's ribald sense of humor.

Or if they did, she was blessed not to be able to understand it.

When Mary Holt had directed the pageant, she'd had Gus as her bunny wrangler. Polly wished she'd had the forethought to shanghai Gus and provide him with a cattle prod to keep her cowboys in line.

"Where's Sloan?" she demanded, having lost sight of him ages ago. The minute he'd arrived, he'd been mobbed. If Polly had thought the crowds during the week had been bad, it was nothing compared to the sea of people who had converged on Elmer this morning.

Spence Adkins had been on duty since 5:00 a.m. At seven he'd called in reinforcements. When Polly had set off for the town hall a little after eight, there were three deputies directing traffic, and several cowboys on horseback were helping people find places to park. She'd passed a crew that was setting up an impromptu large screen TV in the Dew Drop and there was another in the Busy Bee, "to hold the overflow" one of the crew told her.

"They say they can bid from there," Jenny Nichols reported. "We'll have a couple of spotters on site in each location. They can use walkie-talkies to relay the bids. Taggart says it will work."

What did bull riders know about wireless communications? Polly wondered. But then, what had she known about running an auction like this? She realized now that even with all the preparation in the world, she would never have anticipated such things.

Jenny patted her shoulder comfortingly. "It'll be all right. Truly it will. Mace and Shane are working the Dew Drop. Cash and Rance will do the Busy Bee. Alice is recording the bids. Cloris will be backing her up. If you need any kids for runners between places, Tuck will organize them. Jed is taking care of the parking. Charlie is taking pictures. Noah and Taggart are each going to shoot video. Gus will, too, if you want three. We figured we could get someone to edit it later and sell copies— make a little more for Maddie that way."

Polly, dazed, stared at Jenny as she ticked things off. "That sounds great. I...when did you do all this?"

"Earlier in the week when you were dealing with all the

news people. Tess and Felicity and I decided that if you'd be spokesperson, we'd make sure the nitty-gritty stuff got done.''

"I'm supposed to be the nitty-gritty person," Polly said sadly.

Jenny laughed. "I can't think of anything grittier than dealing with all the TV and print people. I'd rather deal with a class of crazy fifth-graders.''

"How about a roomful of cowboys?" Polly offered.

"Sure.''

"You're serious?''

Jenny grinned. "I can be just as bossy as you when I put my mind to it. Besides, Gus was looking for you.''

"Why? Has something happened to Sloan?" Gus had been running interference for him.

"Don't worry about Sloan," Jenny said. "Go find Gus. It's almost eleven. Calvin will want to start.''

Polly found Gus in front of the town hall, which was about to rock off its foundations. "Jenny said you wanted to see me?''

"Thank God. I thought you were in there somewhere." He dug in his pocket, pulled out a small piece of folded paper and stuffed it into her hand.

"What's this?" She started to unfold it, but Gus reached over, pressed it flat again and stuffed it into Polly's pocket.

"Not for public consumption," he said. "It's a blank check. From Sloan.''

"From Sloan? Why?''

Gus took her arm and hauled her around the side of the building where there were fewer people, then bent his head so it was just inches from her ear. "He wants you to bid on him.'

"What! I can't bid on him!''

"Shhh! You have to.''

"I don't have to! I'm not rigging the auction!''

"Come on, Polly. It's not rigging. It's fair. You'd just be bidding on him with his money. Nothing wrong with that. Nothing illegal about it.''

"It would look bad. And why should I?''

"Because he doesn't want to go to a bimbo or a ditz—or some woman in the pay of a tabloid. And because," Gus said flatly, "he wants to take you."

"What!"

Gus shrugged. "He wants you. He said he owed you. Something to do with something he did a long time ago—he said you'd know what."

Gus clearly didn't. Thank God.

"That's ridiculous," she protested. "He doesn't owe me anything!"

"Well, he thinks he does. And you have to do it."

"No—"

"You do," Gus insisted. "I've got to make you agree to do it or...or he'll tell the world my name."

Polly's eyes widened. "He *knows* your name?"

She didn't think Gus had ever told anyone—except perhaps his wife, Mary—what his first name was. He was D. A. "Gus" Holt. And that was that.

"Sloan knows," Gus said grimly. "He was there when I hit a baseball through our living room window. My mother came to the door and yelled at me. She said the whole thing. Out loud." Gus winced at the memory. "C'mon, Pol'. Please. He means it. I'll die."

"I don't—"

"Say you'll bid on him," Gus promised, "and I'll direct next year's Christmas pageant."

It was true what they said—every woman did have her price.

"You're on," Polly said.

The place was jammed. There was hardly room in the town hall to move, let alone raise your hand to bid. Just as well since Jace had no intention of bidding at all.

He probably should have given up his spot against the wall to someone whose presence would mean money in the coffers of Maddie's loan fund. But he didn't move. He was looking for Celie.

He wanted to watch her face, wanted to see her come to

terms with Sloan Gallagher in the flesh. Right now, though, he couldn't see her at all.

There were literally several hundred people of all ages—from the four young Jennings kids in the front row to Maddie herself flanked by Cloris and Alice on one side and a young woman with a wriggling baby on the other—sitting shoulder to shoulder in rows. Lining all the walls were a bunch of standing-room-only hangers-on like himself.

Most of the attendees were young women, many of whom had, like Serena and Kelsey, been hanging around for days. But he could tell that not all the potential bidders were Sloan Gallagher groupies.

In fact, today had brought out a fair number of well-heeled patrons of the arts, interested in Brenna McCall's pen-and-ink-and-watercolor paintings of working cowhands as well as Charlie Seeks Elk's photos, some charcoal rodeo sketches done by Brenna and Jed McCall's nephew, Tuck, and a new display entitled *Cowgirl in Paris,* which Taggart Jones had hung last night.

These were a series of wonderful photos taken by his sister, Erin Jones, who was now a Paris-based photographer. Jace didn't know about Erin's reputation as a photographer, but some of the art patrons seemed to recognize her name and got excited seeing the photos.

People were excited, period. Serena and Kelsey were bouncing in their chairs. He could see them now about five rows from the front. They were saving a seat for Tamara, who waggled her fingers at him as she parted the throng on the other side of the room and came to join them.

Then the curtain moved at the front of the room and there was a sudden heightened buzz of excitement followed by an expectant hush. Once more Jace looked around trying to spot Celie and didn't find her.

Polly was sitting near the back with her mother, who looked avid and excited and thrilled. Polly looked exhausted and on edge. Probably worried that something would go wrong, Jace thought. He caught her eye and gave her a thumb's-up, hoping it would make her relax a little. But she only smiled fleetingly in reply.

He wanted to mouth, "Where's Celie?" But he didn't. She wasn't her sister's keeper. And he didn't want to admit that it mattered.

Maybe Celie just plain old wasn't going to come.

He brightened at the thought just as the curtain opened and Calvin stepped out.

Calvin Hodges had been an auctioneer for a good fifty years. He'd sold horses and cattle, houses and land, beer bottles, blankets and buttonhooks. He'd seen it all. But he'd never seen anything like this. Still, being Calvin, he was never at a loss for words. He beamed out at the crowd.

"Reckon we'll just get started then," he said. "I was thinking how to do this, seeing as how you ain't gonna bid on none of my other cowboys until we get started on what's his name, that Hollywood feller."

All the girls squealed.

Was one of them Celie? Jace couldn't see her anywhere. He wondered if she'd gone to the Dew Drop or the Busy Bee instead.

"So I figured," Calvin was saying, "that we'd start out with Mr. Sloan Gallagher. Just to whet your appetite a bit. We'll go a ways an' then we'll call a halt, and if he gets a little too rich for your blood, could be you'll find another one of these fellers to your liking. How 'bout that?"

More squealing. Shrieking. Clapping. Whistling.

And then Sloan walked out.

If Jace had thought things were crazy before, now the place went wild. If that many women had been screaming and clamoring for *him,* Jace would have turned tail and made tracks as fast as he could run. It was downright scary.

But then Sloan raised his hand for silence and, by God, they shut up. Just like that. Several hundred women stopped mid-shriek and just sat there, leaning toward him, jaws hanging, all of them with their eyes fastened on Sloan.

Jace thought he could hear his own heartbeat.

"Hey, there. I'm Sloan Gallagher," the man himself said

with a self-deprecating grin. "And if you find out what all the shouting's about, I wish you'd tell me."

There were a few shrieks.

But he quieted them. "I thought, before we got started, I'd tell you a little about why I'm here—about what Maddie and Ward Fletcher meant to me."

Polly was startled when Sloan began to speak.

There had been no stipulation that he would, nothing that indicated he might. He gained nothing personally by recounting the story of how he had happened to be their foster child and what they had meant to him. In fact, Polly thought, it could only bring back memories of the worst time of his life.

And yet he did it. He talked briefly about losing his mother, about his father's pain—memories that had to hurt even now.

"My world had shattered," he said. "Then Maddie and Ward helped me begin to put it back together again. I wouldn't be here today if it weren't for them. In fact—" he grimaced a little "—I hate to think about where I might actually be if it hadn't been for them. They taught me that the world goes on in spite of pain. They taught me not to forget, but to put the past in perspective. To go on. To look to the future, to hope, to dream...." And here he paused and looked out across the crowd as if he was searching for something. And then his eyes found her. "To dream," he repeated with a hint of a smile, making Polly squirm in her chair.

"I owe them—and the folks in Elmer—a lot. More than I can ever repay," Sloan said solemnly. Then he winked. "Which is why I'm asking you folks to help."

The bidding was over a hundred dollars in less than a minute.

It got to four hundred in barely more than that.

When it hit seven hundred Calvin called a halt. "We're going to move on and come back to this feller," he said. "Give him a breather while we sell a few more items—and maybe a cowboy or two. Right now we've got some photographs by native daughter Erin Jones sent all the way from Paris..."

Backstage, Sloan stayed out of sight while the interim auctions were taking place. But while he tried to stay out of the way, he also tried to stay where he could keep an eye on Polly.

She was sitting a long way back. Irritated, he thought she could have moved up a little. Surely they would have made room for her. But she apparently didn't try. She seemed to be determined to fade into the background.

How the hell was she going to bid if she wasn't close enough for someone to see her wave her arm?

Jace could see Serena. He could see Kelsey. He could see Tamara Lynd. But not Celie. Not anywhere.

"Where's your aunt?" he asked Jack as the boy slipped past.

"Haven't seen her."

Calvin was auctioning off Cy Williams from Trey Phillips's spread up near Murray. Cy—young, blond and brash—was the first of the bachelor cowboys to come up for bid. And while some of the ones Jace could see in the wings looked ill at ease, Cy laughed and preened and strutted his stuff. A number of young women, Serena included, were bidding furiously.

After Serena won Cy, an art patron from Santa Fe was high bidder for Charlie Seeks Elk's photos, a cowboy wannabe from Denver won Taggart's full weekend at bull-riding school and several local ranchers bought back their own working men who had offered hours of riding fence or haying or moving cattle.

Then Gallagher was back and the bidding went mad until Calvin called a halt at one thousand, five hundred twenty dollars.

"We don't wanta get ahead of ourselves here," he said jovially. "We'll just come back to this ol' broken down cowpoke in a little while."

When the bids on him went over three thousand dollars, Sloan got another break while Calvin moved on to Brenna Jamison McCall's cowboy hero watercolor painting.

Sloan had given Gus a blank check to bid on that. He'd always admired her work, had one original, in fact, in his ranch house near Sand Gap, and while he could afford to buy one anytime he chose, now seemed as good a time as any to bid on another.

He wanted to make sure Maddie's coffers were full.

Gus had apparently deputized Mary to do the bidding. From behind the curtain Sloan watched as she bid against several art connoisseurs. He guessed the painting might have gone for $5,000 in a gallery. It went for over $7,500 by the time Mary beat out the last competing bidder.

"Sold," Calvin proclaimed bringing down the gavel. "You gonna replace the cowboy hero at your house?" he asked Mary.

She smiled and shook her head. "Not a chance." And there was a look of such love on her face that Sloan felt a prick of envy just seeing it. Not for the first time, he wished for that for himself.

He'd begun to despair of finding it, though. Fame gave you almost unlimited access to women who wanted to go to bed with you, but it was no guarantee that you'd find love. Sloan didn't just want to go to bed anymore. He wanted a woman who would value him for more than his fame and his looks and his bank balance.

He wanted a woman like Mary. A strong woman. An independent woman. A woman who would come to him on her own terms and would be willing to put up with the mess that was often his life. That would take an incredibly mature woman.

He wanted Polly.

Of course he'd been fantasizing about Polly for more than half his life. He'd taken her to bed in his dreams for years. But he'd never dreamed about marrying her. At least not until he'd come back to Elmer.

A Cowboy's Homecoming, one newspaper article had called the story of his return, and Sloan had thought the headline inappropriate—after all, Elmer wasn't really his home!—until he'd got here early Saturday morning.

But when Polly had opened the door, even though she'd looked poleaxed at the sight of him, he'd felt the warmth of welcome. He'd felt as if he were home.

The feeling was so new and unexpected that he'd been stunned. He'd put it down to being dead on his feet. Anywhere with a bed would have felt like home, he'd told himself.

But it wasn't true.

The feeling had persisted. Still did.

He looked out through the crack in the curtains and spotted Polly. She was watching intently as Calvin auctioned off yet another of the cowboys.

"Bid on me," Sloan willed her. "Bid on me."

When Polly realized she was crumpling Sloan's check beyond recognition, she desperately smoothed it flat against the knee of her jeans, then folded it and tucked it into her pocket. Her hands were damp. She was hot. Her face felt flushed. Even with ceiling fans going like mad and the heat turned down, it was hot in here.

She wanted to leave, to get a breath of cool fresh air. But Calvin was getting close to the end. He'd finished the photographs and the sketches. They'd gone for high prices, as had the scholarships to Taggart and Noah's bull- and bronc-riding school. There were a surprising number of bidders for the weekend cattle drive to the summer range that Walt Blasingame had donated. And when he saw how high the price went, he'd passed the word to Calvin that he'd be willing to take another "hand" or two, and they'd auctioned the drive again.

Maddie had shaken her head in amazement. Once or twice she'd actually teared up. But she'd managed so far to keep a stiff upper lip, though she blinked a lot and said, "Gracious me," every time Calvin announced the total the auction had brought in so far.

Finally Calvin was down to one last cowboy before Sloan. All the earlier bachelor cowboys had gone for good prices. The girls who had bid on Sloan, but who had dropped out when the bidding became too high for them, did exactly what Calvin had hoped they would—they'd set their sights on the other cowboys.

With the women's enthusiasm, Sloan's example and Jenny's firm hand, the panic-stricken bunch of cowpokes who had been milling around backstage with gray faces and weak bladders two hours before, had managed to transform themselves into reasonable facsimiles of cowboy heroes.

Polly was vastly relieved—until Calvin called the last.

"Logan Reese just come back to Elmer," he boomed as a lean, scowling cowboy took about three steps out onto the stage. He exhibited none of the charm that the others had managed. Instead he stared defiantly at the crowd, which grew quiet and stared back.

Calvin glared at the cowboy. "Give us a smile," he said, then turned to the crowd. "And what do you say, folks? Let's give Logan Reese a real Elmer welcome back!"

There was one clap. Maybe a second. Oh, God, Polly thought.

"Right, then. Let's get to it. Who'll start the bidding?"

No one bid.

There was some whispering. Some muttering. Word was obviously being passed. Girls from out of town who should have been clamoring to bid on such a good-looking cowboy, sat silent, just watching, waiting. The word *ex-con* seemed to float in the air.

Oh, Maddie, this was a mistake, Polly thought. She knew Maddie trusted Logan Reese. But apparently Maddie was the only one. *Please God, let someone bid,* Polly prayed.

"Cat got your tongue?" Calvin asked the crowd. Polly knew Calvin wasn't surprised. She just hoped he didn't make it worse. "Come on, now. You can't all be broke yet. And you can't all go to Hollywood with Mr. Gallagher. Somebody's gotta stick around. So what'm I bid for this handsome feller?"

Logan stood stoically, as if he didn't give a damn what they did.

"Do I hear twenty dollars?" Calvin prompted.

Silence.

"Ten?"

Polly knew it was going to be up to her.

And then from right up front a young boy's voice said firmly, "Twenty-seven dollars and thirty-two cents."

There was a collective gasp. Everyone leaned and craned

their necks. Logan, too, looked startled. He narrowed his gaze on someone in the front row.

"Who is that?" Polly, who couldn't see beyond the horde of surging people in front of her, demanded.

Joyce shook her head.

"Who'll give me thirty? I've got twenty-seven thirty-two! Who'll give me thirty?" Calvin looked around, then, good businessman that he was, took what he had. "Going once. Twice. Sold to…"

A boy about twelve stood up. Three younger children followed him. "Elijah Jennings," he said firmly. "And Emily, Samantha and Stephen."

Polly sat down with a thud. "The Jennings kids bought Logan Reese?"

"Oh, my!" Joyce fanned herself and blinked her astonishment. "What'll Addie say?"

Addie, their half sister and guardian, was all that stood between the kids and foster homes. She was also the last hope for keeping the hundred-year-old Jennings ranch in the family. Their great grandfather, Elmer Jennings, a wealthy rancher, saloon keeper and owner of the first local bank, had been the town's founding father.

But that was then.

Now, a hundred years later, all the town property was gone. The ranch was mortgaged. The herd was small. And last year Addie's father and stepmother had been killed in an accident coming home from Livingston. Addie was left with the ranch, the kids, a mound of debt.

And now, apparently, with Logan Reese.

"Addie is going to kill those kids," Joyce predicted.

"She won't have to honor it. Lije isn't of age."

But Joyce shook her head. "Addie will honor it. God help her, that's the kind of girl she is."

Polly thought it might be interesting to be a fly on the wall of the Jennings's ranch house tonight. But she didn't think about it for long because Calvin had begun the final bidding session on Sloan.

"Five thousand two hundred dollars," Calvin began. "Not

much for a weekend with your heart's desire. Let's show him what he's really worth, ladies. Let's hear fifty-five hundred. Do I hear fifty-five hundred?''

Tamara Lynd lifted her hand.

Calvin beamed. He looked around for higher bidders. He got them. Three other women were bidding against Tamara. Then a bid came in from the Dew Drop.

''Seventy-eight hundred!'' Calvin beamed. ''Now we're movin'. Back to you, little lady.'' He looked at Tamara. ''How about a nice even eight?''

Polly bet Tamara Lynd hadn't been called ''little lady'' since she was four years old.

Tamara said, ''Eight.''

Calvin was delighted. ''Not bad. Not bad. What do you think, Mr. Gallagher? Aren't you worth more than that?''

Sloan grinned. ''Oh, I'd say so.'' Polly saw his gaze move around the room, then stop pointedly when it reached her. She clutched the check, waiting.

Sloan understood that she didn't want to jump in early. He appreciated that. When the bidding picked up again, he didn't mind that she hadn't stuck her oar in yet. But she'd better do it soon.

Calvin had rushed right through the going-going-gone stage with Logan Reese. Sloan didn't want to be hung out to dry because she waited too long.

What if she didn't bid? What if she decided that this was payback time for the evening he'd spied on her and Lew?

They were over ten thousand dollars now. Tamara and Lorena Deckart, a tabloid writer he recognized, who could doubtless afford to keep bidding, with the magazine footing the bill. The fans had dropped out long ago.

''Eleven thousand six hundred.'' Calvin acknowledged Tamara's latest bid, then looked expectantly at the tabloid writer.

''Eleven-eight,'' Lorena said.

''Twelve,'' said Tamara firmly.

''Twelve-five.''

''Thirteen.''

''Thirteen-five.''

It was like Ping-Pong. The bids went up and up and up. Sloan saw Maddie's jaw sagging. He saw Polly sitting on the edge of her chair. He hoped to God she didn't get so engrossed in the "match" that she forgot to jump in.

"Seventeen," Tamara said, but she had hesitated after Lorena's quick bid at sixteen-five, and the rhythm was broken.

"The little lady in red has bid seventeen *thousand* dollars," Calvin called out. He fixed Tamara with a smile.

Sloan saw her swallow. He thought she was looking a little pinched around the mouth. He didn't blame her. He knew she was ambitious. When they'd worked together, she'd been all over him, eager to "get ahead." He knew she still saw him as a ticket to the big time, and even if he never slept with her again, winning the auction would get her plenty of publicity. It might get her auditions, maybe even a part.

But how high was she willing to go? How much did she want to pay for the mere chance?

"Seventeen-five," Lorena said. She smiled at Calvin. She smiled at Tamara. She smiled at Sloan.

He could envision the story she'd be writing. A Weekend Swinging With Sloan. He suppressed a shudder.

Damn it, Polly.

"Do I hear eighteen?" Calvin asked Tamara. "Eighteen? You're not gonna let him get away, are you, little lady?"

Tamara wet her lips. She looked nervous, worried. She looked at Calvin, then at Sloan.

"Only eighteen, little lady," Calvin cajoled. "Go for it. You might just win the weekend of a lifetime and contribute to a good cause at the same time."

Tamara was chewing on her lip.

Calvin waited. The crowd grew quiet. There was a little shuffling of feet. A cough.

Come on, Polly! Sloan sought her out in the crowd. She was inching forward, watching Tamara intently.

"Let's hear eighteen," Calvin called to the crowd at large. "All you people at the Dew Drop and the Busy Bee, here you have it! Chance of a lifetime. Eighteen thousand dollars and you might just be spending next weekend with our very own Sloan Gallagher!''

He looked at Gus and his brother J.D. who were manning the walkie-talkies. They both shook their heads.

"Eighteen," Calvin repeated. He looked at Tamara. "Eighteen? No? Then, seventeen thousand, five hundred dollars going once..."

Polly! Now!

Sloan fixed his gaze on her.

Come on, Polly! Bid!

It was on the tip of her tongue. *Eighteen thousand.*

All she had to do was say it. She would think of the implications later. She would think about next weekend later. She didn't have to go, after all.

She could tell him no.

Right, Polly told herself. *I can tell him no.*

"Seventeen thousand, five hundred going twice..." Calvin was still scanning the crowd for one last bidder.

Polly began to raise her hand. Then, from behind her, she heard another voice. "Twenty-three thousand, seventy-five dollars and fifty-eight cents."

It was Celie.

Jace's head jerked around. He'd been watching Tamara, knowing how determined she'd been to win Sloan, and recognizing how annoyed she must feel to lose to a woman with apparently unlimited funds.

And all of a sudden, out of nowhere, he heard Celie!

He didn't believe it.

He'd long since decided, happily, that knowing she wasn't going to get Sloan, that her fantasies were just that—fantasies—she'd given the whole auction a miss.

Now he stood poleaxed, staring at her as she stood in the back of the room by the door. Her cheeks were red. Her dark curly hair was windblown. She looked absolutely gorgeous.

And more determined than Jace had ever seen her.

Calvin, taken by surprise, caught his breath. Then he gathered his wits and repeated the bid. "We have a bid of twenty-three thousand, seventy-five dollars and fifty-eight cents. Is that correct?" he asked Celie.

Celie nodded resolutely. "That's right."

Then Calvin grinned and wiped his forehead with his handkerchief. "Well now! Did you hear that, ladies and gentlemen. Ms. Celie O'Meara wants to go to Hollywood real bad. Anybody here want to go more?" He looked around.

So did Jace, desperately. But no one else moved. Everyone looked stunned.

"Anyone?" Calvin scanned the room.

Celie stood immobile.

"Going once," Calvin said.

Jace's gaze swung from Celie to Polly to Sloan and back again. Sloan was looking at Polly. Polly was looking at Celie. No one was moving.

"Going twice," said Calvin. He looked at Tamara. He looked at the lady who'd bid against her. He looked at Gus and J.D. who shook their heads. He let his gaze travel slowly once more around the room.

Then he banged down his gavel. "There you have it, ladies and gentlemen! Sloan Gallagher! Sold for the weekend to Miss Celie O'Meara for twenty-three thousand, seventy-five dollars and fifty-eight cents!"

"I don't believe it," Jace heard Maddie Fletcher breathe.

She wasn't the only one.

Chapter 15

She'd won Sloan Gallagher.

Ohmigod, Celie thought as the reality of half a dozen people pumping her hand and Calvin proclaiming Sloan hers—*hers!*—began to sink in.

Mary Holt was looking at her, goggle-eyed. Gus was standing slack-jawed. Her own mother was opening and closing her mouth like a fish.

And no wonder.

Who would have thought a hairdresser from Elmer would spend her entire life's savings on a weekend with a Hollywood actor?

No one.

Not even Celie.

Not until yesterday. Yesterday something had crystallized.

Maybe it was listening to all the local women talking about the groupies from out of town who had come all this way just for a chance. Maybe it was having Sloan Gallagher trying to be nice to her while she tried to avoid his every glance. Maybe it was seeing everyone else in the world doing what they wanted to do—even that stupid, juvenile Jace Tucker who went rolling around in the snow with Tamara Lynd!

Whatever it was, it had made Celie think.

It had made her toss restlessly all night. It had made her get up at dawn and go to the ATM machine at the Mini-mart and check her account balance. She'd stood there staring at the amount for a good fifteen minutes, long enough for Kitzy Miller to ask her if she was all right or if she needed her to call Polly.

Maybe that had been the trigger—knowing that everyone always expected Polly to rescue her. As if Celie couldn't do anything for herself.

And why shouldn't they think that?

She was living with Polly. She depended on Polly. Polly had always been the strong one, the clever one. Polly had always been capable. Hadn't she made a good marriage out of a baby-on-the-way situation? Hadn't she coped with running all over the country with Lew while their kids were little? Hadn't she survived the death of her husband and continued to provide well for her children?

Polly had helped out when Mary Beth was pregnant with triplets. Polly had been there for their mom when their father had died. It was Polly whose no-nonsense attitude had helped Celie make up her mind to go away to Billings and study after Matt had jilted her.

Polly was the one everyone turned to—for everything.

If Celie didn't do something for herself now, it was likely that Polly would be taking care of her in her old age!

"No, I don't want you to call Polly," she'd said flatly. Then she'd crumpled the bank statement, stuffed it into her pocket, marched out the door and headed for the town hall.

All the way there she'd recited the amount in her account over and over. Then she'd stood outside the town hall, waiting, knowing she couldn't go in until the last moment, that there was no way she could stand watching the auction itself.

"How high is it now?" she'd ask. "How high?" when Mark Nichols or Tuck McCall or one of the other boys running back and forth between the Dew Drop and the Busy Bee and the hall hurried past. They kept her posted. She was afraid for a while that the price might well go beyond every penny she had.

And then, at $17,500.00, Mark Nichols told her that "the skinny blonde" was dropping out.

"It's gonna be the other one," he'd said, eyes dancing eagerly. "It's almost over."

Celie had sent a desperate prayer winging to heaven. And then, before she could think about what she was about to do, she slipped in the door, stepped forward and placed her bid.

She'd taken her life into her own hands. Finally she'd made a move.

Now she accepted everyone's congratulations. She tried to smile and look confident. She avoided Polly's gaze. She'd caught a glimpse of her sister right after she'd bid. Polly had looked poleaxed. Celie wasn't surprised.

She couldn't meet Sloan's gaze when he came up.

He looked a little dazed, too. "It's you?" he said oddly. "Not your sister?" As if Polly even had to bid for her.

"It's me," Celie said firmly, raising her chin. "Is that a problem?"

Sloan blinked, then shook his head and leaned forward to kiss her on the cheek. "I'll be seeing you next weekend, then," he promised.

It was all Celie could do not to cave in at the touch of his lips. Sloan Gallagher had *kissed* her?

"Put your arm around her!" yelled one of the photographers.

So Sloan did. And Celie did her best to put on a happy face while a thousand flashbulbs went off. She tried to think of cheery things to say when several dozen reporters stuck microphones in her face and asked her how it felt to know she'd just spent an astonishing amount of money to win a weekend with the most sought-after man in Hollywood.

"It feels great," she said. "Wonderful. Fantastic."

And then she went into the bathroom and threw up.

* * *

"I don't believe it." Joyce said to herself and to almost anyone else who would listen after the auction ended.

She'd been saying the words now for seven hours. She wondered if the real Celie had been stolen away by gypsies and a new person had been left in her place. It seemed as likely as the real Celie spending over twenty-three thousand dollars to go out with Sloan Gallagher!

"That's all the money she has in the world," Joyce muttered to herself as she folded up chairs and carried them to the wall where Walt Blasingame and Charlie Seeks Elk were stacking them. "Twenty-three thousand dollars!"

"If she wants him bad enough," Charlie said, "it's not that much. It's the rest of her life, we're talking about."

Put like that, Joyce thought, he might be right. "But only if he wants her, too!"

But Charlie shook his head. "No. Either way. It's the cost of finding out."

It seemed a huge price. Daunting. Not at all what she would have expected of Celie. But then, maybe that was what made it wonderful—that it was so unexpected—and Celie had done it anyway.

Hadn't she been worried that Celie would waste the rest of her life just dreaming about Sloan and never living?

Celie must have worried, too. And then she'd done something about it. Perhaps something foolish. But maybe not.

For the first time since Celie had won the auction, Joyce smiled.

"I think you might be right," she said to Charlie.

Walt leaned on one of the chairs. "Mebbe she comes by it naturally."

Joyce blinked. "What?"

"She ain't the only one open to new experiences. You are, too."

"Me?"

"If you're still studyin' Spanish."

Joyce laughed. "For all the good it will do me."

Walt shrugged. "You never know."

Joyce, thinking of Celie spending her life's savings to test her dream of life with Sloan Gallagher, smiled. No, she thought. You never did.

"You're leaving?" Sara stared at Flynn as they pulled up in front of her house and got out of the car.

"Got to," he said now. "Got another assignment. Van Duersen's lettin' me out of purgatory. Sendin' me to L.A." Flynn's eyes sparkled at the thought.

Of course Sara knew intellectually that Flynn Murray wasn't going to remain in Elmer, Montana, forever. He'd come, like everyone else, for the story. Of course he would be moving on.

But she didn't want him to. She wanted him to stay—with her. For the rest of their lives.

She'd never felt such desire. The world had simply seemed to throb with it. Every time Flynn looked at her, she could feel a pulse deep inside her. Every time he touched her she was sure he felt it, too.

Wasn't that reason enough to stay?

They hadn't even been to bed together. Not that it didn't sound like a marvelous idea.

It shocked Sara to find herself even thinking that way. But she couldn't seem to help it. She'd never felt that urgency with Gregg. Until she'd met Flynn, she hadn't even understood what true urgency was.

Now she did. Now she wanted to go to bed with him. She wanted to hold him and touch him and kiss him. She had already kissed him—several times. He'd kissed her. His kisses had made her burn.

She wanted more.

These had been the brightest, most wonderful two days of her life. He'd made the whole world come alive for her. She loved to listen to him talk. His soft Irish brogue delighted her. His tales of his Irish village childhood, of university in Cork, of the streets of New York, of shoestring travels to London, Paris, Los Angeles and Rome made her smile. They'd talked about her, too—about parts of her life that had nothing to do with chem lab or biology class. They'd talked about her dad's life as a bullfighter, about growing up in Elmer, about the cowboy myth and mystique.

She'd shown him Elmer and he'd shown her the world.

And now he was leaving?

"You must be starving," she said desperately. "We didn't eat."

After the auction they'd driven up into the hills to look out across the valley, to see the beauty one more time, Flynn had said. They'd also fogged up the windows on his rental car once more. They had kissed and touched with an eager desperation until Flynn had again pulled back, insisting that they needed to get going.

"Your mother will be wonderin' where I've taken you," he'd said.

Sara doubted it, given Polly's memory, but she didn't say anything. She'd just kissed him again. She had never felt such hunger, though it had nothing to do with food.

Still, food was all she could offer him to keep him with her a little longer. So she persisted. "You must want a quick bite. You don't have to be back to Bozeman right away, do you?"

Flynn hesitated, then shrugged. "Guess not." He gave her one of his quicksilver grins. "I'm hungry, all right," he said, and she was sure he didn't mean food, either.

She grabbed his hand and drew him into the house after her.

"Were you there?" Daisy demanded, looking up from the televison where she and Lizzie were surfing channels looking for news. "Did you see Aunt Celie *won?*"

"Yes," Sara said. It was amazing what Aunt Celie had done. But it hadn't seemed any more astonishing than what was happening to her.

"Where were you?" Lizzie demanded. "Did you get in the town hall?"

"Yes." Flynn, with his press credentials, had got them places up front. He'd done his job, had watched the whole auction avidly and had taken lots of notes.

Sara had watched him.

Flynn Murray was the most handsome man she'd ever seen. Far better looking than even Sloan Gallagher. Sloan's hair wasn't black like Flynn's. His jaw wasn't as stubborn as Flynn's. He didn't have that endearing lopsided smile. His eyes weren't green.

She didn't even know what color Gregg's eyes were.

"Come into the kitchen. I'll fix you a sandwich," she said to him.

Daisy and Lizzie bounded up eagerly. "Good idea. We're starving!"

Sara ground her teeth. She didn't need them in the kitchen now. She and Flynn had things to talk about. Plans to make. They needed to talk about when they were going to see each other again. *Without* a couple of little sisters around.

But try telling Lizzie and Daisy that. They were used to Gregg, whom she shared happily with everyone.

"I'll get the mayonnaise. You get the bread," Lizzie said now, heading toward the refrigerator. "Grandma said we could eat all the leftover roast. Want mustard?" she asked Flynn.

"Sure. What can I do to help?"

Tell them to get lost, Sara thought. But there was no way, and while Flynn had been fiercely intent on her only an hour ago, now he seemed happy to simply chat with her sisters.

Sara put up with the communal effort at sandwich making. But once it was finished she said, "Aren't you going to watch the news?"

"I'd rather talk to Flynn," Lizzie said. "I want to go to New York. I want to see a Broadway play."

"When you come, you let me know," Flynn offered. "I'll take you."

"Me, too?" Daisy asked. "If I come to see the Lipizzaner stallions?"

"Whatever you come for," Flynn said. He grinned at Sara. "You, too, of course."

As if she were no more than one of them. Sara stared at him.

"Sara won't come," Lizzie said around a mouthful of sandwich. "She's too busy."

"Well, of course she is," Flynn said. "She's got lots to do. Med school and all that."

"I don't—"

"But you come," he said to her sisters. "We'll send post-cards to Sara wherever she is."

He might have been teasing her, but it didn't sound like teasing. It sounded like he was trying to get rid of her. Sara felt odd. Hurt. Confused.

The back door opened just then, and her mother and grand-mother and Sloan and Celie and Jack came in. All the attention shifted to Celie. Her aunt's face was flushed, her hair mussed, her eyes a little glassy. She looked dazed.

Both Daisy and Lizzie pounced on her. They squealed and hugged her and then, of course, they hugged Sloan, too.

"I can't believe you did it!" Daisy exclaimed.

"Me, neither!" Lizzie chimed in, shaking her head.

"Me, neither," Celie agreed, then laughed a little hysteri-cally.

Flynn got up and came around the table to take Celie's hand. "Congratulations! It was a very gutsy thing you did. I'm look-ing forward to writing it."

Celie beamed. "Are you going to be there? At the premi-ere?"

Flynn nodded. "I'm planning on it."

"Wonderful." Celie looked as delighted that she was going to see Flynn again as she was to be going out with the man of her dreams. She wasn't even looking at Sloan.

The man of Sara's dreams wiped his hands on a paper towel, carried his plate to the sink and said, "Thank you for the sand-wich. Now I really do have to go."

Sara opened her mouth to protest, but Flynn was shaking hands with her mother. "Thank you for your hospitality, Mrs. O'Meara. It's been a pleasure." Then he shook hands with Polly, with Sloan. He tugged Daisy's braid and winked at Lizzie and Jack.

Then he turned to Sara.

"I'll walk out with you," she said.

He got his jacket and pulled it on. Sara did the same, then went to the door with him. She hoped he would take her hand. But he didn't. He just held the door open for her.

The wind had come up when they went outside. It might

snow before morning. "I don't like the look of this," Flynn murmured.

Sara barely spared it a glance. "I'm not all that busy," she said firmly. "With medical school, I mean. I could probably get to New York sometime."

"Sure." He smiled at her, but it wasn't the smile she'd fallen in love with. It was polite, that was all. "That'd be grand."

"And you could come back here, too."

His smile tipped to one side. "Not a lot for me to write about in Elmer."

"But you could come for a visit."

"Maybe someday."

"Maybe I'll go to med school in New York. Maybe at Columbia."

"It's a fine school."

"So I'll definitely be there."

"I'll look forward to it."

They stared at each other. There was something in his gaze she didn't understand. Something she couldn't read, as if he'd dug the moat and shut the castle gate and wouldn't let her in.

"Flynn?" she said, desperate now.

He reached out and touched her cheek. "Don't."

"Don't what?"

He sighed heavily. "It's not... We're not... You're a sweet kid, Sara," he said helplessly at last.

A sweet kid? Was that what he believed?

But before she could ask, he bent his head and kissed her. It was a brief kiss, a brotherly kiss. Not at all like the kiss he'd given her last night. Not like the ones they'd shared just this afternoon. There was no passion in this one. No future. No promise.

His lips were cool. She thought they trembled just a little, but their touch was so brief she couldn't say for sure.

Then he stepped back and touched his finger to the tip of her nose. "Take care of yourself, *a ghra.*"

Then he was gone.

The blank check burned a hole in Polly's pocket all evening. But no more intensely than the looks Sloan had given her since

Celie had won the auction. But she'd had no time to talk to him, no time to explain until finally he'd gone upstairs to pack his bag in Jack's room. Then Polly had gone after him.

He was tossing clothes into the bag when she slipped into the room and shut the door behind her.

He whipped around and straightened up, pasting what Polly had begun to recognize as his public face on. Only when he saw it was her, did his expression change from polished politeness to obvious irritation.

"I'm sorry," she said, thrusting the rumpled, crushed check at him. "I couldn't do it."

"You could have."

"All right then, I wouldn't." Which was closer to the truth. "I still can't believe she did it."

"Neither can I." Sloan looked disgruntled. "Why in hell—?"

Polly hesitated, but realized that, since Celie had been brave enough to step in front of millions and lay her life savings on the line, she wouldn't expect her sister to protect her now.

"She's sort of...fancied herself in love with you. Well, not *you* exactly, but the person you present in your movies, in the magazines, in her heart."

"I'm not—" he began to protest, but she cut him off.

"You were there when she was trying to find a reason to believe something good about men. She was jilted when she was twenty and she went into a shell after that. She felt completely rejected. Worthless. She didn't date after that. She didn't even look at guys for a long time. She didn't trust them. Except in movies. Except you."

Sloan frowned. "Then she expects me to..." His voice drifted off. He didn't look happy.

"I don't know what she expects," Polly told him honestly. "I think she simply wants to find out."

"I can tell her right now. It isn't her I'm interested in. It's her sister."

"Don't say that."

"It's the truth. I've always been interested in you."

"Because you saw…because that day in the barn…" She still couldn't bring herself to articulate the words.

"Because I saw you naked," Sloan said. His voice was frank, but the tone wasn't harsh. On the contrary it felt almost like a caress.

"You were a child."

"I was a teenager. Fourteen. Impressionable."

"Well, hopefully you've grown up," Polly said, trying to dismiss the whole thing. "That was a long time ago."

"But memorable."

She wished he would stop looking at her like that. She wished she hadn't come after him up to Jack's room. It was too small. Too intimate.

"I wanted to take you to the premiere," he said softly. "I wanted to spend the weekend with you."

"Well, I wasn't up for bid," Polly said sharply. "I better be getting back downstairs. I just wanted to give you the check back. And, of course, to say thanks for doing the auction and saving Maddie's ranch."

"That's all you wanted to say?" His gaze was intent, hungry. He pushed away from the bunk beds.

Polly beat a hasty retreat. "That's all."

If Jace stood in the upstairs bedroom of Artie's place and looked down the hill to the east, he could see a part of the McMaster house.

He'd stood there every night since he'd come to stay at Artie's and had stared at the lights in the upper-floor rooms, wondering which one was Celie's. It had made him feel closer to her to stand with his forehead pressed against the glass, looking and longing.

Now as he stood with his fists jammed into the pockets of his jeans and glared in that direction, mostly he longed to spit!

How the hell could she have done it?

How could she have squandered over twenty thousand dollars on a date with a trumped-up, two-bit actor?

What the hell was she thinking?

He glowered down the hill at the well-lit house. Then he

kicked the baseboard, hurt his toes and did a hopping furious lap around the room. "Damn it!" He bent and rubbed his bare toes, winced, then went back to the window once again.

He'd been standing here for an hour. Maybe more. Ever since he'd come upstairs after seeing Serena and Kelsey off. They'd been full of chatter about the auction, not at all sorry they hadn't won Sloan. Serena was gaga over whoever it was she'd won, but who that was Jace couldn't remember.

All he could think about was Celie. With Sloan.

The man she'd always wanted. The one he'd goaded her about bidding on. She wasn't supposed to do it! She'd told him she wouldn't! And then she'd gone and blown her life's savings on one lousy weekend.

Maybe it wasn't one lousy weekend. Maybe reality would be like her dreams. Maybe she'd have Gallagher for the rest of her life!

Jace braced his hands against the window frame and let his head fall forward until his forehead touched the cold glass. He felt achingly, yawningly empty.

"Jace?" Tamara's voice came softly from the doorway.

"What?" He didn't turn around.

Quiet footsteps crossed the bare floor as she came up behind him. Slim arms slid around his waist.

He stiffened.

Warm breath caressed the back of his neck. "She's not the only fish in the sea." Tamara's voice was a soft purr. He didn't know how she knew, but clearly she did. She pressed her whole body against his.

Jace held himself absolutely rigid as her breasts nestled against his back and her hips cradled his. Her thumbs grazed his ribs, her fingers splayed against his abdomen. Her tongue touched the back of his neck.

A shudder ran through him.

"See? It's not so hard to think about something else," Tamara breathed. "*Someone* else."

Jace swallowed.

"It's foolish to care. *They* didn't care. Did they?"

No. Celie sure as hell didn't. At least she didn't care about him.

"So I say we forget together," Tamara whispered. Her fingers slid lower beneath his waistband. They popped the fastener of his jeans, slid down the zipper, freed him, stroked him, caressed him.

And Jace, shuddering, was lost.

It was what she did every Sunday night, Sara told herself as she gripped the steering wheel. She took the car and drove over the pass to Bozeman to study in the lab with Gregg.

"Back in your routine?" her mother had said when Sara had asked for the keys. "It looks like snow, though. You keep an eye out."

"Maybe I'll stay over at Cathy's." One of her classmates, she meant.

"Just as long as it's not at Gregg's." Polly had given her one of those steely-mother looks.

Sara's fingers had closed tightly on the keys. "I won't stay at Gregg's."

"Of course you won't. You know better," Polly replied wryly.

Sara did know better. But that wasn't why she wouldn't be staying at Gregg's. She wasn't going to study with Gregg. She wasn't going to study at all.

She was going after Flynn.

The snow began as she reached the top of the pass going over the interstate to Bozeman. It was falling heavily by the time she reached the motel where she knew he had a room.

She called her mother and said she'd be staying over.

"Smart move," Polly approved heartily.

As she hung up, Sara desperately hoped so.

Thank God she knew which room Flynn was in. She would not have wanted to go to the desk and ask. She didn't want to call him either. She had to see him, face-to-face.

She had stood on the porch after he'd left and wondered if she was going crazy. Had she dreamed all these feelings? Had it meant nothing to him? Was she just going to go back to her day planner and her life before Flynn?

Gregg gave her the answer. "Well, you've had your weekend off," he'd said without preamble when he called. "Now I trust you're ready to get back to work. Our future depends on it, you know."

Sara's future depended on something very different. She needed to talk to Flynn.

She climbed the stairs, found his room, knocked on the door. Half a minute later the lock rattled and the door opened a crack. Flynn, wearing only boxer shorts and holding a bottle of whiskey in his hand, stared, disbelieving, at her. "Sara?"

She swallowed hard. "Was I dreaming?"

Flynn's knuckles were white where he gripped the bottle. "What?"

"What I felt. What was happening between us. I thought—" She couldn't explain. Words wouldn't do. She stepped forward, leaned up and touched her lips to his.

It was the only way she knew of to make sure.

He groaned, anguished. "We can't! Damn it, Sara. You don't want me. You have plans. You have goals. A life! I have—never mind—" He muttered it all while she kept right on kissing him, pressing against his heated body, making him respond, until finally he wrapped his arms around her. "You're going to be sorry. You're goin' to hate me forever."

"I won't," Sara vowed as he hauled her in and shut the door.

Tomorrow was going to be the first day of the rest of her life.

Polly had never been much for slogans, but this one seemed somehow apropos. Tomorrow things would be back to normal. There were would be no television crews, no reporters, no frantic phone calls, no giggling groupies, no fame, no nonsense.

No Sloan.

She felt an odd, hollow sort of ache at the thought. Determinedly she banished it. She wasn't going to get all misty-eyed about Sloan Gallagher.

He was handsome. He was charming. He was everything that made him the heart throb of millions. But that didn't mean a woman like her should be entertaining thoughts about him.

So what if he made her feel things she'd thought had died with Lew? That just meant she wasn't dead, too. And maybe it meant that down the road she might find someone with whom she could share those feelings.

Another man.

Not Sloan.

He was totally and completely out of her league. She wasn't a dreamer like Celie. She knew better than to focus her hopes on a man like him.

In fact, she wished he'd left this evening. She'd thought he would. But after they came back home from the town hall, people kept dropping by. Some came to wish Celie well, to shake her hand and shake their heads even as they supported her. Many came to see Sloan, to thank him for his help, to tell him they hoped he'd come back and visit. Maddie had kissed him and hugged him and even shed a tear or two.

"You come back now," she'd said, squeezing him tight. "You don't be a stranger."

Sloan had promised he would come. He'd said the same to Gus and Mary and the baby when they'd come. And he'd promised to go see J.D. and Lydia on their place outside Murray.

"You won't have time to make movies anymore," Polly said after they left. "You'll be too busy visiting your friends here."

"I could stand that." Sloan said gravely, his gaze fixed on her.

His gaze had once more made her feel those things she'd put aside after Lew's death. Polly had swallowed and hurried out to the kitchen to wash up the dishes in the sink.

She'd told herself she'd come back out to say goodbye to him. She'd be polite and friendly. He was a friend now, after all.

But a little later Joyce had come in and said, "Sloan's staying if that's okay?"

"Staying? Here?"

"It's late and it's snowing. I invited him."

"Of course," Polly had agreed faintly.

So he was back in Jack's room.

"He can stay forever," Jack said cheerfully when she'd gone up to kiss him good-night.

"No, he can't," Polly had said. "Don't start thinking that." She certainly wouldn't let herself think that. Sloan Gallagher, even with his declarations of "interest" and his hungry gazes, was not for the likes of her.

They had nothing in common. If he was "interested," it was because of his memory of her. He might once have been enchanted with the girl she had been. But she wasn't that girl now. No more than he was really the man Celie had been dreaming of for six years.

The seventeen-year-old Polly he remembered didn't exist. This Polly was an adult. A mature woman. With a life here in Elmer.

So even if she liked him, even if he made her smile and laugh and feel things she hadn't felt in a very long while, she was still a realist.

She wasn't a woman who had flings.

She was a woman who had children, commitments, responsibilities. Rabbits.

"So be realistic," she muttered to herself now, "and go to sleep."

She rolled onto her side, drew her pillow close and closed her eyes. The doorknob turned. The door opened a crack.

"Bad dream?" she asked. Jack had them sometimes if he got over excited.

"If I say yes can I get in bed with you?"

She rolled over and sat up abruptly as Sloan slipped into the room, then closed the door after him.

"What do you think you're doing?" Polly clutched the quilt to her breasts and glared at the shadowy figure across the room.

"Well, that depends," he said in a soft, lazy tone. "What do you want me to do?"

"Go away! Now!"

But he didn't. He leaned against the closed door and folded his arms across his chest. Even in the dim light Polly could see that he was smiling at her. It was the same smile that made millions of women's hearts kick over. She'd seen it in *People* magazine just last week. She should damned well be immune to it, knowing that. But it made her own heart beat faster regardless.

"Go!" she insisted. "Go!"

"Ah, Pol'," he murmured, shaking his head. "You don't want me to do that. You want me the same way I want you."

"I don't! And you don't want me. You just remember—" She tried to articulate what she'd just been thinking.

But Sloan cut her off. "I know what I remember," he said. "You. You were beautiful. You *are* beautiful."

"Oh, right. I'm a thirty-seven-year-old, frumpy postal worker."

"Whom I find beautiful."

"Stop!"

"I'm just telling the truth."

How could you argue with someone who wouldn't listen? Polly clutched her quilt tightly. "What do you want, Sloan? Really? A roll in bed? Because I'm not doing that. I don't have flings. I don't have one-night stands."

"I'm not asking for one."

"You're not the guy leaving in the morning?"

"I told Maddie and Gus I'd be back."

"To visit. I'm not going to be your lover in Montana, the woman whose bed you share whenever you happen to pass through."

"Good. I'm glad you're not. I'm glad you won't do it. It isn't what I want."

"Then what are you doing in here?"

"Well, I won't say sleeping with you didn't occur to me. And I won't pretend it doesn't have its appeal." He raked a hand through tousled hair. "It has a hell of a lot of appeal. But I want more."

Her gaze narrowed. "What sort of more?"

"How does marriage sound to you?"

"What!" She stared at him, stunned. No. More than stunned. Poleaxed. "Marriage? *Marry* you?" Polly didn't believe her ears. She half expected him to break into one of those devastating grins and say, "Gotcha!" But he didn't. He looked serious. Intent.

"Is that such a bad idea?" he asked finally.

"You don't even know me! I don't know you!"

"Not well," he agreed.

"So then, what are you doing, talking about marriage?" She was strangling the quilt, totally discombobulated. Sloan Gallagher was proposing marriage? To *her?*

"Because it's crossed my mind."

"It crossed your mind and you proposed?"

"I think you're what I want in a wife."

She was gaping at him now. She was sure of it. "You think?" The mind boggled. "And so you proposed?"

"You said you didn't want a one-night stand."

Her mouth was opening and closing. Why on earth would Sloan Gallagher propose marriage to a woman who looked like a frumpy fish? It didn't make sense.

"You're going out with my sister next weekend," she reminded him.

He shrugged. "Because she's paying a lot of money for the pleasure. That has nothing to do with this."

"It does for me."

"If she weren't, then you'd say yes?"

"No! I told you, we don't know each other!"

"Then we should get to." He sounded so calm, so matter-of-fact, so *sensible!* As if proposing marriage to a widow with four kids and no prospects was an eminently reasonable thing to do.

Polly huddled inside her quilt, shaking her head, telling herself she'd obviously been working too hard. She was overworked, overtired and, today, overstimulated. She screwed her eyes shut, but when she opened them again, Sloan was still there, still looking at her.

"Polly?"

"What?"

"Think about it."

"No."

"Why not?"

"Because it wouldn't work."

"It could."

"No."

He shoved away from the door and came to stand beside the bed, looking down at her. "So what are we? Ships that pass in the night? Twice?" He sounded sardonic, sarcastic almost.

Polly ignored the sarcasm. "That's right."

"We could be more," he insisted. "Give us a chance."

"No."

"You're afraid."

"I'm *not* afraid. I'm realistic! I'm here. In Elmer. Every day. All year. You're not. You're in...in...Tierra del Fuego! We have nothing in common."

"We want the same things. Home. Family. Love. Each other."

Polly deliberately ignored the last two. "I have a home. I have a family," she said stubbornly.

"And I want to share them."

"You want junior high school dances and play practice and Cub Scouts and cranky college students? You're crazy!"

"Am I?"

"Yes! And you're leaving in the morning."

"I am," he agreed.

"There you are, then." It seemed clear and simple enough to Polly.

"But I'll be back. I promise you."

Chapter 16

He wouldn't be back.

Polly was sure.

Oh, someday she had no doubt he'd turn up to visit Gus and Mary. He'd probably drop in on Maddie as he'd promised. He might even come and see her. She might look up someday and find him at the post office window or standing on her front porch.

But he wouldn't be back for her—not the way he'd made it sound.

Polly knew all about "Out of sight, out of mind." The phrase hadn't got to be an old adage without having a kernel of truth.

Just ask Celie.

That was a good part of what had happened to her and Matt.

How many times more likely was it to happen to a jet-setting famous actor who had no real reason to return to Elmer? Matt had at least had family in the vicinity—and a fiancée. But even then he'd barely remembered to come back.

So, no, she didn't expect to see Sloan again. Not anytime soon.

After all, he hadn't even bothered to say goodbye this morning. When she came downstairs to fix breakfast for the kids before school, he had already gone.

"He said he had an early plane to catch," Jack told her. "He said he didn't want to wake you, said you needed your beauty sleep."

So she had looked like a frumpy fish! And that had been his way of telling her so. Needed her beauty sleep, indeed!

"Humph," Polly said, slopping oatmeal into bowls and slapping them on the table. But then, hating herself, she asked. "Did he say anything else?"

"He said he'd see us soon. I asked him if he'd come to my mountain man rendezvous." That was Jack's latest project in school.

"Don't get your hopes up." Polly dumped the oatmeal pot into the sink. "'See you soon' is just an expression."

"But—"

She turned and glared at him. "Don't, Jack."

Jack gave her a mutinous look. "He said he'd try."

"He said he'd come to my play," Lizzie announced, breezing into the kitchen and dumping her backpack on the counter.

"And that I could come to his ranch and ride horses." Daisy bounced into the room after her sister. "That'll be so cool."

All three children gave her bright, sunny, optimistic smiles.

The auction is over, Polly wanted to shout at them. *Elmer isn't famous anymore. Sloan Gallagher is gone. The world is back to normal.*

"Eat your oatmeal," she said crisply.

They ate. They chattered about Sloan, about the play and the ranch and the mountain man rendezvous. They gathered up their books and backpacks, yelled, "Bye, Mom!" cheerfully, banged the door shut and thundered down the steps.

The last words Polly heard them say were, "Sloan said...Sloan thought...Sloan promised..."

Damn him, Polly thought. Damn, damn, damn him. He should know better.

You didn't make promises to kids that you weren't going to be able to keep.

* * *

Sara didn't ask Flynn for promises.

She didn't have to. He'd loved her all night long. He'd shared himself with her. That was a promise—all the promise she needed.

She made up her mind not to cling. She knew he had to go back to New York, that he had obligations. She knew he had to go to L.A. later this week for Sloan's premiere. She understood that.

She had obligations, too.

He admired her determination, her focus, her goals. He'd told her that this weekend. When she'd told him about medical school, about how she'd been working toward it ever since she was fifteen, he'd been impressed. He said he'd never met a girl with more purpose.

She tried to remember that purpose now. To focus on it. It was the only way she was going to get through this, the only way to be bright and cheerful as they sat side by side in the airport and waited for his flight to be called.

She wished he would stay. Or she wished he would say, "Come with me."

But he didn't say anything at all. He stared straight ahead, his expression unreadable. He didn't look at her.

She couldn't stop looking at him. She supposed it wasn't the thing to do, but she couldn't help it. She just sat there and drank in the sight of him, remembering what he'd looked like making love to her, kissing her, holding her tenderly after, saying, anguished, "My God, why didn't you tell me?"

That she'd been a virgin.

She hadn't even thought about it. She'd only thought about him. What had occurred between them this weekend had been so deep, so perfect, so profound, that she couldn't imagine not sharing the rest of herself with him. When they had loved, they'd connected on every level—emotional, intellectual, spiritual, physical. They were a couple now

He might leave. But he would come back. Sara knew that.

So she wouldn't cling, she wouldn't press. She wouldn't smother him with her demands.

"I hope your plane's on time," she said with all the cheer she could muster. And then, lest he think she was trying to get rid of him, she added, "I've got a bio exam at nine."

He glanced at her then and he seemed to come back from a long way away. "You don't have to hang around."

"Of course I'll hang around. I mean, bio's important, but…" She stopped, unsure how important biology was or rather, how important she ought to make it sound. "I'll be all right," she said. "It's just one test. I'll make med school. No fear." She gave him a bright smile.

He grinned back. "Sure you will. Top of the class, no doubt."

"No doubt," Sara said. *And you'll be there to cheer me on, won't you?* she wanted to ask. But that would be pressure, so she didn't. She'd run after him last night. Now it was up to him.

"They're calling my flight." Flynn got to his feet and picked up his bag.

Sara scrambled up, too, and looked up into his beautiful face. They were inches apart. "I—" She stopped, got a grip, smiled. "Have a good flight. I—"

There was turmoil on his face. His jaw worked. A muscle ticked in his temple. "Sara, I— We shouldn't have—"

"Of course we should have," she said, cutting him off. That was the one thing she was sure of. "Don't tell me you regret it!"

He shook his head. "I'll never—"

"Well, I don't either," she said firmly. One more bright smile. *Don't go!*

Flynn dropped his bag, wrapped her in his arms and kissed her, deep and hard.

Yes! Oh, yes!

But then he pulled back. He shook his head, opened his mouth, then closed it again. He sighed, grabbed his bag and, without another word, hurried through the boarding gate door.

Sara watched him go. Desperately she told herself it would be all right.

He would be back.

* * *

The last thing Jace wanted to see this morning was Celie
O'Meara's smiling face.

"Good morning!" she sang, all cheer and bright smiles as
she sailed into Artie's store—late!—and tossed her jacket toward the hook. She missed.

Jace grunted and stared at the column of figures he'd been
adding.

"Ah, in a good mood, are we?" Celie said gaily.

"Just peachy."

She didn't even bother to pick up her jacket, so he bent
down, snatched it up, jammed it on the hook, then went back
to the estimate he was making on some lumber for a local
rancher.

"Thank you." She aimed another smile in his direction, then
breezed past him toward the register.

She was wearing some flowery scent this morning, and it
lingered long after she had passed. He tried breathing through
his mouth.

"You're not catching cold, are you?" Celie asked, turning
to look at him.

"No."

"Because your eyes look a little bloodshot and you look a
little peaked."

"I'm not sick!"

Except inside. He'd felt sick inside ever since he woke up
at five this morning to find himself in bed with Tamara Lynd.

He'd been dreaming about Celie. About making love with
Celie. About touching her and kissing her and easing himself
inside her. And then he'd awakened to find Tamara's hand on
him, his body primed for release at the same time that his mind
rebelled.

Last night he'd given in. He'd been angry, hurt, his dreams
dashed, his hopes thwarted. He'd taken what Tamara had offered. He'd given her release, as well. But that was all it had
been—release.

But he'd resisted that release this morning. Instead he'd
eased himself out of bed and had stood under an icy shower

until his teeth chattered so hard he thought they'd crack. Still his body ached and his mind whirled and his heart ached.

And he damned well didn't need Celie O'Meara waltzing in wearing flowery perfume and humming snatches of some romantic tune!

He couldn't remember whether he was carrying eight or nine. "Damn it!" He slammed down his pencil and broke the lead.

Celie made a tsking sound.

"Go to hell," Jace muttered.

"No thank you," she said quietly. "I've been there."

His head jerked up. "What?"

"After Matt," she said.

It was the first time his name had been mentioned by either of them. Jace swallowed a groan. He did not want to talk about Matt this morning.

But since when had what he wanted ever mattered?

Celie said, "I was in hell after he dumped me. And then I guess I was in purgatory for a lot of years. And now I'm not."

Jace stared at her. "Because you spent your entire life savings on a date with Sloan Gallagher?"

"Yes."

"You really think he's going to...marry you?"

Considering the way his luck was running these days, Jace thought wearily, Gallagher actually might.

Celie shrugged. "I think," she said, "it's time to stop dreaming and find out."

Celie had actually expected to wake up this morning and regret what she'd done.

But when she opened her eyes and stretched and thought about it, she realized she didn't.

She was a little scared, a little excited and oddly relieved.

For years she had carried with her all the ideals of courtship and marriage and family—ideals that she'd never been allowed to test after Matt's defection, ideals that had simply grown with time and fantasy until she hadn't been able to move for the weight of them.

And now it was as if the weight of her ideals had been lifted. She was going to face reality this weekend. She was going out with Sloan Gallagher.

And she didn't care what anyone said—especially not cranky, annoying Jace Tucker—she was looking forward to the prospect.

"Joyce?" The voice on the phone was male and familiar, but Joyce couldn't place it.

It wasn't as if men called her these days.

"Yes?"

"It's Walt Blasingame. I was wonderin'…is it hard, learnin' Spanish?"

Not exactly a question she was expecting. "What? No," Joyce said, confused. "But I don't know how well I learned it, do I?" She gave a little laugh. "I've never tried it."

"But you reckon you could get by? Maybe prove you made the effort?"

"What?"

"I was thinkin' I might give it a try."

"You want to learn Spanish?" That surprised her, but no more than his answer.

"No. Vietnamese." He hesitated, then went on to explain. "I was there in the war. 'Course you know that. We were there together, me an' Gil."

"I remember." She and Gil hadn't been married long. She'd just had Polly. He might have got a deferment because of being married with a child, but Gil had just shrugged and said, "If it ain't me, some other poor sucker'll have to go."

Joyce had been all for the other poor sucker going, but that wasn't the kind of man Gil was.

"I went back last year," Walt said now. "But I didn't know the language. Figured I was too old, but if you can learn Spanish…"

"Well, of course, you can learn some Vietnamese," Joyce said. "I mean, I don't see why you wouldn't be able to. Are you thinking of going there again?"

The war there seemed so long ago. Gil had never much

talked about it. "Got better things to do," he'd always said, and he'd certainly never been interested in going back. Not once, let alone twice.

"Maybe," Walt said. "Reckon I'll order me some tapes or somethin'. Don't suppose you'd want to study 'em with me? Give a guy a little support? You bein' bilingual an' all?"

Joyce laughed at that. "Bilingual? Because I can order a beer and tacos and a room with two single beds?"

"An' you can dance," Walt said. "Don't forget you can dance. How about it?"

Well, why not? What else did she have to do?

Joyce smiled. "All right."

Even if Sloan was out of sight, it was hard for Polly to keep him out of mind when Celie talked about him all the time.

He apparently called several times and talked to Celie, telling her what was going to happen, where they were going to go and what they were going to do.

Every day, it seemed, there was something new to report. Something new Sloan had done to make Celie's weekend a dream come true.

Celie told her the name of the trendy restaurant where they would be having dinner before the premiere. She talked about staying at a posh Beverly Hills hotel.

"For three nights," she said, eyes wide. "I won't be home until Monday. Besides dinner and the premiere, he's taking me around Hollywood and showing me all the stars on the sidewalks. We're going to do a VIP tour of one of the studios. And he said he'd take me out to the beach for an afternoon."

"It's winter in California, too," Polly reminded her, feeling like a spoilsport.

"Not to swim. We'll swim at the hotel or at his place, he said. I guess he must have an indoor pool. He said he'd take me to see his place, too." Celie's eyes were bright and eager. They'd been bright and eager all week.

Polly had thought her sister might have second thoughts, but Celie seemed to be going into this full speed ahead. Sometimes Polly wondered whatever had become of the reticent young woman who had sleepwalked her way through life for the past ten years? Not that she wanted her back, of course.

But she didn't want Celie going out into the world and getting hurt.

"You know he might not, um, feel the same way you do?" she warned, feeling guilty even as she did so and irritably wondering why. It wasn't as if, no matter what he'd said, Sloan was two-timing Celie. Polly hadn't heard a word from him since that night in her room when she'd turned down his proposal of marriage.

Marriage!

And then he hadn't even called!

Celie shrugged. "He might not. But this isn't really about him."

Polly stared.

"It's not," Celie explained. "They were my dreams. Not his. I have to do this, Pol'." She looked at her sister earnestly.

And all Polly could do was nod. "I know."

It was like sending your child off to kindergarten for the first time, Joyce thought.

As she stood by her daughter in the airport Friday morning, she kept wanting to ask Celie if she'd brought her crayons and kept checking to see that she'd tied her shoes.

They should lock me up, Joyce thought.

Celie was doing fine. Much better than her mother. Better than Polly, too, for that matter. Polly had, if anything, been even more worried about Celie than she was. Polly had been fretting all week, worrying more about Celie than about Sara.

Sara had been distracted all week. Joyce thought it might be because of that young man she'd seen so much of on the weekend, the reporter with the lovely accent and the quicksilver smile. But when she'd mentioned it to Polly, Polly had shaken her head.

"Not Sara," she'd said. "Sara will never have her head turned by any man."

Joyce supposed Polly was right. Sara was probably just worried about school. She had midterms soon and she was worried about her chemistry class.

"Do you think Sara is all right?" she asked Celie now.

"What?" Celie seemed to come back from a thousand miles away. "Sara? What's the matter with Sara?"

"Nothing. I just think she's working too hard."

"She's focused," Celie said firmly. "She knows what she wants and goes after it. Sara doesn't dither. You should be proud of her."

"I am," Joyce said. "I'm proud of all of you."

Celie made a wry face. "You don't think I'm an idiot to be doing this?"

Joyce shook her head. "I think you're very brave."

"I should have done something years ago!"

"You weren't ready," Joyce said. "Now you are."

She wasn't really as calm and collected as she pretended to be. In fact, as the plane was landing in Los Angeles, Celie wished her jaw was wired shut to keep it from sagging at the sight of the miles and miles of urban sprawl.

It was so bright, too. The blue of the ocean, white of the beaches, the seasonal green of the Santa Monica mountains...

"The brown of the smog," Sloan laughed when she told him her impression.

He came to meet her at the airport. She'd prepared herself for some studio emissary who would whisk her away to her hotel. But instead she'd got off the plane to find Sloan and a couple of dozen photographers waiting for her.

All week long Elmer had been back to normal, and the craziness of the week before the auction had faded from her mind. The exploding flashbulbs brought it all back.

"Smile," Sloan said, slipping an arm around her shoulder, "and I'll get you out of here."

Celie smiled. *Sloan Gallagher has his arm around me,* she thought and wondered why her knees didn't wobble and she didn't faint.

It became apparent pretty soon.

Sloan Gallagher in person was every bit as gorgeous as he

was in pictures and in films. He was easygoing and casual and friendly. Like a brother.

And that was the truth, right there.

He was warm and friendly and clearly determined to show her a good time. He drove her around Hollywood, pointing out landmarks. He parked and they got out and walked on Hollywood Boulevard. People gawked at him, and lots more cameras clicked. But he handled it all with the same grace and aplomb with which he'd handled the swarms back in Elmer, all the while making Celie feel comfortable and welcome. He was as easy to talk to as she'd ever imagined he might be.

But the spark wasn't there.

Maybe it was because he didn't look deep into her eyes the way she'd once imagined he would. Maybe it was because he was friendly without overstepping some invisible but clearly defined line.

Or maybe it was because while he told her whatever she wanted to know about Hollywood and his films and his next project, when the conversation was left up to him, it invariably went back to one thing—Polly and the kids.

At first Celie was a little annoyed. Who had spent twenty-three thousand dollars to come out here this weekend, after all?

But then she realized that what she'd told Polly was true—she'd bid on him not so much for him as for herself. It was as if she had to do this to win back her life, to get out of her rut and move on.

She'd done that. She could feel it in her bones.

"Did she call?"

It was probably the tenth or twentieth time Polly had asked the question, and it was only Sunday night. She'd gone out to Joneses' with Daisy and Jack so that Daisy could ride horses and Jack could play with Will and so that she wasn't home worrying about Celie all day long and waiting for the phone to ring.

And a good thing, too, because apparently it hadn't. She'd rung only once from her hotel room on Friday simply to say she was there.

"It's fabulous," she'd told her mother. "Like a fairy tale. A dream come true."

Polly's jaw had tightened upon hearing it.

Now her mother shook her head. "Not a word," she said, barely glancing up from the book she was studying.

To keep from gnashing her teeth, Polly focused on something else. She turned her head sideways to read the title. "*Vietnamese in 21 Days?* Whatever happened to Spanish?"

"I'm still studying it. This is to help Walt."

"Walt Blasingame is learning Vietnamese? Why?"

Polly was prowling around the kitchen, needing something to do. They'd eaten dinner with Taggart and Felicity and their family, so she didn't have a meal to fix. Now she started unloading the dishwasher, which at least would give her something to do. What was the matter with Celie? Why didn't she call? Didn't she know people were worried? Well, not worried exactly, but…curious.

"He went back there last year. Said he might go again." Joyce shrugged, and it took Polly a minute to realize that her mother was talking about Walt. "Some men never get over what happened in the war. They need to go back. For closure."

"Twice?" That didn't sound like closure to Polly.

"Don't ask me," Joyce said mildly.

"Aren't you worried about her?" Polly demanded.

"No."

"Well, you ought to be! He's lethal. Persistent. If he wanted her in bed, she wouldn't stand a chance."

"If."

Polly plopped into a chair, then bounced right back out again. "Am I the only one who cares?"

"About what?"

"About Celie, of course!"

Her mother just nodded and went back to her book. "Oh. Of course."

Polly went to the airport to pick Celie up Monday night.

"*If* she's even there," she'd grumbled to her mother on the way out the door. Celie hadn't called since Friday. She might have eloped to Tijuana with Sloan. They might be honey-mooning on the French Riviera or basking with the seals in Tierra del Fuego! Who knew?

Polly didn't. She gnashed her teeth and said pithy things all the way to Bozeman, getting them out of her system, deter-mined to be blasé and indifferent by the time she was face-to-face with the little cree— with her sister.

It worked.

She dredged up the same smile she'd put to such good use during the insanity prior to the auction. It was a little worn and frayed around the edges now, but Polly was sure she could get a few more minutes out of it.

Celie was the first person off the plane. "It's what happens when you come first class," she babbled. "You get great food and hot wet towels and big plush seats and—"

"How's Sloan?"

Celie blinked, then slowly she smiled again. A Cheshire Cat sort of smile. One that said I-know-something-you-don't-know. "Fine. He's fine," she said brightly. "Lovely, actually." She batted her lashes.

Since when did Celie bat her lashes, for God's sake? Polly felt an odd clenching feeling deep in the pit of her stomach. And right on top of it came a powerful surge of anger. How dare he propose to her one day and scant days later make an-other woman—her *sister,* no less!—look like the cat that got the cream?

"How nice," Polly said through her teeth. She turned and stalked toward the baggage claim area.

"Wait!" Celie exclaimed.

But Polly kept right on walking. Steamed. Furious. Hurt.

Celie caught up with her, looking worried. "What's wrong?"

"Nothing." Polly wiped her palms down the sides of her jeans and took a deep breath. "Nothing's wrong. I just…had a long day."

"Oh, right. Still getting the mail leftovers from Valentine's Day?"

Celie thought the post office was her problem? Polly just

nodded. "That's right." She clamped her teeth together so she didn't ask anything else. She would listen. Celie would tell all eventually.

As they waited for Celie's bags, she did. She told Polly about how wonderful Sloan had been to her, how he'd taken her everywhere, shown her everything. She talked about their dinner before the premiere, about the event itself, about the movie. She went on and on about the movie. *I don't need a review!* Polly wanted to scream. But then Celie got to the parties after. She told Polly about Sloan introducing her to so many famous stars she couldn't remember them all.

"It was amazing."

"I bet you were exhausted."

"Oh, no! I was jazzed! Totally. Wired. So he took me back to his place."

Polly nearly bit her tongue. It was all she could do to stand there and smile and say, "Oh, really? Did he? How nice."

It was an acting job worthy of an Oscar. She'd missed her calling at the post office.

"It's a great place," Celie said. "Two stories. Right on the ocean at Malibu. You can go out on his deck at dawn and it's just the most beautiful place on earth."

At dawn. Which presumably meant Celie had slept there. Or *not* slept, as the case had been.

Slowly Polly felt all her anger seep away, and it was replaced by a weary sort of hollowness and a shiver of envy that Celie had gone after what she wanted and, against all odds, had got it.

"Is it?" she said listlessly.

"Oh, yes." Celie babbled on about the size of the rooms, the glorious views, the sunken tub in the master bedroom— another shaft of envy pierced a little deeper—the indoor pool.

"Just for laps, really," Celie said. "So he can stay in shape."

"Of course."

"And he has horses, too. We were going to go riding, but we didn't have time. But he said we'll do it next time."

"So you're going to see him again?" The question was out before Polly could stop it.

Celie looked at her with surprise, as if it were a stupid question, which of course it was. "See him again? Oh, yes."

By the time Celie went off to bed, still smiling, Polly had heard the story of her weekend six times over. Celie had told it to the kids one after the other. She'd told it to Gus and Mary and then to Alice and Cloris. She had been going to stay up until Joyce and Sara got home so she could tell them.

But Polly said, "You must be tired. Surely they can wait until morning."

And Celie, masking a yawn, finally agreed. But her eyes were still sparkling when she danced her way upstairs.

"Oh, what a beautiful weekend," she crooned softly.

And Polly sat in the rocker in the living room and stared at the fire in the fireplace and thought, *It must have been.* And she'd better get used to it, because whenever anyone asked her, "Are you seeing Sloan again?" Celie had always answered, "Yes."

Jack, of course, had been more blunt. "You gonna marry him?"

To that Celie had shaken her head. "We're just friends."

It was like one of those "no comment" statements and Polly knew it. She resigned herself. Sloan Gallagher might soon be her brother-in-law.

"Get used to it," she told herself.

Oh, yes, sure. Some year.

She ought to go to bed and try to sleep. But she didn't think sleep was in the cards.

So she stayed up and waited for Sara to come in. For a panic-stricken moment she thought she might have forgotten her daughter somewhere again. But then she remembered that Sara had said she was going to study late at the library.

"Not with Gregg?" Polly had asked.

"Maybe." Sara had been distant. Offhand.

Midterms, Polly decided. They were the only thing that could stress Sara out.

It was eleven-thirty when Sara returned. She looked surprised to see her mother sitting in the chair.

"I thought for a minute I'd mislaid you again," Polly told her with a faint grin.

Something that might have been a ghost of a smile flickered across Sara's face. "No. I was just…studying."

"Midterms?"

Sara nodded. She toed off her boots, hung up her jacket and started toward the stairs, then stopped. "Did Aunt Celie get back?"

"Yes."

"Did she have a good time?"

"Very."

Sara's eyes widened. "Really? Is she…? Do you think they…?"

Polly wasn't about to speculate. Not for anyone else. "You can ask her about it in the morning," she said shortly.

"Did she…mention Flynn?"

"Who?"

"Flynn. The writer," Sara said impatiently. "The one who was here last weekend."

As if there had only been one. Polly shook her head. "Not that I recall."

Sara's face fell. "Oh."

"What's this?" Polly asked. It was the first time she'd seen her daughter react at all to a member of the opposite sex.

Sara shook her head. "Nothing. I just wondered." She turned away. "G'night." And she hurried up the stairs.

Polly closed her eyes and rocked slowly. Sid the cat sidled up to her and leaped into her lap. He circled and curled and kneaded and, finally, settled. Both dogs sprawled at her feet. All she needed was a shawl and trifocals, Polly thought, and she'd be ready for old age.

Her life was over. It was as simple as that.

The door opened again and another blast of winter air blew in.

Her mother's cheeks were red from the cold. She looked startled to see Polly, too. "What's wrong? Did Celie…?"

"Celie's fine. Celie's *faaaabulous,*" Polly said, quoting her sister in her sister's tone of voice. "She had a *terrific* time."

"Well, thank God for that," Joyce said, unwrapping her scarf and unzipping her coat. "I'd hate to think she was disappointed after all she paid."

"She's not disappointed. I think you can safely count on that."

Her tone had her mother's brows lifting. "Oh? Really? She's seeing him again?"

"So she says."

"Well, my heavens." Joyce considered that. "Amazing," she murmured as she headed for the stairs. "The world is a very strange place."

Isn't it just? Polly thought.

The fire burned down. Sid got up and stretched. He hopped off her lap and stalked around the room. The dogs got up, too, and peered out the window. Roy wagged his tail. Spiffer wagged his whole body. They ran to the door.

"Time to go out?" Polly said. "Such enthusiasm. All right. One last time."

She opened the door.

Sloan was standing there.

Chapter 17

"We have to stop meeting like this," he drawled, resisting the impulse to grab Polly and haul her into his arms.

He'd been aching to do it all week. All the time he'd been hauling her sister around Los Angeles, he'd wished it were Polly in her shoes. Now he grinned at her, and then had to move quickly to jam his foot in the door before she slammed it in his face.

"Hey! Whoa! What's this? I told you I'd be back!"

But Polly was still pushing, trying to shut the door on him. Sloan leaned his shoulder into it, and he was a lot stronger than she was. She didn't have a prayer. Then abruptly she stepped away and he pitched forward into the room.

"Pol'!"

But she was hurrying toward the stairs. Determined to catch her, he shoved the door shut, he vaulted over the dogs and grabbed her by the arm before she could escape the room.

"What the hell is going on?" he demanded. "What are you mad about?" She tried to shake free, but he wouldn't let go. "Damn it, Polly! Answer me!"

Her eyes flashed. "Why should I? What does it matter to you?"

"You matter to me! I told you that."

"Yes, and you also told my sister you'd see her again."

"I will," he said flatly. "Tomorrow at breakfast with luck." He shoved a hand through his hair. "Why? What did you think? That I came on to you and then turned right around and came on to her?"

"She said she had a terrific time. She said she spent the night at your house. She said the sunrise was beautiful!" Polly's voice rose higher and higher.

She was *jealous?* Sloan didn't dare hope.

He said firmly, "And it probably was. I wouldn't know. I was asleep. In *my* bed. And she, I presume, woke up and got out of *hers*—which was in a different room."

Polly didn't say anything for a long moment. Then, in a small voice she said, "Oh."

"I didn't sleep with your sister, Polly. I don't want to sleep with your sister. And she doesn't want to sleep with me."

"I know that's not true! She spent twenty-three thousand and change on you!"

"Cripes." Sloan shook his head. "You make it sound like my price for the night. There was nothing in our weekend about goin' to bed. Maybe at one time she wanted to, I don't know. But, hey, that was before she knew me." He grimaced at his own words. "How's that for a recommendation? Once she got to know me, she changed her mind."

Polly looked doubtful. "Are you sure?"

"We discussed it."

"You did?"

"I asked her why on earth she bid that much money, and she was honest with me. She told me about what's-his-name jilting her. She told me she'd gone into a shell after that and that when she first started looking at guys again, I was the one she looked at. Dreamed about," he added self-consciously.

Polly stared at him. "Celie told you all that?"

"We don't have any secrets, your sister and I," Sloan said, and that was pretty much the truth. Celie had been more than frank with him. She'd even told him when it was she began to think he might not be the one.

"I think it happened after I'd seen you naked," she'd told him frankly, though not without blushing. "It was, um, a shock. But after I thought about it, I realized you were just another man."

That hadn't done a lot for his ego and Sloan didn't tell Polly about it now. Hopefully in the not-too-distant future, Polly would have a different opinion of his naked body.

All he said was, "Celie's got guts. She's willing to take a chance. But she knows which O'Meara daughter I'm interested in. She wished me the best of luck."

Polly didn't reply. She seemed to be mulling it over and Sloan didn't want to push her, unless of course she was mulling her way toward throwing him out again.

"I didn't come back for Celie," he said finally when she still didn't speak. "I came for you. It's always been you."

She pressed her lips together and held herself quite still. But she wasn't trying to pull away anymore. She stayed where she was, inches from him. He could see the rise and fall of her breasts beneath the sweatshirt she wore. There was a pulse beating at the base of her throat. Her lips were slightly parted and he wanted—*needed*—to taste them.

He edged closer, bent his head and prayed she wouldn't bolt as he touched his lips to hers.

Sloan had kissed a lot of women. They'd fill a veritable *Who's Who* of the world's most beautiful actresses, gorgeous models, heiresses, high-society belles. But not one of them kissed like Polly.

There was a sweetness to Polly, a tenderness that he'd felt with no other woman. She was strong—good Lord, was she strong!—but she was vulnerable, too. And that very vulnerability was there in her kiss. It made him go slow when he wanted to go fast. It made him take care when he simply wanted to plunge ahead. It made him savor every moment that their mouths touched, that her body leaned almost imperceptibly into his. It made his grip on her arms loosen and his hands slide in and around to bring her body next to his. He'd wanted this so much, for so long!

She was responding. Opening. Kissing him with the eagerness with which he kissed her.

Now, he thought. Now she could go upstairs and he would go with her. He would join her in the bed where he'd lain alone before, and he would know the wonders of her body and her love—at last.

And then Polly raised her hands between them and pressed against his chest, creating space between them, pushing back. "That's enough," she whispered shakily.

"It's not," Sloan said, and knew it was the truth. "It's not nearly enough."

Polly's smile was strained. "But it's all there's going to be."

"You want it, Pol'," he argued. "You want me."

She didn't deny it. But still she shook her head. "We don't always get what we want."

"I'm not some schoolboy. I don't need a lecture," he said sharply.

"Then think!" Her eyes were bright. "Even if I wanted to, I wouldn't sleep with you here!"

"Why not?"

"Because my children are here! I'm not going to have them thinking their mother just hops into bed with movie stars."

"That's what they'd think, huh? You get a lot of movie stars in this neck of the woods wanting to sleep with you?"

"You know what I mean!" Spots of color were high in her cheeks. She glared at him, then abruptly looked away. "Besides," she said in a low voice, "I haven't slept with anyone since Lew died."

He hoped his gratification didn't show—or his frustration. He should have realized, of course. Polly was not the sort of woman who would sleep around. She might have slept with Lew years ago without benefit of marriage. But there was no doubt she had loved him deeply, and no doubt that her commitment had been total.

That's what lovemaking was to Polly McMaster. Total. Complete. Wholehearted giving. And sharing.

It wasn't casual or recreational. It was far more profound.

And, realizing it, Sloan realized that what he'd thought he wanted, what he'd told Polly he wanted—closeness, intimacy, warmth, sharing, home and family—wasn't what he wanted at all.

Or maybe it was, but it was only part of it.

What he really wanted was more. He wanted the connection that existed between two people whose love embraced more than each other. He wanted to live in a world whose driving force was that love. He wanted Polly to share that connection, that love, with him.

And he knew what that meant.

He sighed. "I'll bunk with Jack."

The world was, indeed, a very strange place, Joyce thought as she tried to get comfortable in her bed. Ordinarily she came home from work and hit the pillow and was out like a light.

Not tonight.

Tonight she was thinking about what Walt Blasingame had said.

He'd been sitting with Artie when she'd dropped by during her dinner hour to visit the old man. She'd been surprised to see Walt. He'd looked glad to see her.

"Hoped maybe you'd stop by. Thought maybe we could practice," he said. "During dinner?"

"Order dinner in Vietnamese?" Joyce had said. "I don't think there are any Vietnamese restaurants in Livingston."

"We can go to Sage's," Walt said.

"Well, I—" Joyce hesitated. She felt awkward all of a sudden.

But Artie looked pleased. "Good idea. Bring me a beer."

Walt winked. "I'll see what I can do."

Sage's wasn't crowded on weeknights. They had a table in the corner where they sat with their phrase books and tried to read them in the flicker of candlelight. Neither of them could do it easily even with their bifocals.

"Ain't life grand?" Walt muttered.

Joyce laughed softly. "Gil always said it's better than the alternative."

"Well, I ain't ready to find out." Walt went back to the phrase book, squinting at it, mumbling, then saying, "How d'you reckon you pronounce this?"

"We need tapes," Joyce said. "I think the language is tonal. Do you remember?"

"A little. There was a teacher I knew there…"

And then he told her about a woman called Sue, and gradually Joyce began to understand Walt's fixation on Vietnam: he had a daughter born to a Vietnamese woman.

"I met her mother before I married Margie," he said. "She was a teacher. Called her Sue. She taught me a little of the lingo. Used to laugh at how bad I was. She was a sweet lady." He got a sad smile on his face. "Kind to a homesick G.I. I was a long way from home. Lonely as hell."

"You don't have to explain," Joyce had said.

But Walt had. He told her about Sue, about his relationship with her, then about going to Hawaii for R&R and Margie, against all odds, meeting him there—*marrying* him there.

"Then I got back to Saigon and found out Sue was pregnant. I didn't know what to do."

Joyce could well imagine.

"I couldn't tell Margie. And Sue wanted the baby." He shook his head. "She said she understood." He shrugged. "What else could she say? I was gone before the baby was born."

"You never knew her? At all?" Joyce couldn't imagine having a child she'd never known.

"Never even knew she was a girl until couple of months back. Sue died—I knew that much—but I went back last year hopin' to find out somethin' more. Didn't happen. When I got home Charlie helped me write more letters. But nothin' happened. An' then outa the blue a couple a days ago I got this." He reached into his pocket and pulled out a thin airmail letter that already looked as if it had been opened and read many many times. He passed it over to Joyce, who opened it and scanned it.

It was an official document, translated, giving the birth name and parents of a child called An, a young woman about the same age as her Polly, who was entitled to call Walt Blasingame Dad.

"Charlie's got someone lookin' for her," Walt said. He paused and got a faraway look in his eyes for a long moment, and what he was seeing, Joyce was sure, was half a world and thirty-some years away. Then slowly his gaze returned to her, and in it she saw light and hope. "I might really find her."

And Joyce smiled. "Yes, you might."

"So I gotta learn this." He tapped the book.

"Yes." She understood his urgency now and his need to find his daughter. She thought, too, about An, the daughter who had never known her father.

Perhaps, of course, she'd had some sort of father in her life. But perhaps she hadn't.

Joyce knew what that was like. Her own father had died when she was just a few months old. She'd never known him. She'd only wished.

For Walt, for An, for herself—for the child she had been and the woman she was—Joyce had nodded. "I'll help."

Some things were just too cool.

Like getting a new puppy or hitting a home run or dragging yourself out of bed on a frosty February morning and discovering that the guy snoring in your bottom bunk was Sloan Gallagher.

Jack was wide-eyed in disbelief, then giddy with joy. "Whhoooo-eee," he breathed, creeping close and peering down at the famous stubble-jawed face. "Coo-ool."

Sloan's eyes opened. He blinked, squinted, then finally got his eyes focused on Jack. Jack beamed. "Hi! Does Aunt Celie know you're here?"

"Celie?"

"She said she was seein' you again."

"She is," Sloan said around a yawn. He shoved himself to a sitting position. "Seeing me. But I'm not here because of your aunt."

"You aren't?" Jack's face fell.

Sloan shook his head. "I came to court your mother."

Some things were even cooler than a guy could imagine.

It was all over town by lunchtime.

"Sloan's come courting, I hear," said Alice Benn when she came to pick up her mail.

"I see Sloan's back," Cloris remarked twenty minutes later.

Loney Bates said, "See yer feller's back in town," when he came midmorning to pick up a package.

Mary Holt came in with baby Mac during the lunch hour. She gave Polly a thumbs-up and a smile. "Good for you."

"What?" Polly said. "What are you talking about?"

Of course she knew. The whole town knew. Short of taping Jack's—and Sloan's—mouths shut with duct tape, there was no way she could squelch the rumors.

"Sloan's back," she agreed.

"And courting you," Mary said cheerfully, cradling Mac in one arm as she opened the post office box.

"He's *not* courting me," Polly objected.

The door to the post office opened and Sloan came in just in time to hear her protestation. "Sez you," he said easily.

Mortified, Polly glared at him.

He gave her an unrepentant grin, leaned through the window and planted a quick kiss on her lips. "I am," he told Mary with a wink, "courting her."

"Celie—" Polly started to object.

"—has given me her blessing," Sloan said firmly. "She thinks I'll be a dandy brother-in-law."

"I'll spread the word," Mary promised. She waggled her fingers at Polly on her way out. "Have fun."

Sloan grinned. "We will."

Jace didn't see Celie Monday night when she got back. But that night at the Dew Drop he heard that she'd had a terrific time. He heard she'd seen the sunrise from Sloan Gallagher's deck. He did his best to rationalize all that, though it wasn't easy and he felt pretty grim.

But when she showed up for work Tuesday morning, smiling brightly at him as he broke up crates in the back room, his spirits sank even lower.

"Had a good time, did you?" he muttered, because he had to say something to her, and it was obvious from her damnable humming that she wasn't contemplating doing herself in.

"Wonderful," she said, giving him the sunniest smile he'd ever had from her.

"Lived up to your dreams, huh?" Jace said, whacking apart one of the crates.

"Actually it was better."

He took a mighty swing and nailed his other hand with the hammer. "Hell!"

Protesting didn't do any good. Polly discovered that pretty quickly. Sloan Gallagher hadn't become a success just because he was a good actor. He'd succeeded because he was determined. He was equally determined, it seemed, to "court" her.

It was such an old-fashioned term that she found it vaguely embarrassing. But as days passed, she found it surprisingly endearing as well. He brought her lunch. He told her jokes. He rubbed her shoulders when she flexed them tiredly at the end of the day. He drove her down to see Artie in the evening and took her to dinner after. Just the two of them.

"It's what you call a date," he told her. "In case you'd forgotten."

She laughed, but in fact she didn't think she and Lew had ever gone out, just the two of them. Before they were married they hadn't been able to afford it, and after they were married, they'd had kids. "It's very nice, thank you," she'd said politely.

She thought he'd get bored and go away, but he never did.

Finally on Friday, when she got home from work and was immediately set upon by Jack needing her to sign his spelling test and Daisy clamoring to tell her about Joneses' new foal, she looked up and saw Sloan coming downstairs with his duffel bag in hand.

The sight gave her a kick in the stomach. *Stop it,* she told herself. *It's only what you expected. He can't stay here forever.*

"Do me a favor?" he asked.

Prepared to give him a ride to the airport, Polly nodded. "Of course."

"Spend the weekend at my ranch with me."

"What! But I can't do that!"

He raised his brows. "You promised," he pointed out guilelessly.

"Out of the question," Polly said. "Jack...Daisy..."

"All of you," Sloan said. "Naturally."

"Cool!" Jack shouted.

"Really?" Daisy's eyes were like saucers. "Can we ride horses?"

Sloan smiled beatifically. "Of course. If your mother agrees."

Tricked.

She'd been tricked. She glowered at him.

He smiled. "You don't want to teach your children that your word can't be trusted, do you?"

God, he was sneaky. There was no way Polly could wriggle off his neatly baited hook.

"Fine," she said grumpily. "We'll come."

He'd see just how much fun having a passel of kids could be.

Sara couldn't go.

Midterms, she said. She looked worried and distracted and Polly understood.

Lizzie couldn't go, either.

Play practice, of course. How could Polly have forgotten?

Daisy herself forgot that she had promised to baby-sit Hannah Nichols and C. J. Callahan all day Saturday while their dads taught bull and bronc riding at Taggart and Noah's rodeo school and their mothers did the flowers for a wedding down in Livingston.

"Can't I tell 'em something came up?" she moaned.

And Polly wished she could say yes because her passel of

kids was dwindling rapidly. But she shook her head. "You made a commitment—just like I did," she muttered as Sloan grinned at her.

"You can come another time," Sloan promised Daisy.

Polly wanted to tell him to stop making promises, but unfortunately, so far he seemed to be keeping them.

At least Jack didn't have other plans.

He was delighted at the prospect of spending the weekend on the ranch. "This is so cool," he said over and over, ripping around the house, getting ready, then reappearing to ask Sloan question after question.

"Can we ride horses?"

"How many cattle do you got?"

"What do they eat?"

"Can I rope one?"

If Sloan thought he was in for a nice relaxing romantic weekend, he was wrong.

Where Polly was concerned, Sloan had stopped expecting romantic anythings. In fact, he'd stopped making plans.

Loving Polly was like the improv class he'd signed up for when he finally decided to take acting seriously. It was like cowboying—riding out on the range where on any given day you never knew what to expect.

He'd liked improv. He'd thrived on cowboying.

He loved Polly.

This weekend he was determined to show her how much.

If Polly had given any thought to Sloan's ranch, she would have expected it to have a modern log house, state-of-the-art appliances, to be the sort of showplace befitting a Hollywood star.

Unlike Celie, Polly hadn't ever read Mariah Kelly's definitive article, Will the Real Sloan Gallagher Please Stand Up? If she had, she'd have known that in Sloan's "modern log house", *modern* meant indoor plumbing, the logs had all been sawed by his ancestors, and that his state-of-the-art appliances ran to a refrigerator run off a generator and a hundred-year-old wood stove.

All the "improvements" he'd made since he'd bought the place back had been on the barns, the fences and the herd.

"That's what makes it pay," he'd said as he pulled to a stop in front of the house. "I'm a rancher. I'm not just throwin' money down a bolt hole."

Polly had been first bemused, then charmed.

There were electric lights, run on the same generator that ran the refrigerator. But he often, he told her, used kerosene.

"Just seems to fit," he said as he ushered them in. "Makes me feel at home. Reminds me of my roots."

Sloan's roots, she discovered, were all here.

"Five generations of 'em," he told her. "My great-great-granddaddy built that barn." He pointed out the window toward the biggest one. "He and his brothers ran cattle up from Texas, did a little horse trading at Miles City, liked the summers here better than in Texas, hadn't really seen the winters yet—" he grinned "—but they decided to stick around. Bought some land when it came up for sale. Wintered over some cattle. Built their herds. They did all right for a fair number of years." He paused and she felt there was a fair amount he didn't say before he went on. "An' now we're doin' all right again." He waved a hand toward the horizon where the snow-covered Bear's Paw rose up above the valley. "What do you think?"

"It's beautiful."

It was.

She would have said Celie was the only one of them who had dreams. But this ranch reminded Polly of her own dream— long forgotten—of a ranch like this of her own. All at once she remembered being a teenager and daydreaming about a place like Ward and Maddie's—a ranch where she and Lew would raise kids and cattle. That was what they'd been working toward.

"Ain't gonna bullfight my whole life," Lew had said. "Reckon we can get us a ranch like that when I retire."

But with Lew's death, the dream had died, too. Polly hadn't even remembered it—she'd never had time. Until now.

She tried to resist it—to resist Sloan. It was a fantasy, she told herself, the sort of thing that Celie had had—and had grown out of. But it was hard to withstand being courted by one of the world's sexiest, most charming men. Especially when he wasn't only charming to her but to her son.

All the way to the ranch Jack had bombarded him with questions. He'd twitched and fidgeted and had asked a thousand things. And Sloan answered every one.

He'd said he would show Jack the horses and the barns as soon as they got there. And when he'd taken them into the house first, Jack had been impatient. Polly had given him a stern look and he'd subsided until Sloan's foreman, a bandy-legged grizzled cowboy called Davy turned up, got introduced, and had some things to discuss with Sloan.

Then Jack had said plaintively, "I thought we were gonna go to the barn."

"Jack!" Polly warned.

But Sloan nodded. "We are. You an' me and Davy. You can come if you want," he said to Polly.

But she declined. "I'll just make a cup of coffee and enjoy the quiet."

"You know how to deal with the stove?" He looked a little concerned. "I can do it for you."

"Artie and Maudie had one for years. I know how to use it. I'll be fine. Go on. Behave," she said to Jack.

Jack looked affronted. "I always behave."

Sloan ruffled his hair. "He'll be fine."

Polly hoped so. She hoped Jack didn't pester. "Would you like me to start some dinner?"

"I didn't bring you to work and wait on us," Sloan protested. "Maria, Davy's wife, keeps stuff in the freezer."

"I'll look," she said.

"Only if you want. Take a rest. Relax," he urged.

Polly wasn't sure she remembered how. But when the door closed after them, she felt a sense of peace settle over her. She looked around. It was a warm kitchen, a homey one. Not at all what she—or most any of those groupies who'd bid on Sloan— would have expected. They might have been appalled at the remoteness of the ranch, at the somewhat primitive conditions. But Polly found it gave her more to like about Sloan Gallagher than she would have imagined.

A dangerous notion, she reminded herself. She was finding far too many things to like.

She began to fill the coffeepot, but her attention was caught by the sight of him and Jack, a tall and dark-haired man with his hand on an equally dark-haired boy's shoulders as they walked with the old cowboy through the snow to the barn. Sloan's head was bent to listen to something Jack was saying. *Asking,* no doubt, Polly thought with a shake of her head. With Jack, everything was a question.

Thank God Sloan was patient. He would be a good father. Someday, she thought hollowly, he'd no doubt have children of his own.

She turned away from the window, drank her coffee, then looked around the downstairs of the house. On the walls and on the bookshelves there were old photos of the ranch in its early days. There were also pictures of several generations of lean, hard men with stubborn Gallagher jaws, and a smiling woman with dark hair and eyes just like Sloan's. His mother, she was certain.

On the mantel there were pictures of Sloan himself as a boy with his parents and another of him about junior high age with a couple of boys she thought were probably Gus Holt and his brother. They were grinning like fools and holding big belt buckles they'd apparently won at some small local rodeo. Just looking at it made Polly smile. The house contained so many early memories.

But there were no later ones. The photos stopped before his mother had been killed. The ranch had been sold only a couple of years later. And only after he'd had success as an actor had Sloan been able to buy it back. He'd restored the early photos—or maybe whoever had bought it had left it the way it was.

But as far as Polly could see there were no photos, no memorabilia, nothing at all of the actor Sloan.

She finished her coffee, then found the freezer and rummaged through it. There were several tubs labeled venison stew and several packs of beef and a couple of casseroles. She got out the stew and put the frozen block in a heavy cast iron pot. Then she worked with the stove until she had a low fire going. Putting the frozen stew on a back burner, she set the table for three, assuming that Davy would go home to his wife.

She thought they'd be back soon, but a couple of hours passed, the stew was ready to eat. She'd found a loaf of bread and had sliced it and set the table. When they still didn't appear, she went looking for them.

Davy's truck was still there, and she could see him in the tack room. But the high-pitched sounds of excited young boys drew her to one of the sheds. There she found Sloan and Jack and another boy messing with a tractor engine.

Jack looked up at the sound of her footsteps. "Hey! Mom, look. Sloan's showin' me an' Eric how to fix the tractor. This is Eric—" he nodded to the dark-haired boy about his size "—him an' me are gonna help feed the cattle tomorrow morning. But Sloan's gotta get the tractor fixed first 'cause they use it to haul the wagons. Davy said maybe he'd let me drive it. If you said it was okay. He said I could practice tonight. An' he said he'd teach me to build a loop an' rope a calf. Eric's got a calf dummy. An' he said I could spend the night. So can I, huh? Please?"

Polly blinked, trying to take all that in. Her forehead wrinkled. "I don't—" she began, not wanting Jack to impose.

"He was invited," Sloan said easily. "And not just by Eric. He's Davy and Maria's grandson. Their place is about a mile over the hill. Eric lives with them, and Davy's turning him into a real fine hand, right?" He grinned in Eric's direction.

The boy beamed and nodded. "Jack can come. My grandpa said it's okay."

"Please, Mom!" Jack implored. He had a smudge of grease on his nose and a desperate light in his eyes.

Polly didn't know when she'd seen him so eager, so happy. Jack wasn't usually *unhappy,* but she realized for the first time how much he was missing with just her and a houseful of women.

"Drive a tractor and rope a calf dummy?" She looked thoughtful as Jack's eyes begged her. "What more could a guy want?" she mused, smiling. "Sounds like a deal to me."

Sloan didn't believe it was going to happen.

There would be some cataclysmic event, some natural disaster—something!—that would come along and prevent him from making love to Polly McMaster.

He was sure of it.

Or if there wasn't, she could always just say no. He could close his eyes and see her saying it, politely but frankly. *Thank you, but no.*

So he didn't dare ask. He didn't want to hear that answer.

And if the truth were known, he didn't know what to say.

It had been years since Sloan Gallagher had had to wonder if a woman actually wanted to go to bed with him.

More often he was tossing over-eager women out of his room, changing his locks and bolting his door. Or, if he was attracted, he played along, whispering sweet nothings that meant exactly that—nothing. It didn't matter because all he and the woman in question really wanted was a roll in the sheets, a physical release and not much more.

Well, some of them had wanted more. Lots thought it would be a coup to be Mrs. Sloan Gallagher.

But Sloan had never been interested.

He'd been carrying a memory of Polly around in his head for twenty years. Whenever he thought of settling down, of having children, of committing himself to a woman—she was the woman he saw in his mind.

He'd obviously imprinted at an early age, he thought wryly. And for a fourteen-year-old, he'd had damn good taste.

Of course, Polly wasn't the same as she had been at seventeen. He didn't need to see her naked to know that. He didn't need to see her naked to know she'd improved with age. She was all that she had been—and more.

And she was here with him in his home—and for the first time since he'd known her, they were really alone.

Sloan had dreamed about this for years. And now that the

moment was at hand, like an awkward teenager unable to ask for a date, he couldn't seem to find the words.

Polly was in the kitchen dishing up the venison stew. "It's ready when you are," she'd said after they'd seen Jack off to spend the night with Eric.

"Right." He'd cleared his throat. "I'll just wash up." That would give him time to think of something to say.

At least, he'd hoped it would. But coming back to the kitchen to see Polly there, her gingery hair like spun copper in the light of the kerosene lamp she'd placed on the table, made him forget whatever he'd thought of.

All he could think then was how right she looked there, how much he wanted to touch her, how little he cared about eating venison stew.

But Polly was dishing it up. "Sit," she commanded, and she sat down opposite him.

He sat. He ate. Mostly he stared at her.

If she noticed his inarticulateness, she didn't comment. She talked enough for both of them—about the ranch, about the house, about Jack. She went on and on, and at some point Sloan realized the same thing was happening to her that had happened to him. She was as nervous as he was—but she dealt with it by talking nonstop while he retreated into silence.

He grinned. In fact he was so relieved he almost laughed.

Polly stopped midsentence. "What?"

He shook his head. "Nothing."

"You're laughing at me," she accused him, but she didn't sound angry.

He shook his head. "I'm not. Or maybe I am. But if I am, I'm laughing at both of us."

She opened her mouth, but no sound came out. Their eyes caught and held, and he felt sure she read in his what he wasn't saying. Flustered, she looked away.

"I don't—" she began.

"Don't you?" he asked softly.

She didn't answer at once. In the fireplace the burning wood hissed and popped. Otherwise there was only silence—and wanting.

"Jack—" she began again.

"Is happy as a pig in slop."

She smiled. "I guess he is." She looked a little wistful. "This has been very good for him. Thank you."

"You're welcome. I didn't do it for him."

Their eyes met again.

"I know," Polly said quietly. And this time she didn't look away.

Polly wasn't sure when she'd made the decision. Had it been when she'd let Jack go to Eric's for the night? Had it been when she'd agreed to come away for the weekend? Or had it been even longer ago than that—after Celie's weekend with him, when he hadn't taken from her sister what he could have, when he'd kept his promise and come back?

Polly tried to sort it out, but she couldn't. She knew it wouldn't last. Knew it was ridiculous to hope.

Yes, he'd once suggested marriage, but Polly wasn't a fool. He'd been in her bedroom at the time. He'd been angling to sleep with her, to satisfy some long-remembered fantasy. He still wanted to satisfy it.

And so did she.

Sloan Gallagher had reawakened desires and needs in her that she hadn't felt since Lew had died. She'd thought it possible that they'd died with him. She'd loved him so long and so deeply that she wouldn't have been surprised if they had.

She wasn't exactly sure she was glad they hadn't.

Waking up in the middle of the night now, she felt longings that she couldn't assuage with memories of Lew. And during the day sometimes she felt a kind of emptiness that didn't simply grow from grief. She felt a need to connect again.

It scared her. She hadn't wanted to lose her memories of Lew. So she'd fought the feelings. She'd fought herself.

And since Sloan had come, she'd fought him.

She was tired of fighting.

She was tired of being lonely.

She didn't expect marriage. She was willing to settle for one night of love.

* * *

In the end Sloan didn't need words. He didn't need to ask.
He got his answer, and could scarcely believe it was true.

They stood on either side of the table, then stepped around
it into each other's arms. He kissed her slowly, savoring the
taste of her, reveling in the softness of her hair as it tangled in
his fingers, then nuzzling her neck, nibbling her jaw, driving
himself wild with wanting her.

And she didn't just stand there. She didn't simply endure his
touch. She touched him, too. Her hands slid up his arms, they
roved over the expanse of his back, they skimmed down his
sides and came up again to rest against his chest. She lifted
her face to his kiss. She opened her mouth to his exploration.
She did some exploring of her own.

And the knowledge that she was as eager as he was made
him even more desperate. He pulled back, bit his lip, groaned.

"What?" Polly whispered. "Is something wrong?"

"Not a thing," his voice sounded ragged even to his ears.
"It's been a long time since everything was so right." He drew
her into his arms again and kissed her once more. And then he
dared to ask the question because he thought he knew the answer. "Will you come upstairs with me?"

Polly touched his cheek with her fingers. She cupped his jaw
and looked a long time into his eyes, and then she gave him
the answer he wanted. "Oh, yes."

Usually when he fell into his bed at the ranch, Sloan's eyes
closed almost before he hit the pillow. He rarely came here
unless he came to work, to put in long hours, to make the ranch
what he wanted it to be, to recontact his roots.

He'd never brought a woman here. He'd invited only one
before—Mariah Kelly—and for entirely different reasons.

Mariah had written a wonderful article as a result of spending most of a week here. But theirs had been a purely professional relationship, though in the course of the week they'd
become friends. Mariah had never been in his bedroom.

No woman had. Except Polly—in his dreams.

When he'd bought the place five years ago, he'd dreamed
of making the ranch the family spread that once upon a time

it had been. He would bring his wife here, he'd decided. They'd raise their children here.

But whenever he considered who that wife might be, whenever he'd daydreamed about it—Polly was the woman in the dreams.

He hadn't seen her in years. It didn't matter. He'd carried her with him always. He'd never imagined anyone else here.

Just Polly.

And now, at last, she was.

They'd brought the kerosene lamp with them, and he set it on the dresser. Then he turned to see her standing by the bed, her hair loose and tousled, a gentle smile on her face. She held out her hands to him, and he moved to grasp them.

"I remember..." he whispered.

But she didn't let him finish. She leaned into him and touched her lips to his. She slid her hands up his arms across his shoulders and down to the buttons on his shirt. Deftly she undid them, and he felt the cool air of the room touch his heated flesh.

He shrugged out of his shirt and tugged her sweater over her head. Then, with fingers far less adept than hers, he began to unfasten her buttons. She held still and let him do it, not brushing his hands away, just waiting, watching him gravely. He caught his lip between his teeth as his fingers fumbled, and he muttered, feeling like the desperate schoolboy he'd been so long ago.

Finally he finished and slid the shirt off her shoulders, felt the silken warmth of her skin beneath his fingers and bent his head to kiss her shoulders. He remembered them golden and freckled. There was barely enough light to see the freckles, only the gold.

Gently he bore her back onto the bed and wrapped his arms around her, eased off her bra and tossed it away. Their legs tangled, denim on denim, and they fumbled together to unzip, unsnap, unfasten and shed their jeans.

And finally they were together, skin on skin, flesh on flesh. Heart to heart. He bent close enough to hear hers beating and pressed a kiss to her breasts.

Polly. His Polly. Here.

As he'd always dreamed of her—smiling up at him, tracing a line down the center of his chest, splaying her hands on his abdomen, arching her hips against the need of his body.

Polly.

His.

She had thought she would feel awkward, inadequate, a far cry from the girl he remembered, a sad disappointment in comparison to the teenager she'd been.

But Polly didn't see disappointment in Sloan's hooded gaze. She saw hunger and desire and passion. She saw reverence, too.

It humbled her and at the same time it made her strong. It made her forget all her supposed inadequacies and made her remember this part of being a woman. She hadn't experienced it since Lew's death. She was grateful beyond words to find it again. It was such a marvelous, wonderful thing.

"Come to me," she whispered.

It was all the invitation Sloan needed.

He settled between her thighs and stroked her, driving her to respond, and trembling himself with the force of his need. And when he was sure she was ready, he came to her, and she drew him down and in.

Sloan felt a shudder run through him. He stilled. Tensed.

And then Polly shifted, arched, and pressed her fingers into his buttocks, urging him on. And he began to move.

He loved her with his body, with his heart and with his mind. He loved her with his memories and with his hopes and with his dreams.

And Polly, in spite of herself, loved him, too.

Chapter 18

They were an item.

And though Polly didn't like people talking and speculating and saying, "Ahhhh," and "Hmmm," in that knowledgeable, smug tone of voice, she could hardly deny it.

It wasn't just that she and Jack had gone away for the weekend with him. It was that when the weekend was over, Sloan didn't go away. He came back with her.

He stayed in Elmer. He said he'd go to Gus's if she wanted him to. But, heaven help her, she didn't want him to. So he moved back in with them.

He did, though, without a murmur, go back to bunking with Jack.

"For now," he said. "Until the wedding."

"What wedding?"

"Ours. You are going to make an honest man of me, aren't you?" He'd given her one of his famous shy, boyish, woebegone looks.

"Don't be ridiculous," Polly said. "You don't want to marry me."

He took her face in his hands and looked deep into her eyes. "Don't tell me what I want."

"But—"

He kissed her soundly. "Don't tell me, Pol'. Believe me. I love you. I want to marry you. I'll prove it."

Sloan could feel the fear in her. And outwardly he knew her objections made a certain amount of sense.

"We live very different lifestyles," she maintained.

On the surface that was true. She lived in rural Montana. He had a home in Malibu, and for the past six years he'd been jetting around the world from Tierra del Fuego to Timbuktu.

But that didn't mean it was what he wanted to do forever or that the ranch he owned didn't matter to him. Other than Polly, it mattered more than anything.

He told her that. "It's my home. It's the place I always come back to."

But he wasn't going to do it forever anytime soon. And he was honest about the rest of his life, too.

He was an actor. He went where he had to. When he married Polly—he said "when," not "if"—he'd still have to do some jetting. Depending on the roles he chose, he'd still spend time in various remote or exotic parts of the earth. He wouldn't be in Montana every day of his life. But wherever he was, he would love her, and he would like her—and the kids—to be with him as much as possible. And in any case, he told her, his job didn't define who he was.

Deep down Sloan was the cowboy he'd always been. In his bones and in his blood he was still part of a long line of Montana men who loved their land and their cattle. He might go other places, do other things, but this was where his heart was.

It was where Polly's was, too.

So, he told her firmly, for all that their lifestyles seemed different, their lives—what they loved and valued—weren't really so different, after all.

"Mmm," she said, and then offered another objection. "But you're a bachelor. I'm a widow with four kids."

"I did happen to notice that," he replied solemnly, then assured her, "I like your kids."

She just looked at him and uttered another noncommittal, "Mmm."

He could tell she wasn't convinced. "I love your kids," he said because it was more than simple "like" these days. The longer he knew them, the more he knew the statement was true.

Jack, equal parts exuberance and innocence, was a boy after his own heart. He loved having Jack trailing after him asking question after question. He liked practicing roping with Jack. He liked offering advice on the Pinewood Derby car. He liked hitting hockey pucks with Jack and feeding cattle with him. He couldn't imagine having a better son than Jack, and he told Polly so.

"Mmm," she said.

But he noticed that she smiled when she watched the two of them together, and he knew, whether she said it or not, that she was glad there was a man around the house for Jack to latch onto.

He loved the girls, too. He'd known a lot of women over the past few years, but he really knew very little about girls. It was endlessly fascinating to get to know them. They were baffling and contrary and absolutely wonderful.

Horse-mad Daisy was so unfailingly cheerful and wonderfully uncomplicated that he wished her mother would take lessons from her. Intense, yet dreamy, Artemis, aka Lizzie, popped up at odd hours and stood watching him in silence, while he was fixing the sink or changing a lightbulb or reading a script, and when he looked up and smiled she'd say, "Can I ask you something?"

She had as many questions as Jack, but of a very different sort.

"How can you tell when boys like you?" she asked him once. And after he'd stumbled his way through that, she'd asked, "If boys don't like you, do you think that will ever change?"

He took her questions as seriously as he took Jack's. He tried to explain how boys behaved and what they thought.

"They don't think," he said flatly. "Not often. They mostly act. And react."

And that had led them to a discussion of the differences between men and women. Sloan couldn't believe he was talking about this to a sixteen-year-old. But when he didn't shy away from her questions, she came back with more.

A week or so later she asked if he thought she should kiss on a first date.

"You're not old enough to date!" he blurted, then realized that she was only a year younger than Polly had been when she'd got pregnant with Sara. "Well, maybe you are," he said. "But go slow. You remember what I said about guys not thinking? Well that goes double when they're kissing girls. They know what they want, and it's not always for the best."

"Like sex," she said.

Well, yes.

Sloan wasn't sure if that was a question or not, but he answered it, anyway. "You definitely don't want to have sex. Not at your age. And," he added, "not just to be doing it. Sex is…well, fun—" cripes, he was blushing! "—but it means a whole lot more when you're in love."

Artemis/Lizzie smiled. "Like you."

He didn't know if that was a question either, nor did he know if Polly would want him to admit that he had made love to her. But the fact was he did love her, and he wasn't ashamed to admit that.

He nodded. "Like me."

If Jack and Lizzie, under whatever name, and Daisy talked at length to him about one thing and another, Sara never said much at all. She left the house early most mornings. She came home late most nights. And when she was there, she seemed to be a shadowy presence, a slim, dark-haired, pale-faced, preoccupied girl.

"Is she okay?" Sloan asked.

"She's fine. She has midterms," Polly explained.

But as February turned into March and March turned into

April, it seemed to Sloan that midterm was lasting a heck of a long time.

"She has papers, too," Polly told him. "Sara's premed. And you know what that means. She's working her tail off. But that's Sara. She's always had more purpose than everyone else put together. She and Gregg are determined to get into a top medical school. Can you believe it? Someday my daughter will be Dr. McMaster."

"Pretty impressive," Sloan agreed, though he hoped Sara was happier about it than she looked.

He didn't have much time to worry about Sara, though. Convincing Polly was a full-time job. He was lucky he had a hiatus before filming started on the picture he was doing for Trevor MacCormack with Becca Reed.

He had finally met with them during the days he was back in California before Celie came for her weekend. Trevor had been delighted with the chemistry between him and the up-and-coming Becca. A slight blonde woman with a surface look of a vulnerable pixie, Becca drew on reserves of tremendous power. She was a born actor. A natural.

"Like you," Trevor had told him. "It works. When the two of you are together things hum."

Fortunately, they weren't going to start humming until the first of May. Becca had commitments on a film in Ireland, Trevor was finishing up work on a project down under, then wanted another rewrite of the script, and Sloan, as usual, had bargained for time to be home during calving and branding—not that he was at his ranch a lot of the time this year.

But when he was, it was heaven. He'd always seen his ranch as a family place—and now it felt that way for real. He and Polly and whichever kids were available went up most weekends. Once or twice Joyce and Celie had come, though Celie appeared to be getting a life, and Joyce seemed to be spending most of her days studying languages of one sort of another.

Sloan didn't miss them. It was Polly he wanted. She made the ranch feel like home. And the kids brought a dimension he hadn't imagined.

He had a great time with Daisy, showing her the horses, then riding out with her. He taught Jack and Eric a lot about calving and branding. And Jack was becoming a dab hand with a catch rope. Those two came almost every weekend. And once the play ended even Lizzie/Artemis came up.

One of those times, she tracked him down in the corral where he was fixing the fence. She watched in silence until he finished, and he wondered what she was going to ask him this time and mentally prepared for it.

But all she said was that she was thinking of changing her name. "Tuck McCall says Artemis sounds affected."

Sloan looked up. "Does he?"

Lizzie nodded seriously. "But at least he knew which goddess she was."

"Good for Tuck." It was more than he did. He straightened up and flexed his shoulders.

"Tuck's pretty smart," she went on. "And he doesn't call me Lizard anymore. He can drive now. He got his license last week."

"Cool."

"He said he might take me to the movie in Bozeman."

A date? Lizzie? "No kissing," Sloan said automatically.

Lizzie laughed. "As if!"

He ruffled her hair and grinned at her.

From the kitchen window Polly saw the two of them grinning at each other. Then, as she watched, Sloan, who was carrying his toolbox in one arm, slung the other arm around Lizzie's shoulders and the two of them walked toward the barn.

Like father and daughter.

He treated them all just like he would his own children. If only...

The thought teased her. Tempted her. It would be so very easy to let it happen.

He was so good with them all. He was a great role model for Jack. He seemed to listen when Daisy went on ad nauseam about horses. He made Lizzie laugh. And sometimes she thought Lizzie talked more to him than she did to her own mother.

He was good for her kids.

He was good for her.

Sloan Gallagher had made her feel like a woman again. He'd made her aware that she was more than a mom. He made her laugh, too. And he made her silly and humble and hungry for his touch.

He said he loved her.

But for how long?

He was here now, but this wasn't his real life. This was an idyll. The first of May he'd be gone to Kauai working on a film.

"Halfway across the world," she'd said when he'd told her.

"There are phones. I called you from Tierra del Fuego. Or you could come with me."

She'd shaken her head. "The kids—"

"—can come along."

"School—"

"—is out in a little more than a month."

"But—"

"Think about it," he said. "I love you." That's what he always said.

Polly thought about it—about him. Sometimes it seemed that was all she did. Day after day she thought about Sloan, about his easy charm and warm smiles and wonderful loving. He was good with her kids. He was nice to her mother. He'd made an ally of her sister. He said he loved her.

But every time he asked her to marry him, Polly couldn't quite manage to say yes.

She was afraid.

A guy could go gray waiting for Celie O'Meara to get her head on straight.

It wasn't bad enough that she'd dithered away ten years after Matt Williams, dreaming about Sloan Gallagher and various other Hollywood heroes. When she finally came to the realization that Gallagher wasn't her forever man, she *still* couldn't see that Jace was.

God knew he gave her plenty of opportunity.

He was right there every day, working his tail off in the hardware store, toting and carrying, stacking and cutting, being helpful and cheerful and not saying, "I told you so," once.

Well, maybe once.

But only because he'd been provoked. Only because it was obvious after Celie returned from her weekend that Gallagher hadn't come back to Elmer for her, but because he'd had his sights set on Polly all along.

But would Celie acknowledge she'd been barking up the wrong tree?

Hell, no. She acted like it was her idea ol' Sloan and her sister were a match. And she seemed perfectly happy about it. That was what galled him—that she could see *now* that Sloan and Polly were made for each other, and she still acted as if *he* didn't exist.

"Well, hell's bells, boy, just ask 'er out," Artie said.

Artie had come home the week after Celie came back from Hollywood. But he hadn't been back on his feet really, so Jace had stuck around. He couldn't work on his corrals anyway until the weather warmed, so he stayed on with Artie, living in Elmer, working full-time at the hardware store and having his nonexistent love life analyzed by a ninety-year-old man.

"No," Jace said flatly. Because he knew what would happen if he did.

Celie would look at him like he was something she'd found on the bottom of her shoe, then she'd curl her lip in disgust, say flatly "No"—and that would be that.

Jace wasn't putting his heart on the line without some encouragement. A flat-out turndown and he'd have no place to go but home. He'd waited too long for Celie to do something stupid like that.

"She'll come around," he told Artie. "Celie's like a skittish mare."

"Celie's like a horse?"

"A skittish one." Jace nodded solemnly. He'd been working with a mare that belonged to his brother-in-law, one that had been trained up wrong. You had to go slow with horses like that, come at 'em sideways. Take it easy. No direct confrontations.

"Sure," he said. "Just gotta go at 'em slow like. Soothe 'em."

Artie rolled his eyes. "Sounds to me like you'll put 'em to sleep."

"Trust me," Jace said with more certainty than he felt. "She'll come around."

"She might not. She might take off," Artie said.

"No. Not Celie." That was one thing Jace was certain of. Celie loved Elmer. She belonged here. He watched her every day when she went outside to look at the mountains. She would just stand there, breathing deep, looking around, letting the breeze ruffle her glorious dark hair. He watched her and longed to go up to her and run his fingers through her hair, longed to put his arms around her.

But whenever she saw him, she turned quickly away and came back in. It had been going on for weeks, and he wasn't getting anywhere.

"Watchin' paint dry is more excitin' than watchin' you court that woman," Artie said.

"I ain't courtin' her."

"I did notice. She ain't gonna wait forever, ya know. Ya oughta ask her to a movie," Artie said. "Or out to a meal."

But Jace couldn't. He'd never had a lick of trouble asking any other woman out, but no other woman had ever mattered.

"Well, suit yerself," Artie said, disgusted. "But she might meet another feller."

Jace did have to consider that. She had come out of her shell after her weekend with Gallagher. She didn't sort of smile vaguely in the direction of her cowboy customers anymore. She looked straight at them and, by God, she batted her lashes and showed she had dimples. She'd even done a little flirting with that kid, Cy Williams, last time he was in.

Cripes, Jace thought, what if she hooked up with yet another wrong one?

"Maybe I could just take her with me down to Billings to pick up the lawn mowers," he said at last. It was early April.

Mowers would be selling soon. He had to go down on Saturday.

"That's romantic." Artie just shook his head.

But Jace couldn't see himself being romantic with Celie. Hell, chances were if he so much as complimented her, he'd get his face slapped.

But a couple of hours, just the two of them in Artie's big truck, might set things on the right road at last. He could come at her sideways then, get her talking, charm her the way he used to charm all those buckle bunnies—if he even remembered how.

So when she came out to the warehouse the next morning as he was shifting a load of lumber, he said casually, "I'm goin' to Billings Saturday to pick up lawn mowers. Artie wants you to come along." Which was only the truth—Artie did want him to ask her out.

But Celie just shook her head. "I'm not going to be here."

"What the hell do you mean, you're not going to be here?" That Wiliams kid hadn't lined her up for something, had he?

"I'm going on a singles cruise."

A flea on roller skates could have knocked him over. "A what! A *singles* cruise? What the hell are you going to do a stupid ass thing like that for?"

Celie blinked rapidly, took a step back, then squared her shoulders and lifted her chin. "To meet men, obviously."

"But—"

But she didn't give him a chance to object. "Now that I'm over Sloan, it seems like an excellent idea."

"But—"

"Artie said it was fine with him."

"Artie *knew?*" That blankety-blank son-of-a-gun!

"I thought he told you. But he probably figured it wouldn't matter to you," Celie said offhandedly.

Jace felt as if she'd punched him in the gut. "You can't go."

"What do you mean, I can't go? Why not?"

"Because…because you can't afford it! You bought Sloan!"

"Well," she admitted, "he helped me out there. He paid my

bid. Said it was the least he could do. I always knew he was a good guy," she added with a grin.

Jace sputtered furiously. "You don't—you can't—"

But Celie went on just as if he weren't strangling on a reply. "But I am. I'm not going to sit here all my life and wait for the right man to come along. I've wasted ten years. So I decided, if I was willing to spend twenty-three thousand dollars on the wrong man, I might as well spend a few thousand to find the right one."

"On a *singles* cruise?"

"You never know. I'm leaving Wednesday. So if you need to know where anything is, be sure to ask me before then."

"But—"

But Celie didn't wait to hear any more sputtered, furious objections. She smiled, waggled her fingers at him and was gone.

Joyce figured she had a vocabulary of about thirty-seven Vietnamese words now. She knew basic equivalents of *please, thank you, yes, no, I need a taxi, how much does it cost?* and *I'm looking for my daughter, An.*

She didn't expect *she* would ever have to use that last one. But it had been the one Walt was most eager to learn. And she didn't mind learning it, either. She liked spending time with Walt a couple of mornings a week. It gave her a focus, a sense of purpose beyond her job. She looked forward to him coming.

He came about ten and they sat at her kitchen table and drank coffee and listened to the tapes and tried to say the words. They were both pretty bad at it. Mostly they laughed at how bad they were. And then they talked about other things—about life and their kids and her grandkids. Walt envied her her grandkids.

"Maybe someday," he said.

"*Nietos,*" she told him. "That's grandkids in Spanish." They checked their book, but they couldn't find the word in Vietnamese.

"You should learn Spanish," she'd told him last week.

"I didn't get any Mexican girls pregnant," he'd said with a rueful smile.

The smile was evidence that things had changed. After his heart attack, Walt told her, he'd been lost and depressed and then desperate to find his other daughter. He'd felt guilty and bereft. It had become a quest.

In a way it still was. But he'd come to understand it better. He told Joyce last week that he knew he might never meet the young woman he had sired. He knew that, no matter what he wanted, she might not want to meet him.

"I just have to try," he told her.

And Joyce nodded. "Yes."

So she practiced with him, and then, later, she'd practiced her Spanish with Celie whose ship was going to make stops in Panama and Puerto Vallarta.

"You know, you could go on a singles cruise, too," Celie had told her when she'd first brought brochures home.

Joyce had been startled, then laughed at the thought. "I'm sure you'd love to go with your mother."

"Not with me," Celie said. "With people your age. They have them. You should think about it, Mom."

Joyce was thinking about it now as she mixed up a batch of cookies. Celie was probably somewhere along the coast of Mexico right now. She had gone off on Wednesday, determined and smiling.

"More power to you, sweetheart," Joyce murmured. Everyone else was gone. Polly was at work. Sloan had driven up to the ranch to make sure everything was taken care of before he went to Kauai the day after tomorrow. The kids were all in school.

"What do you think, Gil?" she said out loud. "Can you see me on a singles' cruise?"

If he were here, she thought, he'd probably fall on the floor laughing.

"Me, neither," she said with a wistful shake of her head. Still Celie's plans had made hers seem possible. Maybe a week at a beach in Cancun.

There was a tap on the door.

Carrying the mixing bowl, Joyce went to open it. "Walt!"

He usually came on Tuesdays and Thursdays. It was Wednesday. It was only nine in the morning. "What's wrong?"

Walt looked chalk-white as he held out a letter. "It's from her."

Her.

Joyce dumped the bowl on the counter and took the letter, then opened the door wider and beckoned Walt in. He came in, pulled off his hat and stood crushing the brim of his hat while Joyce stared at the letter in her suddenly trembling hands and felt as nervous as she was sure Walt must have been.

"Read it," he urged her.

Joyce slid the thin paper out of its envelope and unfolded it. In a small, neat careful hand, Walt's daughter had written in English, "I have dreamed of this for years—to know my father, to know he has not forgotten me."

She wrote that her mother had shown her his picture, but that she never knew his last name. "She didn't want me to know in case I had the idea to disturb your life," An had written. "She said you did what you had to do."

Joyce looked at Walt. His eyes were shimmering with tears. Still holding the letter in one hand, she reached out with the other to take one of his in hers. It was cold and rough, but it grasped hers fiercely and hung on.

"I am so glad you have written to me now. I hope we can be friends. I am a teacher of English. I learned it so someday I might be able to talk to you."

Their eyes met again. Walt grinned wryly. "Guess her mother must've told her how bad I was at languages."

"Not so bad," Joyce said, but she smiled a little damply, too.

She went back and read the letter again, digesting it slowly. Walt's daughter was a widow. Her husband, a policeman, had died two years before. She had two children, a boy, nine, and a girl, five.

"Grandkids," Walt said, dazed. "Can you believe it?" He was grinning again, this time with delight. And Joyce shared his joy.

"It seems," she said, "as if you've been a grandpa for years."

"Seems so," he agreed with considerable relish.

The letter ended with an invitation. "I hope you will come to Vietnam to visit us. I and my children will be so happy to welcome you."

"So when are you going?" Joyce asked, folding the letter and handing it back to him.

Walt took it, unfolded it and read it silently to himself before answering. Then he looked up and met Joyce's gaze. "As soon as I can talk you into comin', too."

Stunned, Joyce simply stared.

Go to Vietnam?

Her first instinct was to say no. She was sixty years old, for heaven's sake. She'd never traveled abroad before. She might manage Mexico. Mexico was on the beaten path. She might even decide Mexico was a bit much. Maybe she would start with Canada. She would be able to use more than thirty-seven words.

Said you wanted to travel, didn't you? she could almost hear Gil's voice in her ear.

But…

Vietnam?

With Walt! What about that?

Women her age didn't travel with men who weren't their husbands. Did they? Joyce was so out of touch she really didn't know.

"If you'd rather not," Walt said now, after what was probably a very long stretch of utterly flabbergasted silence, "I'll understand. I just thought…well, you were sayin' you wanted to go somewhere different. Travel a bit. I know you thought Mexico, but I figured maybe if you didn't have your heart set on that, you might want to think about comin' along."

"Well, I…" Joyce was still a little overwhelmed by the notion. "I don't know," she said. "I hadn't thought— You and me? I'm not…we aren't— Oh, heavens. Old habits die hard," she said at last.

"They do," Walt agreed solemnly. He took her hand again

and rubbed his thumb along the side. "Would you come if we were married?"

If she had been astonished before, it was nothing to this. "Married?"

"I been thinkin' about it a lot lately. Thinkin' about you." He rubbed a hand over his short hair, then kneaded the taut muscles at the back of his neck. "I haven't got a lot to compare it with, what I been thinkin', what I been feelin'. Just what I felt for Margie and what I felt for Sue. But I'd say it ranks right up there. I reckon I love you."

Abruptly Joyce sat down.

"If it's gonna make it harder," Walt said quickly, "just forget I said anything."

Forget? Just turn off her mind and forget?

"Are you crazy?" Joyce demanded.

Walt grinned. "Maybe a little. Hell, Joyce, I wasn't expecting to fall in love with you. I wasn't lookin' for anything like that. But it sure does feel like that's what's happened. And well, it doesn't have anything to do with goin' to Vietnam— unless you want it to. Reckon I shouldn't've said 'em together. You can come or not. But either way, I'd be honored if you'd be my wife."

Joyce was still in shock. Getting a proposal of marriage was as shocking as Walt's hearing from An. She'd never thought about marrying again, had never even considered it.

What would Gil say?

She smiled. No question there. Gil would say, *If that's what you want, go for it, babe.* She knew Gil. He had always grabbed life with both hands.

And she? What was she going to do?

She'd started to move forward. She'd taken baby steps. Did her macramé. Studied her Spanish. Planned vaguely for "someday."

But never a someday like this.

"I'm stunned," she said to Walt. "Amazed. Astonished."

"But not sayin' no," Walt asked quickly.

But not saying no.

She could hear Gil in her ear now. *Come on, Joy-o, fish or cut bait.* She closed her eyes and saw Gil smiling at her. She opened them and saw Walt looking worried.

"I'll go to Vietnam with you," Joyce said, and felt a quickening deep inside at the joy in Walt's sudden smile.

He reached for her, took her in his arms, and for the first time since Gil died, she felt the solid warmth of a hard male body against hers. Walt was taller than Gil. He stood straighter. He was broader through the shoulders. His jaw was bristlier. And his lips...

She didn't compare his lips. She didn't think at all, she simply savored the kiss. It was tender and gentle and experienced. It offered. It didn't take. It gave, but it didn't insist.

It wasn't young love—eager and fierce and passionate. But it was deep and strong and abiding. It felt real.

They both came with families, with baggage, with memories. They each had too much past to pretend they were just starting here. It was the past that made them who they were today. And they would help make each other who they were tomorrow. They weren't finished yet, either one of them.

For the first time, Joyce thought, she could smile as she faced the future.

"Yes, to Vietnam," she said again, smiling into those wise, gentle faded blue eyes. "And I'll consider your other offer seriously."

A part of Polly expected it to end right here.

Sloan was leaving today. Going to Kauai. Going to paradise, according to one of the magazine articles about his next film that she read. Celie had given it to her before she left last week.

"Nice place for a honeymoon," her sister had suggested.

It was. The photos showed Kauai to be gorgeous. Romantic. Secluded. And based on the pictures, Polly allowed herself a romantic fantasy or two. But she really wasn't anticipating anything like that.

"How can you be if you won't set a date?" Celie had complained.

"I'm busy. He's busy. We have—"

"Commitments. Responsibilities," Celie said before Polly could. "I know. But there's more to life than that, Pol'."

Yes, there were also singles cruises. But Polly didn't say that. She knew she ought to be glad that Celie had taken her destiny in her own hands and was actively doing something for a change. Winning The Great Montana Cowboy Auction had given Celie more confidence than she'd had in years.

"There's love," Celie went on. "Sloan loves you. You love him."

"Yes."

"Then what are you waiting for? The apocalypse?"

"Something like that."

Celie stared. "What?"

Polly shrugged helplessly. "A sign."

Not the apocalypse necessarily, but some assurance that marrying Sloan was really going to work, that it wasn't going to end in disaster, that discounting all their differences and believing in love really did make sense. It was too big a leap—like jumping the Grand Canyon—and Polly couldn't, simply couldn't, do it.

"I just need a sign," she said. "That's all."

But the choirs of angels were all busy the afternoon she took him to the airport. Every one of God's obvious messengers was busy delivering other lines. No celestial being went, "Pssst!" in Polly's ear, then having got her attention said, "It's okay for you to marry Sloan Gallagher." No minister showed up at the airport to give them his blessing.

It was just Sloan and Polly—and a hundred or so interested onlookers in the departure lounge, all poking each other and whispering, "There's Sloan Gallagher!" and "Isn't that Sloan Gallagher?"

Sloan was polite, but he wasn't "on" the way he had been during the auction.

It amazed Polly the way he could do that—be totally involved with a crowd of people on one occasion and on another be polite but slightly remote, thereby creating an oasis of personal space. Somehow he sent the message that they could watch, but they couldn't intrude.

"I've got something for you," he said to Polly. He reached into the inside chest pocket of his jacket, pulled out a fat envelope and handed it to her.

Wordlessly she opened it. In it were eight plane tickets to Kauai, one for each member of her family. And one for Walt. The flight was in two weeks' time.

Polly stared at them, then at Sloan.

"Celie will be back by then," he said. "Sara will be finished with finals. Lizzie, Daisy and Jack can miss a week of school. And it will get Walt and your mom halfway to Vietnam. I'll arrange whatever else needs to be arranged. All you have to do is show up—and marry me, Polly." Deep-blue eyes locked with hers.

And for a split second Polly dared to believe she saw a sign.

He called her every night.

"I miss you," he said.

And Polly wasn't lying when she said, "I miss you, too."

She'd grown used to having Sloan around, to seeing him, talking to him, laughing with him, touching him. Now she went to bed early with memories of what it had been like loving him. She woke up thinking about him, she went to bed thinking about him. She went through her life in a Sloan-filled daze.

It worried her, though. It felt like she was courting disaster. But as each day passed and the disaster didn't happen, she began to hope. She even began to plan.

She dared to buy a few summery things to wear on the beach. She even got a new bathing suit. Celie had brought her back a nightgown that was simply shocking.

"I can't!" Polly protested, face reddening furiously.

But Celie said, "You have to. I bought it in Puerto Vallarta. I certainly can't take it back. And think how happy it will make Sloan when he gets to take it off you."

When he was gone and she was working at the post office, it was impossible to imagine. Polly shook her head. "You're shameless," she accused her sister. "I suppose you bought one for Mom, too."

"As a matter of fact..." Celie grinned widely.

"You didn't!" Polly was shocked.

Surprisingly, Joyce liked hers. She and Walt weren't married yet. They were engaged, though. Walt had given Joyce a ring. Polly saw her mother look at it sometimes as if she were surprised to see it on her finger. But then she'd fold her other hand over it and get this small secret smile on her face as if she were both delighted and amazed.

Polly was pretty amazed herself. She still couldn't believe it was happening, even as she packed her bag the night before they were to leave. Tomorrow at this time, she'd be with Sloan. The next day she'd be marrying him.

It was like one of his movies—complete with happy ending.

And then the door opened and Sara came into her room, white-faced and raccoon-eyed. She'd finished her finals last week, and Polly was glad she was coming with them. Sara, of all of them, looked as if she needed a rest.

"All packed?" she asked cheerfully.

And Sara shook her head. "I'm bleeding."

Chapter 19

Pregnant and bleeding.

Which Sara had somehow, until that moment, failed to mention. Now she sat shivering, knees drawn up and arms wrapped around them on her mother's bed. She looked exhausted and young and very, very scared.

Polly felt like she'd been hit over the head with a brick.

"You're *pregnant?*" Polly stared at her daughter. Sara? *Her* Sara?

"Don't look at me like that!"

But how were you supposed to look when everything you thought you knew about your child suddenly turned totally upside down? "I'm just...surprised."

"And disappointed," Sara said, jaw jutting.

"Worried. How much are you bleeding? How far along are you?"

"Three months," Sara said in a small voice.

"Three?" Polly gaped. She'd seen Sara almost every day for those three months. How had she missed the signs? *Why on earth didn't I know?*

Of course Sara was gone a lot, always studying, always in

class or at school or in the library. Polly had noticed her daughter looking gaunt and stressed and sleepless lately. But she had attributed it to how hard Sara was working. She'd never once thought Sara could be pregnant.

Not Sara.

Never Sara.

Sara planned everything. But she certainly hadn't planned this!

Polly had a hundred questions. She couldn't ask one. And the past didn't matter, anyway. What mattered was what was happening to Sara and the baby now.

"I started a little spotting yesterday," Sara said, her voice quavering. "I read in a book that it sometimes happens around when you would have been getting your period, so I didn't think too much about it. I thought it would stop, Mom, but it…it hasn't! And there's more now. What if I lose the baby?" Sara wrapped her arms around her legs and rocked, turning her anguished eyes on Polly.

Make it better, Mom.

Polly folded her in a fierce hug. "Get your jacket. We're going to the hospital."

The E.R. doc called Sara's obstetrician.

"You have an obstetrician?" Polly asked her daughter as they sat in the small examining room.

"Of course." Sara looked surprised that she would even ask. "I know the value of prenatal care. I'm not totally stupid." Then she winced and added, "Only selectively stupid."

"Takes one to know one." Polly put her arm around Sara's thin shoulders and gave her a squeeze. It was all too easy to remember the panicky early days of her extremely unplanned pregnancy with Sara.

"At least Dad loved you," Sara said, which was certainly true.

Polly stroked Sara's hair away from her face. "Don't you think Gregg loves you?"

Sara blinked at her, then she shut her eyes. When she opened them she shook her head. "No," she said in a hollow voice. "But it doesn't matter. This isn't Gregg's child."

It was a good thing there was a chair where Polly sat. She stared at Sara. "Not...?" She couldn't finish. Horrible things that could have happened to Sara were flashing through her head.

Sara must have realized it from the expression on her face, because she shook her head fiercely. "It's not that," she said. "I wanted to do it. I went to him. I love him! It's...it's Flynn's."

Flynn?

Who the heck was Flynn?

For more than a few seconds Polly couldn't think. And then she remembered a lean handsome raven-haired young man with an Irish accent and a gift of blarney.

"The writer?" she asked to be sure.

Sara nodded. "Yes. That's him."

"And he and...and you..." Polly could almost not say the words. She felt so hopelessly inadequate. Her daughter had *slept* with this man and she'd barely even noted his existence!

What kind of mother was she?

The door opened and the obstetrician came in. He nodded at Polly, but his focus was entirely on Sara as he smiled and said, "Ah, Sara. Let's take a look and see what's going on with you."

Polly got to wait outside. She got to sit in the waiting room and stare at a magazine and not see a word. Sara, her Sara, was pregnant! She'd had sex—made love, she imagined Sara would say—with a man her mother barely even realized she knew. She thought she was in love with this man, this... this...*Flynn!*

And where *was* Flynn?

Polly hadn't asked, but it didn't seem as if Sara knew.

The doctor came out of the examining room right before Polly wore a rut in the floor. She grabbed him by the arm. "Is she—"

He folded a hand over hers. "She needs to go to bed. To stay there. To rest. A lot. I'm keeping her overnight. We'll

see about tomorrow. She's exhausted. She needs to stop stress-
ing herself out.''

"She will." Polly was determined. "And the— What about
the...baby?''

The word sounded almost foreign on her tongue. She hadn't
thought about babies since Jack. It seemed impossible that Sara
was having one.

"The baby seems to be holding its own. So far so good,
anyway." He gave Polly's hand a pat. "If the bleeding stops,
things should be okay. Even so, a perfectly normal pregnancy
is a big thing to handle on your own. I'm glad Sara finally told
you.''

"She should have told me months ago!" Polly said, anguished.

"She said you had plenty of other things to think about,"
the doctor told her. "She said it was her problem. Not yours.''

"Yes, but—''

"You know now," he said gently. "Just give her your support." He turned to go, then looked back and winked at her.
"Grandma.''

Oh, good Lord.

Sloan had called Polly every night since they'd been apart.

Partly it was because he missed her so badly. Every day he
thought of a hundred different things he wanted to tell her. He
wanted to talk with her, listen to her, laugh with her. He wanted
to share his day with her and to be allowed to share hers.

But that was only part of it. The rest was that he was afraid
that, left on her own, Polly would get some bee in her bonnet,
rethink the whole notion of marrying him and toss him out on
his ear.

Until he had the ring on her finger, he wasn't going to rest
easy. Once they were married, he knew Polly would honor her
commitment—even though he also knew she would never love
him the way she loved Lew.

Over the past three months he'd thought about it a lot, and
he knew he couldn't possibly compete with Lew McMaster.

He'd never be her first love. Never be the man she most wanted. But he could live with that.

He had to live with that if he wanted to live with her.

Still, they weren't married yet. So he called her every night, just to talk, to touch base, to remind her that, no matter how she felt, he really did love her.

Last night they'd talked for half an hour. She was packing her bags, she'd said. Wait until he saw the nightgown Celie had bought her, she'd said. She made his blood run hot just talking about it, laughing about it.

And today—in a few short hours—she would be here.

All day long Sloan was like a kid on Christmas eve—distracted, excitable, tense. His mind was on Polly, not on Becca Reed or the treasure they were supposed to discover buried on this deserted island, a treasure that everyone else wanted to steal. But he knew his job and, distracted or not, he did it.

Polly would be his reward at the end of the day.

And finally it came. He was off like a shot when Trevor ended the shooting.

"Don't do anything I wouldn't do," Trev called after him with a grin.

Since Trevor had a gorgeous wife with whom he was madly in love, Sloan didn't see any problem there.

He stopped back by the house he'd rented, grabbed a shower and changed clothes before heading to the airport. The house was built of native wood and stone. It sat on a cliff overlooking the ocean above a secluded sandy beach. The real estate salesperson who'd found it for him had promised that it was a garden of Eden setting. She hadn't lied. Sloan knew Polly would love it. He could hardly wait to share it with her.

He grabbed his cell phone on the way out the door in case Polly called to say the plane was going to be late. Trevor had banned them from the set saying he couldn't get anything done with a hundred ringing phones. Now, as he headed toward the door, Sloan saw the message light flashing. He punched the button.

It was Polly. Breathless. Agitated.

"Sloan? I'm sorry. I'm…not coming." A large desperate

gulp. "It's Sara. Well, no...it's not Sara. I mean, it not *just*
Sara. It's...oh, hell, it's hard to explain on the phone." Another
shaky breath. "I wish—" She broke off, stopped short. Then,
firmly, "No. No, I don't. I...you're better off without me. It
wouldn't work. It wouldn't be fair to you. Trust me. Have a
good life. You'll be glad I didn't come." There was a click,
then silence.

Sloan stood stock-still staring out at paradise.

Have a good life? You'll be glad I didn't come.

What the hell was going on? Couldn't he trust her on her
own for a minute without her having a crisis of confidence in
their love?

Or maybe, he thought raggedly, there really wasn't that
much love. Maybe his fears were even more real than he had
imagined. Maybe it wasn't just that she didn't love him as
much as she'd loved Lew.

Maybe she didn't really love him at all.

Thank God for her mother and Walt and Celie. They took
over at home while Polly stayed with Sara.

In her mind she knew Sara wasn't in serious danger and,
after twenty-four hours, during which the bleeding slowed and
Sara's body seemed to relax and the contractions stopped, the
chances of her losing the baby lessened as well. Sara was getting along fine.

Polly didn't need to be there every moment for Sara. She
needed to be there for herself. She felt guilty for not seeing,
for not knowing, for not being aware.

"I didn't know when you were pregnant with Sara," Joyce
tried to tell her. "You can't know everything. And even if you
did, it's not your life."

They weren't words that Polly wanted to hear. She felt so
inadequate, so lost, so guilty. Her daughter had needed her for
weeks—months—and she'd only been thinking about herself.

"What about Sloan?" her mother said.

"What about him?"

"Haven't you talked to him?"

Polly shook her head. "I left him a message."

Joyce's brows lifted. "A message? That you weren't coming to your own wedding?"

Polly shrugged. "It never would have worked."

"What!" Joyce looked scandalized. "What do you mean it won't work? You love each other!"

"That's not...it's not enough," Polly said helplessly. "There's more to life than that. There's Sara. There's a baby! He's not going to want to marry a grandmother!"

"Did you ask him?"

"Don't be ridiculous." How could she possibly ask him a thing like that? And how could he ever give her an honest answer? She wasn't going to trap him into something he didn't want, wasn't going to force her family on him. "It's over," she said.

"But—"

"Over, Mom. Drop it." Then she spun away and hurried out of the hospital. She wasn't going to cry. Lew dying had been something to cry over. Sara losing the baby would have been something to cry over.

She wouldn't cry over losing Sloan Gallagher.

It wasn't paradise when you were alone.

Sloan guessed Adam in the garden had probably known that. Adam had probably figured out pretty quickly that without someone to share paradise with, it didn't matter how beautiful it was.

Without Polly to share it with, the world was an empty place. Sloan sat there a long time. He played her message over. He listened to it again and again. He wallowed in the unfairness of it.

He loved Polly, damn it! He'd loved her for years! He'd almost had her.

And now...he felt like the little boy who, promised a long-awaited gift, got a stocking with a hole in it instead. He felt rotten, miserable, deprived.

And then he realized that this really wasn't about what he wanted and didn't have. It wasn't about whether or not Polly loved him. It was about loving her, about being there for her when she needed him. *That was what love was*—even when she thought he ought to be glad she wasn't coming.

He wasn't glad. He cared, damn it! About all of them. He loved all of them—not just Polly, but Jack and Daisy and Lizzie. Even Sara, whom he barely knew.

And now something was wrong with Sara. Something serious. Something important because Polly didn't panic. Polly always coped.

But Polly wasn't coping now. He'd heard that in her voice. She was in a panic. She needed help.

He picked up the phone and punched in a number. "Trev? It's me, Sloan. I've got to go to Montana. Now. Tonight."

Sara was going to come home. The baby was all right.

The doctor had told Polly the good news just a few minutes ago. Then he'd vanished back into Sara's room. "Just wanted you to know," he'd said.

Now as she stood in the corridor of the hospital, Polly drew a deep breath and said a prayer of thanksgiving. It had been a harrowing thirty-six hours. But it was going to be all right. Things would be back to normal—or as normal as they could be, considering this new development. It was taking some getting used to, but Polly was getting used to it.

She would see that Sara had plenty of rest, good food, whatever she needed to keep things going well. That was what mattered now. Whatever happened between Sara and Flynn—well, that was out of her hands. Her job was to take care of Sara, to pay attention to the rest of her kids. Not to go off half-cocked anymore and—

"Pol'?"

The voice, low and rusty sounding, came from right behind her. And Polly spun around to find herself face-to-face with Sloan. She stared, her breath caught in her throat. "What are you doing here?"

He looked worse than she had ever seen him—his dark hair tousled, his eyes bloodshot, his jaw unshaven. He looked like any worried husband or father—and gorgeous, to boot.

It was all Polly could do not to throw herself into his arms and hang on. She'd become so accustomed to talking to him, sharing with him. Now she desperately wanted to burden him with her burdens, load on the responsibilities, divvy up the commitments.

But she knew it wouldn't be fair.

"I got your message," he said simply. "Where else would I be?"

She didn't know. But she didn't expect him here!

"I said I wasn't coming to Kauai. I didn't expect—I didn't ask you to come here."

"You don't have to ask, Pol'. I want to be here. I want to help. To do whatever I can. I love you." He made it sound so simple. So true.

Oh, God. Oh, please don't tempt me this way!

"Daisy said Sara's pregnant."

"She *told* you?" But of course Daisy would. Why wouldn't she? She didn't understand. "Then you know," Polly said flatly.

He shook his head. "Is she okay? Daisy said she'd had some problems. Bleeding?"

"She's okay. She needs to rest. To take it easy. She's been…dealing with it alone. Putting way too much pressure on herself."

"Sounds like she needs a vacation," Sloan said easily. "I know just the place." He grinned. It was that mischievous, boyish grin that invited Polly into a conspiracy.

She resisted it. "She needs to stay here and go to bed."

"There are beds in Kauai."

She wrapped her arms across her breasts. "No."

"Why not?"

"Because we're not coming to Kauai. I told you that!" God, she'd thought it had been hard to say the words on the phone. It was harder by far to say them to his face. She started to turn away, but he caught her arm.

"You said you weren't coming because something was wrong with Sara. I understood. But Sara's okay now. Stressed, but okay. She needs rest. We'll give her rest. We'll give her the vacation she needs. What's wrong with that?"

"It isn't just the vacation. It isn't Sara. I can't, Sloan. I just...can't."

"Can't what?" he challenged her. Blue eyes bored into her.

"I can't marry you." She forced herself to say the words.

Sloan's jaw tightened. A muscle ticked in his temple. He looked as if he were in pain.

"Because you don't love me?"

"Of course not!"

"Then, damn it, why?"

They were attracting, as always, lots of curious onlookers. Two young nurses were hovering close with pens and papers in their hands, ready to swoop in and get Sloan's autograph the moment he indicated it was okay. But he showed no signs of doing so. His gaze was fixed on Polly. She doubted he knew anyone else was there.

"I love you," he said to her now, his eyes locked on hers. "I know I've said it before, but I think I really know now what it means. It means I'm willing to do whatever needs to be done for you and for your kids and mother and sister and your dogs and your cats and your rabbits and—hell, I don't know— maybe even your squirrels! It means I want to spend the rest of my life doing that. It means I want to share everything I have with you. And it means, by God—that whether I get it or not, I want you to share with me." His chest heaved. He let out a long, shaky breath. Then his voice dropped. "What do you say, Pol'?"

She held herself absolutely rigid. She couldn't move. If she had she would have flung herself into his arms. But it would be so wrong to burden him with all her baggage, to lay her troubles on him. So wrong...

She shook her head.

Sloan just looked at her. There was a shuttered expression on his face. The naked longing was gone, replaced by weariness, sadness, defeat.

"I can't make you love me, Pol'. I can't make you trust me. I want to spend my life with you. It's all I've got. I can't offer more than that."

He went in and saw Sara before he left. He told her that whatever she needed, she could always call on him.

Joyce and Walt arrived while he was in there. He wished them well, shook Walt's hand and kissed Joyce on the cheek. He called Jack and Lizzie and Daisy and told them he hoped he'd see them soon, that he had to get right back to Kauai to start filming again, so he couldn't stop in.

Then he came back and found Polly staring out that same damn window, her shoulders stiff, her face composed. "If you want me," he told her quietly, "you know where to find me."

Then he drove to Bozeman, got on the plane and left.

It was the hardest thing he'd ever done.

If you want me, you know where to find me.
Polly wanted him. Every day. Every night.

But it was selfishness, she told herself. It was foolishness.

That's what she told Sara, too, when her daughter confronted her about it. No one else would. No one else did. Everyone else let Polly wallow in her self-righteous misery.

But Sara, home from the hospital two weeks, with a hint of color back in her cheeks and the tiniest of bulges at her waist, said, "That's stupid."

Polly stared at her. "What do you mean?"

Sara shrugged. "You love Sloan."

Polly didn't deny it. "That's not the point. I have other commitments."

"Me? The baby? No. We're important to you. But we're going to have our own lives, Mom. So are Lizzie and Daisy and Jack."

"But not yet."

"No, not yet. But Sloan isn't asking you to give them up, is he?"

"Of course not!"

"Then why are you afraid?" Sara shook her head. "I don't understand you, Mom. This isn't what you taught me."

"What do you mean?"

Sara wrapped her arms around her knees and looked at her mother intently with Lew's beautiful dark eyes. "You taught

me that when you really care about something—about someone—that you can't just play it safe.'' She swallowed. ''Like
loving Flynn.''

''You're saying it's my fault you're having this baby?''
Polly said, raising a brow.

Sara shook her head. ''No. I'm saying what you always
taught me—that some things are worth the risk, Mom—even
though there are no guarantees.''

Out of the mouths of mothers of babes.

You spent years trying to make sure your kids knew what
they needed to know to get along in life. And just when you
despaired of them ever getting it—not only did they get it, but
they turned around and tossed it right back at you.

Polly knew that Sara was right. She'd just forgotten. She'd
been so desperately busy since Lew's death, taking care of
everything and everyone, that she had only focused on that—
on the caring. She had been so busy conserving and protecting
that she'd forgotten that there was more to life than that.

Once upon a time she'd taken risks.

At thirteen, as horse-mad as Daisy, Polly had begged her
father to buy a half-wild paint horse because she'd admired his
spirit.

''He'll throw you on that pretty face of yours, Pol','' her
father had said.

But Polly had been determined. She'd called him Thunder
because she could hear the sound of thunder in his hooves
when he ran. She'd dared to train him, to saddle him, to ride
him. And yes, she'd been thrown more times than she wanted
to remember. But in the end Thunder had been the best horse
she'd ever owned.

She'd taken other risks. She'd gone out with Lew when other
girls wouldn't give him the time of day.

''You don't want to date guys from Fletchers','' her friend
Cynthia had said. ''They're losers.''

But Lew hadn't been a loser. He'd been down on his luck.
He'd had a few hard knocks. Like Thunder, he'd been a little

wild. And like Thunder, he'd responded to her interest, her care, her love.

"You reckon I'm like one of your ol' horses?" he'd teased her once when she'd said so.

"You think you love me as much as Thunder does?" she'd countered, because Thunder would have gone through fire for her.

"Damn right I do," Lew vowed.

And when she'd gotten pregnant with Sara, he'd been there for her. His entire life, Lew had never let her down. And after it, she'd been determined never to let him down, to always do the best for his children.

And she'd tried.

She could honestly say that since Lew died, she'd done everything she needed to do to take care of them all. And that was fine. It was good.

But it wasn't enough, Polly realized.

There was more to life than conserving. More to life than protecting. More to life than clutching what you had to yourself and never daring to reach beyond it.

Sara, God bless her, had learned that. For good or ill, Sara had risked loving Flynn Murray.

And Sara wasn't the only one.

Celie had dared spend her life's savings on one date with Sloan, and having taken that step, was daring to take others. Even their mother wasn't huddled inside a protective shell waiting for death to come and reunite her with her husband.

She was actually going to marry Walt.

"I love him," she'd said, sounding a little surprised at her own vehemence. "And Gil wouldn't expect me to curl up and die—even though I tried," she admitted a little shamefacedly. "I owe him—and myself—the effort to keep on going."

Last night she'd cornered Polly in the kitchen. "Lew wouldn't expect you to stop living either," she'd told her daughter.

"I know," Polly said.

It was true, she did know. And she knew, too, that as she

had loved Lew, so she loved Sloan. Deeply. Passionately. With all her heart.

And she knew that, as she'd taught Sara, there were no guarantees.

Loving Sloan was a risk.

She could take it—if she dared.

Becca Reed called his trailer "the cell."

Trev referred to him as "the monk in paradise."

So he wasn't the life of the party these days. So his furnishings tended toward monastic simplicity and his life toward the celibate ideal.

So maybe someday he'd get over it—over her.

He wasn't there yet. He still thought about her constantly. He still wished he hadn't been so damned self-righteous, stalking off, telling her she knew where she could find him.

But really, what else could he have done?

Nothing.

He still talked to the kids now and then. It felt like a divorce, almost, talking to them, keeping in contact because it wasn't their fault that he wasn't the right man for their mother.

He'd kept it low-key and casual. He asked as indifferently as he could, "How's your mother?"

But the answers, no matter what they were, never satisfied because he didn't really know. He didn't talk to her. He didn't get to see her.

Except at night. In his dreams he saw her. Sometimes she was young and golden the way she had been that first time in the barn so many years ago. Sometimes he dreamed of her as she'd been in his bed at the ranch. Sometimes he dreamed they were just laughing together, talking, touching.

And when he woke up, he ached even more than before.

He'd fallen asleep in his trailer when they'd finished shooting this afternoon. He was tired and he'd declined Trev's invitation to dinner at Becca's and to join a few of them later for drinks at a local bar. He didn't feel social.

"Oh, come on," Becca urged him. "You never come."

"Nope. Thanks."

"How about if we stop back later and see if you've changed your mind."

"I won't change my mind."

But Becca was determined. "You're not only monastic," she grumbled. "You're turning into a hermit, too."

He thought about going up to the rental house, but it held no pleasure for him now. He'd rented it to share with Polly and the kids. It just echoed when he was there alone. So he often slept in his trailer.

He was lying on his narrow bed, staring at the ceiling when the first tentative taps on the door came. He lay still, hoping that Becca and her friends would go away.

They didn't. The tapping continued. Determined. Annoying.

Finally he hauled himself up, stalked to the door and jerked it open, his expression thunderous. "Go—"

"—away?" Polly finished for him.

He stared, blinked. Disbelieved.

Polly McMaster stared back at him. She stood two steps below him, her gingery hair a messy halo, her wide mouth in a nervous smile, her eyes saying things he only dared dream.

Was this a dream? He closed his eyes and opened them again, but she didn't go away.

"Pol'?" His throat ached.

"I love you," she whispered. "I love you so much." Her voice broke. Her eyes filled. And as he reached for her and hauled her up the steps, into his trailer, into his arms, the storm broke and they shuddered and clung together.

"Oh, God, Pol'!" His arms wrapped her, held her tightly to him. He could scarcely believe she was here. Here! Polly. His Polly.

He'd given up. He hadn't called. He hadn't pushed. He hadn't tied her to him. He had let her go.

And here she was.

Sloan rubbed his face against her hair. He kissed her ear. He drew in the soft summery scent that was Polly's alone. They rocked, clinging together, each needing the strength of the other.

"I'm scared," she whispered. "But I'm more scared of life

without you than with you. I never thought I'd love anyone like I love Lew. But I do. I love *you,* Sloan. I was a fool. I'm so sorry I sent you away!''

"Don't be sorry!" He kissed her hair, her cheek, her lips. He knew a great sense of relief, as if a weight on his chest had lifted, as if the road to the future had opened up before him and a light shone that made life brighter and more promising than he'd ever dreamed.

Polly loved him!

"It's okay," he murmured. "It doesn't matter. Nothin' matters, Pol'. Now that you're here!"

It was almost paradise.

It would be, Polly told him, if they had four kids, some dogs, a cat, a bunch of rabbits and a squirrel.

"A squirrel, huh?" Sloan said, nuzzling her cheek. They were lying in bed together, the sound of the surf in the distance and an ocean breeze blowing lightly through the open window.

"And a grandchild," Polly said, smiling impishly. "Or two."

Sloan's brows hiked up. "Two?"

She laughed, wriggling down into the tumbled bedclothes and drawing him with her. "I don't know. I just said that. I just wanted to get a rise out of you."

He took her hand and placed it on a strategic portion of his anatomy. "You've always been able to do that."

"Sloan Gallagher!" She feigned shock.

He laughed and rolled her beneath him, felt her settle and draw him in. And as he looked down at her, golden and beautiful and loving and his, his breath caught. "Did I ever tell you how much I love you, Grandma?"

Polly tickled his ribs and he squirmed and they rolled over and she ended up on top. "Once or twice, Gramps."

Sloan laughed, delighted.

"You really don't mind?" Polly said, suddenly serious. "I mean, what's it going to do to your image?"

"Who cares?" He grinned. "Think of the fun the tabloids will have with it." But then because she really did look worried, he shook his head. "I'm glad. I love you," he repeated. "All of you. Mother-in-law. Sister-in-law. Kids. Grandkids. Dogs. Cats. Rabbits. Squirrels. Believe it, Pol'."

And looking at him, seeing the love in his eyes and believing in it—and in him—Polly nodded. "I do."

"You just keep practicin' that line, sweetheart," he told her, and then he eased himself into her again and they began to move.

Polly laughed. Dear God, she loved this man and the joy he had brought into her life—into *all* their lives. After Lew she hadn't ever thought to love again. Now she couldn't imagine not loving Sloan.

He had taken her heart by storm. But in the end he, too, had risked by giving her the choice.

Thank God she'd found the courage to take it.

Polly smiled and touched her lips to his. "You know who really won The Great Montana Cowboy Auction? Me."

* * * * *

Will Jace and Celie ever get together?
Find out in

A Cowboy's Pursuit,

a new CODE OF THE WEST
book coming June 2002,
only from Silhouette Desire.

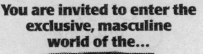